Tiger Heart

A Chesapeake Bay Mystery

Vivian Lawry
and
W. Lawrence Gulick

iUniverse, Inc.
Bloomington

Tiger Heart
A Chesapeake Bay Mystery

Copyright © 2013 Vivian Lawry and W. Lawrence Gulick

All rights reserved. No part of this book may be used or reproduced by any means, graphic, electronic, or mechanical, including photocopying, recording, taping or by any information storage retrieval system without the written permission of the publisher except in the case of brief quotations embodied in critical articles and reviews.

This is a work of fiction. All of the characters, names, incidents, organizations, and dialogue in this novel are either the products of the author's imagination or are used fictitiously.

iUniverse books may be ordered through booksellers or by contacting:

iUniverse
1663 Liberty Drive
Bloomington, IN 47403
www.iuniverse.com
1-800-Authors (1-800-288-4677)

Because of the dynamic nature of the Internet, any Web addresses or links contained in this book may have changed since publication and may no longer be valid. The views expressed in this work are solely those of the authors and do not necessarily reflect the views of the publisher, and the publisher hereby disclaims any responsibility for them.

Any people depicted in stock imagery provided by Thinkstock are models, and such images are being used for illustrative purposes only.

Certain stock imagery © Thinkstock.

ISBN: 978-1-4759-8642-6 (sc)
ISBN: 978-1-4759-8643-3 (hc)
ISBN: 978-1-4759-8644-0 (e)

Library of Congress Control Number: 2013906849

Printed in the United States of America

iUniverse rev. date: 5/2/2013

When beholding the tranquil beauty and brilliancy of the ocean's skin, one forgets the tiger heart that pants beneath it; and would not willingly remember that this velvet paw but conceals a remorseless fang.

Herman Melville

Acknowledgements

We appreciate the many people who supported and encouraged us during the writing of this book: Barbara Baker, Patrick Grieb, Patty Grieb, and Winifred Gulick.

We are especially indebted to those who read earlier versions of the manuscript and offered information, insights, and opinions that we found invaluable. These include Lawrence Greenberg, Donald Makosky, Bennett Shaver, and the members of the Central Virginia Chapter of Sisters in Crime critique group.

Chapter One

EVERY NIGHT IS THE SAME. Richard comes awake when she snicks off the hall light and then he sees her every move—in spite of the walls, in spite of the darkened room, in spite of his closed eyelids. He sees her sitting on the toilet, elbows on knees, compact belly resting on firm thighs, heels raised so that her weight rests on the balls of her feet. He sees her at the sink, holding her toothbrush under the faucet, flicking off excess water with a snap of her strong wrist. He cannot escape her reflection in the mirror, the short brown hair with a natural wave and a few strands of gray. She turns her face from side to side, chin elevated, lips drawn back, examining big, even teeth. Revulsion stabs him. Carol would be surprised if she knew. And terribly hurt. He has no right to hate her.

Carol moves stealthily in the darkened room, from the bathroom door to the bed. Richard clenches his teeth, wills himself to stillness. With the deft economy of long practice, she feels all three pillows and puts the firmest one between her updrawn knees. She lies on her side, facing outward. And then, as she has done every night for the last decade or more, she twists her upper torso to the right until her spine cracks. She sighs softly, nestles into her pillows, pulls up the sheet, and pushes down the blanket.

As she settles into sleep, the sole of her foot touches the back of his calf. Richard does not kick her foot away. He inches closer to the edge of the bed, willing his body smaller, begging the powers of the dark for oblivion.

* * *

Standing in the steamy shower, Richard rubs in shampoo, eyes closed against the cascade of soapy water. His mind will not stay blank. Several strands of brown hair come away in his fingers and he tries to drown speculation about how soon he'll be bald. He rolls the soap in his hands, lathers his broad shoulders, arms, and chest. He washes methodically, moving down the wedge of his torso, front and back, armpits and belly. He pulls back the foreskin of his soft penis, washing the groove around its head.

A vision of Allie explodes into his consciousness.

* * *

He was at baggage claim in the Portland airport. She was concentrating on retrieving her suitcase. Pixie tendrils of blonde hair fit her head like a baby bonnet, emphasizing her wide blue eyes and the three-inch gold loops in her ears. He said, "May I help you with your bag, Miss?" and without even a glance she said, "No, thanks. Someone's meeting me." He said, "Are you sure you don't need help with your bag?" Her head snapped up. She whirled and flung herself into his arms. She smiled radiantly and euphoria surged through him. They held each other a long time.

* * *

Richard chokes off the sob that threatens to strangle him. Tears sting his eyes, but he turns his face into the hot spray and does not feel them on his cheeks. Twenty-five years ago, they really believed they had a future. Richard shudders, remembering how anxiety and guilt immobilized him during the months after Allie's visit.

*   *   *

When he married Carol, he'd promised to take care of her. After their separation he helped her move, bought a new car for her, filled out her tax returns. When Carol took an overdose of tranquilizers and called to tell him what she'd done, he called 911 and held her hand on the way to the hospital. She kept saying she didn't want to live without him, couldn't stand the thought of him with "that woman." He didn't go back to Carol then. But he didn't move forward with the divorce, either. His therapist said he was doing fine, but Allie sent two novelty buttons for Christmas—no letter, no note, just two buttons: "Not To Decide Is To Decide" and "If Not Now, When?"

*   *   *

Richard makes the water hotter, nearly scalding his skin.

*   *   *

The next time he called Allie, she sobbed. She said she had to get on with her life, had to know whether he was in it or not. He said nothing, pain and dread stopping his words. After a long silence, she said, "I can't go on like this. If you ever get a divorce, let me know. I'll always love you." He managed to choke out something like "If that's what you want," and then the line went dead. Why could she not give him the time he needed to extricate himself from Carol's clinging devotion, to deal with the guilt of abandoning the woman he'd promised to care for?

Eighteen months later, Allie called. It was nearly one o'clock in the morning. Her words were soft and fuzzy at the edges, an echo of nights when they had drunk long and she wanted to be loved to sleep. She asked whether he was living with Carol again, then said "I'm getting married in two days." The call was brief, her words piercing his gut like knives.

When he returned to bed, Carol brushed his shoulder with her fingertips. "Richie? Richie, was that Allie?" He did not hit her. He never hit her. But his tight snarl stopped her quavering voice as effectively as a blow: "Yes. She's marrying a man named Buck Brady." That was the last time either of them spoke Allie's name to the other. Since then, he hears her name only in his dreams, sees it only in his journal.

* * *

Richard begins washing his legs, his feet, his toes. He stands in the steamy spray, muscles tight, apprehensive. Soapy water runs off his body and swirls down the drain. It carries away the tears, the fallen hair, the dead skin cells. Every day more of him dies. Every day more of him washes away.

Soon he will see her again. It's unavoidable—as unavoidable as the years passing—as unavoidable as his pain. Did Allie try to persuade her husband not to serve on the Board of Trustees? Did she suggest he befriend another college? Surely she knows I'm on the Board. But West College is her alma mater. Maybe she'll make excuses, not attend the Trustees' social functions. No, she isn't a coward. Never that. But maybe she no longer cares.

Chapter Two

Nora steers *Duet* down the Chester River, wondering how quickly the new West College trustee will learn the rudiments of sailing. Buck Brady is big, burly, and middle-aged, with sandy hair, a well-trimmed mustache, a quick smile, and a deep voice. Her glance takes in his unbuttoned cotton shirt, beefy leathered hands, the yachting cap set low over his left eyebrow. New boat shoes strike the only discordant note in his old salt appearance. If she didn't know better, Nora would expect him to spin a yarn of his early sailing days. She scans the sky. Dark clouds are forming in the west. "Buck, take the helm. I'm going below to catch a weather report." They are in the middle of a wide, open space at the mouth of the Chester River, no other boats in sight, nothing ahead but the red channel marker pointing the way to the Chesapeake Bay. "Leave the channel marker to port and head for the open water."

Buck says "Aye, aye, skipper."

She senses that he's checking out her ass as she starts down the companionway.

* * *

Nora pitches headfirst into the cabin bulkhead. Chart book, pens, glasses, hat, jacket—everything that isn't fastened down—slides and skitters toward the bow. For an instant she confuses the blow to her head with the thunk and grinding crunch of the impact. She pushes herself up and scrambles topside.

Buck sits at the tiller, looking surprised but not alarmed. The drum of the seven-foot-high channel marker scrapes along the hull as the light wind and gentle current carry the sloop down the river toward the Chesapeake. He smiles sheepishly. Nora looks around. *How the hell did he manage to ram a channel marker? The damn thing's four feet wide! Shit, shit, shit!* She does not trust herself to speak.

As *Duet* clears the mark, Nora goes forward to inspect the damage, throwing over her shoulder, "Keep her southwest." Her tone is tight as a violin string, high and thin. She leans over the bow pulpit and sees a jagged wound the size of a baseball glove eighteen inches above the waterline. But there is no hole through the hull. She moves silently to the port side.

"Any damage?" Buck sounds casual, like an innocent bystander. When she does not reply, he continues with an undertone of belligerence—or maybe defensiveness. "Don't worry. Whatever it costs, I'll pay for it. But, hell, we were hardly moving. How bad could it be?"

Nora counts to five before saying flatly, "We have a nasty gouge in the stem and two deep scratches in the gel coat just below the port gunwale." She feels violated, as if her own body has been pierced. Her stomach clenches and a gorge rises in her throat. "But we aren't taking on water. We can get back to port all right."

Buck chuckles, "Great! No big deal, then."

Nora stares at him, trying to get a grip on her anger. *This is my baby you battered. Don't you get that?* His hand rests lightly on the oak tiller. His posture is relaxed. Nora turns her gaze to the open channel. *How could a man who's climbed to the top of the corporate ladder be so careless? Why the hell didn't he watch where he was going?*

*   *   *

"Van, I wanted to kill him. If I have to spend another day with that man, I *may* kill him—with my bare hands."

Hendrick van Pelt watches Nora pace from fireplace to window, throwing her hands up, her head back. She came directly from the boatyard to his house on Faculty Row. Copper-colored tendrils, escaped from the single French braid down her back, curl around her ears. Scarlet streaks her high cheekbones, disguising the dusting of freckles usually clear on her pale face.

Van has never seen her so angry. Nora Perry in high dudgeon is truly formidable—beautiful but formidable. Van likes her broad shoulders and muscular build. He thinks her 5'10" and 165 pounds statuesque. But if *he* had caused those wide brown eyes to flash fire, those capable hands to clench and unclench spasmodically, he would be paddling like hell to get out of the way of the hurricane. As it is, he sits quietly, nods sympathetically, and lets her rant. She will get over it faster that way.

"Three days I've been out with him—just *three days*—and I can't think of a single novice-sailor mistake that Schuyler Buckner Brady *the Second* hasn't made! He insists that he wants to learn to sail but he sure as hell doesn't act like it." She whirls toward Van and raises her fingers one at a time, counting off Buck's weaknesses and sins. "He doesn't *concentrate* when he has the helm and ends up luffing the sails or going through an uncontrolled gybe. He *won't* slow down on the approach to a dock or a mooring. And he doesn't cleat the lines properly, no matter how many times I show him." She pauses to draw breath and continues at lower volume.

"Of course, lots of people have trouble with that. And it's easy for a beginner to misread the compass." Van grins as Nora's inherently fair nature asserts itself. Her fairness is just one of the reasons her faculty colleagues respect her and students flock to her classes.

She reaches the fireplace and turns sharply on her heel. "But to actually ram a channel marker! Who knows how long he was daydreaming or watching the shoreline or whatever the hell he was doing?"

Van's affection for his sailing partner inclines him always to be sympathetic. In this case, his experience teaching sailing lends extra empathy. "I can see that it was frustrating. Is there anything I can do to help?"

"I only wish!" Nora stops and faces Van, feet planted, arms akimbo. "I think the real issue is that he doesn't believe the basics of sailing are the same in a twenty-seven foot sloop like *Duet* as in a hundred-and-thirty-six-foot schooner like the one he's chartered. He *says* he wants to understand what's going on with the schooner, but he dismisses half of what I say as irrelevant." Nora shakes her head.

Van smiles. "Many people have difficulty comprehending the physics of sailing."

"Don't defend him! He just isn't interested. And besides, he is disdainful of anything small or slow—and he's pegged *Duet* as both. He has the mentality of a power-boater," she concludes, disgust thick in her voice. Van chuckles.

"Okay, okay. I know I'm on a rant. But I really do have problems with Buck Brady. And the biggest one is that I'm a woman—more or less his own age, neither his underling nor a potential conquest. Buck is used to being in charge, and taking instruction from a woman galls him. I can feel it. He ignores what I say about the importance of keeping the lines tidy and the gear stowed properly and then budges in and tries to take over when I'm hauling sail or setting the anchor." Van's own first sail with Nora wasn't much more than a year before, the memory of his initial discomfort with a woman skipper still fresh. He feels a spurt of empathy for Buck Brady—but knows better than to say so. Nora stops in front of Van. "I think it was his need to be macho that let him—*caused* him—to be so casual, so *negligent*." Suddenly her eyes fill with tears. "And now my beautiful boat is mangled." She drops onto the sofa beside Van. "Repairs will cost hundreds. Maybe a thousand or more. And by damn, I'm going to let him pay for it!"

Van pushes a fall of brown sun-bleached hair off his forehead and speaks in measured tones. "It seems to me that you have two alternatives. You can put a lock on your feelings and continue with the sailing lessons, or you can tell him to go to hell."

"Damn it, Van, don't tell me what I can do! I want you to pat my hand and say, 'Poor baby. I know just how you feel.' I want *comfort*, not some manly attempt to fix it!"

Van laughs and pats her hand. "Poor baby. I know just how you feel."

Nora laughs, too, and playfully punches his shoulder. "Nice try. A little lacking in sincerity, maybe, but … Listen, if you really want to help, take over Buck's sailing lessons." Van starts to demur but she stops him with an upraised hand. "No, really. He only came to me because Sky told him I'm a good sailor and I know the Bay."

Sky is Buck's son, and as a senior at West the previous fall, was tangentially involved in the Slater murder case, when the investigation, the president's resignation—the whole debacle—had roiled the college the entire academic year. Van shakes his head and again tunes in to what Nora is saying. "But you would be perfect. Really. Just think about it. You're a man *and* you have credentials.

He would love having private lessons from a yacht club instructor who also happens to have a Ph.D. in physics. And as someone who does this as a summer job, you could charge him an arm and a leg. He's the sort of person who values anything that costs him a lot of money."

"You know I have no boat."

"No problem. He's already offered to charter one while *Duet* is being repaired. All you'd have to do is line it up. But get something bigger than *Duet*. I'm sure that would help. You could do a whole male bonding thing." She grins. "And at the same time, you could be a good role model for him—a masculine man who isn't sexist."

Van isn't sure he wants to be a model of anything. He rubs his brow. "How about just telling him to go elsewhere?"

"Van, think about it. We're faculty members. He's a trustee—a brand new trustee. That means he's going to be involved with West College for *at least* the next six years." She shakes her head. "Antagonizing Buck Brady would be cutting off our noses to spite our faces."

Van needs a little time to consider this turn in the conversation. He looks at her hand, curved quietly on the cushion between them, and pushes aside an urge to stroke her fingers. He'd have to be sure of her response before he'd put himself out there with Nora. That isn't a tangent he wants to pursue. "So why did you agree to do this?"

Nora shrugs. "He caught me off guard. He asked whether I would do it as a favor, because he's chartered a schooner for a week in August and invited trustees and their spouses—to welcome President and Mrs. Sloan—even though he's never been sailing in his life! He won't be sailing her, of course, but he said he doesn't want to look like a complete idiot. One thing for sure about Buck Brady: he's a man who never wants to appear ignorant. I can understand that. And ... well, I just wanted to be helpful." Nora laughs. "Besides, he can turn on the charm when he wants to. And just then, he wanted to." She shifts to face him and takes his hand in both of hers. "I really need you to get me out of this. If I have to spend one more day trying to instruct that—that *man*—I'll end up doing the college more harm than good. Not to mention developing ulcers and high blood pressure and maybe having a stroke!" She grips his hand.

Van grins. "You make it sound so very inviting! How could I resist? But perhaps he will refuse my instruction."

"Not to worry. He's set aside this entire week to learn everything there is to know—or at least, all he feels he needs to know—about sailing. You can just take the last four days. He'll be as pleased with a change of instructors as I am. I'll call him now and set it up!" Nora smiles broadly and plants a playful kiss on his cheek before bounding up and heading for the phone.

The warmth of her lips lingers on Van's cheek. When they started this sailing season, Van had admitted his love for Nora—to himself. But in the weeks since, she has persisted in treating him with sisterly affection, throwing up a barrier he has not yet breached. What would he not do for the woman he loves?

Chapter Three

VAN HATES ARRIVING LATE—FEELING APOLOGETIC, starting off one down to Buck Brady—but unexpected road construction added twenty minutes to his trip to Rock Hall.

He scans the deck at Waterman's, packed with people eating crabs at wooden picnic tables. Buck Brady is sipping a martini at the outdoor bar. His booming voice carries clearly to Van. He's informing the occupant of the adjacent stool that he's learning to sail and that he has only a week to do it. "I'm waiting for my instructor now. He usually teaches sailing at a yacht club, but I've commandeered him. My first teacher quit when I knocked a hole in her boat." Buck's grin and his cavalier attitude ignite a flash of anger on Nora's behalf.

Buck's neighbor laughs. "Are you putting me on? It isn't easy to knock a hole in a boat." He chuckles again. "Wouldn't it have been easier just to fire her?"

"Probably. And less expensive, too!" Buck lifts his glass. "Here's to better luck this time." He looks up as Van works his way toward the bar. "Professor! Good of you to take me on. Appreciate it." He swings off the stool.

Van has met Buck Brady only once before. He winces at the familiar tone, acutely aware that he is actually only an associate professor—and reminds himself that outside academe, the distinction doesn't mean much. The two men shake hands, the grip a little harder than it needs to be, and eye each other appraisingly. Buck looks like a man who takes care of himself, more athletic than Van remembered.

"I am pleased to see you again, Mr. Brady."

"Call me Buck."

"Buck, then." Van pauses, expecting Buck to ask by what name he should be addressed. He believes in maintaining a clear line between student and teacher. In his physics classes that includes a certain formality of address. He doubts that this would be effective when the student is ten years older, four inches taller and weighs sixty or seventy pounds more than his teacher. Finally he says, "You may call me Van."

Buck doesn't seem to be listening. "Where's the boat?"

"The one I have reserved is at a marina at the mouth of Swan Creek—a couple of miles away."

Buck slaps a ten on the bar, swallows the residue in his glass, and says loudly, "For you, Charlie. See ya soon." Everything about Buck Brady seems bigger than life—louder. If Van hadn't known better, he'd have thought Buck a regular at Waterman's. Buck pushes his way out of the bar, Van trailing behind. Much in Buck's manner reminds Van of his father. He pushes aside the uncomfortable thought.

"Where's your car, Professor?"

"I parked over by the ice house." Van glances in the direction of his decrepit Toyota Corolla. "I could leave it there for a few days."

"Right. We'll go in mine, then. You navigate."

On the drive to Gratitude Marina, Buck glances toward Van. "I hope *you* can get the job done, Professor." Something in his tone sounds like a criticism of Nora and Van stiffens, readying a retort. But when Buck continues, his tone has turned confidential: "Learning this sailing stuff is important. I mean, no one wants to look like a fool, right? And my wife, Allie—Have you ever met Allie?" Van shakes his head. "Allie's an alum and I want to help her *alma mater*. That's why I chartered the schooner, and invited the other trustees to help me welcome President and Mrs. Sloan. We get away from our offices for a few days, get to know each other, and I'll be one step ahead when I come to my first Board meeting this fall."

On the surface, Buck radiates confidence. But his easy self-disclosures sound a little off-key. Van eyes all the gadgets in the new Lincoln Town car. *What sort of man needs all of this—if his confidence is real?* Van points and says, "Turn left here."

Buck swings onto the potholed macadam. "Whoa! Better slow down. Christ, doesn't Rock Hall have a roads department?" Van begins a mental list of things Buck feels free to criticize. *And we have been together only fifteen minutes.*

"Is an Island Packet any good? You said there wasn't a lot available on such short notice. And it didn't cost that much. I just hope it's bigger than that little boat of Nora's."

Van would give his eyeteeth to own a boat like *Duet*—someday, if he ever gets through with his kids' college debts. His ex-wife makes no financial contribution. But then, she hadn't done so before she left him, either. He pulls his thoughts back to Buck's question. "The Packet is a fine boat—thirty-five feet, well built, and commodious. The cabin has about a six and a half foot head clearance."

"Good. Maybe I won't crack my fuckin' head every time I go below." Van cracked his head often the first time he sailed with Nora. But he won't say anything that might be taken as criticism of her or her boat. He and Buck walk out the dock in silence.

Buck eyes the boat and guffaws. "*Knot a Clew*. That's rich. You think they named her in my honor?"

Van grimaces. He dislikes cute names for boats. He says only, "I checked her out with the charter representative on my way to Waterman's. Everything seems to be in order. Are you ready to sail?"

"Yeah, Professor, ready as I'll ever be."

Van's movements are sure-footed and efficient, a man at home. He drives *Knot a Clew* out into the channel and relinquishes the helm to Buck. As they follow their route along Eastern Neck, Van says, "The United States has adopted the international system for navigational aids. Once you learn them, they'll serve you no matter where you sail."

"Yeah, yeah, yeah. Nora made me memorize the shapes and colors and numbering of channel markers—all that stuff." Buck stares into the distance. "She must've said, 'Red right returning from the sea' a hundred times." His imitation of Nora's voice is uncanny. He glances at Van and resumes in his own voice. "Like I couldn't remember to keep red to starboard without some stupid saying."

"'Red right returning' may sound childish but it is familiar to every sailor, a convenient mnemonic to remember the most basic rule of the lateral system."

Buck looks sideways at Van. "Do you always talk like you've got a stick up your ass?"

Van flushes. "I have been told often that my speech is somewhat stilted."

"That's an understatement!" Buck laughs. "But not to worry. I like it. It suits you."

Van can think of no appropriate response. Silence stretches between them. His thoughts scatter. He contemplates his reaction to Buck's criticisms of Nora's boat, the implied criticisms of Nora and her teaching.

Buck says, "Did I piss you off?"

"No, not at all. I was just musing."

Buck grins. "No shit." He extends his right hand. "Professor, you're okay."

* * *

When they get to the southern end of Swan Point Bar, Van says, "Okay. Bring her right to a course of 240." Buck seems momentarily confused about which direction to turn the wheel. Van says, "Just like a car."

Buck says, "Just when I'd gotten used to a tiller!" Once they are on course, he says, "How about if you steer and I put up the sail? I just pull on that rope, right?"

"Mr. Brady—Buck—if you wish to make a good impression on your trustee colleagues, not to mention the crew and skipper of the schooner you have chartered, you must remember that there are no ropes on a sailboat, only lines. That particular line is the main halyard." Pointing to the double block off the boom, he adds, "That line is called a sheet."

Buck laughs. "Sailors are so full of *sheet*! Why can't you call a rope a rope? And if you have to call them lines, then why call them anything else?"

Van laughs, too. "Like so many professions, sailing has its own vocabulary. It is an efficient shorthand." He glances at Buck's puckered brow and adds, "No one would expect you to know all of the jargon. Just start by remembering that on a sailboat, ropes are lines."

Buck steers in silence for awhile. Suddenly he grins. "What the hell? I can talk lumber camp and I can talk board room—not to mention a little French and a smidgen of Italian. Just give me a dictionary or a glossary or something—and by damn, before this week's out, I'll be talking sailor, too!"

Van laughs with him. "I am sure you will." He thinks Buck can probably do just about anything he sets his mind to.

*   *   *

Buck breaks their companionable after-dinner silence by saying, "Well, Professor, it's time for me to go below. I think I'll read awhile and then turn in."

Van remains topside, looking at the night sky. The stars hover low and clear. He traces the pattern of the Big Dipper, then searches out the other constellations. He recalls nights like this on *Duet* with Nora, and longing washes over him. She can have all the men she wants. And has, if rumor can be believed. But she has given him no reason to believe he could be one of them—at least, not on terms he can accept. *If you know what is good for you, van Pelt—if you don't want to end up a lonely old man—you will find a woman your own age who is not so committed to remaining single.*

*   *   *

The sun comes up in pastel ribbons. The smell of brewing coffee wafts aft on a warm breeze. Van hands Buck a mug. "Time to get underway?" Buck sounds eager.

"Wait a few minutes for the coffee to work its magic."

Buck grinned. "You mean crap time?"

"That is the idea. Meanwhile, get the NOAA weather report on the radio. Try channel two."

Van says, "It sounds like a perfect day. While I'm in the head, you plot a course from the mouth of the Magothy River to the bobble off Love Point." Buck looks uncertain. "Just do it the way I showed you. I will check it before we leave."

Van looks over Buck's notes on their course. It is the first time a novice has gotten it absolutely right on the first try. His only comment is, "Perfect."

Buck throws up his right arm, punching the air. "Yes!"

They depart under power. When *Knot a Clew* clears the last channel marker before the open bay, Buck raises the main and unfurls the genoa. "Take the helm," Van says, relinquishing the wheel.

On their way across the Bay, Van explains the essentials of sail trim. As they come around the bobble off Love Point and head for Castle Marina, Buck tightens the genoa. Van says, "Perfect," proud of Buck's progress.

They sail in silence until Buck blurts, "Christ."

Van jerks to attention. "What?" He doesn't see anything amiss.

"Hitting that channel marker was the last straw for Nora. I'm damned sorry about it—of course I am—but she didn't have to get *that* bent out of shape. It's not like I did it on purpose. She was so mad she wouldn't even talk to me. Even when I said I'd pay for repairs. I mean, it's just a goddamned boat."

Van wonders whether Buck's defensiveness is because he really doesn't understand what he did or because he wasn't able to make amends. "A skipper's boat is a highly personal thing—almost an extension of the self. I imagine some people feel that way about cars or thoroughbred horses. But what is done is done. It will be all right."

Buck looks skeptical. "Yeah. Well. All I can say is, I'm glad you took over the lessons. You're an okay guy. Not that I have anything against Nora. She's a fine little lady."

A vision of Nora, tall and sturdy, standing with feet planted, fists on hips, cursing a blue streak, makes Van grin.

Buck continues. "But I never knew what she was going to do next. She sails just like a man—just like you. But when I fucked up her boat, I didn't know whether she was gonna punch me out or cry!"

Van laughs. "She probably didn't know either." Buck's scowl fades and he lightens his grip on the wheel. Van says, "When we get to R-6 in the Chester River, we will furl the sails and drive her into the marina. I will take her in. You can take her out."

"Whatever you say, Professor."

*   *   *

In spite of a few poor landings and running aground once, by the end of the week, Buck has mastered the rudiments of sailing. As they are off-loading their gear, Van thinks *I do not believe he will steer West College far off course while he is learning to be a trustee.*

Chapter Four

At 3:15, West College President Jim Sloan slides his feet into highly polished loafers and heads downstairs. He pauses in the hall to check his appearance one last time, then runs his hands over his pockets, checking the contents—wallet, eyeglasses, keys, directions to the Roths' house.

He fumbles with the ignition, not yet used to the college-owned car that came with the job. The exhilaration he felt when he won the West College presidency has begun to fade. Right now he wishes for the comfort of the known. Anxious about this first social engagement of his presidency, he heads to Baltimore to pick up his wife.

Jim double-parks in front of her office building, punches the warning blinkers, scans the pedestrian traffic, and sees Rebecca standing by the door. "Christ, she doesn't recognize the car." He taps the horn and waves out the window. When she sees him, she strides to the car, briefcase in hand.

"You're late," she says, tossing her briefcase onto the back seat. "What happened?"

"I made a wrong turn and got screwed up because of a couple of one-way streets." He hands Rebecca directions to the Roths' house.

They drive in silence except for an occasional prompt for a turn until Rebecca says, "This is the street." Pointing, she adds, "That must be the house over there."

Jim whistles. "Not too shabby."

Rebecca bristles. "Having dinner with the chair of the Board Finance Committee could affect your entire presidency." She grips his arm. "Don't act like an awe-struck hayseed."

Approaching the door, Jim keeps his face blank as a drawn curtain. But Rebecca's lack of confidence in him hurts. "Successful presidents have supportive wives," he snaps.

Rebecca narrows her eyes, mouth drawn razor-thin. But she says nothing.

* * *

Nathanial Roth opens the door. Jim thinks he looks like a model in *Esquire*—an ad for Sutton Place tailor-made shirts, perhaps: slim, tall, dark hair combed straight back.

"Come in, come in," Nate says, gesturing toward the foyer. He takes Rebecca's elbow and guides her into the hall, chatting amiably. He is a man of grace and style, with an easy manner—the sort of man Jim has always tried to be.

Jim's darting glances take in the chandelier, the oriental carpet, the antique Chinese vases—and Mrs. Roth, standing still as a statue, hands folded delicately in front of her, smiling, awaiting an introduction. *Not very attractive. Hips too wide, a pug nose, and frizzy dyed hair, almost orange in this light.*

Nate says, "This is my wife, Priscilla—my guiding star."

Jim swallows his surprise and says, "How do you do?" He doesn't know what he expected, but not this mismatched couple.

Priscilla smiles. "I am so pleased to meet you both. I've heard a lot about you, Jim. And I look forward to knowing more about you, Rebecca."

Nate glances at his watch, exposing a monogrammed shirt cuff. "We thought we'd have cocktails on the patio if that suits you."

"Show the way," Jim says.

*   *   *

"Everybody's drink okay?" Nate asks. Everyone nods. He chooses three almonds and slides the crystal dish toward his guests. "So what's the good Mr. Brady done now?"

Jim scoops a handful of nuts up the side of the bowl and adopts a poker face. "He wants Hendrick van Pelt to join us on the schooner. I gather they got pretty chummy earlier this summer. I told him there'd be hell to pay—a trustee singling out a faculty member as his fair-haired boy like that."

Nate smiles and shrugs. "No doubt it's good for him to have his preferences thwarted occasionally."

Jim grins. "Well, he wasn't exactly thwarted. He'd already invited him and Van had accepted! So I suggested he also invite Nora Perry. She sails, too, and she's Chair of the Faculty for the next couple of years. Van's the new faculty representative to the Board. We could present it as having the faculty leadership represented—which would make Van's inclusion go down better. Buck ranted a bit about not pandering to prickly academic egos. But I insisted."

Nate lifts his chin and looks down his long, narrow nose at Jim. "We all admire the self-made man," he says. "But Brady may have more dollars than sense. If you're not careful, you could end up with a rogue trustee."

Jim studies Nate's face. *Does he just dislike Buck? Does he even know him well?* His gaze moves to Rebecca and Priscilla, now talking quietly as they walk through the herb garden. He says, "I don't think he'll be as bad as all that. He just needs a little mentoring in the role of a trustee and the culture of West College. Perhaps you could take him under your wing, Nate."

"Not bloody likely!" Nate laughs. "Can you imagine any two trustees who are less alike?" Jim pictures the slim, elegant Nathaniel Roth playing big brother to the loud, burly Buck Brady and sees the absurdity. Nate shakes his head. "He has rough edges. And no feel for the done thing. You need to bring Brady into line pronto or you might as well just hand him the reins. You're right that someone needs to take him aside—tell him what's what. But I'm not your man—more a job for the Chairman of the Board. He seems actually to like Brady."

Rebecca returns from contemplating the herb garden while Nate is speaking. Her voice is low-pitched and cool when she says, "I can understand that. I met him only briefly, but I rather liked him myself." She traces the crease of her beige pants along one slim thigh. "He's certainly smart, high energy, and successful. He must be exceptionally capable, too, to have amassed so much wealth when he's barely over fifty." Rebecca shifts from her summing-up-for-the-jury tone to one with a hint of laughter. "Besides all that," she says, lifting the long mane of dark brown hair off her neck, "a lot of women would think he's sexy."

"No doubt a lot of men would think so, too," Nate says dryly. "But this isn't about sex appeal—or even about having more money than any three other trustees put together. It's about knowing one's place. If the most junior hire at your law firm took it upon himself to host a party for the new senior partner, without so much as a by-your-leave, there'd be hell to pay. Many trustees feel that Buck Brady was presumptuous, appointing himself a one-man welcoming committee for you and Jim."

Priscilla Roth rolls her eyes. "Oh, Lordy. Let's not get bogged down in an interminable discussion of Bulldozer Buck."

"Priscilla!" Nate sounds pained.

"What?" She looks at Nate, her blue eyes open wide. "Everyone calls him that." She flashes a smile at Jim and Rebecca. "Well, *I* don't—except in very special company. But tell me it doesn't fit, the way he rides roughshod over everyone, flattening all opposition, drowning out every objection."

"You're mixing your metaphors," Nate says, patting her hand and chuckling. As he draws his hand back, he moves Pris's drink glass to the serving tray.

Priscilla glances away and busies herself resetting one of her hair combs. Jim wonders whether she suffers from a delusion that pulling her frizzy orange hair back on both sides disguises the moon shape of her face. Mostly it calls attention to her graying roots. She stands abruptly, smoothing the long black skirt over her wide hips, bumping the patio table and making the tray of glassware tinkle as she turns toward the house. "I'll go check on dinner. It's Celia's day off. George is magic in the kitchen but he is absolutely *hopeless* at table."

Jim shifts his gaze from Priscilla to the flowerbeds, acutely aware that of the four, he is the only one who grew up in a house without servants. The hired hands on his parents' farm in Minnesota were something else altogether. He looks around the table, wondering how he will handle the faculty, the trustees—and whether he will be able to handle his wife any better than Nate seems to handle Priscilla.

Rebecca glances at Jim. "Do we know yet who will be on the schooner? I mean, besides the four of us, the Bradys, and Van?"

Jim looks at her. Wasn't she listening when he talked about it last night? Priscilla's call to dinner cuts off whatever he might have said about the guest list.

*   *   *

Nate and Priscilla close the door behind the Sloans and return to the living room. Pris feels the warm glow of a job well done—enhanced, perhaps, by the several glasses of wine. "That seemed to go well," she says.

"The evening did go well. I appreciate your part in that." Nate sips the last of his brandy.

"I enjoyed meeting Rebecca." She cuts a sidelong look at Nate. "She's very attractive."

"I suppose she is."

"Suppose? As if you didn't spend half of the evening looking at her, smiling, holding her chair, pouring her wine …"

"Priscilla, be reasonable. I was just being a courteous host. There's nothing to be jealous of." He holds her gaze till Pris looks aside. Something in his tone tells her this isn't the time to bring up his constant flirting—not if she wants the evening to end well.

Nate continues. "Jim's new, but he should make a decent show—given a little behind-the-scenes guidance. Together, we can handle Buck Brady."

"You want to be the power behind the throne!" Nate scowls. "Not that there's anything wrong with that." She bites her lip. "Anyway, one nice thing about Rebecca is that she doesn't put on airs. A big-time contracts attorney could easily look down her nose at a woman like me, with no career beyond volunteer work. But there's no hint of that. And she's funny as anything." Nate shakes his head. "What?" Pris asks, patting her hair.

"You're too hard on yourself. You make important contributions to the community. Besides, she isn't 'big time'—not yet, anyway. She only got the job after Sloan was hired at West, has been with the firm less than a month. But who knows? Someday she *may* be big time—on a par with her father, even. She doesn't seem the sort to 'look down her nose' at you, but even if she did, I doubt you'd know it. She's old money, after all—third generation at least."

Nate's dissenting opinions make her temper flare. "If having old money puts people somewhere between perfect and flawless, what's *your* problem?"

"Not having enough of it."

"There you go again!" Pris rolls her eyes. "You have *plenty* of money. Your salary as CEO of The Roth Foundation. *And* you have a lifetime income from your parents' trust."

Nate sighs. "I have plenty of *income*, Priscilla. The trust principle goes to the twins. I don't even control it. It isn't at all the same as having money of my own." His mouth twists into a bitter smile. "I find it ironic that the money I come closest to controlling is the money I give away! But even there, the Foundation Board could overrule my grant decisions if it wanted. They could fire me if, in their collective wisdom, that seemed warranted. And then where would we be?"

"Right where we are now! Income is the money that counts, Nate. And my trust is even bigger than yours."

"No doubt you think that's very comforting." He stands abruptly and smoothes his sleek hair. "I'm going to bed." He turns toward the stairs. "Don't drink too much, Pris."

Priscilla looks at his slim straight back as he leaves and wishes she could start again and turn the conversation in a different direction. Her gaze lingers on the place where he had been. *We seem to have more and more run-ins these days, blowing up out of nowhere. It wasn't always that way.* "Of course," she mumbles to the empty room, "nothing's the way it used to be." Pris pours another nightcap. *What difference does it make? I won't be going to Nate's room anyway.*

When she and Nate started dating, it felt like a fairytale come true: she was thirty-five and in love for the first time. At thirty-three, the only heir to the Roth furniture fortune would have been a good catch barring anything but two heads and a criminal record. But Nate was good looking, witty, and a romantic suitor as well. Priscilla Twitmeyer wasn't the only one who couldn't believe she had captured his heart. They were married as soon as she could arrange the ceremony. She went into such a frenzy of planning that even the cousins who were her bridesmaids giggled behind their hands that "Prissy Twit isn't giving him much time to reconsider." They thought she didn't hear.

She stares into her bourbon. "But it wasn't like that!" she whispers. "He wanted it as much as I did—back then."

Before marriage, Priscilla's only sexual experience had been with Joe, a Franklin and Marshall undergraduate who invited her to be his date for a big party. She was thrilled. And pleased to see that not all fraternity men put a premium on beauty. Most of the women at the party were quite plain. Everyone drank. One of the guys took pictures. And after the party, Pris and her date had sex. She didn't remember the sex very clearly, but she remembered the hurt when she didn't hear from him in the following two weeks. She called and was told he was in class, at soccer practice, "out." Finally his exasperated roommate said, "Look, he only invited you to the party as a joke. It was our Fifteenth Annual Dog Show. He doesn't want to see you again—not even in the dark." The hurt and humiliation made her wary of any man who showed an interest in her. But Nate had persisted, had overcome her defenses.

Pris refills her glass and stares into the fireplace, feeling middle-aged. *Maybe he just doesn't love me anymore.*

On her wedding night, she discovered how good sex could feel. She and Nate made love nearly every night—or day—in those early months. She felt almost pretty. But her libido waned when she got pregnant. She'd been grateful that Nate was so accepting. He'd insisted that he didn't really mind. But after the twins were born, it was never the same. The delivery was hard and she was depressed for the better part of a year. Nate was gentle and solicitous and understanding. He assured her that she was as desirable as ever. But they seldom made love. She came home one evening from a meeting of the Outreach Committee at church and found that he had moved his bedroom to the third floor. He said he couldn't get any sleep with two crying infants next door. When she said that she could move to the third floor, too, he said firmly that a mother needed to be near her babies. The twins are now nineteen. But Nate had so many reasons why their sleeping arrangements should remain separate that she'd stopped bringing it up years ago.

It's amazing how much distance separates the second floor from the third. Pris tells herself they both are content with the arrangement of their lives—that sex isn't everything. Still, she is very aware that this year their anniversary will fall during their time on the schooner. They will be sharing a cabin for nearly a week. Priscilla smiles and pours another bourbon.

*   *   *

Rebecca doesn't look up from her papers. "Hmmm?" She jots a note in the margin of a contract and bites down on the end of her red marking pen, hoping Jim will take the hint and leave her alone.

"I said, 'I hope this sail isn't a total disaster.'" Jim stands by the fireplace, fists in the pockets of his robe. "Some of the trustees are irritated about it. You know, setting it up so late and expecting people to change their plans comes across as arrogant. Others think Buck did it that way on purpose, knowing a lot of people would have unbreakable plans, so he could appear magnanimous but get by on the cheap."

Jim moves to where Rebecca has set up her favorite workstation, a brown leather club chair with matching ottoman. He stands at the corner of the lapboard across the arms of her chair, nudges the pile of papers sticking out over the edge. Rebecca glances up. "You're hovering."

"Sorry." He turns aside, bumps her briefcase standing open on the floor, and sloshes seltzer with lime onto the lamp table at her elbow. "Sorry," he mumbles.

Rebecca pushes her reading glasses onto the top of her head and folds her hands on the lapboard. *Dammit.*

Jim holds up his right hand. "I know, I know. You're going to say that they brought Buck onto the Board before I even got here and if they find him too strong willed—well, they need to deal with it. All very logical. But the bottom line is that if the members of the Board get into a pissing contest, I'm the one who's likely to get caught in the cross-fire."

Rebecca arches one eyebrow, hoping her disgust doesn't show. "Not a pretty picture."

"No, I guess not." Jim picks up the snow-scene paperweight they bought on their honeymoon and tosses it into the air a couple of times before returning it to the shelf. He paces back and forth beside the window. "It's just—I don't even know these people. I need to get on top of the job quickly and a week on a sailboat seems like a waste of time."

"Well, you'll just have to deal with it." Rebecca watches Jim stop beside an end table and straighten the magazines, cross to the bookshelves, pick up a framed snapshot of his children and put it down again. She feels like screaming "Stop fidgeting!" but says,

"There's nothing preventive you can do." She shifts her weight and puts her glasses back on. "Getting yourself all worked up tonight serves no useful purpose." She keeps her eyes on the contract while Jim walks around the room, straightens pillows, moves things a fraction of an inch. Finally she says, "You're prowling." *How can you not know that your dithering drives me crazy?*

He stops where he stands. Rebecca glances at him, then back at her paperwork. He says, "So you think Buck Brady is sexy, huh?"

"What I actually said was that a lot of women would think so. But now that you ask, yes, I do. It's just an observation." *Surely you know the kind of man I'm drawn to. Strong, decisive men, like my father—or Nate—or Buck Brady.* Rebecca turns a page of the contract.

"You work too hard, Becca. It's after 11:00. Are you coming to bed soon?"

Rebecca takes a deep breath and exhales slowly. "Jim, I've asked you a hundred times not to call me Becca. Only my father calls me that. And I'm the new kid at the firm. I've got to work hard. I told you yesterday that I had contracts to review before I return to Baltimore Sunday night."

"This is only Friday."

"You know I don't like to leave things to the last minute." Jim turns toward the hall. Rebecca scowls at the contract until she hears the closing of their bedroom door. Then she rests her head on the chair back, draws another deep breath, and relaxes into the aloneness.

Once upon a time, Rebecca liked everything about Jim, from his easy-going nature to the leather elbow patches on his tweed jackets. He'd seemed a welcome contrast to her hard-driving father and fiercely competitive coworkers. *There was a time when I thought being a brilliant scholar made everything else unimportant.*

But ultimately, every man she's ever met is measured against the standard of her father. It is becoming increasingly clear that Jim isn't anything like her father. She taps her pen on the contract. Rebecca hates it when extraneous thoughts press into her consciousness, get in the way of her work. Anger begins to surface. *Maybe I made a mistake marrying Jim.*

Rebecca turns her thoughts to the dinner party with the Roths. *It wasn't bad, actually. Nate is exceedingly good looking, and suave— not to mention a little flirty. How did he come to marry Miss Piggy?* Priscilla's frizzy hair, pug nose, and little squinty eyes made the nickname inevitable in Rebecca's mind, though never in a thousand years would it cross her lips. *She's awfully nice. And probably smart enough. But still ... I wonder whether she has a drinking problem.* Rebecca shifts in her chair and sips her seltzer. *Nate could be very helpful to a new president. I'll have to encourage that relationship.* Weariness settles on her bones. *But where am I going to find a friend? Strong, capable women probably aren't plentiful in Centreville.*

Chapter Five

RICHARD EMORY TRUDGES ALONG THE Annapolis harbor dock, a black canvas duffel bag in each hand. His broad shoulders and chest are out of proportion to his short legs and slim hips. He leans into the weight of the bags. Carol, half a step behind, scurries to keep up. He should have told her about Buck Brady coming onto the Board. He should have told her that Allie would surely be on the schooner. But he couldn't stand Carol prying into his thoughts, his feelings—couldn't bear hearing Allie's name on her lips. He curses himself for not finding a way to keep Carol off this sail.

Anticipation and dread have shredded his sleep for nearly a month. *Will Allie still be hurt? Angry? Maybe she'll pity me—or despise me—for staying married to Carol. Or worse: maybe she won't care.* He breaks out in a sweat. His heart hammers his ribcage. He aches to see her smile again, to feel her soft tapered fingers on his arm, his chest, his body. *What if she still loves me, too? How the hell will I live with that?*

Thoughts he has tried to suppress now assault him. *There's probably more than one man in the world named Buck Brady. And* even if this is the one she married, they might have divorced years ago. No one's mentioned Allie. If I weren't such a godforsaken coward, I'd have asked someone about her. Approaching the schooner *Endeavor*, he is afraid to stop or even slow down lest he turn back. He dreads Allie's scorn—or her fury—but he dreads her absence even more. His pace quickens. When Carol bleats, "Richie, slow *down*," he turns on her. "If you can't keep up, the boat will wait."

Stepping onto *Endeavor's* gangway, Richard scans the deck for Allie. He sees a shoulder that might be hers, but the woman is mostly obscured by two men standing on deck. One man steps forward and says, "You must be Richard Emory. I'm Buck Brady. Glad you could make it." He holds out a beefy hand. Richard drops the duffels and shakes hands.

The man Richard has tagged as the captain says, "I'm your skipper, Mike Marcy. Welcome aboard."

The men's words hardly register. The skipper must be six-six and Brady only a couple of inches shorter. Both men have full heads of hair. Richard is suddenly very aware that his own balding pate barely tops five-seven. *What would Allie think of the comparison?*

"And this is my wife Allie," Brady says, turning to put his arm across the shoulders of a tall slim blond and draw her forward.

More than two decades, but he would have known her anywhere. Her hair still forms a cap of short, wispy tendrils. She still stands with both feet firmly planted and tilts her head ever-so-slightly to the right. She holds out her hand and Richard feels her long, cool fingers across his hot palm. Her blue eyes hold Richard's brown ones in a steady gaze. She says, "I'm pleased to meet you, Mr. Emory." Her voice is soft and low. Did he imagine a note of intimacy? The slight pressure before she let go of his hand? "I'm glad you could join us."

Richard nods, trying to breathe around the pain in his chest.

So, that's the way she wants to play it. He turns to block Carol's passage, his glare hard and stone dead. She sucks in her breath and looks wary. "Come meet our skipper, Captain Marcy. And our hosts, Buck and Allie Brady." He grips her elbow and turns back to the others saying, "My wife, Carol."

Carol emits a tiny moan, quickly stifled. She looks from Allie to Richard and back again. She draws away a little and Richard tightens his grip on her arm. Allie smiles thinly and holds out her hand. "How do you do?" The press of Richard's fingers is forward and Carol takes the proffered hand, then snatches hers away as if burned.

Mike Marcy looks sharply at Carol. "Are you all right, Mrs. Emory?"

"Oh, yes." Her voice is faint. "Just a little queasy—from the heat, I think."

"Well, let's get you below then. Your stateroom is cooler. Maybe you should take a Dramamine." At his gesture one of the crew steps forward. "Take the Emorys below."

The mate picks up their duffles and leads Carol down the companionway. Richard follows, suppressing an urge to wipe his sweaty palms on his pants. Grabbing Carol ... He's never lost control like that before. The spurt of violence has left him shaken. But his heart and mind still reach out to Allie. *Christ, why didn't I marry her when I had the chance?*

*   *   *

Van rests an elbow on the varnished oak rail and sniffs the salt air, relishing the prospect of a few days sailing. He admires Captain Marcy's ease and assurance as he greets arriving passengers. Van has difficulty interacting with strangers—especially people of wealth and power—and knowing that's what this sail entails casts a pall on his mood. He runs his hand along a manila line coiled on a stout wooden peg, then smells his fingers. A whiff of the pungent oil preservative reminds him of his year at the Maritime Academy, of his youth, of the scent of seaweed and tidal pools, and the musty smell of sun-baked salt—of a time when everything seemed possible.

Van watches the waves and listens to the chatter among passengers and crew. He learns that Captain Marcy skippered *Endeavor* when she carried cargo from Rockland, Maine to Boston, before she was refitted for passenger charter—and that he's a proud man, proud of his Master's license and of his local reputation as a top-notch skipper, a man happy in his own skin.

Nora steps on the gangway and Van's tension drains away. He steps forward. "Hello, Nora."

She looks up and the sun flashes copper in her hair. "Have I missed anything?"

"Not really. I have been enjoying the air, checking out the schooner's rigging, people watching."

Nora laughs. "People watching, huh? An astute observer like you must have picked up some interesting tidbits. So, give. What did I miss?" She looks at him, eyebrows raised.

Van shifts his weight and glances at the other people on deck. He does not mention the most telling exchanges: Rebecca Sloan's chagrin that she can't get a writing table in her stateroom; the disturbing way Richard Emory treated his wife; Priscilla Roth's request for a double bed because she and her husband will be celebrating their anniversary in two days—and, as she spoke, Nate Roth's face flaming crimson. Van feels like a voyeur—unintentional, but a voyeur nevertheless—embarrassed, and sordid by association. He says, "Well, Buck Brady has asked the skipper for a turn at the helm once we are underway."

Nora rolls her eyes and whispers, "God help us. Let's talk later.

Right now, I need to get below and find my billet." She disappears down the companionway. Van's mood dims with her leaving.

* * *

Endeavor is well out into the Bay, traveling south in the main shipping lanes toward Bloody Point on a circle sail to accustom the passengers to the ship. Traffic is light. Nate Roth paces the afterdeck, wearing dress whites and a scowl. *Maybe he is thinking about his upcoming anniversary.* Van feels alone, assaulted by memories of his own failed marriage—of his wife leaving with another man while he was at a meeting of the Acoustical Society, taking most of their belongings, leaving little but a note on the mantel. He mentally shakes himself and turns from the rail.

Nearing the companionway ladder, Van hears voices coming from below. Not wanting company, he pauses.

Speaking quietly, the first mate says, "That prissy old fart—Livingston?—kicked up a hell of a fuss, demanding to know why the Chairman of the Board is bunking with a faculty member when there's a perfectly good bunk available in his cabin. I said cabin assignments aren't my job. He didn't like it."

"He'll get over it." Captain Marcy's voice is a low rumble.

"Who's gonna sit at the head of the table with you? The Bradys and the Sloans?"

"Who else? Nobody outranks the honoree and the moneyman. But if I had my druthers, I'd have Nora Perry on my right and Melissa Nelson on my left. Nora is a fine figure of a woman, and I've heard she's a good sailor, too. And Melissa Nelson's a real beauty." Van recalls Melissa Nelson coming aboard. A good looking brunette—mid-thirties or so—some job high up with CNN in New York. Marcy chuckles. "Not a sailor, apparently, but sleek as a cat. You can't have everything!"

"As your trusty first mate, I could take care of those two ladies for you. I'd be happy to do it."

"You wish! You're between Priscilla Roth and Carol Emory. They need a little TLC. See they get it. I'd be damned surprised if Mrs. Emory doesn't have bruises." Van hears a deep sigh. "I sure as hell hope I don't have a wife-beater on board."

The voices fade but Van waits a couple of minutes before he descends the companionway, his step lighter than his heart. *Right now, I wish I knew a little less about my fellow passengers.*

* * *

Richard is flat on his back, staring at the ceiling. Carol has been weeping and bitching by turns. Right now she weeps. "How could you do this to me, Richie? How could you?" Richard says nothing and she raises her voice. "You *knew*. Admit it! You knew and you never told me."

Richard doesn't look at her. "I didn't know anything." The words come out flat as planks.

"You're a liar! A goddamned fucking liar!" She pummels his chest with her fists until he catches her wrists and pushes her away.

"Believe what you want. I won't discuss it." He still hasn't looked at her. "And if you don't stop carrying on, everyone on board will know you're a jealous, hysterical bitch."

"I don't care!" Carol hisses. "I don't care if the whole world knows you and Allie Brady had an affair. That whore almost broke up my marriage and now the two of you want to act like you never even met!" She throws herself face down on her bunk, the pillow muffling her sobs.

Her crying rakes his soul. *I should try to comfort her. Jesus Christ, what kind of a sonofabitch am I?* Richard rises from his bunk, moving like a man wading through wet cement. "Carol, hush. Everything's going to be all right." He strives to be matter-of-fact, the words falling like stones.

Carol jumps up and buries her wet face against his neck. "Oh, Richie, I don't know what I'd do if you ever left me."

He puts one hand on her back and unclenches his teeth. "I've told you, Carol—over and over: I'll take care of you."

"Do you mean it? Oh, Richie, if you mean it, make love to me. Make love to me now." Carol kisses his neck and rubs her pelvis against him.

Richard's stomach turns over, but he nods.

Carol tears off her clothes and lies naked on the bunk. Richard strips from the waist down and reaches for the bottle of body oil Carol holds. He drips oil onto her mound, and Carol smoothes it into all the places it needs to go. But when she reaches for him, he steps back. He oils himself until his organ is thick and stiff, wishing Carol would close her eyes, but she doesn't. He flips her onto her stomach. Carol crouches on her knees, her forehead resting on her crossed wrists. "Come on, Richie," she whispers. "Love me. Come on, baby."

Richard kneels behind her and drives into her body. He can fuck anytime, anywhere, all day, all night. *But I haven't made love since the last time I was with Allie.* He bites down on his lip to keep from crying out and draws blood. He slams into Carol again and again, punishing them both.

* * *

Nora surveys the table. Captain Marcy is holding forth to half the diners while keeping an eye on the other half. "I'm out of Camden, Maine myself, but my first mate came up from the British Virgins. Of course, that means he doesn't know a thing about potato navigation." The skipper pauses. Nora suspects that he tells this story on every charter.

Rebecca Sloan says, "And just what is 'potato navigation, Captain?'"

"Potato navigation is unique to the coast of Maine—the natural child of Maine potatoes and Maine fog. When the fog rolls in thicker than oyster stew, so thick you can't even see your bowsprit, you send a deckhand forward with a bag of potatoes. Every two minutes he heaves a potato dead ahead as far as he can. He listens for the splash. If there's no splash, you're in big trouble. And you better change course before you hit the rocks."

Jim Sloan says, "You must be joking."

Marcy turns to the Bradys. "As the only other New Englanders here, it's up to you to vouch for my sincerity."

Buck guffaws. Allie smiles and says, "This much I can vouch for: potato navigation is part of the lore Down East. At the very least, it makes a good story."

Marcy grins broadly. "And like any good story, there's a lot of truth in it. The coast is rough and not at all forgiving if you run aground—not like your soft-bottomed Chesapeake. In Maine, you can sail close enough to the rocky shore to scratch a match and still be in forty feet of water. But if there's no splash, you could punch a hole in your hull or tear off your keel."

Nora scans the table. Pris is laughing and chatting with the first mate. Her eyes are a little too bright, her color a little too high, her comments a little too loud. Nate's eyes are on his plate, his lips clamped tight. Carol Emory seems to be trying to engage her husband's attention. He says little, his brooding eyes on the captain's end of the table. Nora wonders whether everyone will remain civil. Melissa Nelson says something to Van that Nora can't hear. She seems to be taking every opportunity to vamp Van. Van tilts his head toward Melissa, smiling. He seems a lot happier than when Nora saw him on deck.

She turns to Bill Baxter on her right. The Chairman of the Board is a widower in his mid-fifties. He's done good things for West over the last five years, leading a successful campaign to renovate campus buildings and update the science labs. Seeing him in action at Board meetings, Nora has been impressed. But she knows virtually nothing of him socially. Now she says, "So, is your brewery a family business?"

"It is now. Both my sons are involved in the operation already. But my father was a regional VP with Sherwin-Williams, headquartered in Cleveland."

"Paint to beer seems like a big leap."

Bill hunches one muscular shoulder. "In college a friend turned me on to expensive Belgian ales . Dad kept me on a tight rein, so I was in no position to buy them. I picked up a brewing kit for free at a yard sale—a fermenting bucket, a bottling bucket, some basic tools, and instructions—and started making kit beers at the frat house. A kit's like using a cake mix for baking. The beers weren't half bad, though—it's actually pretty hard to really screw up a batch of beer—but they were nothing special, either. My friends didn't complain."

"I'll bet you were the life of the party."

"I don't know about the life, but certainly the spirit!" Bill chuckles. "I was lucky. I found a way to be a geek *and* be popular. Beer's all about the chemistry."

"And the rest is history?"

"Pretty much. Dad was footing my college bills, so I could spend summers working for free at breweries to get some experience. I knew early on that I wanted to make a living doing something I love. A fifty thousand dollar loan and lots of hard work later, Baxter Brewing was off and running. I developed a proprietary yeast strain we guard like liquid gold. And I still create most of the recipes."

Nora says, "The oldest written recipe discovered to date is for beer. It's on a four-thousand-year-old clay tablet found in Mesopotamia. But I suppose you knew that."

"I did, actually. But I'm surprised you do. I thought I was talking to a brewing novice."

"You are. But I collect cookbooks."

"How about a stroll on deck after dinner?" Bill's tone is soft and inviting.

Nora flashes a broad smile. "I'd love to." .

As the passengers linger over coffee or a last sip of wine, Marcy taps his glass to gather their attention. He invites everyone to participate in sailing the schooner. He goes over the Do and Don't List and explains the safety features of *Endeavor*. "The Coast Guard requires us to instruct you in the life jacket drill, the lowering and launching of a lifeboat, and procedures to follow if we lose someone overboard. My first mate will review these topside, while there's still daylight. Don't hesitate to ask questions."

The safety orientation ends a few minutes before 20:00 hours as *Endeavor* heads toward her anchorage in the outer harbor at Annapolis. The crew does the cross-check. The night damp drives all but a few passengers below. Nora and Bill walk the deck. At the stern, they pass Richard Emory in tense conversation with Nate Roth. Nora thinks, *Huh. I wouldn't have taken them for chums. But maybe there's kinship in unhappy marriages.*

Nora is inclined to leave them their privacy but Bill pauses and adopts an exaggeratedly severe tone. "Don't tell me you're discussing Finance Committee business. This is supposed to be a holiday from all that."

Both men look momentarily startled and Nate murmurs something that includes the words "nothing serious."

Bill says, "You're missing a great evening for a stroll." Nora's speculation ends as Bill draws her hand through his arm. She's surprised that his forearm is so hard-muscled, and realizes that she's only ever seen Bill in a suit. He's wearing a navy blazer now, but surely he'll get more casual as the sail progresses. They turn to take the starboard route forward to the bow. She hears the strumming of a guitar and sees one of the crew, guitar in hand, singing in a quiet baritone. *With that face and that voice, by this time tomorrow, he'll be the darling of all the female passengers.*

Nora hums along with "Flow, Sweet River Flow." She sees Melissa slide her hand through Van's arm and hears her say, "Can you think of anything more romantic than this?" *She doesn't hesitate to go after what she wants!*

Van nods in Nora's direction. He and Melissa pause at the railing near Nate and Richard.

Nora and Bill lean on the rail, silently watching the western sky work its way toward dark as it swallows the day's last light.

Chapter Six

NORA STANDS TOPSIDE IN THE morning light, the sun painting the east in ribbons of lavender and pink. The ship's clock strikes eight bells. *Endeavor* is anchored near the mouth of the Severn River. She savors the familiar view of Annapolis a mile upstream—the church spires, the domes of the State Capitol and Bancroft Hall at the Naval Academy. Her mood doesn't fit the idyllic setting. She is bunking with Melissa Nelson—"Call me Lissa"—whose incessant questions about Van wear on Nora's patience. *Is he always so courteous? Is he married? How long has he been divorced? What does he do besides teach physics and sail? What are his favorite foods? Don't you think he's just the handsomest thing? Is he seeing anyone in particular?* Lissa's infatuation with Van might be entertaining in smaller doses, but the constancy of its display is plucking Nora's last nerve.

The crew is preparing for departure. Few of her fellow passengers have come topside. Eastward, the open water toward Kent Island is sun-struck and *Endeavor* seems to ride at anchor on a sea of fractured mirrors.

Captain Marcy puts the rudder amidships and shouts, "Weigh anchor." The Singing Deckhand—as Nora had privately dubbed him—strides forward to haul the anchor, inviting Van, Lissa, and Buck to take the other spokes of the capstan. Nora leans against the rail nearby, watching.

Lissa murmurs, "With all the muscle around this wheel thing, you guys won't even know I'm here."

Buck chuckles and winks at her.

Van says, "You would always be noticed."

Nora marvels that a woman of Lissa's experience and achievements fishes for compliments so blatantly.

As they circle the capstan, the deckhand breaks into a sea chantey. The other three join in the refrain, Van's fine bass carrying clearly.

> Well, a hundred years on the eastern shore
> *Oh yes, Oh.*
>
> ...

By the time they get to the last verse, their actions suit the words:

> Well, I thought I heard the old man say
> *Oh, yes, Oh*
> Well, it's one more turn and then belay
> *A hundred years ago.*

When the red chain link comes through the chock, signaling that the anchor is out of the water, the deckhand shouts down the wind, "Anchor aweigh." He peers over the rail at the anchor. "Clean as a whistle," he says. His handsome face always seems to carry a mischievous smile. He grins at Lissa. "Sometimes bottom mud hangs on the hook like guilt on a novice sinner." She laughs and flutters her lashes. He whistles a few bars of "What Shall We Do With A Drunken Sailor" as he hauls the anchor aboard.

Does she really think making eyes at the crew will draw Van in? Nora wants to stomp over there and shake some sense into the younger woman. The vision of such an unseemly act nails her feet to the deck. She keeps her eyes on the water, but wonders what Van does think of Lissa's flirting.

Endeavor moves majestically out of Annapolis harbor, past the radio towers, toward the Bay Bridge and Baltimore. The power of the schooner under full sail overcomes Nora's irritation. She stops at the helm near the first mate. "She sails beautifully."

"Aye, she does. A grand lady—despite her age. She was built in 1938." The mate glances at the main mast's pennant. "With the wind out of the southwest and the ebb current, we'll likely get more chop before long." Van joins them. The mate shifts his gaze from the ship's compass to his visitors. "So you guys are the professors who sail, right?"

Nora nods. "How do you know?"

"We always try to know something about our passengers." *Endeavor* clears a mark. The mate checks the compass and the fathometer. "Would one of you wanna take the helm?"

Van says, "I am sure we both would like a turn. You first, Nora."

Nora takes the helm, relishing the feeling of leashing the elements, concentrating on keeping *Endeavor* on course but aware of Van and the first mate at her back. Her body moves in counterpoint as *Endeavor* breaks through the mounting waves. Spray wets her face. She runs her tongue over her lips to taste the salt.

They sail in silence until the mate says, "Nice going. You steer small." Nora smiles, pleased at the compliment that she held a steady course. The three chat about *Endeavor's* size, speed, and handling. After fifteen minutes or so, she relinquishes the helm to Van. She watches his strong, steady hands on the wheel, understanding the grin that lights his face. Memories of their sails together on *Duet* surface—memories of fighting heavy weather, sharing galley duty, enjoying the night sky. Their companionship is more important than any other friendship she has. She looks at Van. He's looking at her—a long glance with an expression that Nora thinks says, "We understand each other."

The mate interrupts her thoughts. "For a couple of professors, you guys have a real feel for the helm."

Captain Marcy joins them topside. "Cold front coming through on Wednesday. We'll have a northwest breeze by Wednesday night and all day Thursday. Could be we'll get some weather."

* * *

The singing deckhand gathers Nora, Priscilla Roth, and Adrian Livingston for the twice-daily deck scrub, each armed with a stiff, long-handled brush. "We need to keep the deck planks wet so the wood stays swollen and watertight." He demonstrates. "Always across the grain. Always across the grain."

Priscilla giggles. "I guess we all better get to it if we don't want to end up like the Ancient Mariner: 'Water, water everywhere and not a drop to drink. Water, water everywhere and all the boards did shrink.'"

Livingston sniffs. "I believe the correct quotation is 'Water, water everywhere and all the boards did shrink; Water, water everywhere nor any drop to drink.'"

Priscilla rolls her eyes at Nora. "Whatever."

* * *

Nora stands on the port side, shielded from the spray amidship, enjoying the rhythm of the schooner breaking through the blue-grey waves.

"Hi."

Nora turns at Van's greeting and nearly bumps into Lissa, who smiles sweetly. "I was just telling Van how happy I am that we're bunking together. I've admired you forever—ever since I was an undergraduate."

Nora remembers Melissa Nelson as a frivolous student—capable but unmotivated for anything more intellectual than being a cheerleader. Recalling her grandmother's injunction that "if you can't say something nice, don't say anything at all," she settles for, "Really?"

"Yes, even back then."

Nora looks at Van, who is grinning broadly. Did he think the snide allusion to her age funny?

Buck Brady strides by with half a dozen trustees and spouses in tow, pointing to aspects of the standing rigging, describing the functions of some of the lines, explaining some of the basic terms in seaman's vocabulary. When Buck demonstrates how to belay a line on a cleat, Nora's eyes meet Van's and they exchange grins, a flash of their easy understanding.

*　　*　　*

Just before noon *Endeavor* docks at the concrete seawall in Baltimore's Inner Harbor. Nora watches several people scramble ashore and turns to Van. He's wearing khaki shorts and a red polo shirt that reveal his summer tan and muscular build. Nora eyes him appreciatively. "What's your pleasure?" she asks, the sweep of her arm encompassing shops, restaurants, jugglers, street musicians, and paddle boats.

"I believe I shall visit the aquarium."

Melissa speaks over Nora's left shoulder. "That's where I'm going! It'll be great to have company." She steps past Nora and loops her arm through Van's. She, too, wears khaki shorts, and a tight navy tank top. She presses close to Van's bicep.

"Er, yes." Van flushes and shifts his weight, drawing slightly away from Melissa. "What about you, Nora? Will you come to the aquarium?"

Nora glances from Van to Melissa and back again, stifling a grin. "I'm not up for the shark tank today. I think I'll take the water taxi to Fells Point. Maybe I'll be able to replace some of my broken Depression Glass." She turns on her heel and strolls away, hands in the hip pockets of her chinos, French braid swinging under her yachting cap.

* * *

Jim leans on the starboard rail, surveying the Inner Harbor. Nate claps him on the shoulder and says, "Why don't you and Rebecca join Priscilla and me for lunch ashore? I have an appointment later this afternoon, but we have plenty of time. There's a great seafood restaurant just across the way. Where is Rebecca, anyway? Is our first lady bored?"

Jim flushes. "Lunch would be great. Rebecca's below. I'll get her."

He stands in the doorway to their stateroom, his stomach in a knot. "What do you mean, you're going to your office?"

Rebecca snaps the latches on her briefcase. "I mean, *I'm going to my office*. It's less than two blocks away. I'll be back by evening."

"Rebecca! This charter is in our honor. You can't just duck out."

Rebecca faces him, both hands on the handle of the bulging briefcase hanging against her thighs. "People have scattered every which way. No one will notice whether I'm wandering around the Inner Harbor or not, so why should I waste the time?"

"This is not wandering. This is a luncheon invitation."

"I can come to the Inner Harbor for lunch any day of the week."

Jim feels like shouting but hisses instead. "Rebecca! The Roths have invited us. You're the wife of the president. Is it too much to ask you to act like it?"

"The Board doesn't want another president whose wife has no life of her own. Bill Baxter said so."

"Well they don't want a phantom wife, either! Rebecca, I've been on the job only a month. This is important."

Rebecca looks at him coldly. He looks steadily back at her.

Finally, she heaves a sigh. "Oh, all *right*. If you're going to make a big deal out of it ... "

Relief floods through him. He tries to push aside the remnants of his anger before going topside to meet the Roths.

*   *   *

Richard stows his journal in the locker and pulls out a clean shirt. He feels Carol's hands and lips on his naked back in silent invitation. He says, "No," and pulls on his shirt. He turns, stepping back from her fluttering fingers, from the pained look in her eyes, and tucks in his shirttail.

"Oh, Richie, what's wrong?" Her tears glisten in the dim cabin light.

He wants to yell *Everything in the whole fucking world is wrong!* He reaches for the doorknob, glances back at Carol. Her hurt—and her need—are almost enough to pull him back. *But I've got to talk to Allie—alone—now. I've got to know where we stand.* He leaves without answering Carol.

Richard hurries down the gangplank, trips into a post resting loosely on the brick walkway along the seawall. "Christ, slow down," he mutters. His heart pounds as he circles the waterfront shops and restaurants. *Where is she, damn it?* A flash of regret about leaving Carol is smothered by recollections of times with Allie, and thoughts of what might have been. An hour passes. Finally, he catches sight of Allie outside the Barnes & Noble on Pratt Street.

He follows her in but hangs back as she wanders from the poetry display to the shelves of bargain books to the cooking section. Her every move is fluid, graceful—the music in motion so vivid in his memories. He follows her along the wall labeled Literature to the back corner. Finally, he says, "Hey."

Allie glances up in surprise. "Hey, yourself." She smiles. "It's been a long time."

Richard wants to say, "Too long." He wants to fold her into his arms and not let go. Instead he says, "How have you been?"

"Good." She speaks again, with more emphasis. "Life's been good."

Their eyes lock. Finally Richard says, "How about going to the Rusty Scupper for a glass of wine? Or a cup of coffee. We could … talk."

Allie nods. "We have a lot of catching up to do."

They walk in silence. Their shoulders touch and Richard remembers one spring day, standing next to Allie on a crowded bus, going up an escalator, waiting in line at a movie theater, brushing against her every chance he got. Her voice, her scent, her *presence* were magnets he couldn't resist. He'd said, "I've been walking around all day with half a hard on," and she'd laughed. Does she remember?

They take seats in the bar as far as possible from the noon crowd. She orders a California chardonnay. He has a draft beer.

Finally Richard says, "Buck doesn't seem to—I guess you never told him about us."

Allie's lips quirk into the lopsided, impish grin he loves. "Somehow, the right occasion to tell my husband that I had an affair with a married man never presented itself." The grin fades. "We just weren't something to share." Allie shifts restlessly. "So. What's been going on with you? I mean, I know about your accounting firm. Besides that." She turns her wine glass. "Do you have children?"

"Can you imagine the neurotic bastards Carol and I would produce?" The joking tone he intended comes out sounding bitter. Richard shrugs. "I never wanted children with anyone but you." He hasn't smoked in fifteen years but now he desperately wants a cigarette. "So, what about you?"

Allie smiles. "Two sons and a daughter. My older son, Sky, graduated from West College last spring." Richard looks at her, mentally doing the math. As if reading his mind, Allie says, "Yes, I was pregnant when I married Buck. He insisted on doing the right thing." Their eyes lock for a moment. "I called you two days before the wedding. You were back with Carol. How long—after us—before you two … ?"

"A year. We lived apart for a year." Richard closes his eyes. "I'd promised to take care of her."

"Back then, I wondered, what about taking care of me?"

"You've always been strong, Allie. You never needed me. Not like she does. You were never unstable, never tried to kill yourself."

"No, I didn't need you like that. But I needed what we had, how you made me feel. No other man ever made me feel so totally—so completely *accepted.*"

"I don't think there's been a single day that I haven't thought of you, that I haven't longed to be with you." Richard takes her hand. "Your last phone call left me feeling as if some essential organ had been ripped out of my body. Through all those years apart, knowing you were somewhere in the world sustained me. I always knew I'd see you again. Somehow. Somewhere."

Allie looks startled. "I felt that, too. I mean, knowing we'd meet again."

Richard grips her hand as if it's a lifeline. "You see? Nothing's really changed. Nearly twenty-five years are gone, but not the feeling that this is home—here—wherever you are. Just seeing you gives me peace. You make me whole."

Allie looks startled. "Oh, Richard. You can't be serious. You can't have been obsessing about us all these years!" Tears glint in Allie's eyes.

"I mean it, Allie. The last twenty-five years have been hell. I don't want to live without you any longer."

"You need to grow up, Richard. Our time has passed." Her tone is gentle, and she smiles raggedly. "I'm married now. Very, very married." She looks at her watch. "Oh, my gosh. I've got to get back. Buck had some conference calls but he'll be wondering …" They stand, gaze into each other's eyes. Allie puts her hand lightly on Richard's chest. "You'll always have a place in my heart." Richard draws her close. "Richard, don't." She steps back, looking into his eyes. "You need to move on."

Richard's eyes search her face. "We need to talk again. Soon. There's so much we haven"t said."

"Not a good idea." Allie squeezes his hands and hurries out the door.

Richard sinks back onto his chair and orders another beer. He replays their conversation, examining everything she said and how she said it. *Things are a hell of a lot more complicated now. But she still cares. She's got to give me a second chance.* He orders more beer and sips slowly, filling in the time until dinner, until he can return to *Endeavor* and have other people around to cushion his encounter with Carol.

Walking back to the boat, he hears a loud whistle and sees Simon Hummel hailing a cab. Nate Roth claps him on the shoulder as Simon gets into the taxi, then turns toward the waterfront. Richard slows his pace and drops back, hoping not to be seen.

Chapter Seven

ENDEAVOR SAILS OUT OF BALTIMORE harbor in time to catch the morning thermals, heading for the Chester River. The wind catches Nora's hair as the sails fill and she thinks, *West wind, easy passage. We'll arrive in good time for the Beach Boil Dinner.* Nora and Van stand on the foredeck, awaiting orders from the skipper.

"When we clear Bodkin Point, haul and set the foresail."

Nora shouts, "Aye, aye, Skipper." Side by side, she and Van haul in the sail.

Van speaks without pausing in the task at hand. "Did you find any Depression glass?"

"Only one piece. But it's a beauty! A pink footed goblet. It's the first one I've ever seen in my pattern."

"That burglary last winter—the senseless vandalism. It will take a long time to restore your collection."

Nora secures the foresail, looking at Van out of the corner of her eye. "How was the aquarium?"

"It was great! Did you know that Lissa was a biology major? Seeing the exhibits with her was a very different experience."

"I'm sure." Van doesn't seem to notice her dry tone.

"We talked about sensory systems. From my research on audition, I know that the ears of fish develop out of the first cervical vertebra, but I did not expect Lissa to know that." Nora has seldom heard Van speak so animatedly. She can't think of anything appropriate to say. He doesn't seem to hear her silence. Van slacks off on a windward line. "Lots of people think that horseshoe crabs are related to edible crabs, but in reality they are closely related to spiders. Did you know that?" He glances in her direction.

"Yes, actually."

"Well, did you know that at sexual maturity, salmon need more oxygen? Fresh water has more oxygen than salt water, so salmon leave the ocean and migrate up rivers to fresh water ponds. Procreation happens."

Nora turns, fists on hips, unable to contain her amusement. "If I'd known the mating behavior of sea life was such a turn-on, I'd have told you about the stickleback a long time ago. It's a small fish, sort of like a seahorse. A mature male gets a bright red spot on his belly, which triggers elaborate sexual displays in the female." In her mind's eye, she sees Van's red polo shirt and Lissa Nelson clinging to his arm. "Researchers can get those sexual displays with a red dot on a stick!" Van's mouth drops open. She turns and saunters away.

But having moved as far from Van as the boat's dimensions allow, Nora leans on the port railing, reflecting on that exchange. *Nora Butcher Perry, get a grip. One minute you're feeling protective as a mother hen. The next, you're teasing him mercilessly.* Nora gazes at the wake fanning out behind *Endeavor*, her cheeks aflame at having acted so childishly.

*   *   *

When *Endeavor* is off Eastern Neck Island, Van crosses to Nora just as Marcy joins them. "You two are fine sailors. I couldn't have done a better job on the foresail myself. He slaps Van on the shoulder and smiles at Nora.

"What is our next anchorage?" Van asks.

"A sweet spot at the mouth of the Corsica River."

Nora thinks, *About thirty-three nautical miles from our anchorage by Fort McHenry.* She casts an eye at the sky. "Weather coming in? I've noticed clouds forming in the west."

"Yes, but it'll probably be fine. I hope so, anyway." Marcy grins. "These folks are more interested in the Beach Boil Dinner than in sailing—present company excepted." He touches his cap and heads to the helm.

*   *   *

Richard joins Nate and Buck for the twice-daily deck scrub. Buck distributes the long-handled brushes. Nate says, "We should work from bow to stern."

Buck adds, "And port to starboard."

Nate says, "Brady, you haul water. Richard and I will man the brushes."

Richard whistles tunelessly, his gaze fixed on the far horizon while the other two men jockey for position like competing drill sergeants. He wields his brush mindlessly. He spent the long hours of the night mulling over every word Allie said, hearing her every inflection, seeing her every look and gesture. His heart hasn't changed. But everything else ... *I've got to see her again—alone.* Buck's voice breaks into his thoughts. "So, where did you meet Allie?"

Buck's question catches Richard flat-footed. "Meet Allie?"

"Yeah. How did you two hook up?"

Christ. She said she hadn't told him. Why now? Buck's casual tone confuses Richard. He searches for the most cautious response.

"We worked at the same accounting firm in Portland—the first job for both of us."

Buck looks surprised. "You knew Allie back in Portland? Hell, that was in another life-time."

"You didn't … ? What are we talking about here?"

"Yesterday. You and Allie."

"Oh. Yesterday." Beads of sweat glisten on Richard's forehead. He licks his lips. He glances at Buck. "We bumped into each other at a bookstore."

Buck cocks an eyebrow in Richard's direction. "Small world."

Richard returns to swabbing the deck, hoping the conversation is over. The day has been hell already. When Carol questioned him, he told her he'd walked around the shops, stopped for a beer. He glances around, hoping she hasn't overheard this exchange.

Buck leans on his long-handled brush the way a farmer might lean on a pitchfork. "So you and Allie worked together in Portland? That's a real kick in the pants. I'm surprised she never mentioned it."

Richard shrugs. "It was only over coffee that we realized we'd worked together back when. We didn't keep in touch."

"Well, that's about to change! Now that we're both on the Board."

"Uh. Yeah." Richard's gut churns. Images of Board dinners and cocktail parties flash into his mind. He imagines Allie trying to be discrete, and Buck's fury if he ever tumbles to their affair. *How the hell will I ever keep a lid on Carol?*

Nate calls, "Hey, Emory. It's across the planks. Always across the planks."

"Yeah. Right." Richard makes a great display of vigorously swabbing the deck, moving out of conversational range ASAP.

* * *

Four miles past Castle Marine, Nora leans on the starboard rail, looking for Queenstown Harbor. She glances at her watch: 1300 hours.

An hour later, with the skipper's okay, crew looking on, Buck drops the anchor. He looks proud of himself—inordinately so, Nora thinks, given that gravity and the brake on the capstan did most of the work. The tender shuttles passengers, crew, and everything necessary for the boiled dinner to the riverbank on the northern corner of Corsica Neck. The process takes more than an hour.

Sun time is late enough in the afternoon for Nora to wear a swimsuit, though she keeps the protection of a white cover-up and hat. The suit is one-piece, navy blue, with a skirt, and white piping laced through grommets around the scoop neckline. It looks nautical and suits her sturdy figure. She feels good about it until she sees Van laughing with Melissa—slim and supple, two scraps of orange fabric rich against her tanned flesh, barely covering the essentials. Nora grimaces at her own alabaster skin, fuming at the injustice of sun poisoning, of having to wear hats and long sleeves and long pants and sunscreen.

She busies herself helping the cook with dinner, layering ears of shucked corn, scrubbed sweet and white potatoes, and raw clams into two big cookers.

Nora surveys her fellow passengers. Some walk the riverbank, others wade or swim in the shallows. Couples fascinate her, both as a psychologist and as a woman who has chosen to remain single. Richard Emory sits on a beach towel, gazing across the river, while Carol flits and fusses around him, bringing cold drinks, offering sunscreen, talking to his silent profile. Jim Sloan sets up a chair for Rebecca, then sits on the sand, leaning against her knee. She reclines the chaise and puts her hat over her face, the picture of a woman about to take a nap. Looking from one couple to another, The Principle of Least Interest pops into Nora's mind: in relationships, the person with the most power is the one who is least interested in maintaining the relationship. Nora looks again at Van and Lissa, hoping he knows what he's getting into.

Bill Baxter spreads his towel next to Nora's. "Nice bathing suit."

Nora looks at him sharply, but sees no sign that he's being facetious. "Thank you. You look pretty good yourself." *Whoa, girl. You don't know him that well. Yet.* She rushes to add, "You're a strong swimmer."

Bill laughs. "I work at it. I started ten years ago, as a way to cope with my wife's death. I worked with a trainer and a nutritionist—cheaper than a therapist or anger management classes. It turns out I like a daily regimen of exercise. It gets addictive, you know?"

Nora's gaze takes in his green eyes, salt and pepper hair, and chiseled torso. "I feel that way about sailing."

"I love the water, too. My sons and I bike and hike, but I like surfing and kayaking more. We should sail together sometime—if you're willing to teach me a thing or two."

His eyes twinkle and the possibilities stretch into the unknown. Her stomach does a little flip and she says, "I'd be happy to."

Nora turns her gaze to Priscilla Roth, wading thigh-deep in the river, holding aloft her flowing beach cover-up. *What does she think it really covers up? Certainly not her weight. Not her age. If anything, it just attracts more attention—sort of like my long pants and long-sleeved shirts in high summer heat.* She wonders, not for the first time, how Priscilla ever came to be married to Nate. Thoughts of older, unattractive women quickly turn inward. Nora runs her hands over her hips, down the skirt of her bathing suit. If it weren't for Bill, she'd be feeling downright dowdy right now. *Get a grip, Nora. You are not ugly.* Still, her heart goes out to Priscilla.

Suddenly Priscilla screeches, "Oh! Oh! Help! Something's got me!" She jumps up and down and struggles toward shore as quickly as the water allows, all the time whimpering, "Eh, eh, eh."

Nora meets her at the river's edge, takes her hand, and leads her across the sand. "What happened?"

Pris looks at her legs as if amazed that no blood flows. She sits heavily on the sand, shaking her hands, bouncing her knees up and down, tears streaming. "It was everywhere, all over my legs." As she speaks, faint red welts bloom on both thighs and one calf.

"Shhhh. Shhhh," Nora says soothingly. "It'll be okay. I think you had a close encounter with a jellyfish. One got me this summer. It felt like a curtain of razor blades, billowing against me. There's a good reason they're called sea nettles." The cook hands Nora a first aid kit. She pulls out cotton balls and a bottle of ammonia and dabs the liquid on Priscilla's welts. "This is going to sting for awhile—maybe a few hours."

Priscilla whimpers. "It hurts so bad. It stings—like—like hundreds of electric shocks." Tears stream down her cheeks. She can't seem to hold her legs still. The dimpled flesh quivers around her knees. Nora glances at the people who've gathered round, hoping no one else notices the jiggling.

Adrian Livingston sniffs. "I thought jellyfish were salt-water creatures."

Van stands at his elbow. "They are. The Chesapeake is tidal—and so pretty salty at its mouth, and brackish as far up as Fairlee. We are almost twenty miles south of that."

Everyone except Nate drifts away. When Nora catches his eye, he looks out across the river, embarrassed, perhaps. He says, "Calm down, Priscilla. A jellyfish sting isn't fatal.".

As Nate walks away, tears again flood Priscilla's eyes. She whispers, "How can he just walk away on our anniversary?"

Nora pretends not to hear, but she takes Pris's hand, and stays by her, offering such comfort as she can, until the cook shouts, "Dinner's ready!"

*   *   *

The sandy shore holds the sun's heat, and the air feels warm on Nora's exposed legs. Everyone raves about the food— except Adrian Livingston. *He* complains about everything, from the inconvenience of getting clams out of their shells to the messiness of corn on the cob. Nora is developing a hearty dislike of the man. His only pleasures seem to come from being the fly in the ointment.

Buck bangs a piece of driftwood against one of the metal cookers. "Hear ye, hear ye! Raise your glasses and toast the new president and your lovely first lady. To Jim and Rebecca!" Nora catches the look Buck casts in Nate's direction, his expression seeming to say, "Look who's king of the mountain!" Nate nods curtly and Nora wonders about the source of the tension crackling between them.

Nora glances at Priscilla, who appears calm now but unhappy. *She's so painfully uncomfortable in her own body. The way I feel about myself when I look at Melissa.*

As they finish dinner, the sky to the west turns dark and the wind picks up. Nora assesses the sky. On the Chesapeake, half an hour can be the difference between calm and a full blow. Captain Marcy says, "It's pretty late in the day for a storm, but something's brewing. It'll probably pass to the south, but we'd better get back to *Endeavor*, just in case." He turns to the cook. "Douse the fires." Everyone pitches in, quickly gathering equipment and debris. Marcy claps his first mate on the shoulder. "I'm anxious to pick up the NOAA weather. You've got shore duty." The first group, including Marcy, leaves for *Endeavor* within minutes, the water already choppy.

Rain pelts down. When the tender returns for the last load, the mate brings slickers for those still on shore. The blow has begun in earnest. Lightning strikes all around. Horizontal rain hammers them, sending small cold rivulets down Nora's neck. Waves wash over the gunwales, nearly swamping the tender. Nora gasps, fighting to keep her seat.

Suddenly Van yells, "Man overboard!"

The mate shouts "Hold on!" and turns the tender hard right to come about.

Buck leans far over the side and grabs Richard's unbuckled life jacket. He yells, "Don't fight me, man!" Together Buck and Nate haul Richard aboard.

The mate throws the transmission into forward and races for *Endeavor*. Richard coughs and sputters. "Jesus Christ! Who pushed me?"

Buck throws his arm across Richard's shoulders. "Take it easy, man. The wave washed you overboard."

The passengers most experienced with boats are in the last group shuttled back to *Endeavor*. They scramble aboard and set about helping the crew. Nora and Van lash the mainsail to the boom, struggling to keep the wind out of the canvas. Driving rain bruises their faces and bare legs. Nora's hood blows back and a rope of wet hair whips across her cheek. Van grabs the mast with one arm and Nora with the other. "Sweet Jesus!" she yells. "We must have a fifty-knot blow here!" The wind snatches her words away. Two men are aft, wind at their backs, checking the lifeboat webbing, lashing down the oars. Another man, incognito in rain slicker with hood laced down, battens the forward hatch.

Nora fights the wind and follows Buck below, where Captain Marcy is listening to NOAA weather. The cook is securing the galley, getting everything moveable into bins and lockers. The double gimbaled stove swings with the roll and pitch of the boat, whacking his elbow. One deckhand checks portholes, another checks that everyone's still wearing a lifejacket. Passengers in the main salon sit ashen faced, or stand swaying, trying to keep their footing.

Carol wrings her hands and whimpers, "Where's Richie?"

Buck says, "He's topside," and struggles up the companionway. Nora tightens her life vest and follows him, looking for Van.

Lightning flashes—sky to ground, ground to sky, and sideways—weaving bright threads in a black curtain. Nora shouts to Van, "I hope to heaven we don't take a hit."

He says, "You feel the anchor dragging?" Nora nods, assessing the likelihood that they'll be driven aground.

Marcy comes topside, hunched into his slicker, his life vest only partially fastened, and shouts to his first mate, "Two crew forward! Let out another eight fathoms of chain. And get these people below!"

The crew hustle everyone down the companionway. Marcy brings up the rear, closing the hatch behind. Lissa catches Van's hand and pulls him into the seat beside her. She looks pale and shaken. Nora takes one of the few remaining seats, beside Bill.

Marcy stands easily and speaks calmly to the white-faced passengers. "Just hang in a little longer. These blows are vicious but they don't last long."

Jim Sloan looks apprehensive. "How bad is it?"

"We've got sixty knot winds out there—that's about seventy miles an hour." Marcy grins. "I've only seen this a few times on the

Bay." Nora and Van exchange smiles, sharing Marcy's thrill in a contest with the elements.

Many of the passengers sit mute, a few moan, several are white-knuckled. Bill Baxter leans against Nora's shoulder, smiling. "Nurse, cook, deck hand. You do good work."

Nora smiles back, grateful for his warmth.

Rain leaks around the hatch and water drips off slickers. The cabin air hangs heavy and hot. Lissa is pale and trembling. Van takes her hand and says, "The situation is a little precarious. But we will not capsize." Nora watches him from across the salon, well aware that capsizing isn't the only possible disaster.

Jim Sloan grips Rebecca's hand.

Buck puts his arm across Allie's shoulders and draws her closer.

Nate says, "Give me space to *breathe*, Pris," and moves a few inches away.

Carol looks frantically around the salon and wails. "Richie? Richie, where are you?"

Endeavor pitches and rolls. Bright white light fills the salon. A fraction of a second later, an ear-splitting thunderclap, then a rush of air throws everyone off kilter. Adrian Livingston—a retired minister—drops to his knees and starts praying just as Buck cries "Jesus fucking Christ"—his first public fall from boardroom to lumber yard language since coming aboard.

Lissa covers her face with her hands. "Oh, Lord. I'm not ready to die."

Carol sobs, "Richie, Richie."

Nora hears a sizzle and smells ozone. Marcy grabs a fire extinguisher and heads for the NAV station.

Chapter Eight

When the lights go out, Carol Emory screams, "I have to find Ritchie!" She fumbles with the hatch.

Captain Marcy scoops her up like a child and holds her, kicking and sobbing. "There was no one topside when I came below. He's got to be down here somewhere." Carol writhes and beats his chest. "Mrs. Emory! Settle down. You can't go topside till this blows over!" Carol whimpers and goes limp. Marcy sets her gently on one of the benches.

The storm is done in less than an hour, start to finish. Nora says to Bill, "Storms are like that on the Bay—brief and sometimes vicious."

"Now what?"

"Wait for Marcy's orders. When we do get some lights on, they won't be much, just lanterns and such. The best we can do is stay out of the way unless instructed to do otherwise."

Bill squeezes her hand. "I admire a woman who keeps her head in a crisis."

The crew distributes flashlights and lanterns to passengers, hangs anchor lights topside to mark their position. Marcy says, "Anybody with a cell phone, check whether you've got a signal. The storm scorched our electronics and we gotta call the Coast Guard."

People scramble toward their cabins or search their pockets to no avail. Nora says, "I've got nothing here, Captain, but let me go topside. The reception is probably better there."

"Sure thing. Follow me. And watch your footing." When Nora says she has a signal, Marcy calls the Coast Guard. "This is Captain Sebastian Marcy, the schooner *Endeavor*, requesting assistance. We're disabled near the mouth of the Corsica River." He gives their last coordinates. "We've dragged some, but I think that's close enough." He reports the particulars: length and condition of the boat, the number of passengers and crew. "No serious injuries, some bruises, maybe a sprain or two.

As he cuts off the call, Carol Emory scrabbles up the companionway. "I can't find Ritchie! He isn't anywhere!"

Marcy says, "Calm down, now. Just stay calm. He's gotta be here somewhere." Nora thinks his expression belies his words.

She puts her arm across Carol's shoulders and leads her below. "Shhh. Shhhh. The captain will do everything possible."

Marcy organizes the crew and passengers to search the ship, everything from the cabins to the lifeboats. As each person reports, Carol grows more and more distraught, moaning, "He's gone. He's gone."

When the first mate says, "Captain, we've searched everywhere. He isn't on board," Carol flies at Allie. "You whore! This is your fault! I know it!" Nora holds Carol back as she strains toward Allie. "The minute you come back into our lives, he's gone! You goddamned fucking whore! What have you done to my husband?"

All color drains from Allie's face. Buck looks like he's been poleaxed.

Marcy says, "Mrs. Emory, you'd best go to your cabin. Even if the storm washed your husband overboard, he was wearing a life jacket. The water's warm. The Coast Guard will launch a search and rescue operation. We'll find him."

Nora remembers that when Richard was on the tender, he was wearing his life jacket but the straps weren't fastened. She says, "Carol, come lie down. Do you have anything that will help you sleep?"

Carol looks at her, wide-eyed.

Pris says, "If she doesn't have anything, I do. I have Ambien."

Nora says, "I'll stay with you till you fall asleep."

Marcy calls the Coast Guard again. "One passenger is missing. We believe he went overboard." Marcy recounts their search efforts aboard, and why they can't search the water till morning.

Chapter Nine

Van calls mid-morning. "Can you come for coffee? I want to talk some things out."

"Sure." *Van isn't a spur-of-the-moment kind of guy.* Nora says, "What things?"

"Richard Emory."

"Oh." Realizing it's nothing personal, she shifts mental gears. "Okay. Your place in twenty minutes?"

Settled at Van's kitchen table over steaming mugs, Nora says, "I'm glad you called. I've barely slept for the last week, wondering—you know."

"Believe me, I do know." Van covers her hand with his. "Every time I think about the storm I am reminded of the line from *Moby Dick*: "When beholding the tranquil beauty and brilliancy of the ocean's skin, one forgets the tiger heart that pants beneath it; and would not willingly remember that this velvet paw but conceals a remorseless fang."

"How apropos! Not just to the Chesapeake, but to so much of life." Nora picks up her mug. "The worst thing is, he hasn't been found. I mean, the Coast Guard has done some dragging, sent down divers. Why didn't they find the body?"

"The Coast Guard was patrolling other parts of the Chesapeake during the week right after Richard went overboard. I heard the news report just this morning. Apparently there was a terrorist alert, a threat to blow up both the Chesapeake Bridge Tunnel and the Bay Bridge."

Nora whistles. "Wow. If they'd taken out the main connectors from Norfolk to Cape Charles *and* from Kent Island to Sandy Point … I can only imagine."

"The Coast Guard from Still Pond and Annapolis were damned busy. My theory is that while the threat alert occupied the Coast Guard and delayed the search for Richard, the especially high and low tides that followed the storm carried the body out of the search area." Van grins sheepishly. "This may sound like pure hubris, but I have been trying to figure out when and where the body might surface. I did a little research. A body sinks first, then resurfaces when gasses from decomposition make it buoyant. All sorts of things affect when the body floats—everything from foods last ingested to body weight to clothing. Given the water temperature this time of year, the body should have floated again within a week."

"I'm impressed." Nora punches his shoulder. "Leave it to a physicist."

"Solving a puzzle with one unknown is easy. But this—this is more like guess work. It has been fascinating, actually. I have done some calculations—I will spare you the details—that involved wind velocities and directions, salinity, the effect of the moon on tides, and river currents and flow rates over the past week. Bottom line: I think the body may be near Tilghman Neck."

"Van, that's fantastic!"

"Of course, if it got hung-up on something—or if I miscalculated—it may not be there. I have not looked."

"Well let's go find out!" Nora leaps up.

"Perhaps we should call someone?"

"Who? And what are the chances anyone would take us—you—seriously? If we find him, we'll call." Nora grabs Van's hand and heads for the door. "Let's take Corsica Neck Road down to Spider Webb Road. From there we can tramp through the woods to the water."

* * *

They thrash through thick underbrush, dodging trees—Red Cedar, White Oak, Black Cherry, and Sycamores—to get to the tall brown and green sea grasses at the water's edge. Knotweed grows in the grasses and climbs the trees, the sharp prickers clinging to Nora's pants and punishing Van's bare legs. She grins. "One of the few times I'm glad to be wearing long pants in summer heat!"

Van eyes the welts reddening his legs, "Too bad I did not know to do likewise. This stuff is everywhere!"

"It's the bane of gardeners. It spreads over everything, sometimes choking trees, and grows so fast, it's called Mile-a-Minute. If I'd realized it was here, I would have warned you."

"Nice afterthought."

At the water's edge, Van says, "You go right, I will go left. Call me if you find anything. If we find nothing, we will meet here in two hours."

Less than half an hour later, Nora's phone rings. She squishes along the bank toward Van. By the time she sees him, the putrid odor has assailed her. She stops, the olfactory memories taking her back to finding Ted Slater's body last year. She shudders. She forces her feet to move forward. Van, a tinge of green showing through his tan, stares at the water's edge.

This close, the smell of rotting flesh is almost overwhelming. She swallows her rising gorge and looks. The body is bloated and distorted, hunks of flesh missing, little left of his head but the skull. Shreds of cloth wave in the water like mutant seagrass. She says, "Do you remember what Richard was wearing?"

"Swim suit. Some sort of shirt. I do not remember his shirt." Van runs a hand down his face. "I am not about to search for ID. But as best I can judge, this is a male, more or less the height and build of Richard Emory."

"Who else *could* it be? How many bodies could wash up—now—where you calculated Richard would be?" They are standing on Tilghman Neck at Gordon Point, only a mile and a half from *Endeavor's* anchorage. Nora stands at the water's edge, her hands locked together. "Leaving him in the water feels—wrong. Callous or something. But I don't think I can touch—him." She swallows hard.

Van takes a step back. "We should not touch him anyway. Evidence and so forth."

Small waves from the wake of a passing workboat lap a nearly fleshless leg bone. Nora turns her back and fumbles for her cell phone. "I'm calling Frank."

*   *   *

Captain Franklin Jefferson Pierce, chief deputy in the Queen Anne's County Sheriff's Office, slogs through the muck. "So you've done it again. What is it with you two and dead bodies? I thought you'd had enough last year with Slater."

Nora listens for hostile undertones. Frank hasn't spoken to her for months, not since the Slater business wrapped up—not since she visited him in the hospital. *He was really pissed that Van and I didn't stay out of his murder investigation. And now Richard*

Emory. Former student, former lover, dear friend—three reasons she doesn't want Frank to write her off.

He glances at the grizzly remains. "And it would have to be a floater." He sounds disgusted.

Nora faces him, fists on hips. "Suck it up, Frank. We're in your jurisdiction."

She follows his gaze to the body caught in tree roots, legs swaying in the water. He sighs. "Have you touched him?"

"You gotta be kidding." Nora glances at Van, then back to Frank. "You aren't likely to find ID in a swimsuit, but we're pretty sure it's Richard Emory—for all the reasons I told you on the phone." She shifts from one foot to the other. "But he's … How could he be so—so—so mutilated?"

Franks says, "When a drowned body sinks, it goes face down. The torso has more fat, so it's more buoyant than the arms and legs. Plus, shoulders and hips just naturally hang in one direction. So the face, arms, and legs get dragged along the bottom by the current until the gasses make it float again. But part of the damage is probably from crabs."

Her stomach heaves. "I don't think I can ever eat crab again."

Frank arches one eyebrow. "You've never stopped to think what crabs eat? Not that it's usually *human*, but …" He shrugs. "I'd have thought that after a week, the body would be well down the Bay."

Nora says, "In rivers that feed the Bay, like the Corsica and the Chester, high tides reverse the flow. Van thinks it may have traveled toward the Bay and then came part way back."

"When I got here, there were birds. Lots of birds." Van sounds subdued.

Frank nods, his eyes still on the body. "Birds seem to like floaters more than other bodies."

Nora wills herself not to see beaks dipping into eyeballs.

Van says, "What now?"

"We don't touch anything. And we call the Natural Resources Police."

"The poacher patrol?" Van's surprise is evident as he voices the question that leapt to Nora's mind, too.

"They do a lot more than game and fisheries."

"But it's Queen Anne's County! That's why I called you."

"We're standing in Queen Anne's County now. But all water deaths are investigated by the Criminal Investigation Division of the Natural Resources Police. I'm sure their Search Support Units were involved already, so they'll hit the ground running. I'll call the Commander, Captain David Olsen."

"That's it? We just walk away without knowing what happened? We knew this man!"

Frank takes in a lungful of air and slowly expels it in what Nora has privately labeled his be-patient-with-dimwits sigh. "Noni, these are the facts of life." He uses his old nickname for her, an echo of the relationship that was, all those years ago. "There isn't much to know. Assuming this *is* Richard Emory, he fell, jumped, or was pushed from a boat in the middle of a storm. And like I just said, that makes it a case for the Natural Resources Police."

Chapter Ten

NORA CLOSES THE FOLDER FOR the October meeting of the Board of Trustees. The first item on the agenda is reading the Board's resolution of appreciation for Richard Emory. *And then everyone will be thinking about the storm, the inquest ... Two months and I still feel haunted.*

She drops into her recliner, closes her eyes and leans her head against the back of the chair, waiting for the Extra Strength Tylenol to kick in. Fragmented scenes from August and September batter her aching brain. Carol Emory hysterical, screaming that she had to find Richie, then flying at Allie Brady. *If the trustees had had any inkling that Allie and one of the other trustees had been lovers, Buck would never have been appointed to the Board.*

Nora remembers the frantic search for a workable cell phone, recalls Adrian Livingston's acid tone as he said, "If Brady had set the anchor as he should have, it wouldn't have dragged. Surely we would have found him." *He just wouldn't drop it, even when Captain Marcy explained—twice—that, using the capstan, the anchor would have been set the same no matter who did it.* Nobody wanted to continue the sail, even if *Endeavor* hadn't been disabled. Nora starts to shake her head but a throb of pain stops her. *I hope to heaven I'm not coming down with the flu!*

Dental records proved that the body was Richard. No explanation for the lack of a life vest, though Nora suspects that it wasn't properly secured. From the water, sand, and grass in the lungs, the ME concluded that the man was alive when he went into the water. There was no sign that he had been struck by lightning.

Nora thinks often of Carol Emory. The entire inquest was a nightmare. The ME's gruesome photos and testimony. Carol Emory saying, "Buck Brady did this. He pushed Richie overboard because of his whoring wife. He wanted Richie dead!" She admitted that Richard had been depressed—had been seeing a therapist—but denied that he might have committed suicide. Then she shouted, "But if he ever did, it would be because of *her!*" She pointed at Allie Brady as she spoke. Buck put his arm around Allie, who sat stiffly erect, tears streaming down her cheeks. Nora overheard Nate Roth whispering to Jim Sloan: "When Buck and I pulled Richard back into the tender, Buck said something about not fighting him and Richard said something about being pushed."

When all was said and done, they were left with the open verdict Frank had predicted: Richard was dead—but with no ruling of suicide, murder, or accidental drowning.

She'd called Carol a couple of times over the last two months. She and Bill had taken flowers after the inquest. But Carol's ranting frazzled Nora's nerves.

Nora yawns. She didn't sleep well and got up about six o'clock to review the meeting materials. *I hope Carol is pleased with the framed citation—that it doesn't make everything worse. Who knows how she will behave? I just hope there are no new disasters. After Ted*

Slater's murder last year—and everything that followed—West College deserves a break.

*   *   *

By the time Nora enters the meeting room her headache has eased. She puts an apricot muffin and grapes on a buffet plate and draws a cup of coffee from the urn marked "Decaf." She looks among the dozen or so early arrivals but sees no sign of Van. Images of him and Lissa play along the edges of her consciousness. *They've been together a lot since Endeavor. I just hope he knows what he's doing. A faculty member dating a trustee is risky business.* Nora thinks about a recent conversation with Bill Baxter. When she'd hesitated to accept a dinner invitation, he'd said, "You're a tenured full professor. It isn't as though I have any influence over your future or well-being at the college." And so they have seen each other several times. She likes him enormously. Still, she'd prefer their relationship remain discreet.

Most of the trustees near her are talking about the Emory tragedy. "I didn't know him well, but he seemed a competent member of the Finance Committee." "What a waste." "Why didn't someone prevent it?" Another scene from the storm flashes through Nora's brain: all the scurrying figures in storm slickers.

A familiar voice says, "Good morning, Nora."

She turns, smiling. "Frank. Welcome to the first Board meeting of the year." She waves a hand. "Try a muffin. The food is the biggest benefit of this job." Frank chuckles and Nora breathes more easily. His irritation over Richard Emory's body seems to have passed. *I hope being one of only three black trustees doesn't turn out to be painful for him.* "I hear you have a baby girl."

Frank grins, deepening the shallow crows' feet at the corners of his eyes. "Yeah. A real beauty. We named her Jessica." He runs a hand across his close-cropped hair, a little gray at the temples.

While Frank talks about his wife Claire and the new baby, Nora thinks how handsome he looks in civilian clothes—a gray suit well-tailored to his muscular build and military bearing, shoes polished to a high gloss. *Closely trimmed mustache, strong chin, perfect teeth—he looks more like a bank executive or an actor than a cop.*

"The twins don't know what to do with such a tiny baby—and a girl at that. They keep dropping dump trucks and baseball gloves into her crib."

"Good show! Your sons seem to have all the right egalitarian instincts." They laugh and drift toward one of the large dormer windows. As they turn to face the view, Nora says, "So, what do you think about Richard Emory's drowning?"

Frank looks at her quizzically. "What should I think about it? I mean, even in my line of work, you don't expect the sudden death of someone you are about to meet and work with."

"Aren't you involved in the case?"

"I told you. That's Natural Resources Police."

"Well that's unfortunate! It seems to me that this whole case has been handled very—um—very *casually*." She lowers her voice to a murmur. "If you were investigating this, you'd look at every angle."

"Well, it's a moot point." Frank shifts his weight and seems tense when he gazes out the window. "Sheriff Bentley's already concerned that my being on the Board at West College might be a problem—potential conflicts of interest and so on. I'm just as happy not to be involved in another criminal investigation involving the college." He looks back at Nora. "Have you done much sailing recently?"

"Some. But never as much as I would like."

"With van Pelt?"

Nora glances aside. "Not often. He's developed other interests recently." Just then Van steps out of the stairwell, smiling and chatting with Melissa Nelson, his head tilted as if trying to catch her every word.

Frank looks from Van to Nora and says, "Oh. I see."

"What's that supposed to mean?" Nora flushes. "Van deserves to find the woman of his dreams. I hope he does. I'm just not sure that's Lissa Nelson."

*   *   *

Frank takes his seat at the long conference table and rehearses the names of his fellow trustees, most of whom he's just met. *What the hell is an alumni trustee supposed to do, anyway?* He glances across the table at Nora. *I have a lovely wife and three great kids. But I'll always have feelings for Nora. If van Pelt hurts her, I may have to take him out behind the shed.*

All around him, the room buzzes as trustees who were on *Endeavor* field questions from those who were not. The pounding of Bill Baxter's gavel commands Frank's attention and brings the meeting to order. Bill's voice resonates around the room when he asks Adrian Livingston to offer the invocation. The prayer isn't entirely by rote, but it contains all the usual phrases about the Almighty, the well-being of West College, and the duty of trustees to exercise wisdom.

When the prayer ends, Bill says, "The chair recognizes Nathaniel Roth."

Nate rises and holds out a hand to Carol Emory, drawing her forward to stand beside him. He adjusts his tie and clears his throat. Light gleams on his carefully cut dark brown hair. "On behalf of the Board, I wish to read a statement of appreciation for our departed member." Stiff, elegant, with measured cadence, he reads the citation: "West College has lost a strong and valued colleague: Richard James Emory. The Board of Trustees offers deep sympathy and condolences to his wife, Carol, and to his other family and many friends." Frank looks at Carol Emory, clothed in unrelieved black, fists clenched, as Nate continues. "He served West College well as a term trustee, most recently as member and Vice Chair of the Committee on Finance. The Board will miss his business acumen and his familiarity with the important role that schools such as West College play in the day-to-day workplace he knew so well." Nate looks solemn, but Frank detects no hint of real grief.

Nate pauses to pass the printed resolution to the recording secretary and continues in a less formal tone. "Richard was a conscientious trustee and a pleasant companion. One time when we were talking about our families, Richard said that his success in Baltimore surprised him, that he was just a Midwestern farm boy, born and bred. That was typical of his modesty. But we all know that his success was no accident. He worked long and hard to build his accounting firm, always with his dear wife's support." Here Nate nods toward Carol. "After an early apprenticeship, he launched Emory & Associates, now arguably the premier accounting firm in Baltimore." Turning toward Bill, he adds, "Mr. Chairman, I move that this resolution be entered into the minutes, and that this framed copy be presented to Mrs. Emory."

Bill bangs the gavel and without calling for a vote says, "By acclamation."

Carol grips the framed citation with trembling hands. "Thank you. Richie would be very pleased to know how much you valued his dedication to West and his—his long hours—especially this last year—in service to the college." Her voice cracks. "Thank you." She shakes hands with Bill Baxter and walks quickly from the room, tears in her eyes.

Frank looks at Buck Brady. Buck stares at the notepad in front of him, his forehead creased, his mouth set. *Probably remembering the gossip about his wife's affair with Richard Emory.* Frank feels a pang of sympathy. *There was sure a hell of a lot of gossip about me and Nora, back in the day. Poor bastard.* Brady looks for all the world like a man who'd rather be anyplace else.

*   *   *

Van walks with Nora through the soft, fragrant air toward Chums. The October sun glints on her copper hair, twisted into a figure-eight at the nape of her neck—her typical on-campus style. Nora strides easily, her mid-calf wool skirt swinging free, her tweed jacket reflecting all the colors of fall. Walking across campus with her feels like old times to Van. They've scarcely seen each other since *Endeavor*. The fall is always hectic, what with the start of classes and getting his children off to college. And this year, he's spent chunks of time with Lissa as well. But in spite of all the busyness, he's missed the comfort of his times with Nora. He smiles contentedly. "So how was the Finance Committee?"

"Good. Once they got past talk about Richard Emory's drowning, everyone felt the next thing to euphoric: the portfolio earned over seven percent." She laughs. "Buck was funny. He's Richard's replacement on the committee. He said, 'I can't believe these returns. This manager—this Simon Hummel—must be a wizard. The market's been in the toilet.' Nate said, 'Get used to it. Simon's been beating the market for two years now—ever since we turned the portfolio over to him.' Having something positive to focus on was good. How was the Committee on Faculty and Academic Affairs?"

"Lots of concern about freshman attrition last year. Amazement that there is controversy over the proposed revisions in the faculty handbook. A long discussion of what sort of pay raises the faculty might hope for next year." He grins. "It was a learning experience."

"Isn't that what you say when there's no other redeeming value?"

"How well you know me." Van feels an odd lurch in his chest. He regrets losing their easy camaraderie. Nothing has been the same since the schooner sail. "Marcy is lucky *Endeavor* didn't have more damage."

"Yeah. The brass grounding plate discharged most of the lightning strike into the water."

Nora sounds bemused, and Van takes it as a reflection of how upsetting the storm and Emory's death have been. Right after the inquest, they talked at length about the drowning, about what—if anything—could have been done to prevent the tragic accident. Marcy swore there was no one on deck when he came below, so Richard must have gone overboard while others were still topside. The clanging of cable and rigging against deck and bulkhead, the groaning and grinding of timbers, the shriek of the wind—who could have heard a human voice? Van says, "Everything was so hectic, it is a wonder we remembered to breathe."

Lunch tables and a buffet fill the Chums ballroom. Early arrivals are already seated, plates piled high, when Van and Nora join the buffet line. As they finish serving themselves, Lissa calls, "Van! I saved a seat for you." She pauses almost imperceptibly. "There's a seat for you, too, Nora. If you want."

"Thanks. But I need to talk to … " Nora scans the room. "To Bill." She nods to Van and carries her plate toward a table in the far corner. Bill stands to hold a chair for her.

Van walks toward Lissa. *Is something going on between Nora and Bill Baxter? He certainly seemed to seek her out aboard* Endeavor. *Wealthy. Sophisticated. He has a lot to offer.* Van has felt occasional twinges of guilt over the last several weeks, wondering whether not making time to sail with Nora constituted neglect. *But if Nora has Bill in her life ...* Lissa touches his arm and Van smiles warmly. Lissa's obvious interest is flattering, albeit a bit disconcerting. *She is a gorgeous career woman, coming after me full-tilt, visiting Centreville, inviting me to New York. She would have gone to bed with me a month ago. I know it. But sex ...* Van's first full sexual experience resulted in Sheila's pregnancy, marriage at age eighteen, four children, and divorce twenty-three miserable years later. During those twenty-three years, he had one abortive affair. *The next time I get into bed with a woman, I will do so with the intention of making a lifetime commitment.*

Frank carries a loaded plate to the empty chair beside Nora. For the hundredth time, Van wonders about Nora's relationship with the good-looking black man—exactly what it had been, what it is now. He turns back to Lissa.

Chapter Eleven

Allie leans close to the mirror and dabs make-up over the lavender circles under her eyes. Her face looks as bloodless as a peeled potato. *The lighting in public restrooms make me look more dead than alive.* She pats her ivory hair into a silky cap and tweaks the wispy tendrils around her face. As she moves, light winks on her gold loop earrings, and gold bangles on her right wrist jingle. She steps back for the long view. *I look like one of those big-eyed waifs on sappy greeting cards.* She last wore this dress in mid-summer. She gathers a handful of black fabric from across her hips. *How could I have lost so much weight?* Always slim, she now looks gaunt.

Allie hasn't seen these people since the inquest. She cringes at the thought of facing them now. But her absence from Buck's first Board meeting would just fuel the gossip, and she can't do that to him.

She stares into the mirror, remembering that night. When Carol attacked her after the storm—called her a whore and lunged at her with fingers curled into talons—Buck stepped between them, grasped Carol's wrists and fended off her blows. Pris Roth said, "I'll get a sedative," and Nora led Carol to her cabin. Buck took Allie's arm and steered her to their cabin, gently closing the door. He spoke quietly. "It isn't that you had an affair before we met. Or that you didn't tell me about it before. But why deceive me now? There's no way in hell you two didn't recognize each other the minute he set foot on board! Why lie about that?" Allie had never before seen such pain on his face. Tears rolled silently down her cheeks. "I'm sorry, Buck. I never meant to hurt you and I'm sorry. That's—all I can say." He said, "Christ, Allie," and pulled her into his arms. He held her while she sobbed. And in the morning he said, "It's over. We don't need to talk about it again." He stood by her at the inquest, too, when Carol screamed that she was a home-wrecker and that *whatever* had happened to Richard, his drowning was Allie's fault.

Since then, he's been silent and watchful, but unfailingly gentle and solicitous. He's made no demands—not even sex—so when he asked her to come with him to the Board dinner, she had to agree. *But everyone will be staring, speculating about me and Richard. How am I going to get through this night?*

The depth of her feelings shocks Allie. After that last phone call, shortly before her wedding, she never tried to get in touch again. Once, she looked him up in the Alumni Directory at the library. He and Carol both held degrees from Michigan, so the directory told her not only where *he* lived but also that Carol lived at the same address. She hoped they had found happiness. She always assumed that someday, somehow, their paths would cross. When Richard joined the West College Board of Trustees, his affiliation with her *alma mater* reinforced that expectation, even though nothing really changed. When her son, Sky, matriculated at West, she made no effort to be on campus during events that trustees were likely to attend.

When Buck joined the Board of Trustees, she knew it was going to happen—she was going to see her first love again. She wondered whether he had changed much, whether he was happier than before. She thought that surely he wouldn't still feel hurt or angry after so many years. She looked forward to tying up what felt like a loose end from her past. She debated telling Buck about Richard, but eventually decided that it would be less awkward if they—she, Richard, and Carol—just pretended it had never happened. They had stayed married all these years. Surely Carol was over it by now.

When they met at the bookstore and went to the Rusty Scupper—when Richard said that he had always loved her—Allie could hardly speak. He said he didn't want to live without her. A flood of emotions had washed over Allie. Shock. Guilt. Pity. Confusion. She left as quickly as she could manage, trying to buy time to think. He seemed so fragile, and so hopeful. Before she could get back on an even keel, could figure out how to let him down gently, he was gone.

Sometimes, in the night, she tells herself that he never knew. But the look in his eyes when they parted said that he did. In her darkest moods, she is convinced that Richard killed himself, and he did it because she rejected him so harshly. The pain of knowing that she can never make amends weighs on her. And there is no one with whom she can share her grief, her fear. If it were anything else, she would turn to Buck. But she cannot hurt him again. Looking at her reflection in the women's room mirror, tears sting her eyes. She blots them carefully with a square of toilet tissue, trying to preserve her mascara.

Laughter floats in from the ballroom, along with the sound of the College String Quartet starting its program. Nora pushes through the women's room door. Allie draws back. *Too late to hide in a stall.*

Nora smiles. "Hi. The music is a nice addition, isn't it?" She peers into the mirror, patting the bouquet of copper curls piled precariously on top of her head. "I think their whole program is going to be Haydn and Mozart minuets—light, and easy enough for student musicians. I think the viola is especially good, don't you?"

Nora's vitality fills the space, buffeting Allie. "Yes. Very nice," she murmurs and escapes to the ballroom.

*   *   *

Buck pumps Simon Hummel on his investment strategy for the college's fixed income portfolio, but remains aware of Allie's every move. He sees Nate smile at her when she approaches the portable bar, hears him say, "May I bring you a glass of wine?"

Allie smiles at Nate. "Thanks. But make it gin and bitters on the rocks."

Both Buck and Simon watch when Nate hands Allie her drink. Both see Nate raise his glass and hear him say, "To a beautiful woman who knows her own mind."

Simon chuckles. "Nate's quite the lady's man, isn't he?"

With effort, Buck keeps his expression bland. He says, "Seems to make a career of it." He continues his interrogation of Simon without missing a beat but his thoughts roil. *What is it about Hummel that pisses me off?* He looks from Simon to Nate and back again. *Shit. He's a younger, paler version of Nate Roth! Same hair style in a lighter shade of brown, both of them looking like models for G.Q. or something.* Buck laughs silently. *Poor bastard. What a cross to bear. I'll have to be careful not to hold it against him.* He looks surreptitiously at Nate. *And now that S.O.B. is putting the moves on Allie. She's so fragile now.* Pain stabs his heart. *If he does anything to upset her, I'll break his pretty-boy neck!*

Simon claps Buck on the back. "How about another drink?" As

they walk toward the bar, Simon says, "I'm glad you're so interested in College finances. I look forward to working with you on the committee."

Buck smiles. *Maybe Roth hasn't contaminated him yet.* "Thanks. It's mutual. So, I hear you're a skier." They drift into a discussion of the pros and cons of short skis and various boot bindings.

*   *   *

Nora stands in the ballroom, scanning the assembly for Frank or Bill or *someone* interesting to join. Her glance lingers on Allie. *Why do I feel so sorry for her?* She mentally shakes herself. *Stupid question. Married or not, she's lost someone important to her. Her marriage has to be rocky now. And she's the target of vicious gossip.* Nate is smiling, his arm across Allie's shoulders, handing her a drink. Nora is close enough to hear Nate's toast to Allie just as the Mozart stops. The volume of conversation between Buck and Simon drops like a stone. *Did Buck hear Nate?* As Buck and Simon resume their conversation, Nora studies Buck. *What thoughts does his smile hide? His pain over Richard and Allie? Resentment of Nate flirting with his wife? Or is it genuine? Maybe appreciation of the classical music.*

Two trustee wives—one a bottle blonde, the other dripping diamonds—pause near Nora, their eyes on Nate and Allie. "Would you look at that?" the blonde says. "Skinny as a New York model and flirting with Nate Roth, bold as brass, and Pris right here in the room, too." Both women look from Allie to Priscilla, who is glaring at her husband. The blonde continues, "If looks could kill, Richard Emory wouldn't be the only one dead. You heard that they were lovers, didn't you? Allie Brady and Richard Emory, I mean. At least, that's the polite version of what Carol said at the inquest. She said Buck killed him but his death was her fault—Allie's fault, I mean. *Buck* isn't looking any too happy now, either." Both women look toward Buck. "He could make quite a career killing off his wife's lovers. Nate better watch his back."

Her diamond-bedecked companion giggles. "Oh, Marcia, how you do go on! That's ancient history! Besides, didn't they return a verdict of accidental drowning?"

The two women start toward the hors d'oeuvre table. "No, it was an open verdict. But mistakes do happen."

Nora's face flames. *Is it just the Bradys they tear apart or do they go after everyone? What are they saying about me and Bill? Or Van and Lissa?* She turns angrily toward the portable bar and nearly bumps into Frank, Van, and Lissa. "Did you hear that?" she hisses. "Why don't they leave well enough alone? Vicious gossip doesn't do anyone any good."

Lissa turns to face Nora. "Of course gossip is unkind. But you've got to admit, where there's smoke, there's usually fire."

Nora's eyes narrow but her voice softens. "I don't have to admit any such thing. And doesn't anyone just stick to the facts?"

Lissa rolls her eyes. "The fact is that Richard disappeared from the boat. *Something* happened to him. And I, for one, don't believe it was an accident."

Nora wonders why Lissa seems to be spoiling for an argument tonight. She keeps her tone level when she says, "Frank, you saw the body, and you know the medical examiner's findings. What do you think?"

Frank shrugs. "I didn't actually see any reports. My jurisdiction is Queen Anne's County." He glances at Lissa and says, "But determining whether a drowning is accident, murder, or suicide is next to impossible."

Lissa smiles triumphantly. "There you are then. It could have been murder."

"Or suicide," Van adds.

Frank says, "I've heard that Emory was depressed, seeing a counselor. Who knows what went through his mind when he went overboard? It could have been, 'Who's the SOB who pushed me over?' Or it could have been, 'Finally, a resting place.' It *could* have been one of those. But statistically, neither one is likely. Suicidal drowning is uncommon and most often it's in a bathtub. The body is clothed, and it happens under the influence of drugs or alcohol. There's usually a note. And signs beforehand. Most people don't suddenly become suicidal during a storm and jump overboard to drown."

Lissa says, "So, then, why not murder?"

"For one thing, it's difficult to make sure a healthy person drowns. Holding the head under water leaves bruises. If you put an unconscious body in the water, there'd probably be signs of whatever led to the victim being unconscious."

"But no one had to hold his head under water or drug him," Lissa protests. "This was in rough water—in the middle of a gazillion knot storm! I doubt there are many healthy, conscious people who could survive that."

"A storm is entirely consistent with accidental drowning. Most drownings *are* accidental. The cause of a drowning death is determined based on surrounding circumstances. In this case, there were no known threats to his life, no suicide note or anything of that sort. Hence the ME's verdict."

For reasons Nora doesn't stop to examine, she finds herself compelled to argue against any position Lissa takes. She says, "But even if a murderer is suddenly overcome by the urge to kill *and* is quick-witted enough to seize the opportunity offered by the storm, he—or she—would still need motive and opportunity. And Richard was never alone."

Lissa's stance becomes subtly more rigid. "Then why didn't

anyone see him go overboard? Besides, Buck Brady *had* motive. Richard Emory was his wife's lover."

Nora snorts. "A quarter-century-old affair is hardly a motive for murder."

Lissa sniffs. "I suppose you would know. But maybe it started then and they were picking it up again now."

Van says, "I read somewhere that sex, revenge, and money are the most common motives for murder." Nora turns angry eyes on Van. *Is he saying Buck did it? Some scientist!* Van catches her look and flushes. As if he'd heard her thoughts, he says, "Of course, regardless of motive, no reasonably intelligent person planning murder would count on a storm at sea."

Lissa turns on Van. "You're siding with her?"

Van shifts from foot to foot. "This is not about taking sides. One should draw conclusions based on sound reasoning."

Nora smiles. *That's the Van I know.*

"So now my reasoning is unsound!" Lissa shakes her head. "I'm gonna go bite something." She pivots and marches toward the hors d'oeuvres table. Van looks from Nora to Frank and back again before following Lissa.

Frank tilts his head toward Van and Lissa. "So what do you think about the proper professor and the city sophisticate?"

"I think that faculty members dating trustees is a bad idea." Nora realizes that her words exploded with more force than the question warranted. Frank looks pointedly from her to Bill and back, but says nothing. "Not that it's unethical to date a trustee. But campus politics make it risky—especially for someone who hasn't yet been made a full professor." Frank cocks one eyebrow. She forces a smile "Don't we have better things to talk about? Where's Claire?"

"The baby's running a fever. Claire thought she should stay home with her."

Sick baby or post-partum depression? A soft gong sounds. "Hmmm. The dinner hour is upon us."

*   *   *

Jim Sloan puts stockinged feet on the coffee table. He says, "One day down and one to go. If the rest of my first Board meeting goes as well as today, I'll be a happy man." Rebecca sips a seltzer with lime and says nothing. "The resolution of appreciation for Emory didn't disrupt the meeting much at all. The fixed income portfolio is strong, admissions look promising, and alumni giving is up nearly fifteen percent over last year—all of which makes the Board very happy. If I could just smooth things out with Buck, there might be fewer clouds on the horizon."

Rebecca yawns. "So what's the problem with Buck now?"

"More of the same. Give him a few drinks and he gets a little loud, his humor a little heavy-handed. Even without alcohol, he's pushy and opinionated and questions everything. He just doesn't seem to get it: as the new kid on the block, he ought to hold back a little. Also, Adrian Livingston seems to have decided that one way or another, Buck is responsible for Richard Emory's death, so practically everything he says includes sly comments or innuendo. Nate is even worse. He baits Buck—makes comments about what a 'swell' sailor Buck is, how smooth he is, how astute his observations, but in a voice that drips sarcasm."

Rebecca purses her lips. "Buck's wealth really galls Nate."

Jim looks surprised. "Buck's money? You think that's relevant?"

Rebecca rolls her eyes. "It's *the* central issue. Haven't you noticed how prickly Nate is about not having inherited the family fortune outright? And even if he had, his net worth wouldn't match

Buck's. I'd give long odds that that's why he's putting the moves on Allie."

"Moves on Allie? Who?"

"Nate, of course. Jim, open your eyes! He was hardly two feet away from Allie all night. And every time Buck looked their way, he moved closer. Or made a toast or took her arm to go into dinner."

"Really?"

"How could you not notice?" Rebecca shakes her head. "Sometimes you're hopeless. Priscilla certainly noticed. She was watching like a hawk. And drinking too much. Nate may be your bosom buddy, but you don't know him at all."

Jim shifts his body and glances aside. "Yeah, well. A president has a lot on his mind at Board events. How was your day?"

"It could have been worse. Your biology chairperson upheld the honor of the department and didn't show his pain." Jim's puzzlement must have been written on his face for Rebecca's tone is condescending when she continues. "At having to spend the better part of his day shepherding trustee spouses around. But an outing to the A&P with a lecture on supermarket botany was novel—and more interesting than I expected. The weather was perfect, too, and that always helps."

Jim smiles sourly. "Well strike up the band! A duty of the president's wife that you could get through without grinding your teeth."

* * *

Nate shows no public disapproval of Priscilla's drinking, even though it pains and embarrasses him. He pleads a sudden headache as reason to skip dessert. At home, he helps Priscilla into the house and up to her room, trying not to make noise in case the twins are in. Twice she stumbles on the stairs.

"It's so nice to have you in my room tonight," she mumbles. He takes her clothes off and drops them on the chaise where the maid expects them to be. Priscilla puts her arms around him. "We're gonna have sush a good time. Jus' like we use to."

Nate disentangles himself. "Come on, Pris. Put your arm through here."

"But I don't wanna nightgown. I want *you*." She smiles loosely and bats her eyelashes, drawing his attention to the mascara now smudged around her eyes. She again tries to put her arms around him.

Nate unwinds her arms from his body. "Put on the damn nightgown!" Tears spring to Pris's eyes. A geyser of anger spurts within him. "For the boys' sake—for the servants—try to appear less drunk than you are!" Priscilla raises her arms above her head and stands mute. Nate drops the nightgown over her like a parent dressing a child. Tears course down her cheeks, and she sways slightly. His voice is gentler when he says, "Get into bed before you fall." He steers her toward the bed, arranges the sheet over her.

As Nate trudges wearily to the door, Pris whimpers, "I love you, Nate."

Nate mumbles, "Love you, too." He climbs the stairs to his room and locks the door behind him. Guarding his privacy is a habit. He sinks into a chair by the open doors to the balcony. Wind rustles dried leaves. *I should have been gentler with Pris. But the way she carried on at dinner ...* The wine he drank at the reception and dinner nibbles at his defenses. Thoughts he usually holds at bay press on him. *Pris was as good a choice as any to be the mother of my children. My parents were thrilled. But they didn't change the trust—not in my favor, anyway. So, it's a good thing I married money. Where would I be today without Pris's money? Still, on nights like this, I wish I hadn't.*

*   *   *

Buck watches Allie getting ready for bed, moving from her suitcase to the motel bathroom. *She's so thin!* For the last two months, he's vacillated between concern for his wife and fury that there is anything to be concerned about. When he asked about Carol's accusations, Allie said only, "I never saw Richard after you and I started dating." He assured her they could put the affair behind them. He can't bring up it up again now. But when he mentions that she isn't sleeping well, seems depressed, is losing weight—anything like that—she refuses to discuss it.

And now that sonofabitch Roth … He doesn't really give a rat's ass. He's just coming on to her to get my goat. But what if Allie falls for him? She's so needy now. And whatever she needs, I don't seem to have it. Buck punches his pillow and turns over, weighed down by his old doubts about Allie's love. He fell for her the first time they were together. She wasn't as taken with him, though she seemed eager enough to go to bed. The sex was great. But she wouldn't have married him—not then, anyway—if she hadn't gotten pregnant. Nights like this, he wonders whether she would have married him at all.

Buck gets up for a glass of water. In the next bed, Allie lies without stirring, but he doubts she's asleep. He looks at his reflection in the mirror. *Not a bad body. Women still come on to me. But I've never been tempted. Well, not seriously. Allie is all the woman I need. All I want.* He gets back into bed. *We've had a good life together—except for that one bad patch with Pete Fitzroy. With my know-how and Allie to smooth the rough edges, I've been more successful than I ever imagined. But the rough edges are still there, damn it. And Roth is smooth incarnate.* His last thought before sleep washes over him is, "I'll be damned if Nate Roth—or any other sonofabitch—is going to ruin my marriage."

Chapter Twelve

THE MORNING IS PLEASANT, WARM for early November—a nice respite from the cold back home in Center Sandwich, New Hampshire. Buck sits at the desk in his hotel room, naked except for his reading glasses. He flips the pages of his presentation file. Satisfied that he's ready, he dresses for his meeting at Mast and Mallet: starched white shirt, double-breasted navy pin-striped suit, black Italian loafers polished to a high gloss. He wants Gig Thomas, the up-and-coming owner of the boatyard, to feel that he's an important client.

Stepping out on the balcony overlooking Annapolis harbor, the remains of a mug of lukewarm coffee in his hand, Buck glances at his Rolex. No hurry. From his fourth floor balcony, he sees the grounds of the Naval Academy, the anchor basin, the harbormaster's quarters, and the old Middleton Tavern where he had steamed crabs and beer last night. Directly below, the sight of the schooner *Woodwind* tied to the wharf at Pusser's Landing, her main mast almost three stories high, kicks Buck's heartbeat into high. His breathing turns fast and shallow. This is his first trip to

Annapolis since *Endeavor's* return in August. *If I'd had any idea the hell that charter would raise ...* He takes one last look, gathers his gear, and heads for the lobby.

"Was everything all right, Mr. Brady?"

"Everything was perfect." Buck pauses, imagining what the young desk clerk would look like naked. She's tall and blonde, much more buxom than Allie. He and Allie haven't made love in nearly three months. Since Richard's drowning, she hasn't been interested in much of anything, certainly not sex. *I'll be damned if I ever force myself on any woman. Or beg for it, either.* He's never cheated on his wife, but lately he's thought about it more often. He smiles at the clerk. "I'm going to Mast and Mallet on Beach Drive Boulevard. What's the best way to get there?"

While she gives directions, Buck glances surreptitiously at her breasts, then shifts his gaze to her name tag. "Thank you, Tammy. You've been very helpful. And charming." He smiles again. *What a pair.* Tammy smiles broadly in return, a dimple winking in her left cheek. When she turns to retrieve his receipt from the printer, Buck examines the black fabric stretched taught across her backside. *An ass to die for.* In a flash, he conjures an image of Tammy naked in his room, his hands on her hips, moaning her pleasure while he pumps into her. He imagines the fullness of her breasts in his hands. That thought flips the guilt switch in his brain. Suddenly his hand is on Allie's breast, small and troubled but the source of nourishment for his psyche. *Fuck it. I should have jerked off with a sex video last night.* He takes his receipt and turns toward the automatic door.

*   *   *

Buck and Gig Thomas shake hands, each sizing up the other. Thomas is a tall blond with leathered skin, probably in his late thirties. He wears scuffed boat shoes and grey denim overalls with "Gig" embroidered above the breast pocket. *I was right: he's definitely hands-on.*

"How about we start with a tour of the plant and shops?" Thomas asks.

"Great idea." Buck leaves his suit jacket behind, taking the tour in shirtsleeves. One advantage of over-dressing is the opportunity it offers to get casual, to signal a move to a less formal footing. To further that end, he offers an occasional mild oath. By the third "Hot damn," Gig is clapping him on the back and laughing that his "pretty little boatyard" can impress the big exec.

Back in his office, Gig says, "I was surprised that International Paper wanted to bid on my plywood business."

"International Wood and Paper would be more fitting, but we're too busy getting bigger to think about a new name." Buck leans back. "The fact is, we have a new product. You're a custom boat builder with a great rep. You'd be the ideal showcase." Buck explains the recent innovations his company has made and the advantages of the new plywoods with plastic laminated layers. "Gig, we'd like nothing better than to be your exclusive supplier. And here's what I'm ready to do for you." He hands over the proposal.

Gig glances over the product specs, reads the schedule of prices and payments twice. He rubs his chin. "You know, Buck, I'd really like to do business with you. But I gotta tell you, I have a better bid than this on a very similar product. My profit margin isn't big enough to eat any costs I don't have to."

Buck leans back in his chair. "I suppose you're talking about that product Pete Fitzroy's come up with for Seattle Wood." Gig's eyes widen and Buck knows he hit the mark.

"What makes you say that?"

Buck laughs. "Pete and I go way back. We've been butting

heads and swiping each other's customers for years. What kind of a contract is he offering?"

"Well, now, I don't think I ought to be handing out details on a competitor's confidential bid."

Buck rests his right ankle on his left knee and rests his chin on his fist, looking speculatively at Gig. "I tell you what. Hold off signing with Fitzroy until you've tried our product. I'm telling you, you'll find ours is better." Buck plants his feet on the floor and leans forward, then realizes that his eagerness to close the deal might be too much. *Ease up man. Ease up.* He takes a deep breath and sits back. He smiles and points to blueprints tacked to the wall. "That your newest design?"

"Yeah. The whole yard is proud of her." Gig gives a big thumbs up.

"She's a real beauty. I'd sure like to see her sporting our ply. How about this? Whatever price Pete quoted you, I'll match it."

"Match it?" Gig shakes his head.

It's now or never. "Look, Gig, I really want this demo. I'm making a one-time-only offer, good till I walk out the door today. Whatever price Pete quoted you, I'll beat it by three percent the first year and guarantee to at least match him thereafter. We should be talking transportation, delivery schedules, who pays shipping and delivery."

Gig smiles ruefully. "Three percent, huh? You're making this mighty tough." His smile fades. "Mr. Brady—Buck—I like your confidence in your product. I like you. But I just can't do it."

Buck says, "You haven't signed anything, have you?" Gig shakes his head. "Think about it over lunch." They leave for O'Brien's Oyster Bar and Restaurant back on Main Street, Buck delivering his best pitch all the way.

Finally Gig says, "In all good conscience, I just don't see how

I can back out on Fitzroy. He was first in line with a fair proposal and I told him the contract is a go."

Buck tents his fingers. "What about your slim profit margin?"

Gig shakes his head. "I'd love that extra three percent. But I guess I'll just have to eat it this first year. A man's word is his bond."

Shit. Buck knows better than to burn bridges. He backs off and they talk of other things over lunch. After a second cup of coffee, Gig says, "I've gotta be getting back. But if your new plys are as good as they sound, I guess we might be seeing a lot of each other. My commitment to Fitzroy is for one year." They shake hands like old friends.

*   *   *

Buck orders a martini and thinks about his afternoon meeting with Peter Fitzroy, ostensibly about West College Board of Trustees business. Pete, too, is on the Finance Committee.

Fitzroy has been a boil on Buck's butt for two decades. They went head to head during their early years together at IP. Buck worked longer and harder, and in the end, he was promoted over Pete. But it had come at a price. He was on the road half the time and working fifteen- and eighteen-hour days when he was in town. Allie stayed home with three young children, coping as best she could.

Buck signals for another martini, his black thoughts turning inward. He still feels the pain of that Monday morning, taking out the trash—of the bag breaking and spilling its guts onto the curb—of finding the letter in Pete's neat, tiny print, saying that he didn't understand Allie's change of heart, that he thought they were great together, that one weekend really wasn't time enough—but that, if she wanted to end everything between them, he would honor that. Buck sips his martini, flooded by remembered emotions: the hurt of Allie's betrayal, his relief that she had ended it with Pete, his determination to mend his ways—and never let either of them know that he knew.

Buck thought hard about whether to join the West College Board of Trustees. West is Allie's *alma mater*—and their son's—and it is a logical choice for his philanthropy. Buck knew up front that Pete was on the Board. He hadn't seen Pete face-to-face in fifteen years or more. He thought he could handle it. His snort of laughter is mirthless. *Little did I know there could have been two ex-lovers on that charter. Were there others?*

Now, Richard Emory is dead, but knowing he's about to see Pete, even if it is just to talk about Board business, makes his gut churn. *If we're going to work together on the Board—see each other three or four times a year—I'm gonna have to keep a lid on it.*

Telling Pete he'd scooped Seattle Wood's deal with Mast and Mallet would have felt like an Olympic gold medal. Securing the right platform to launch a major new product line *and* getting Pete's goat–definitely a winning combination. *Damn.* Buck empties his glass and leaves O'Brien's.

Buck checks his watch. He has time to spare. He glances in the window of Hats in the Belfry. He chuckles. *Almost as funny as naming a boat* Knot a Clue. He whistles through his teeth, buoyed by alcohol. *Maybe I'll get a little action on for tonight. Maybe I've earned a little tail, a little payback for Allie and Pete, Allie and Richard.* He heads back to the Marriott, but Tammy is already off duty. *A blessing in disguise?* He passes through the lobby, rambles along the canal, and turns back up Main toward the Treaty of Paris Restaurant. He orders a martini and waits for Peter Fitzroy.

*   *   *

A middle-aged man of average height, slight of build but physically fit, strides briskly toward Buck. "Peter. Right on time." They shake hands, sit at a small round table in the corner, and order. The waitress brings mugs of steaming coffee. Buck takes a sip and winks at the waitress. "Strong enough to stand on its own legs. Just the way I like it." She laughs and turns away.

Pete adds half the jug of milk and two sugars to his mug. He says, "Jesus. How do you drink this stuff black?"

"A simple drink for a simple man. Besides, it matches my soul: black as the ace of spades."

Pete smiles, his mouth a razor line across his square, angular face. "Now tell me something I don't know." They sip their coffee in silence. Buck notices a little grey at Pete's temples, glinting in his otherwise black hair.

They talk for an hour on two motions they expect President Sloan to bring to the Board at its January meeting. They disagree on everything from the appropriate presentation to the desirable outcome. The exchange is reasonably civil but with enough jibes to add an edge. As they close their folders, Buck says, "So, can we hope you'll honor us with your presence in January? Or are you going to blow off all your trustee responsibilities?" *Christ. I shouldn't have had that last martini.* But Pete is a pompous ass and Buck can't seem to help himself.

Pete flushes. "What's that supposed to mean? October was the first Board function I've ever missed."

"The first *meeting* maybe. But you refused my invitation last August."

"You should have scheduled the damn sail sooner! I had other plans."

Buck snorts. "Plans can always be changed. What's more important for a trustee than welcoming the new president?"

"Jim Sloan doesn't seem to have a problem with it. Besides, the way I hear it, that sail was no place for any man Buck Brady might have a beef with." Buck flushes and Pete leans forward, elbows on the table. "You know what's going around among the trustees don't you? They say you pushed Emory overboard on the way back to the schooner, that Nate pulled him out of the drink—that first time. Word is, Emory and Allie were an item and Big Buck just couldn't handle it. What do you think they think happened then?" Pete leans back again. "Not that I'd ever believe such a thing about my old pal Buck."

Buck feels murderous but finally unclenches his teeth and smiles sourly. "Glad to hear it."

"So, when did you start wooing Gig Thomas?"

Buck glances sharply at Pete, swallows the last of his now cold coffee. *What gives him the least edge?* He examines his burly hands, folded on the little table. "I met him today. What about it?"

Pete shrugs. "I got a call from Gig a couple of hours ago. I faxed him a contract for our new plywood this morning. He apologized for not getting back to me sooner, said he was tied up, mentioned lunch. He signed the contract, by the way. So I guess that means you lose."

Pete's smile burns into Buck. He says, "No, Thomas didn't bite. And, given his verbal commitment to you, I admire him for that. But this is only the first round. This time next year, he'll be doing business with me. I underbid you by three percent." Pete looks stunned. Buck feels a surge of exhilaration. "Enjoy the year you've got. In the end, I'm gonna kick your sorry ass."

"No way in hell you could underbid me by three percent and clear a profit." Pete's half glasses frame worried eyes and his forehead shines with sweat.

"Who said anything about profit? Let's just call it a loss leader, in the service of establishing a long-term relationship."

Pete's creamy baritone is steady, hate oozing like the sweat on his brow. "I could handle losing a rinky-dink contract—even to a shit like you—*if* it comes to that. But what I can't handle is a friend who does me more dirt than any enemy ever did. I'll never forgive you for screwing up my future with International Paper."

"All I did was point out that you weren't producing for us. I was your supervisor. That was my job." Buck picks up his mug. "I didn't screw up your career. You did that yourself."

"Yeah. Right. Which is why you've been out to get me ever since."

Buck's eyes bore into Pete's. "And just why would I be out to get you, *friend?*"

Pete looks away, clears his throat. "I don't think we have anything more to discuss. And I've got a pile of work on my desk." They part without shaking hands.

Buck heads back to the Marriot. *Damn Fitzroy.*

Chapter Thirteen

"So, Buck, what's up?" Jim Sloan tries for a cordial, interested tone as he scrolls through the list of his e-mail, the telephone clamped between his shoulder and his ear.

"I've been going through the materials for the January Board meeting. And I gotta tell you, the numbers for the fixed income portfolio are off."

Jim swivels away from his computer screen and focuses on the conversation. "What do you mean?"

"The income's too high."

Jim laughs, relieved. "The college is making too much money?" Buck's wealth flashes into Jim's consciousness, cautioning diplomacy. He adopts a serious tone. "Exactly what makes you think there's a problem?"

"Just that the returns are too high. And too steady. Doesn't anybody else have a problem with that?" Buck sounds offended.

"Nobody's said anything to me." Jim scowls at the bare branches waving outside his window. "Buck, I respect your opinion, but you *are* new to Board finances. I'll take your concerns to Nate and

Stan. If there's a problem with our summary, or with the report we received from Simon Hummel, one of them will see it, too." Jim spends a few more minutes chatting—about the Board meeting coming up in two days, about business, about the weather—and in the end, Buck seems calm.

But after the call, Jim rereads the report. *Is there a problem? Finances aren't my strong suit.* He calls Nate. After summarizing Buck's comments, he says, "So what do you think?" Nate sounds concerned and questions him closely. Jim fidgets, and after his third "I don't know" he snaps, "I've told you everything he said!"

If Nate hears the irritation in Jim's voice, he gives no sign. "So the bottom line is that Brady has the wind up on a hunch that something's wrong."

"He seemed very sure."

"Well, *I'm* sure there's nothing irregular here. I'll grant you that Buck's smart, but he's also a pain in the ass. He thinks he's the only person on the Board who knows anything about business. But so far, his performance on my committee has been unimpressive. He's no more an accountant than he's a sailor. He's probably just stirring the pot."

"Trying to make trouble? Why would he do that?"

"For one thing, he hates my guts. And for another, he wants to chair the Finance Committee—and to do it sooner rather than later."

"Chair the Finance Committee?"

"Absolutely." Nate pauses. "Besides, everyone knows he and Allie aren't getting along. He's strung tight as piano wire."

Jim clears his throat. "Well, you aren't helping matters in that regard." He drums his fingers on his desk. "I say this as a friend, Nate. Maybe you should stop flirting with Allie—especially right under Buck's nose."

"Relax, Jim. It doesn't mean a thing. I'm just being kind to the walking wounded. But if it makes you feel better, I'll bestow my attentions elsewhere."

After ringing off, Jim sits in silence. *He and Priscilla have been married a long time. And nobody could think Pris is a beauty. But she's smart enough, and thoughtful and good-hearted. What is it with Nate and other women? Doesn't he see how much it upsets her? And why did he take Buck's comments on the finance report so personally?* Jim massages his left temple. *I hope Nate's right—that all of this is just Buck's invention.*

Jim walks across to Stan's office and recounts his conversations. Stan looks serious, lines up his pencils, mentions the sterling reputation of Simon Hummel's firm and the years Nate has chaired the Finance Committee. In the end he concludes, "The fact is, our portfolio manager is beating the benchmarks by a fraction—and doing it consistently. Maybe our investments are doing better than Buck's and he can't handle it."

Jim breathes easier as he packs his briefcase for home. Nate might have an ax to grind with Buck, and Stan's performance might still be a little shaky, but knowing they agree that there is no problem relieves Jim's anxiety. He decides to call Bill Baxter before heading out. *It wouldn't do for Nate—or worse, Buck—to say something to Bill when I hadn't.*

Bill seems inclined to agree that Buck is mistaken, but takes a kindlier view of his intentions. "He has the welfare of West foremost—and he isn't being shy about it."

When Jim passes along a laundered version of Nate's criticisms, Bill bristles. "Nate is hardly an impartial observer. Either he's seriously interested in Allie or he's trying to get under Buck's skin. In either case, his flirting just makes the situation worse."

In spite of his own concerns on the matter, Jim says, "Perhaps he thinks—uh—that Allie needs some attention. Carol Emory's comments about her and Richard—well, it must have been hard on the Brady marriage."

"Whatever Nate's motivation, if he keeps it up, he'll be courting trouble. I'll talk to him."

"That won't be necessary. I already spoke to him. It was a little awkward, but he took it well enough." Jim clears his throat. "And speaking of awkwardness with Board members … When Frank Pierce was a student here, Nora Perry was the director of his honors thesis. They've been—um—good friends since then."

"So?"

"As Chairman of the Board, I just wanted to give you a heads-up. I thought you should be aware of any possible—entanglements—even past ones—between Board members and our Faculty Chair."

"I see. Yes. Thanks for letting me know." Bill sounds almost distracted. Jim brushes back his hair, pushes up his glasses, and wonders how best to get on with the conversation. Eventually Bill continues. "Last fall we offered condolences to Carol Emory. And then you had to hire a new VP for finance. It's the devil's own luck that your first months at West have been so beleaguered. I hope you know that you can count on me—whatever you need."

"Thanks, Bill. It's good of you to say so."

They ring off and Jim swivels slowly back and forth, vastly relieved that there is no financial problem at West, thinking about how to tell Buck he's mistaken and then smooth his ruffled feathers. Thoughts of Buck turn to thoughts of Nate. *His comment about bestowing his attentions elsewhere—Is he thinking about getting something started with Nora Perry? I know she's preparing a grant proposal for his foundation. If there's one thing I don't need, it's to have the Chairman of the Board and another trustee interested in the same faculty member. I can see the attraction. She's good looking in an Amazonian sort of way. Not exactly in the first bloom of youth, strong-willed and opinionated. But she's keen and witty, and easy to talk to. Surely she and Frank Pierce are ancient history. Not that the race issue matters to me, but it matters to a lot of other people—not to mention that he's a married man. I thought Adrian Livingston would burst a blood vessel when he told me they were an item in the past. Where does that man get his information?* Jim shakes his head. *Little did I know that so much of my job as president would be keeping up with which Board members, spouses, and faculty are sleeping together—or have done so in the past—or might want to do so in the future.* The grandfather clock strikes six. *Enough. I've got to get home.*

*   *   *

Buck sits at the bay window, papers for the up-coming trustee meeting piled on his lap. An oversized thermometer on a silver maple a dozen feet away reads 20 degrees. Pretty typical for a January evening in Center Sandwich. The sun at twilight painted soft orange on the underside of wispy clouds, but the sunset lasted hardly fifteen minutes before darkness closed in. Now logs settle in the fireplace behind him, sending dancing shadows across the floor.

His conversation with Jim Sloan earlier that afternoon still rankles. Buck recognizes a soothe-the-raging-beast move when he gets one. He isn't accustomed to having his concerns brushed aside.

Allie went to see her elderly aunt in Gladstone, New Jersey, two days ago, with plans to meet him in Centreville for the Board meeting. Perhaps it is the silent house, but he can't keep his mind from visiting things past. *If she hadn't gotten pregnant, would she ever have married me? Why didn't she tell me about Richard Emory? What would have happened if he hadn't drowned?* His thoughts skip: weather warnings from NOAA, the Coast Guard reports of winds in excess of 60 knots, the dark turbulent waves with long overhanging crests, the skipper's searchlight glinting on the water. Images of Richard drowning haunt him. He shakes his head, pours a double shot of whiskey, and picks up the reports.

Propping his right ankle on his left knee, his pant leg hikes up exposing his bare ankle. *New Hampshire shins, white as dry bone. When I was a lumberjack, my skin was leather.* For the last twenty years, he's spent more time in boardrooms than in lumber camps. *But whatever I lost in that move, it wasn't as good as what I got. And I couldn't have done it without Allie. My manners were rough as pine bark when she took me in hand, sanded off the splinters, and told me I could do anything I set my mind to.* He is halfway through the report of the Committee on Student Life when Allie calls.

"Are you eating?" she asks.

"Oh, yeah. And drinking, too."

"But not too much of the latter," she says.

He chuckles. "Right. Look, I'll get a ride to Manchester airport tomorrow. I expect to be in Baltimore by 3:00. Can you pick me up at baggage claim? You can't miss me. I'll be the guy with polish on his shoes." Allie laughs, but it seems to Buck that her heart isn't in it. "Would you rather I rent a car?"

"I can pick you up. It's just …"

Buck says, "Never mind. I know how you feel about urban traffic. You stick to the state roads. I'll rent a car. Do you have the confirmation number for the motel?"

"It's in the car." Silence stretches between them.

Finally Buck says, "So I'll see you tomorrow around four o'clock. Drive carefully." He pauses. "I love you." He looks at the wall, counts to three.

"I love you, too," Allie says. The line goes dead.

Buck hangs up slowly. *Will things ever be right between us again?* He dreads the board meeting—everyone in the room watching them, Allie smiling at Nate, people snickering behind his back. *She's so vulnerable now. So needy.* Buck sighs. He doesn't know what to do to make things better. He picks up the reports for the Board meeting. He sighs again. His wife mourning another man is a stone weighing on his heart. *But I swear, whatever it takes, I'll protect her.*

Chapter Fourteen

FRANK STRAIGHTENS HIS TIE AND takes one last look in the full-length mirror—Claire's mirror. *God, honey, I miss the old you. You could make these damned college events bearable.* Half of the bed is reflected behind him in the mirror—the half where Claire sleeps. And sleeps. Will she ever get over her depression? Since Jessica was born … He turns his back on the thought and steels himself for a difficult evening. *At least Nora will be there. I couldn't have asked for a better friend these last few weeks.*

On his way down the hall, he looks in on Jessica, already asleep. He pauses to watch her breathe, then gently pulls her blanket up. He closes her door, swallowing hard around the lump in his throat.

The light is still on in the twins' room. "Daddy, Daddy! Will you read to us?"

Frank smiles but shakes his head. "I told you I have to go out tonight. Grandma will read to you tonight. But I'll read to you Sunday. I promise." He tucks them in and kisses each good night in spite of their protests of, "Ugh. No mushy stuff!"

* * *

Frank enters the Formal Lounge at Chum's and scans the crowd of trustees and spouses, searching for Nora. When he sees her standing by the French doors, looking out on the black velvet evening, the tension in his shoulders ebbs. He joins her, a glass of wine for each of them in hand.

Nora smiles. "Thanks. How are things at home?"

Frank winces. "Mama thinks it's high time for Claire to 'pull herself together.' But she also thinks it's scandalous for a husband to be 'dressin' up and steppin' out' while his wife suffers. Otherwise, everything's fine." Nora purses her lips, tilts her head, and seems to be trying to read his face. Frank has to control an urge to squirm. "What?"

Her voice is low and gentle. "Your mother loves you and the children—and Claire, too. She's a good woman, even if she is still set against our friendship."

Frank forces a grin. "I'd be lying if I said otherwise. But you're the best damned friend I have. The only one I can talk to. So Mama will just have to like it or lump it." Frank scans the crowd. Several people seem to be looking toward him and Nora.

A tiny frown creases Nora's brow. "She's always been so proud of you—your education, your achievements. I think you've always been her favorite child."

Frank holds up one hand. "Yeah, yeah. Mom always loved me best." He grins. "Which is why I know she'll come around in the end. Besides, she's been so busy—tending the kids, helping me find a sitter, just being there with Claire … She—We—There's always the possibility that Claire might try to harm herself." He hurries on, before Nora can react to the hint of suicide. "So Mama's got her hands full, and all the time she's calling Pops to make sure everything is okay in Philadelphia. I doubt she's had time to give you much thought." As he tells Nora the latest details of his children, he becomes aware of Van looking in their direction. "Van is here. Behind your left shoulder. You still seeing him?"

"Not so much." Nora shrugs. "I suspect he's been spending all his free time in New York."

Frank listens for the feeling under the casual words. "Noni, I'm sorry."

Nora lays her hand on his forearm. "It's okay. Seriously. When someone develops a serious love interest, other friendships take a back seat. It's human nature." Her voice is low. Frank glances away. Adrian Livingston catches his eye and smiles tightly. Frank smiles back. *The old goat always looks like he's just tasted something rotten.* Frank imagines him thinking, "And Claire not here?"

Nora says, "Here comes Bill."

Frank turns to greet Bill Baxter.

"Frank, how's Claire?" Bill smiles sympathetically.

Frank glances at Nora, wondering what she might have said about Claire's postpartum depression. Or is it just the byproduct of small town, small college? "Thank you. Knowing family and friends are wishing her well is a comfort."

Bill acknowledges Frank's comment with a nod and turns to Nora. "And how are you tonight?" His tone and his look are unexpectedly intimate, and Frank shifts mental gears. Maybe it isn't just Van who's developed new interests.

Before Nora can answer, all three of them turn as Pete Fitzroy hisses at Buck: "You don't know what the hell you're talking about!"

Buck looks belligerent. "Like hell I don't. I've read the documents. Seattle Paper is so far from sustainable lumbering, you could drive eighteen-wheelers through the gaps." Buck drains his martini.

Pete steps closer to Buck but speaks louder, his face mottled purple. "You and your bloody International Paper! You act like you're the world standard on everything! And all the time you're lying, cheating, stealing clients in every underhanded, double-dealing—" Those near enough to hear him fall silent and watch. Frank sets his glass on the windowsill, ready to step in if things get out of hand.

Buck says, "What's your problem? You're the one who got the Mast and Mallet contract." Frank relaxes a little. *At least one of them is trying to be reasonable.*

"Any decent man would have respected his commitment, not tried to bribe Thomas to break it. Is that the way you usually do business? Or are you just out to get *me*?"

Buck's face is unreadable. "Why would I be out to get my old pal Pete?" he snarls. "I offered Thomas a better deal—not to mention a better product—*when your contract's up*. You can't expect to keep clients when you're peddling crap."

"There's not a nickel's worth of difference between our plastic laminates and yours and you damn well know it! We've had them in the pipeline for more than two years. When I find out how you stole our formulas—." Pete leans toward Buck, fists clenching spasmodically.

Frank steps forward and puts a hand on Pete's shoulder. "I think you boys ought to go to your corners and not come out fighting."

Van comes up behind Buck, says, "Buck, I haven't seen you all day. Why don't I buy you a drink and you can tell me all about the Finance Committee meeting." Frank nods in Van's direction.

Buck turns toward the open bar. "No need to babysit. If Pete and I have anything more to say to each other, we'll take it outside."

Pete shrugs off Frank's hand, glowers at Buck's back, and strides away, leaving Frank and Van in the middle of the room. Van says, "I am sorry Claire is having such a difficult time."

Frank wonders how many people know. He clears his throat. "Thank you."

"Frank!" Priscilla Roth touches his arm. Van steps away as Pris launches into effusive conversation with Frank. Frank only half listens to her, just enough to murmur something appropriate or nod when she pauses. Pris repeats herself for the third time and Frank realizes she's tipsy. *How much did alcohol fuel that blow-up between Buck and Pete? Or was there something else? In the past, maybe.*

Pris stops speaking abruptly and Frank follows her gaze to where Nate is greeting Nora, taking both her hands in his, kissing her on each cheek. His hands still enfold hers when his low chuckle drifts toward Pris and Frank. Frank would have called Nate's half-hooded gaze "bedroom eyes" even if he hadn't heard him say "The most fascinating, beautiful woman in the room. I haven't been able to get near you all evening." Nora blushes and smiles but looks uncomfortable. Her comment is brief and inaudible.

Pris stirs and Frank turns back to her. Tears glitter in her eyes. She finishes her drink. "Just when I was beginning to feel thankful that he's ignoring Allie Brady." Her voice is acid.

At the mention of Allie, Frank searches the room. She's standing next to the wall, tossing down a martini, looking miserable. *Alcohol. The anesthetic of choice tonight.*

* * *

Frank and Nora pause under the old oak tree outside Chum's. She says, "No, really. I have my car. There's no need to see me home. But thanks." She kisses Frank's cheek, squeezes his hand, and is gone.

He leans against the tree trunk, dreading the thought of home. The other departing diners don't seem to notice him there. Adrian walks past, stiffly erect, handling his cane like a caricature of an English gentleman. Frank smiles. *Ass.* Several couples leave. Pete Fitzroy comes out. He heads for his car and Frank looks for signs of intoxication. *Should I give him a breathalyzer? No more reason than for half the people here tonight.* While he hesitates, Buck and Allie come out and walk in the same direction as Pete. Frank follows, just in case. Buck draws Allie's hand through his arm as they walk into the mild night, Frank a few feet behind.

Allie says, "The president seemed in especially good spirits." Frank can hardly hear her. She seems to be speaking very carefully.

Buck says, "Could be. But that bastard Fitzroy is a royal pain in the patoot. Did you hear him? If Pierce and van Pelt hadn't stepped in, I'd probably have pasted him one." He sounds more amused than angry now. "I just hope I didn't embarrass you too much."

Allie says, "Here he comes. Buck, be nice. Don't start anything."

Pete's body language shouts anger and he's heading straight for Buck. Frank tenses and stops in the shadow of a nearby tree. Buck seems to feel Pete's anger, too, for he steps between Allie and Pete. He glances toward the shadows under the tree. Frank can't tell whether Buck sees him or is just checking out his surroundings in preparation for dealing with Pete. Pete stops under the streetlight—an arm's length away from Buck—breathing hard and scowling. Buck extends his hand. "No hard feelings, Pete."

"Bah!" Pete glares at Buck, ignoring his hand. "Did you spike my tire?"

Buck's hand falls. "Huh? What the hell are you talking about?"

"I've got a flat."

"Christ, Pete, give it up. A good brawl is what makes us lumbermen. Hell, we didn't even draw blood. Do you really think I'd do something that petty?" Frank has never heard Buck use an awe-shucks tone before. It doesn't ring quite true. He can't decide whether Buck is cajoling or disdainful.

Pete glances from Buck to Allie and back again. "Probably not. I guess."

"You can bet on it." Buck claps him on the shoulder. "Come on. I'll help you with the spare."

Pete snorts. "It *is* the damn spare! I loaned the car to my next-door neighbor a couple of days ago and he blew a tire. I haven't picked up a new one. Christ, it's been years since I had a flat. And now two in one week."

Allie says, "Oh, dear. Twenty-four-hour road service isn't exactly easy to come by in Centreville. It could be hours before you get home."

"Hey, not a problem." Buck turns to Pete. "Take my rental. Allie drove down in her car, so this one would just sit in the college parking lot tonight anyway." He holds out the keys. "It's the green Merc with Maryland plates. Just drop it back here tomorrow so I can return it to the airport after the meeting."

Pete doesn't meet Buck's eyes, but he takes the keys. "Thanks." Pete walks toward the parking lot without looking back. Frank breathes more easily.

Allie takes Buck's arm. "I'm glad you didn't get into a fight. And lending him the rental was the decent thing to do."

Buck shrugs. "Let's get back to the motel."

Frank steps off the grass and walks heavily after the Bradys, his steps crunching the gravel. Allie looks startled but Buck shows no surprise. *Maybe he knew I was there all along. Maybe a witness makes Buck a whole lot friendlier.* Franks says, "Have a good evening. And drive carefully."

Winding through the empty streets of Centreville, Frank realizes how bone tired he is. *Not that I'm likely to get much sleep.* Frank bangs his fist on the steering wheel. *Damn it! Claire, why can't you pull yourself together? I need you!*

*   *   *

Even though it's a Sunday morning, Frank stops by his office to clear a little paperwork before the last half-day Board session. The week after Claire started therapy, Sheriff Bentley suggested, ever so gently, that maybe Frank needed a little time off. Frank declined and buried himself in his work.

The dispatcher at the Queen Anne's County Sheriff's Office pops his head in the door. "Frank, call Queenstown police. Something about an automobile accident."

"I don't do traffic accidents," Frank says.

"I know. But a man's dead. They need your help."

"Okay, okay. I'll call." Frank reaches for the telephone, knocking over a picture of Claire and the kids, less patient and more judgmental than usual. He rights the photo and suppresses a spurt of anger at all the reckless or drunk or speeding sonsofbitches who cause them. He dials. "This is Frank Pierce. What's up?"

"We had a fatal car crash here last night. But it doesn't smell right. The dead guy's driver's license says Peter Fitzroy, age 52. The car was rented."

"Pete Fitzroy? Jesus, I just saw him last night."

"He's a friend of yours?"

"He's a fellow trustee of West College. So what was it? Alcohol?"

"Naw. The booze was secondary. We don't think it was an accident. From the tire marks it appears that the driver swerved—

maybe to miss something, lost control, and hit the bridge abutment. We found a trail of brake fluid on the road for three hundred yards, none at the site of the crash. It looks like the master brake cylinder had been tampered with."

Frank recalls Buck handing Pete the keys to his rental car. "So you think homicide."

"You got it."

"Where's the car now? Impounded? I'll get the techs working. Anything else?"

"The car was rented at Marshall Airport. The contract in the glove compartment is in the name of a Schuyler Buckner Brady from New Hampshire. So maybe Fitzroy's using two names. Or he stole the car. Or maybe Brady fled the scene." Frank sees again Pete's clenched fists, hears again the false goodwill in Buck's words. The Queenstown officer says, "Pierce? You still there?"

"Yeah, I'm here. I know Brady, too. He loaned the car to Fitzroy last night."

*   *   *

Frank glances at his watch and knocks on Jake's door. "Got a minute? I need to talk to you." Jake waves him to a chair on the other side of the desk. Frank grins at his boss, hoping to take the edge off what's to come. "You should never come in on a Sunday morning, Jake. Bad things happen."

Frank reports his conversation with the Queenstown police officer. "So the question is, who was the intended victim? If somebody was out to get Brady, who and why? If they meant to get Fitzroy, how would they know he was in Brady's car? Unless it was Brady who wanted Fitzroy dead. I tracked Brady down at his motel a few minutes ago. As soon as I said who was calling, he said, 'God, it *was* Pete Fitzroy.' Just like that. No questions. He said he'd heard about the accident on the morning news and guessed it was Fitzroy based on the description of the car, but I don't know." Frank looks at Jake. "Brady loaned the rental to Fitzroy. I saw it. Pete's car had a flat, Brady and his wife had two cars, hers and the rental. So maybe it was no big deal. But they—Brady and Fitzroy—were practically brawling earlier." He recounts their argument over cocktails before the trustee dinner.

Jake scowls over reading glasses low on his nose. "Frank, given your role on the Board of Trustees, maybe you shouldn't be investigating this one. If this case turns out to be a homicide—which seems likely—the potential conflicts of interest are enormous."

Frank sits up a little straighter. "You don't need to remind me of the dangers of friendships. But these weren't friends. More like acquaintances." He smiles thinly. "If we can't investigate people we know, you won't have a man on the force who can investigate anything anywhere in the whole damn county!"

Jake scowls, "Yes, well, there's some truth in that. But somehow it's more likely to come to voters' minds when it's West College and big wigs on the Board." Jake holds up a hand, forestalling Frank's protest. "But it's still pretty early to make a call on your involvement in the case. We'll let things unfold a little first."

Back in his office, Frank stares out the window. Of course he is flattered to serve his alma mater as an alumni trustee, and his parents bask in the reflected glory. *But damn it, I can't let Jake pull me off the case. With Claire so depressed, work is the only part of my life where I have any control at all.*

Frank heads for the 9:00 meetings, stopping on the way to send two men to go over Fitzroy's car. He arrives at Old Main a scant five minutes before Bill calls the meeting to order. Pete Fitzroy's name is on everyone's lips.

When Bill opens the meeting by saying, "I'm sure we all are profoundly saddened by the sudden death …," Frank only half listens. *Homicide. It's got to be. And I'm the guy who will prove it.* The thrill of the hunt tingles up his spine. In all his years of police work, he's never left a homicide open. He looks at Buck, who stares at his notepad, doodling. *He did the same thing during the Emory memorial. Jesus.* He glances across at Nora and returns her nod. Frank massages his forehead, hoping to fend off a headache. If anyone were to ask, he'd say, "I'm fine," knowing it to be a bald-faced lie. *But I have to hold it together till Claire gets better.*

Chapter Fifteen

LEAVING OLD MAIN AFTER THE meeting, Frank ducks his head and belts his trench coat against the driving January sleet. The campus is deserted as only a foul Sunday can make it. When the Board meeting ended at noon, Frank announced that a team of officers was waiting at the student center to question trustees and spouses before they leave campus. Striding toward the Chalmondeley Student Center—usually called Chums—Frank remembers the classmate who gave the money for the building five or six years earlier. Shalindar Chalmondeley was from India and spoke English with a pleasing lilt. They were roommates for three years. *I've never had a better male friend. I'd give a lot to have him here right now.* The task before him weighs heavily on Frank as he pushes through the door. Dealing with strangers would be a hell of a lot easier.

Jim Sloan meets him there. "Is this really necessary, Frank? People have planes to catch, places to be …"

Frank feels himself stiffen but keeps his voice level. "I know it's inconvenient, Jim, but sudden death is like that. Everyone present last night has to be questioned, the sooner the better."

Jim rubs his chin as if it has a three-day growth of beard and shakes his head. "But is turning the Student Center into a police interrogation facility really necessary?"

Frank stares at him stonily. "If it would make you more comfortable, I can haul everyone down to the Sheriff's Office and question them there."

"Why, for God's sake? It's an automobile accident!"

"Or maybe not."

"You mean … ?" Jim frowns, his face turning the color of a half-ripe tomato. "Okay. Here and now is the lesser evil. But for heaven's sake—oh, never mind," he mutters and stalks away.

Frank strides to the front of the ballroom and scans the assembly, waiting for the buzz of conversation to die down. Nora sits near the back looking calm and sad. He catches her eye. She nods and gives him a small, sympathetic smile. Buck and Allie Brady sit three rows ahead of Nora. Buck looks pale and distracted. Allie looks as if she might faint. *Those* could *be natural reactions to having loaned the car to the victim.*

When the room is quiet, Frank says, "We'll make this as fast and easy as possible. We'll start with those who have planes or trains to catch. Please identify yourselves, and we'll get you on your way as quickly as possible." Frank gestures to the two men standing near him. "Sergeant Joe Jamieson and Detective Sy Brown will help with the questioning." Frank knows the impressions his colleagues are likely to make. Joe Jamieson is in his early forties, with thinning hair, a small paunch, and a mild manner that does not inspire confidence in new acquaintances, but Frank trusts his judgment and his skill. Sy Brown matches his name: straight brown hair combed back, brown pants and a well-worn brown tweed jacket.

He is in his late twenties and very fit. The people he questions are likely to find him judgmental and slightly abrasive. In this opinion, Frank concurs.

"Sy, when you line up the interviews, put the Bradys on my list, near the end." Sy's eyebrows shoot up and he opens his mouth, but closes it again without question or comment. Perhaps he's slowly learning not to antagonize his superior.

As Sy divvies up the interviews, Joe says to Frank, "We found Fitzroy's car parked near that dorm that's being renovated, a metal peg stuck in the tire. There's a ton of construction junk around, and no way to tell whether Fitzroy drove over it or someone spiked the tire using what was at hand."

Frank frowns. "No help in deciding whether the intended victim was Fitzroy or Brady. Question accordingly."

Most of the trustees are happy to cooperate, some showing telltale signs of morbid pleasure at being on the fringes of a murder investigation. A few grumble at the inconvenience. Frank finds the grumblers easier to deal with than those who start their interviews by inquiring about Claire's heath. Keeping a lid on his situation is difficult enough without being reminded of it time and time again.

Adrian Livingston insists on speaking only with Frank and on doing so *now*. After suffering one concerned inquiry after another, Frank finds Adrian a welcome relief. "Well, Pierce, I can't say I'm surprised. I'm not a man to say, 'I told you so.' But I did tell Bill that Buck Brady would be nothing but trouble on the Board. And here we are, embroiled in another death. If you ask my opinion, it's another *murder*. Two in a matter of months."

Frank tries to ignore Livingston's querulous whine. "And what makes you say murder, Adrian?"

"Well, just look at it," Livingston sputters. "I mean, what are the chances it's all just coincidence? Speak to Nate Roth. He'll tell you. Brady was arguing with Richard Emory the day he went overboard. *And* he was the one who set the anchor—the anchor that dragged, making it impossible to find Emory. Now this. Brady argues with Fitzroy and Fitzroy dies in Brady's rental car. You can't tell me that's coincidence. You'd see it yourself if you weren't so distracted by your wife's condition."

Frank hides his spurt of anger under a bland tone. "What makes you think it was Brady's rental car?"

"Well he said so, for heaven's sake! During the coffee break. So who had a better chance to tamper with the car?"

Frank's head snaps up. "Do you know something about the car being tampered with?"

"Nothing. Nothing at all." Adrian squirms in his chair. "Just what Jim Sloan said a few minutes ago, that maybe it wasn't an accident."

Frank fights to contain his exasperation. "I can see how you'd be tempted to add two and two. But about last night—apart from the argument during the social hour—did you see or hear anything that might be relevant?"

Adrian sniffs. "How should *I* know what's relevant? Sorting that out is your job, isn't it? All I can tell you is that Peter Fitzroy was in a sour mood all through dinner, grumbling about 'the high and mighty Schuyler Buckner Brady.' That's a quote, mind you. He hardly seemed in a mood to be taking favors from Buck Brady—assuming Brady was in a mood to offer one. Which I doubt! Every time he looked in his wife's direction, he cried in his beer—so to speak."

"And why do you think that was?"

"Oh, come, Pierce. Everyone knows their marriage has been strained—to say the least—ever since Carol Emory let the cat out of the bag about Allie and Richard. Now Allie seems quite taken with Nate Roth." Adrian leers. "And last night, Fitzroy seemed to be dancing attendance, in spite of his hostility toward Buck. One can't help wondering how many men are in her past—or in her future."

Further questioning just confirms that Adrian is willing to repeat the same gossip and speculation as often as Frank is willing to listen. He neither saw nor heard anything relevant. Frank extricates himself as diplomatically as he can and calls in Buck Brady.

If anyone can shed some light on this, you're the man. Would you set Pete up to die just because he beat you out of a contract? Are you that small? Or that competitive? Or was Pete a mistake? Frank says, "Have a seat."

As he sits down, Buck says, "I was sorry to hear about your wife, Frank. Depression is a nasty business, but everyone says she's a fine woman. This must be hell for you."

"Thanks for your concern. It's been difficult. But work helps me get through the days. Unfortunately, right now that means dealing with Pete Fitzroy's death. Tell me about your argument last night. It sounded pretty hot to me."

Buck grins sheepishly. "Yeah, well, I guess we got into it pretty good. But it didn't mean anything. Pete and I have been—were—competitors for years. But a blow-up like that, it just blows over. You were there. You know that, right? So when I found out Pete's car had a flat, and we had two cars right here—well, I'd have offered it to any of the trustees."

Frank makes a tent of his fingers. "When you and Pete were arguing, he said something about you stealing clients, product specifications. What was that about?"

Buck raises his eyebrows. "Pete's paranoia! We developed our own plastic laminates—the best on the market. Pete just had his britches in a twist because we started R&D after Seattle Wood did and still beat them to production."

"And stealing clients?"

"Hey, it's business. You make the best deal you can to get where you need to go. He got the Mast and Mallet account for a year but I was damned sure going to take it away from him. I underbid him, that's all. It was just business."

"Hmmm. Yes." Frank stares steadily at Buck, who looks defiant. *What's he hiding?* "Remind me why you weren't surprised when I called this morning."

"Like I said. I'd heard about the green Merc rental on the morning news." Buck licks his lips. "And the accident happened on 301—Pete's likely route. I couldn't help thinking ... you know." Frank presses him but gets nothing more.

"So, why did you have two cars?"

"Allie and I came to the Board meeting separately. I was coming from New Hampshire and she was visiting her aunt in New Jersey."

Frank waits for Buck to continue. Most people under interrogation do. When Buck remains silent, it raises a flag: Buck is not behaving like most people. "Tell me about the rental car. Don't leave anything out."

Buck runs a hand over his hair. "I got it at the airport on Friday, drove to the motel to check in, left it there and came back here with Allie in our car for Friday night's dinner. Then yesterday morning, Allie wanted to do some antique shopping along Rt. 301, so I drove the rental in for the Saturday meetings. I planned to leave the rental here last night, pick it up today, and drop it off at Marshall on the way home. I had no way of knowing Pete was going to need a car."

"Unless you put his out of commission."

"How could I? I didn't even know which car was his. Plus, I didn't leave from cocktails to dessert. Ask anybody. Anybody saying otherwise is lying." Buck looks straight at Frank. "Besides, it was my rental. If this was intentional, it was intended for me. Have you thought about that?"

"Assuming you were expected to be the next person driving the rental, can you think of anyone who might have wanted you to have an accident?"

"Hell, no! Who would have something against me?"

Frank looks at Buck. *He's giving me the ol' shuck an' jive. Every self-made corporate executive has enemies.* "That's what we're trying to find out," Frank says. "What about business enemies? Loan sharks? Gambling or drug debts? Family feuds? Who would benefit from your death?"

Buck shakes his head at each question. "Sure there are people who don't like me. But I can't believe anybody would want me dead. Aside from a couple of charitable gifts, Allie and the kids get everything when I die." He grins with what looks like genuine amusement. "But they've got pretty much everything now! And I'm still making money for them hand over fist."

"Money isn't the only reason a wife might want to get rid of a husband." Frank pauses. "Just how bad are things between you and Allie?"

Buck's smile fades and he looks away. "If by bad you mean unhappy, it's been hell. Richard Emory's death has been hard on her. Her mourning another man has been hard on me." *Those sound like the truest words he's uttered today. Is he using the truth to play me?* Buck looks back at Frank and speaks quietly, "But if by bad you mean hostile, then not at all. It's a tough time for us, but our marriage is solid. We love each other." *Wishful thinking?*

Frank says, "That'll be all for now. I may be in touch later."

He brings Allie in immediately, before Buck can coach her on the interview. She looks gaunt and plucks at the fabric of her pantsuit fretfully. *Upset?* He remembers Allie tossing back a martini. *Hungover? Needing a drink?* She confirms all that Buck said about the cars. Frank goes over it twice before moving on. "What can you tell me about your husband's relationship with Fitzroy?"

Allie looks wary. She focuses over Frank's shoulder when she says, "Buck and Pete? We've known Pete practically forever. They were coworkers at IP in the early days and we lived in the same housing development. But then ..." Allie seems to be looking everywhere except at Frank. "Oh, lots of things happened. Pete and his wife separated and Buck got a promotion over Pete. Pete left IP. Since then, we haven't seen Pete. I mean, maybe Buck has seen him at business conferences or something. But see him to talk to—that's only since Buck joined the Board."

So what's she hiding? Something big. But is it relevant to the case? "The word on the street is that you and Buck have been having a tough time of it since last summer." Allie looks away, color draining from her cheeks, and says nothing. "Is it true?"

She looks at Frank. "I don't see that the state of my marriage has anything to do with Pete's accident."

"What if it wasn't an accident? What if Pete Fitzroy wasn't the intended victim?"

"I've thought of that. The idea scares the bejesus out of me." She plucks at the crease of her pant leg. "But I can't think of anyone who would want to hurt Buck."

"Just how bad are things between the two of you?"

Allie looks startled and then she laughs, a tight little bark. "Surely you aren't suggesting that *I* tampered with the rental!"

"It's been known to happen."

"I hardly know a wrench from a screwdriver. If I wanted my husband dead—which I don't—I'd choose some method I know something about—maybe a drug overdose or something nonviolent like that. Or I'd hire a hit man—assuming I knew how to go about that. In any case, I wouldn't let a bystander be killed instead if I could stop it. Last night I could have stopped it." Frank cocks an eyebrow at her. "One word from me and they would have been at each other's throats again. Buck would never have offered the car after that."

When Allie leaves, Frank pauses a few minutes to mull over the interview. *Basically, she said she wouldn't have killed him that way—and she would have intervened to save a bystander. But it's only her word.*

Frank's interview with Nathaniel Roth yields little. He noticed no one leaving early. He knows nothing of who Pete talked with or what was said. "Apart from his argument with Buck. But everyone heard that. Otherwise, I didn't see or hear anything of Buck Brady, either." Nate eyes Frank coolly. "I think Buck is an arrogant asshole. Any time we are in the same room, I try to be on the other side of it."

"You don't seem to feel that way about his wife."

"Allie Brady is lovely, in every sense of the word."

Frank looks at him steadily. "Would she be even lovelier as a rich widow?"

Nate laughs. "Even Buck must know enough to tie up his fortune in trusts for the children and grandchildren."

"Is it true you overheard a fight between Buck and Richard Emory the day he died?"

Nate laughs again. "Is this your attempt to keep me off balance or something?"

"Adrian said you'd overheard an argument between Brady and Emory."

"Adrian's got the most gossip and the fewest brains of any man I know! Surely you don't believe everything you hear from that old maid in pants!"

"I don't believe everything I hear from anyone. That's why I asked. Is there some reason you haven't answered?"

Nate shrugs. "None at all. I never heard an argument between Brady and Emory. What I *did* hear was when Buck and I hauled Richard back into the tender on the way to *Endeavor*. Buck said, 'Don't fight me, man,' and Richard said someone had pushed him." Nate shrugs again, his tone sounding carefully casual: "It does make one wonder."

* * *

Back in the office, Frank calls in Joe and Sy. "What did you get?"

"Not half enough! Especially from that Melissa Nelson." Sy sniggers. "That broad has one hell of a body."

Frank scowls. "Stick to the point, Sy."

"What's the big deal, Frank?" A flush creeps up Sy's neck, and Frank wonders again at the source of Sy's long-standing antagonism. *Would he be this insubordinate with any captain, or just with a black captain? Or is it just with me?* Sy says, "You want the straight dope, quick and dirty? Nobody saw or heard anything besides that fight before dinner." He snaps his notebook shut and stares at Frank.

"You know I want more detail than that."

"I just don't want to waste your time with things you don't want to hear. You ask me what you want to know, I'll tell you." He continues to stare at Frank.

Frank refuses to rise to the bait. He patiently asks questions and ignores the surly tone of the answers. All he gets for his efforts is a longer version of the same.

Joe clears his throat. "I talked with Perry, van Pelt, Mrs. Sloan, Hummel, and Priscilla Roth. Hummel said he thought Brady had left the ballroom while the tables were being cleared but was back for dessert. He said he didn't know how long that might have been—not long—maybe Brady'd just gone to the gents. Other than that, I didn't get anything really on point. Everybody gave basically the same account of the argument before dinner. Mrs. Sloan kept saying, 'The College is not responsible for this dreadful accident. We have no liability here.' Mrs. Roth is really pissed that her husband was flirting with Nora Perry, and didn't seem to be paying attention to much of anything else. Professors Perry and van Pelt were clear and to the point—they'd be good witnesses except they didn't see anything!"

When Joe and Sy leave, Frank sits at his desk a long time. His thinking about the case comes down to one question: Who was the intended victim? Everything depends on that.

More thinking isn't going to answer the question, but he lingers. Should he go home or to Nora's? *No, that isn't the question. I should go home. But, God, I dread walking in that door. Claire's sadness fills the whole damn place. And the little ones make me feel so helpless! But Mama's handling everything just fine. She keeps saying she's got to get back to Philadelphia, but dynamite wouldn't get her out of here until I have good childcare lined up. If I go to Nora's, I can put my feet up and unwind. She's a good listener and a wise counselor. Mama would give me hell sure as anything. She never could see Nora's good qualities, has always thought that 'that Perry woman' will bring me to grief.* Frank sighs, remembering his history with Nora.

He was a junior psychology major at West when Nora came for her campus interview. He was impressed. The following fall, he lobbied to be her undergraduate teaching assistant. Having topped his social psych research methods course, he got the job. She agreed to direct his honor's thesis.

Spring semester, having finished his thesis, Frank invited Nora to a play on campus, pointing out that he was no longer her student and, as a graduating senior, never would be again. Nora said, "As long as you are a student at West, it would feel unethical to see you socially. It's a small department and a small school. It would not be good for either of us."

At the conclusion of Commencement exercises, Frank introduced Nora to his parents and handed her a folded sheet of paper on which he had written:

You've had excuses by the score
But I'm a student here no more.
We'll dine in Philly
And maybe get silly.
Shall I pick you up at four?

Nora laughed and accepted. They had several dates over the next couple of months, in spite of his parents' objections to interracial dating. It was something of a scandal in Centreville. About the time Frank realized he was well and truly in love, Nora said that continuing to date him would be unfair because she felt like she was dating her kid brother.

Hell, I'm only three years younger than Nora. Now she's been seeing van Pelt and he's nine years younger! The thought tastes bitter.

When he returned to Centreville ten years later, neither of them ever having married, Frank renewed his suit. They enjoyed a lot of good times, a mutually satisfying sex life, and a close friendship. But when Frank pushed for marriage, Nora said, "I've seen too many women turn into wives. If marriage is what you want, you'd best look elsewhere. I don't expect ever to marry." And she hadn't. Five years later, Frank married Claire Weston, a black woman from a wealthy suburb of Philadelphia. His family was pleased, her family less so. He and Claire had a good marriage.

Frank seldom saw Nora. He didn't move in academic circles. Then the murder of a West College faculty member last year brought her back into his life. The bonds of their friendship held firm, though sometimes strained by her stubborn interference in his case.

Nora was the first person I turned to for advice about Claire. Frank shakes his head and sighs. *Maybe I should feel guilty, turning to Nora. But why? I'd never be unfaithful to Claire.* Frank taps his yellow pad with the eraser end of a pencil. *Bill Baxter has taken Nora out. Nate Roth is hitting on her. If anyone is right for Nora, it's van Pelt. Why don't the two of them see it?* He pushes back from his desk and gathers his things. *Frank, old man, you're lucky you aren't walking down that road again.*

He heads for home, thoughts swirling from Pete Fitzroy to Buck Brady to Richard Emory. From Carol Emory to Allie Brady to Pris Roth. Who was angry enough and vengeful enough to commit murder?

Chapter Sixteen

NORA'S COAT SWIRLS IN THE February wind as she pushes through the revolving door and enters the lobby. She searches the directory for The Roth Foundation, and strides down the polished terrazzo hall toward Suite 111. The calmness and confidence she felt on the drive to Baltimore drain away as she approaches the mahogany door. She takes a few deep breaths, braces herself to make the best possible presentation of her grant proposal, and turns the knurled brass doorknob.

Her eyes sweep the reception area. *Quietly elegant but not opulent. And definitely cold.* An attractive middle aged woman looks up from her tidy desk. "Hello. You must be Professor Perry."

"Yes."

"I'm Mrs. Middendorf. Let me take your coat."

While the receptionist hangs Nora's coat in the closet, Nora examines the room more closely. She is especially impressed by the inset mahogany panels on the walls and the carved dentalium design beneath the cornice. *Van would love it.* Thinking of Van nudges her bruised feelings. This Christmas he left *The Mariner's*

Book of Days on her front stoop. When she called to say thank-you and invite him to dinner, she learned that Melissa Nelson was spending the holiday in Centreville. *He hadn't even told me.* Coming from someone she considers a dear friend, that omission is painful. She wonders whether Lissa is driving a wedge between them on purpose or whether it's just a byproduct of their intense involvement.

The secretary in the far corner says, "Would you like coffee, Professor?" She smiles.

"No, thank you." Her stomach is tight as a knot. She tries to talk herself down. *So what if you've here to ask the Roth Foundation for research money? The worst Nate can say is no. Small children would not die. It wouldn't be the end of the world.*

The receptionist tap-taps from the closet to her desk, her passage across the waxed parquet floor echoing off the bare mahogany walls. The only adornment hangs on the front wall near the entrance: a bronze plaque revealing the establishment of The Roth Foundation with monies from The Roth Furniture Manufacturing Company of Baltimore. The last line reads, "for the Betterment of Mankind."

Mrs. Middledorf hangs up the phone and says, "Mr. Roth will be with you in a moment."

As she speaks, the inner door opens and Simon Hummel strides into the reception area. He says, "Professor Perry, good to see you. You seem to be weathering the winter well."

"So do you."

As they shake hands, the door swings wide and Nate steps into the reception area. "Great to see you, Nora."

Simon nods to Nate, says, "I'll be in touch." To Nora he says, "I'll see you at the next Board meeting, if I don't have the pleasure sooner." He heads for the door.

"You're looking as lovely as ever." Nate embraces her in that warm but perfunctory way that accompanies a kiss on the cheek, and steps back smiling.

"Thank you." Nora scans his tall, slim frame, his finely chiseled features, his elegant navy blazer. *I bet those gold buttons are really gold.* "You must be having a West College day."

Nate's eyebrows shoot toward his hairline. "Oh. You mean Simon." He takes her arm and guides her into his office. "He wasn't here about West. He manages most of the Foundation's investments." Nora turns toward a straight backed chair but Nate says, "Here. This one is more comfortable," gesturing with a long, manicured hand. "Actually, that's how he came to manage funds for the college—by doing such a good job for the Roth Foundation."

Nora settles into a soft leather chair of the kind one might find in the library of an exclusive men's club. Nate's office is beautiful, elegant, and warm: impressionist paintings—mostly Renoir—leather-bound books on the sideboard, two Egyptian vases, a large Persian rug covering most of the floor. The contrast between this and the reception area is stunning. Nate reaches into the drawer of a table centered in the room and the beginning strains of Mendelssohn's Scottish Symphony fill the room, soft and soothing.

Nate smiles and takes the chair opposite Nora's. "So, what do you think of my digs?"

Nora moves her briefcase from her lap to the floor. "Your office is beautiful. I love the woodworking in both spaces, but I must say, the contrast between reception and this is extraordinary." Her gesture includes the entire office.

"I'm glad you like it. I favor contrast and surprise—in almost everything."

Nora expects something more by way of explanation, but when

he says nothing else, she doesn't ask. They chat for a few minutes about the Baltimore Symphony, city traffic, parking, and the winter weather. Nora feels drawn to Nate, and wonders fleetingly about living with such a man—sophisticated and witty. Her fantasy halts before it really begins when Nate says, "Pris and the twins are off skiing in Colorado. I'm looking forward to joining them this weekend." Nora shakes her head and smiles at her own musings.

"What's funny?" Nate pulls the sleeve of his blazer over the monogram on his shirt cuff.

"Just an aberrant thought that I found amusing."

Nate leans forward, elbows on knees, hands clasped loosely. "Before we get down to foundation business, I want to tell you how much I admire all you do for West College. Serving with you on the Finance Committee has been very revealing." Nora covers her surprise and says nothing, wondering where this is going. "First, I think you did an excellent job in persuading the Committee to recommend a significant bump in the pool for faculty salaries. I just regret that the Board took President Sloan's recommendation instead of the one you and I favored."

Nora tries not to show her anger about the final decision. *Why would a new president who came up through the faculty ranks himself recommend a smaller pay raise for faculty than the Finance Committee thought feasible—and desirable?* Finally, she says, "Regardless of the outcome, I appreciate your support—as would all of the faculty, if they were privy to these things."

Nate nods. "And *I* appreciate the good opinion of someone as astute and well-respected as you. No wonder your faculty colleagues elected you their chair. No wonder your students voted you outstanding teacher of the year again." He smiles and sits back in his chair. "As a trustee of West, I especially like that your preliminary proposal specifies working with an interdisciplinary group of faculty to improve the learning environment for students."

Nora tries not to let Nate's compliments raise false hopes that the Foundation will fund her grant proposal. "Thank you. You do a lot of good work through the foundation, too."

"Indeed. We support a lot of higher education projects, but also art and music and other cultural activities. We try to remain open to good ideas from any quarter. As a psychologist and a sailor, you might be especially interested in two of our more unusual programs. First, we support a half-way house for the rehabilitation of ex-convicts. And, second, we fund a facility on the waterfront to support merchant seamen whose ships dock in Baltimore."

"That's even broader than I thought." Nora again feels Nate's magnetism. His philanthropy is wonderful. She smiles, feeling more relaxed than earlier. "Tell me about the waterfront facility." Nate looks pleased at her interest. "Why did you fund such a thing?"

"To benefit mankind—in this case, in the form of merchant seamen. A clean bed. Laundry. Hot meals. And access to the internet for messages home. The Association of Maritime Unions gives us high marks, so the big investment's worth it." Nate's smile looks satisfied.

"I'm sure." The mention of investments reminds Nora of Simon Hummel and college business. "This has nothing to do with the Foundation's good works, but have you received the revised budget projections for West College?"

"No. But our chairman was pretty adamant that what Stan gave us at the last Board meeting was—insufficient. The revisions should be along soon."

Bill has said nothing critical of Stan to her, but from Nate's guarded tone, Nora infers that Stan Gosser's performance is an issue with at least some trustees. *So, I'm not the only one who thinks the new business VP is an incompetent ass!* She keeps her face blandly pleasant but internally she seethes, remembering her most recent encounter with Stan. When she'd asked him for some simple comparisons between the Psychology Department budget and the budgets of other departments, he'd acted as though she wouldn't understand them if she had them. When pushed, he finally said he couldn't produce them. *With luck, he'll be gone before he can do too much damage.* She says only, "I hope so. The department chairs have had some problems with their departmental budget reports. Current projections would be very helpful." Nate stands. *Good grief! Is he ending the meeting? What about my proposal?*

As if hearing her thoughts, Nate says, "I assume you brought your proposal."

Nora nods and hands him three copies. He glances at the cover sheet as she closes her briefcase. "This looks complete. If I have any questions, I'll call."

His abruptness is startling. Nora expected to discuss the proposal in detail. She stands and extends her hand. "Thank you for your time. I look forward to hearing from you."

Nate holds her hand a little longer than necessary, looking into her eyes. "You are a very attractive woman. I'm surprised you never married."

Nora snatches her hand away and glances aside, her body tense. *That's none of your business* comes immediately to mind, but prudence rules the minute. She forces a chuckle. "Why should I marry? How many really happy marriages do you know? Besides, I like my independence."

A frown pinches Nate's brow. "I believe I made you uncomfortable. My sincere apologies." He opens the door for her and Nora walks into the reception area, her face flaming. Nate says, "I'll notify you as soon as the Foundation Review Board makes its recommendation. That may take a month or more. But I'll be in touch."

*   *   *

Six weeks later, Nora parks near The Rusty Scupper. She is in Baltimore for a lunch meeting with Nate. When his secretary called to make the appointment, she said, "Mr. Roth would like to meet with you personally to discuss the Foundation Review Board's recommendation for your proposal." She gave nothing away.

Nora has waffled between opposite interpretations of the lunch invitation: either the recommendation is positive and Nate wants to share the good news personally, or the recommendation is negative and he wants to let her down gently. Somewhere in the middle is the possibility that they want her to rewrite and resubmit. *Well, I'll know soon enough.* As she walks toward the restaurant, she thinks about her previous meeting with Nate. *Everything was great until that one awkward moment at the end. Whatever possessed him? Maybe I was giving off subtle cues or something—somehow telegraphing my attraction to him.* These are not new thoughts. She puts them aside and hurries toward the stairs.

She enters a little before noon, ahead of the lunch crowd. The maitre d' shows her to a table with sweeping views of the harbor. He whisks away a discrete white tented placard with "Reserved for Mr. Roth" written in flowing black script.

Today Nora has traded her usual tweeds for what she privately labels her banker look: two-inch black heels, a sage-green wool gabardine suit, a cream silk blouse, and pearls. A black attaché case has replaced her shoulder-bag briefcase. Of her usual campus look, only the figure-eight twist of rich copper tresses remains.

Nora glances around at the other diners and is glad she made the effort.

While she waits, she thinks about her proposal. *I shouldn't have asked for so much money. What if they thought the budget was padded? It isn't! But West College isn't exactly the big time.* She stares out the window at the Inner Harbor, feeling as anxious as the restless water.

A waiter arrives with an ice bucket and a bottle of French chardonnay. He presents the bottle to Nora. "This is the wine Mr. Roth suggested, but if you would prefer another, I'd be happy to show you the wine list." His voice is thick and rich as velvet, his enunciation careful.

Nora looks at the tall, rugged waiter as he proffers the wine bottle. The hand holding the bottle is missing two fingers. She catches her breath and looks away from the scarred stubs. She glances up and the waiter smiles broadly. *He seems completely unselfconscious about his missing fingers. I admire that.* She barely glances at the label. "That will be fine, I'm sure."

As he pours, he says, "My name is Sam. I will be serving you today. Would you like an appetizer with your wine?"

"No, thank you. I'll wait for Mr. Roth." Nora sips the crisp wine with a hint of oak and gazes over Baltimore harbor. She never tires of watching water.

"I hope Sam has been taking good care of you." Nora starts. Nate is at her elbow, handsome and dapper. He takes the chair to her left, smiling. "I thought I would be here first."

Nora smiles. "I haven't been here long. I try to allow for contingencies."

Sam reappears, pours a glass of wine for Nate, and glides away. "Yes. That is one of the things Bill admires about you."

Nora shifts in her seat. *What does he know—or think he*

knows— about Bill and me? "You certainly get the royal treatment around here."

Nate laughs. "I come here often. Besides, Sam likes to show his appreciation." Nora looks at Nate questioningly. "You may remember that The Roth Foundation funds a halfway house for ex-convicts. Sam is our 'poster child'—a great example of what rehabilitation and a helping hand will do. I got him the job here. His street name was Three-finger Sam—for obvious reasons—but here he would be better known as Suave Sam. He's been an exemplary employee for over a year."

"Do you know what happened to his fingers?"

Nate shakes his head. "Not exactly. Only that he lost them years ago, while he was in juvenile detention."

"And now you're giving him a second chance. The Roth Foundation is living up to its mission."

"We try. Which is why you and I are having this celebratory lunch today." Nora's heartbeat spikes. Nate pulls an envelope from the inside pocket of his suit. "Congratulations. The Board voted to award you the grant. A hundred thousand a year for four years."

Nora gasps. "I can't believe you funded the whole amount!" Nora skims the letter. "Even the money for summer stipends so faculty can be trained. Thank you!"

Nate smiles. "Your eyes spark fire when you are excited."

Lunch passes pleasantly—good food, good service, good humor. Over coffee, Nate touches her hand in a way that might be accidental. As they part, he says, "And when can I see you again?"

Nora laughs, high on chardonnay and success. "There's always the May Board meeting. I look forward to telling you about my progress organizing the grant project."

Nate inhales deeply. "Do I have to become Chairman of the Board before you will see me socially?"

Nora looks at him levelly. "It isn't that Bill is chairman. It's that he's single."

*   *   *

Driving over the Bay Bridge doesn't hold its usual magnetism for Nora. Her thoughts roil. She's half flattered, half offended by Nate's behavior. He flirted outrageously with Allie Brady at the January Board meeting. Nora doubts any serious affection on his part—for Allie or for herself. He's magnetic and charming. Under other circumstances, perhaps. But she's been there and done that and married men are definitely off limits.

She has seen Bill several times now. He's better company than she would have expected before their time together on *Endeavor*. He talks about his brewery only when asked, he's smart, and he has a sharp sense of humor. Not to mention a great body. They move together exceptionally well on the dance floor—the best partner she's had, barring Van. She savors the developing relationship.

Approaching home she thinks, *I got the grant. Dinner and a concert with Bill this evening. I'm queen of the mountain!* She bites her lip and tightens her grip on the steering wheel as she swings onto Route 213 toward Centreville. *Maybe I'll have time to give Van a call when I get home, share the good news.*

Chapter Seventeen

"Thank God it is Friday," Van mutters and locks his office door. He trudges toward the bookstore, briefcase swinging, half-knowing that he won't start grading the contents till Monday. He recalls a favorite graduate professor at Princeton saying, "Always carry a book, Mr. van Pelt, always a book. That's what I do. Of course, it's just for show." Van smiles. He always takes his briefcase home. But the mild spring weather is as inviting as a maiden's kiss. He knows he'll be out in it.

The doors of the bookstore stand open to warm April air. Paying for his copy of the *Kent County News*, Van thinks *What a great day to be on the water. I wonder whether Nora will take* Duet *out this weekend.* As if conjured by his thought, he sees her standing in the doorway, talking with Clyde Barnes. *Maybe she has time for a cup of coffee. We have hardly talked since the January Board meeting. But probably Old Motor Mouth would invite himself along. What sort of conversation could we have with the biggest gossip on campus at our elbows?* Everything about Clyde grates on Van's sensibilities: his bushy mustache needs trimming, the plaid necktie hanging over his corpulent belly is too loud, and the tweed cape folded off one shoulder is pure affectation.

Van is still waffling when Clyde sees him and half bows, both hands on his brass-capped walking stick. "As I live and breathe, the good Dr. van Pelt. I was just about to ask after you." Behind Clyde's back, Nora rolls her eyes and shrugs.

Van tamps down his irritation and keeps his voice neutral. "Good afternoon, Clyde. Nora."

Clyde peers over his half-glasses from one to the other. "So, what do you two have going on this weekend?"

Nora looks annoyed but speaks civilly. "Sunday's up for grabs, but I expect to spend tomorrow getting *Duet* ready to launch."

Clyde chuckles and turns to Van. "I guess you've got your Saturday mapped out for you. I, for one, eschew manual labor. I'm taking my better half to Longwood Gardens. The spring bulbs should be at their peak. See you around." He waves and walks away.

Van watches his retreat, acutely aware that Clyde is seldom behind the curve on campus gossip. *No doubt he knows that Nora is dating Bill Baxter and that I am spending most weekends with Lissa.* He suspects that Clyde feigned ignorance of the situation just to stir the pot. "As usual, Clyde is minding everybody's business but his own."

Nora shrugs one shoulder. "Leave it to Clyde. He's nothing if not consistent."

Between teaching, research, and time with Lissa, Van's seldom thought about the changes in his relationship with Nora, but now he feels the distance keenly. He says, "Prepping *Duet* sounds like a great way to spend a Saturday. Would you like a hand tomorrow?"

When Nora says, "Sure—if you're free. That would be great," Van's good mood kicks up another notch.

*   *   *

Nora drives them from Centreville to Kent Narrows. Van feels awkward at first, trying to bridge the months of non-communication, but by the time they pull into Mears Point Marina, their old camaraderie has returned. *Duet*, hauled for the winter, looks bereft. Her bare mast pierces the air between two tarps draped like pup tents over the fore and aft decks. A dozen lines, once taut but now loose from months of wind and weather, run under the hull and hold the tarps in place. Nora starts at the bow, Van at the stern, each wielding a reefing knife to cut the weathered lines and recalcitrant knots.

Winter grime has grayed the white decks. Nora tunes a portable radio to WBJC and strains of Beethoven's Fifth Symphony float on the soft air. They wash *Duet's* topside with boat soap and brushes. Water from the hose chills Van's fingers, though laboring in the sun warms the rest of him. He hums along with the music. They work mostly in silence, broken by the occasional request to pass the soap, a crevice brush, or the hose. Seeing the clean boat emerge from the grime is gratifying. *A year ago, when I helped Nora prepare Duet for launch, I knew I would be sailing with her. Maybe she will be sailing with Bill this year. And Melissa ... Can I hope to sail with Nora this summer?*

When they break for lunch, Nora says, "Hey. You've got soap on your face." The touch of her icy finger on his warm cheek burns like a brand.

They sit on stools at The Red Eye Bar eating burgers washed down by draft beers, talking about classes. The rolled-up isinglass curtains let in balmy air. Nora talks about progress with her research grant, and asks Van whether he would like to be on one of the interdisciplinary teams. Van agrees, and talks about his latest woodworking project, a musical jewelry box he's making for his daughter's birthday.

Van filches a French fry from Nora's plate and eludes her playful slap. "Have you heard anything more about Richard Emory?"

"Not a blessed thing! I asked Frank the other day. We were at the grocery store and he had the twins *and* baby Jessica with him, so he wasn't inclined to chat. He said Claire was under the weather. We know what that means. I do hope her depression lifts soon. Anyway, basically, he said that with no evidence to the contrary, Richard's death is presumed to have been an accident and anyone who might investigate a murder is busy doing so elsewhere!"

"Ummm. I suppose a case must go cold at some point."

"And still no progress on Pete Fitzroy's death, either. They know that wasn't an accident, but there are no leads to the perpetrator. Even the question of whether the intended victim was Fitzroy or Buck is still open. But I have this gut feeling that those two deaths are linked."

"Not in any obvious way."

"No. But it's been bugging the hell out of me." Nora finishes her fries. "Somehow the unnatural deaths of two people I know—it just feels as though they're linked. But I can't see how, other than that they both were trustees." She drains her draft. "You know, there's a lot more to beer than I ever knew before I started dating Bill." She blots her lips with the napkin. "But back to Richard. I'm not buying accident. I mean, there was just so much high emotion on that sail. Maybe suicide or maybe murder, but Marcy was too careful for someone to go overboard accidentally."

"Ummm. But I gather there is no way to determine that."

"Maybe. But proved in a court of law or not, I need to know."

Walking back to *Duet*, Van's step is light. He cocks one eyebrow.

"To speculate wildly: suppose Richard Emory was pushed and Buck was the intended victim both times, the other two just incidental damage. Or perhaps Buck knows something about Richard's death and was the intended victim when Fitzroy was killed.'

Nora laughs. "I love the way you think!"

While Van's hands guide the electric polisher back and forth along the hull to finish off the waxing, his thoughts swing between Nora and Lissa. *I could watch Nora's sure, capable hands all day.* He looks at her, carefully applying metal polish to the stanchions, affection welling up unbidden. A wisp of her hair floats on the light breeze. He remembers seeing her laughing in the passenger seat of Bill's Mercedes convertible, her hair swept up in a cluster of loose curls that caught the wind. *How would I measure up against Bill—against all the men in her past?* Chagrined at the self-doubt the thought reveals, he applies himself to the electric polisher with renewed vigor. Somehow, with Lissa, sex doesn't feel like a life-long commitment. Sometimes he feels a touch of shame, acting against his stated values. *But her reckless, anything goes attitude makes me feel free to explore. And I do not care if she realizes how much she's teaching me.*

Lugging the polisher to the other side of the hull, he thinks *Some of the happiest times of my life have been on this boat. I feel a oneness with Nora I've never felt with anyone else. But Lissa holds The Big Apple in the palm of her hand. It is a world I would never have known on my own.* Van recalls when Lissa met his children last Christmas, everyone seeming determined to make the visit a success. *I cannot delude myself that it was love at first sight. But they got along all right. And they will like her more when they know her better. Familiarity breeds comfort.* Van coils the cord of the electric polisher and lays it aside. *During the two summers I sailed with Nora and the academic year between—when she was the totality of my social* life—the children accepted her easily. *On balance, I am happy to be here today and not in New York.* Van climbs the ladder to the foredeck where Nora is preparing to work on the teak. *Okay, van Pelt, it is time to get your head around the task at hand.*

Van whistles *Oh, What a Beautiful Morning* as he brushes a coat of Semco preservative onto *Duet's* port-side teak. Nora works the starboard side, her rich alto providing the lyrics. The music feels companionable. The April sunshine kisses Van's cheeks while soft breezes eddy around the boat, high and dry on her stands. They spend nearly two hours cleaning the topside teak, the last task of the day.

Van loathes for the day to end. As they stow the gear, Nora says, "You've earned yourself a dinner." He feels reprieved. She continues, somewhat tentatively, he thinks: "I have plans for tonight. But how about one night next week? Would that work for you?"

Van stifles his disappointment and grins. "Sounds like a plan to me."

When Nora drops him back at his house, they part with a hug and cheek kisses and vague plans for dinner sometime next week.

Chapter Eighteen

The Philadelphia Orchestra is performing *Appalachian Spring*. Bill has a reservation at Bookbinders. Preparing for her date, Nora thinks she ought to feel more enthusiastic. Perhaps the efforts of the day have sapped her energy.

* * *

Back at her house after the concert, ensconced side by side in Adirondack chairs on the patio, Nora and Bill sip brandy and enjoy a soft breeze off the river. Over dinner they'd talked of the upcoming Board meeting—everything from college finances to Richard Emory's death. Nora admires Bill's discretion. He said nothing to discredit the new VP for Business, so she said nothing of Nate's comments. Only once did he skirt the edge of disclosure, saying, "I just hope Buck Brady isn't at the center of anything more."

But now they talk of the soft spring night. Bill says, "I feel like I could touch the stars."

"Ummm. That's how I feel on *Duet*."

Bill traces the curve of her jaw with the back of one finger. "I'd like to sail with you sometime."

Nora's breath catches. "Well, then, we'll see what we can do."

Bill's right hand massages the nape of her neck. Warmth suffuses her body. Bill leans in. When his lips settle softly on hers, something in Nora's belly does a little flip. It's been a long time.

*   *   *

Nora is making breakfast when she hears the knocker. Van is the only person she knows who uses the knocker rather than the doorbell. She cinches her robe tighter and opens the door, smiling broadly. "Van. Good morning."

Van smiles in return. "I apologize for coming by so early, but I wanted to catch you before heading out today."

"Come in." Nora swings open the door.

Van steps into the foyer and stops. Nora follows his gaze to where Bill is sitting at the oak table by the patio doors. Her spare white terry robe gapes, exposing several inches of bare chest and a flash of thigh.

Van stiffens. "I did not know you had a guest. I apologize for the intrusion."

As he turns toward the door Nora says, "Not a problem. Join us for a cup of coffee."

"Another time, perhaps." His face is shuttered, his voice low and level. Only the pale pink blooming on his cheeks and the pulse throbbing at the base of his neck betray emotion.

Nora puts her hand on his arm. "Van, join us. It's okay."

"No, thankyou. I should have called first." He turns on his heel and walks quickly to his car.

She bangs the door shut and drops into the chair across from Bill. "He is such a stick sometimes!"

"I'm sorry. I didn't mean to embarrass you."

Nora's scowl slides into a look of affection. She shrugs. "It was just a little awkward. Don't give it another thought."

Bill picks up her hand. "No problem. My thoughts can easily go elsewhere."

The look in his eyes holds the promise of a very enjoyable morning.

Chapter Nineteen

Nora stands and arches her back, grateful that the weeding is done. She wipes sweat from her brow and glances toward the Corsica. The water is as gray as the sky. The air is heavy, the temperature already ninety in the shade. She walks through the patio doors, pulling off her straw hat and gardening gloves, lifting the wet curls pasted to her forehead. Even with the air conditioner set at seventy-seven, the first wave of inside air feels icy on the damp shirt clinging to her back. The soggy waistband of her pants chaffs tender skin. She pours a tall glass of iced tea, feeling righteous for having weeded the long flower bed between the brick patio and the river. According to the early morning forecast, the weather should improve by mid-day. With luck, the Fourth of July will remain glorious. And the next several days are supposed to be terrific. *Rebecca and I should have a great sail.* She heads for the shower.

In anticipation of the cookout, Nora skips lunch and tries to ignore her rumbling stomach. *What kind of a shindig is this anyway? One thing's for certain: it will be different from any party the Howards ever threw.* The Sloans' predecessors were gracious but formal. By contrast, as far as Nora knows, anyone is welcome to attend Jim and Rebecca's party—as long as the guest dresses in red, white and/or blue and brings something for the potluck. Beer and wine, hamburgers and hotdogs will be provided. Nora pulls on white clam-digger pants and, in deference to her vulnerability to sun poisoning, a long-sleeved blue shirt. She slips into white sandals and ties a red, white and blue silk scarf around her waist like a pirate's sash. She fastens her unruly curls into a high ponytail and grabs an oversized white visor. On her way out the door, she retrieves an enormous bowl of Tuscan white bean and tuna salad from the fridge.

* * *

When Nora rounds the corner of Ozmon House, Rebecca says, "Hi, there. Welcome to the Red, White and Blue party."

Nora waves the bowl of salad. "I've been looking forward to it. You certainly lucked out on the weather."

"I almost always do! Though I have to admit, I was a little worried last night in spite of the forecast. You know what they say about weathermen: they were invented to make economists look good."

Nora grins and gazes across the sloping lawn. "Your lily beds look absolutely gorgeous. How many varieties do you have?"

"I don't know. At least a dozen. I guess my predecessor gardened quite a bit, but the grounds crew takes care of all that now. Frankly, I don't have much interest in gardens."

"Oh. Well. They're beautiful anyway. I suppose you're aware that Bill Baxter set up an endowment to establish and maintain these gardens? He has a special interest in the physical plant." Rebecca says nothing, but her long, hard look brings a pink tinge to Nora's cheeks. *Is she wondering how close Bill and I are?*

As if on cue, Bill steps off the deck with a handful of small

U.S. flags. He smiles warmly. "Hello, Nora." He kisses her cheek. "Great day, isn't it?"

"Couldn't be better."

He half turns toward Rebecca. "I'm not much of a cook, but I trust the beer covers my obligation. Also, I took the liberty of bringing a non-food contribution to the festivities. I thought I'd plant some flags in the gardens—if you don't mind."

"Knock yourself out." Rebecca cocks her head to one side, looking from Nora to Bill and back again. Nora feels another wave of warmth wash over her face. "Help yourself to something to drink, Nora. Soft drinks, iced tea, beer—courtesy of Bill—and wine are in the ice tubs." Rebecca turns to greet the next arrivals. "Well, look who finally dragged in. You're late, Mr. Roth."

Nate looks both patriotic and nautical in white ducks and a navy and white striped polo shirt. A red bandanna is knotted around his neck. Nora's struck again by how handsome he is—and how mismatched he seems with Pris. She, too, wears white pants. They are not flattering to her thick waist and wide hips. Her orange hair clashes with her red T-shirt.

Nate laughs. "I'm always late, Rebecca, and this auburn-haired beauty will testify to it, won't you Nora?" Nate hugs Nora and kisses her cheek.

Priscilla, Bill, and Rebecca look at her. She laughs and shrugs his arm away. "My, how you do exaggerate. If you all will excuse me, I can hear an iced tea calling my name."

Nora walks to the far side of the lawn, imagining four pairs of eyes boring into her back, and nearly bumps into Frank. He smiles warmly. "Hi. An interesting gathering, wouldn't you say?"

"You can say that again. There must be a hundred people here." They look over the crowd—a mixture of faculty members, trustees, administrators, and townspeople. Off to one side, a dozen people play volleyball, Van and Lissa among them. When she flubs a return, Lissa laughs and Van punches her playfully. *At least she isn't athletic, too.* No one could help admiring Lissa's body—trim and youthful. Feeling decrepit, Nora turns her back to the game and smiles at Frank. "How are your children? Is Mrs. Brown working out well?"

"The kids are great and Mrs. Brown's a godsend." The volleyball players yell and cheer. He looks in their direction and shakes his head. "My God, it must be ninety-five degrees out here." He shakes his head again. "I'm going in search of a cold drink. Bring you something?"

Nora says, "An iced tea would be great." Frank walks toward the nearest ice tub. Her glance falls on Rebecca. What must life be like as the president's wife? Separated from the larger Centreville community but with unwelcome demands to join community volunteer groups, college duties intruding on her law practice. *She must long for the company of another professional woman. Getting better acquainted will be good.*

*   *   *

Long picnic tables and benches are scattered under the trees. Nora carries her plate to an empty one under a big oak near the water. She's scarcely taken a bite when Frank and Bill join her, one on each side. The Sloans and the Roths follow, Nate sitting across from Nora. Lissa says, "Here's a shady spot," and heads for Nora's table, Van in tow. Simon Hummel takes the last seat, next to Nate.

Van catches her eye. "Nora, the peer tutoring and facilitation classes are going well. How is the rest of your grant coming along?"

"Great. Just—great."

Simon laughs, a bit raucous. "What would you expect her to say when the head of the Roth Foundation is within earshot?"

Nate scowls. "Simon!"

"Just kidding. Nora knows that, don't you, Nora?" He laughs again, the others join in, a scene avoided.

Nora wonders how much Simon has had to drink. She turns to Rebecca and says brightly, "We're still on for Wednesday's sail, right?" Rebecca nods, her mouth full. "If we leave early we can make it to Queenstown in time for lunch and be back at the mooring basin just before dinner. Is that okay with you? *The Dink*—my dinghy—is being painted, but I've asked Paul Zimmerman to take us out to *Duet* in the college skiff. We're set for 8:00. I'll get everything ready the night before."

Rebecca grins. "I'm looking forward to it."

Nate says, "If the forecast holds, you'll have good sailing." The table talk meanders from the weather forecast to the admissions picture, from gardening to the Orioles, and Nora sinks thankfully into the background. Simon glares, says little, and drinks steadily.

* * *

Flares bloom over the Corsica like allium—lighting the night sky, reflected in the rippling water. The last fireworks boom echoes off the river at quarter before ten.

The picnickers linger on the riverbank. Nora picks up her salad bowl. Bill says, "Shall I come by later?"

She smiles. "I'd like that."

As she rounds the hemlock by the corner of the house, someone grabs her from behind, knocking her salad bowl to the ground. A hand clamps across her mouth. For an instant she is too startled to struggle, but keenly aware of hard muscles and the strong smell of alcohol.

"Shhhhh. Quiet." His whisper stirs the hair by Nora's ear. He loosens his hold and Nora spins around.

"Simon!" is all she manages before his kiss silences her. She pushes him away and scrubs her wrist across her lips. "What do you think you're doing?"

Simon chuckles. "Surely you don't have to ask." He tries to kiss her again.

"Stop it!"

His lips cover hers again and Nora pushes him so hard he hits the corner of the house. He grabs for her but she steps away.

"Simon Hummel, cut it out!" she hisses. He takes hold of her upper arms. "Don't touch me!" She tries to twist away.

His face is in shadow. He speaks quietly, his voice tight. "You're willing to put out for everyone from the Chairman of the Board to the local constable. No one would fault me for expecting the same."

He's drunk as any three men ought to be. "Who I see is none of your damned business! And if you so much as lay a finger on me again, I'll have you up on assault charges. Don't think I won't!" He loosens his hold and Nora steps back a pace, her heart pounding.

Simon leans into the corner of the house and Nora wonders whether he is too drunk to stand unsupported. "Not a good idea. Think of the talk. Besides, I thought you wanted me, the way you were flirting."

"I have no idea what you're talking about."

"Why don't we agree that we've had a mutual misunderstanding and let it go at that?" His words slur around the edges.

Nora hesitates, squints, tries to see his face. Finally she says, "Fine."

"Great. We'll let bygones be bygones." He turns toward the back garden, his step unsteady.

Nora's breath comes painfully. She looks around but sees no

one. *I did nothing to encourage him. I'm sure of it.* But her hands shake as she picks up her bowl.

Driving home, she reviews her previous encounters with Simon, thinking about anything she said or did that could have made him think she would welcome such advances. *There was nothing—nothing at all.* But given their roles at West and the necessity of working with him on the Finance Committee, she decides it is best to just let it go. *If he wants to save face by claiming a mutual misunderstanding, fine. As long as it doesn't happen again. It isn't as if he's the only person whose personality changes under the influence of alcohol.*

By the time Bill arrives, Nora has put it aside. She has decided not to mention the encounter. Bill would want to fire Simon's firm, or at least Simon, and there is no denying that the part of the portfolio Simon manages is doing exceptionally well.

* * *

The Wednesday morning air is heavy as Nora loads the cooler in the trunk of her car and drives to campus. The overcast sky depresses her enthusiasm for the trip to Queenstown. *So much for the good forecast. Maybe Rebecca won't show up. I half hope she doesn't.*

Paul Zimmerman, wearing a yellow oil skin, is in his little office at the dock. "Mornin', professor."

"Good morning, Paul. Looks like you're expecting rain."

"Well, now, you never know. Sometimes the weathermen get it right." He smiles, his hands cupping a struck match to light the cigarette dangling from his weathered lips. "Where's Mrs. President?"

Nora smiles at the Mrs. President—the title he uses for every first lady of West College. "I told her we'd meet her on the dock at eight o'clock."

Paul yanks up his left cuff and glances at his watch. "Guess we better start walkin'. What ya got in the buggy?"

"Only a cooler in the trunk. We're just going for the day."

As they walk out the dock, the cooler suspended between them, Nora says, "How's the summer sailing camp going?"

"Fine and dandy. The kids like the boats, but most of 'em don't know spit about sailing. After a few more weeks, they surely will."

"Maintaining the boats keeps you pretty busy."

"The boats take time. But I've got other duties, too, you know."

"Don't we all! The College is lucky to have you." Paul says nothing but he smiles broadly.

Rebecca is standing by the skiff.

"Mornin', Mrs. President."

"Good morning to you, Mr. Zimmerman. Hello, Nora."

After an exchange of comments on the doubtful weather, Paul says, "Well, are you ladies ready for a lift out to *Duet*?" He boards the skiff, cooler in hand, not waiting for their unison "Yes."

*   *   *

Nora grabs *Duet's* lifeline and hauls herself aboard, feeling more graceful and at ease than on land. Rebecca declines assistance with a stiff, "No thanks. I can do it." Nora and Paul look busily elsewhere while she makes three attempts before finally managing to get her body over the gunwale. Paul hands up the cooler, wishes them a good trip, and turns back toward the dock.

Nora hauls the cooler below. Returning topside she says, "If you go forward and drop the mooring line, I'll take us out." Rebecca hesitates and Nora adds, "Take the loop off that bow cleat and drop it by the mooring buoy."

*   *   *

Paul is about fifty yards away when an explosion splits the air and his skiff bobs violently on the churning river. He whirls to look astern over the smelly outboard. "Jesus, Mary and Joseph!" He turns the skiff and speeds back toward *Duet*. A cloud of blue smoke drifts toward him. *Duet* lists to starboard. The stench of gasoline and melted plastic burn his nostrils. The caustic air stings his lungs. He blinks rapidly to clear his tearing eyes but sees no one on board. *Duet* continues to heel. He chokes off the outboard and cups his hands around his mouth. "Professor! Mrs. President! Professor!"

"Here! Here!"

He spots Nora's head, her right arm clutching a floating cockpit cushion. He throws a life jacket toward her. "Are you okay?"

"It's just my arm. Where's Rebecca?"

With four strokes on the oars, Paul has the skiff beside Nora. "Let me help you."

Nora motions with one arm, as if trying to push the skiff away. "Help me find her. I've got to find her." She ignores the thrown life jacket and swims amid floating debris toward *Duet's* sinking bow. Another cockpit cushion, a white docking fender, a small piece of singed Dacron sail bob on the oily water.

Paul brings the skiff around the bow, where Nora holds a half-conscious Rebecca around the waist with one arm and treads water. Rebecca's head lolls back on Nora's shoulder.

Paul rigs a sling to haul them aboard. Rebecca's right arm hangs at a crazy angle and her legs bleed profusely. Nora's shirt is burned nearly off the left side of her body. She tears a remnant off to put pressure on Rebecca's wounds. "Jesus, Mary and Joseph, Professor. Look at your arm! Your face! Let me do that."

Nora glances at her left arm, raw and oozing, as if noticing it for the first time. "I can handle it. Just call 911."

Paul pulls a cell phone from the pocket of his slicker, calls 911 and the College infirmary for help at the dock. He turns the skiff toward the dock and tries the engine again. The boat jumps forward before the engine sputters twice and dies. Paul swears and takes up the oars.

* * *

Nora leans heavily against the starboard side, staring at the life jacket drifting down the river. Slowly she realizes that *Duet* is sinking. Helpless tears sting her eyes and scald the wounds on her left cheek. Searing pain in her left arm pierces her consciousness.

* * *

Frank responds to the 911 call as stretcher-bearers carry the two women into the parking lot. A small crowd from across campus have run to the landing dock, craning their necks to see what happened. He hears excited voices—that mixture of horror and curiosity typical of bystanders at disasters and crimes.

"What's happening?"

"Nora's been killed."

"No, it's Mrs. Sloan."

"It's both of them. They drowned."

Frank rushes to the stretcher, sees the rise and fall of Nora's breast. "Thank God, Noni! Are you … ? What happened?"

Nora turns dazed eyes in his direction. "My beautiful boat. I turned on the ignition and she just—exploded. My poor beautiful boat."

The paramedic says, "Step back please."

Frank struggles to breathe. His heart pounds painfully. He turns to the paramedic. "How bad is it?"

"She's got some pretty nasty burns on her left arm and hand and on the left side of her face. Lucky for her, the water was cool enough to help." He nods toward Rebecca, unconscious on the other stretcher. "She's got a broken arm, severe lacerations on her legs, and probably a concussion."

Just as the ambulance pulls away, Frank sees Van running out the dock. He looks at the mooring where *Duet* has settled on the bottom. He turns to Frank, all color drained from his face. "Nora. Is she…?"

"She's burned but she'll be all right."

"Thank God!"

"They've taken her to the hospital. Rebecca Sloan, too. Nora said the boat exploded." Frank follows the direction of Van's gaze. The only visible sign of the boat is fifteen feet of mast piercing the surface of the water at a crazy angle. "How could that happen? What would make a boat explode?"

Paul stands at Frank's elbow. He says, "*Duet* has a gasoline engine in the hold. You gotta blow the bilge to get rid of gasoline fumes before turning on the ignition or else an engine like that'll explode." As Paul talks, his voice steadies. "You could blow a hole in the hull, sink the boat. Some people've killed themselves that way."

Frank looks at Paul. "You think Nora forgot to blow the bilge?"

Van seems to jerk to attention, the movement catching Frank's eye. "Absolutely not! That may be the most common cause, but Nora is far too experienced for that sort of mistake. Blowing the bilge is a habit, like putting on your watch in the morning or combing your hair before you leave the house."

"But sometimes people forget those things." Frank holds up a hand, stopping Van's protest. "Okay, okay. Assume she blew the bilge. What else, then?"

Van's jaw has a stubborn set. "There could have been a defect in the air blower system. Nora would not start the engine unless she *thought* the bilge was blown. But if something happened to the conduit that runs from the bilge blower to the transom—if it became disconnected somehow—then she would have heard the blower and thought it was clearing the gas fumes when, in fact, it was not. When she started the engine, the fumes would ignite."

Frank scowls. "Is that a common sort of problem? This conduit coming loose?"

Van says, "Not at all." The three men stand, fists in pockets, looking out over the water to *Duet's* mast.

Frank says, "And we can't rule out a bomb."

*   *   *

Frank sits by Nora's hospital bed, her unbandaged right hand in his. Nora says her burns are mostly second degree, that she's doing well, and will be released soon. Frank says, "So tell me what happened."

Nora shakes her head. "I wish I could. I don't remember anything from the time I told Rebecca to cast off the mooring line till I was in the skiff on the way to the dock. The doctor says maybe it will come back to me. Some of it, anyway."

Frank clears his throat. "I talked to van Pelt about it."

"Van?"

"Yeah. He got down to the dock just as the ambulance pulled away. He said the most common cause of an explosion like this is not blowing the bilge."

"Van said I didn't blow the bilge?"

Frank can't tell whether she is incredulous, indignant, or insulted. "No, no. Don't get riled. He agreed with Zimmerman that that was the most common cause, but said you would never forget to do that."

"Damned straight. I *always* blow the bilge. *Duet* must have been sabotaged."

"It could have been an accident. An equipment problem."

Nora shakes her head. "No way. I'm very careful about maintenance. And in all my years of sailing, I've never had a conduit come loose. I've never even known anyone it happened to."

"Well, when you get your boat afloat again, we'll check it out. Until then, relax and try to get well." His voice turns husky. "Noni, I don't know what I'd do if anything happened to my best friend." He grips her hand.

"Oh, Frank." Nora brushes her bandaged left hand lightly along his temple. Tears well and spill down her cheeks.

*   *   *

The thought of Nora injured makes Van's throat tight. He drives to the hospital, oblivious to everything but his grip on the steering wheel. His heart pounds and he wills his thoughts away from the cause. He arrives before she's been assigned a room. He picks up a vase of yellow roses at the hospital gift shop and paces the waiting room until an aide tells him she's in her room.

At her door he stops. She isn't alone. How did Pierce get in?

"Nora, thank God you will be okay." He brushes her forehead with a kiss and deposits the flowers on the windowsill. He turns to Frank. "I could not get in until just now. And the nurse said I could stay only a minute. How did you manage?"

Frank grins. "The power of a badge."

Van gazes at Nora's battered face. "How are you feeling?"

"Like I've been chewed up and spit out." Her smile looks forced.

A motherly-looking nurse bustles in. "You all need to leave now. We need to tend to our patient." She's smiling but firm.

"But I just got here!"

"I'm sorry, but we need to do procedures. If you were family, that would be a different matter. But as it is, you can come back tomorrow, after she's had some fluids and some rest."

Frank releases Nora's hand and rises.

Van says, "Do not worry. We will find out what happened."

"Thank you both for coming. It means a lot." As they turn to leave, she adds, "Will one of you call Bill? You can tell him what happened, maybe dampen some of the gossipy exaggeration."

Chapter Twenty

Nora lies in the hospital bed, fighting back tears. Her left arm and the left side of her face throb and burn. Pain radiates to her neck and shoulder. She declines medications that deaden the mind as well as the pain, and tries desperately to remember.

When her nurse comes in, Nora asks for a mirror. The nurse says, "Your burns don't look too bad right now. The antibacterial jelly is keeping them moist." She hands Nora the mirror. Nora takes one look at her mottled face and wonders what the nurse *would* call too bad. "Honey, don't get upset now. They're gonna turn dark—blue-black—in a couple of days. But you're gonna be just fine."

Tears course down Nora's cheeks—again. It seems she's been crying ever since she got to the hospital. She needs to block out that face in the mirror. "I'll take that pain pill now."

Her doctor comes by. He looks middle-aged and harried. "You have first and second degree burns over twenty percent of your body, but only one patch on your arm might require a skin graft." *Skin graft?* "The cool river water minimized the burn damage but exacerbated your loss of body heat. Over the next twenty-four hours, we'll be giving you five liters of fluids and substantial quantities of antibiotics."

Nora nods. Her left arm and hand are immobilized by bandages, and pain accompanies every move. IV tubes are attached to her right arm. She feels helpless.

Jim Sloan stops by mid-morning. He darts sideways glances at her face and Nora winces, knowing what he sees, wondering whether her face has already begun to blacken. "You saved Rebecca's life. Paul told me." He seems to search for words and push them out around a lump of emotion. "How can I ever thank you?"

"Paul is the real hero. Thank God he was nearby. I still don't know how he managed to get Rebecca and me into the skiff." She shakes her head, tears stinging her cheeks. "I'm so sorry for what happened. I feel so—so *responsible*."

Jim touches Nora's shoulder gently. "All I can say is thank you." He glances aside, as though embarrassed by the emotion in his voice. "How are you doing?"

Nora manages a crooked smile. "I'll be in here for at least another day. They want to replace fluids and stabilize my body temperature. They say I suffered a little hypothermia. But I'll be fine." Nora shrugs one shoulder and immediately wishes she hadn't. "How's Rebecca?"

Jim straightens his back, hands in pockets. "They had to suture her right leg, but the doctor said she probably won't have a scar. She has a badly broken arm and a slight concussion, but nothing to worry about. Thank God."

"That *is* good news. I'll check in with her as soon as they unhook me." Nora gestures with her IV arm.

When Jim leaves, Nora's thoughts turn to *Duet*. She desperately wants to arrange to get her boat refloated but can't do a damned thing about it at the moment. The nurse tells Nora that she'll have the use of her right hand soon, but for the time being, she can't even use the phone. *If only Van were here. He'd know what has to be done about Duet.*

Every flat surface is bedecked with flowers: white carnations from Jim Sloan; a dish garden from her departmental colleagues; mixed bouquets from Frank and Bill; a dozen red roses from Nate and Priscilla, with a note wishing her a full and speedy recovery. And the yellow roses from Van. She can't complain of neglect. But right now, she needs Van here. No doubt he's in the lab.

Lying in pain, feeling helpless, she stares at the flowers intended to cheer her. Cut flowers in elaborate arrangements always remind her of funerals. A flash of her own mortality gives way to a personal accounting. *I'm a good teacher. Students and colleagues respect me. I work hard and I'm successful. I'm loyal to friends and family. I look for good in everyone and logic in the world. I try to be kind.* A smile quirks her lips. *On the other hand, I'm hot-tempered and stubborn. I procrastinate. And my love life ... A lot of people would not approve.* Nora tries to focus on *Clair de Lune* drifting softly from the radio, tries to put painful thoughts aside. The drugs to which she finally yielded help. She drifts toward sleep. But her last thoughts are about how *Duet* blew up, and whether there's someone out there who wants her dead.

When the aide brings her lunch, Nora asks her to dial the Meers Point Marina and hold the phone. "Sid? It's Nora Perry."

"Hi, Professor Perry. How're ya doing?"

"Not so good. Not good at all, actually. That's why I'm calling. There was an explosion on *Duet* this morning. I'm in the hospital and she's at the bottom of the Corsica River, in the West College mooring basin."

"Holy shit! Are you going to be all right?"

"Yeah, it looks like it. I've got some burns but I think they're more painful than serious. Listen, I can't talk long. But I need to get *Duet* refloated. Can you arrange it for me?"

"Sure thing. There's a marine salvage place I work with all the time." Sid pauses, and his next words come in the rhythm of a man talking around lighting a cigarette. "These guys're good, so they're busy. They won't get to it for at least a couple of days. But they'll do it right and do it fast enough to keep the cost down. Sort of." He chuckles. "Maybe it'll just cost you an arm instead of an arm and a leg."

Nora tries to laugh, too. "That sounds good to me. I'm not using my left arm right now anyway. But in case they aren't taking pay in body parts this season, I'll check with my insurance company, see whether they'll be paying you and the salvage team directly or reimbursing me."

"Hey. Not to worry. I know you're good for it."

"I want to be there. I won't get out of here till tomorrow at the earliest, so try to schedule accordingly. Let me know. When she's up, tow her to your place. Haul her and assess the damage. See if you can make her right." Her voice quavers.

"Don't you worry about a thing. You just get *yourself* right. I'm sure we can fix *Duet* up good as new—in time for you to get in a lot more sailing this season, too."

Nora lies back, relieved to have made arrangements for *Duet*. But every time she closes her eyes, she relives the explosion. Over the next few hours, bit by bit, she remembers telling Rebecca how to drop the mooring line, the sound of the fan blowing the bilge, turning the key in the ignition, the wall of compressed air slamming into her body an instant before she recognized the blast. At first, the need to find Rebecca had filled her consciousness. But once she had hold of her, the feel of Rebecca's clothes scraping raw burns, the sting of the river, the oily water in her mouth, the weight of her limbs treading water—all these assaults on her senses overcame her.

Van and Bill come by that afternoon, Frank close behind. She tells them all she can remember.

*   *   *

When Nora gets to the college dock three days later, the first thing she sees is the big orange float tied to *Duet's* mast. Depression weighs on her heart.

Paul Zimmerman hurries from his office. "Professor! What are you doin' here? Are you supposed to be out already?"

The white bandages on Nora's arm and face make her feel like a half-wrapped mummy. She smiles as best she can. "Hi, Paul. I'm fine. Really. I was even able to drive myself over to watch the salvage."

"They're gonna refloat *Duet* this morning?"

"That's the plan. Did you put the orange buoy on the mast?"

He nods. "And I collected the cushions and stuff that floated up. They're in my office whenever you want to get 'em."

"Yet another thing to thank you for—besides hauling me out of the river! Rebecca and I were lucky you were still close by."

"Aw, anybody would've done the same. How's Mrs. President doin'?"

"Very well. We left the hospital together. What a pair! My left arm in a sling and her right one in a cast. She will recover, but I doubt she'll want to go sailing again any time soon."

The barge from Kent Narrows Salvage Company chugs into view. The barge carries the driver and a diver and tows a floating platform. Nora can see the air compressor on the barge, along with flotation devices. The barge slows as it approaches the orange buoy. "Well, now, this could take a right long time," Paul says. "How about I bring out a chair for you? And some kind of sunshade. You really shouldn't be out in the sun, you know."

At his words, Nora notices the stinging under her bandages. She turns the full brilliance of her eyes on him. "Paul, you are a godsend. Thank you. I didn't even think to bring a lawn chair."

*   *   *

Van arrives while Nora is watching the diver don his gear and jump into the Corsica with the two deflated bladders. The skipper throws over a black buoy to signal a diver in the water. She can't see the diver but she knows he's fixing the flotation devices to the port and starboard sides with connecting belts under the keel. She relishes Van's companionable silence. No need to explain to him what is happening or why.

The activity at the mooring basin is the biggest show in town and Nora and Van are seldom without company on the dock. The process is slow, with little visible from shore. Most passersby gaze out over the river while they inquire about her health. They are gone in a matter of minutes.

When Clyde Barnes strolls out the dock, she sighs. *I really don't need the biggest gossip on campus trying to pry information out of me.* Clyde doesn't even pretend interest in the salvage operation but goes straight to the news with the greatest potential for gossip. "I hear Rebecca Sloan's still in the hospital—broken arm, concussion, all that. What happened anyway?"

Nora doesn't look at him. "Rebecca's out of the hospital. And I don't really know what happened." Clyde seems to be waiting for her to go on. *If I don't say something, he could be here forever.* "When the explosion occurred, *Duet* heeled over—fast—and sank. My best guess is that Rebecca was thrown against the shrouds and fell on the gunwale."

"Yeah, but what caused the explosion?"

"How the hell am I supposed to know? The boat isn't even out of the water yet!" Nora shifts in her chair, trying to ease the pain in her burned arm.

Clyde holds up both hands. "Hey. Don't be so pissy. I'm just asking what everybody is wondering."

*   *   *

When Frank arrives the mast stands almost vertical, but the boat still rests on the river mud ten feet down. "What's happening? What's all the racket?" Nora notices Frank's glance at her bandages, the sad look on his face.

Van says, "The air compressor. They need to get *Duet* afloat and vertical so they can tow her."

They look at the barge and the floating platform for awhile. Frank says, "How long will this take? Is it going to be hours or days or what?"

Nora says, "She should be up by noon. But we won't know the extent of the damage till she's hauled. I'm having her towed down to Mears Point Marina. They should be able to tell what happened."

"If I drive you down to Kent Narrows, we can look at her together and maybe get a bite to eat after."

Nora smiles. "Sure, if you can take the time. I'll call when she's up."

"I'll take the time." He sounds grim.

"What is it?"

Frank runs a hand over his hair. "Nothing important. Jake's on my case about—things. I reminded him that this is an active investigation, of a crime in his jurisdiction. No problem."

"I would like to join you at the marina if that is all right." Van's tone is as tentative as his words.

"Actually, the fewer civilians the better." Frank tucks a stray wisp of hair behind Nora's ear. "Call when you're ready to go."

As he walks away, Nora turns sympathetic eyes to Van. "I'll let you know what we find."

*   *   *

Getting *Duet* afloat takes nearly four hours. Finally the deck breaks the surface, water draining away. The horse-shoe shaped jim buoy is still fastened into its frame at the stern. The mainsail still wraps the boom. Nora wonders how badly burned it is. She sighs. Replacing the main would be $1200 at least. Nora mentally ticks off the possible damage, everything from the engine to the cabin carpet. She wonders for the hundredth time how she will ever get the boat put to rights. The barge heading out into the river, towing *Duet*, diverts her thoughts. They'll probably be pumping her bilge all the way to the marina. She heads for Paul's office to call Frank.

*   *   *

Sid has *Duet* in the slings when Frank and Nora arrive at the marina. On the starboard side, halfway between the gunwale and the keel, is an irregular hole as big as a basketball. The chine confirms what Nora's memories and injuries had led her to expect—that the explosion blew out on the starboard side. *Oh, Lord. I could have been killed.* Suddenly her legs feel rubbery and she has to concentrate to remain upright.

Sid lights his next cigarette from the butt of the last one and talks around puffs. "I haven't been on board yet—just got her up. I can see you're not in any shape to climb up there, but maybe you want to wait around while I take a look-see."

Half an hour later, he is back. "Well, now, I've seen worse. But I gotta say, it's bad. Pretty much everything in the starboard locker burned. You're probably gonna want a marine surveyor to inspect her, but I can tell you right now what happened. The conduit from the bilge blower to the transom was cut. Your blower was blowin' but your gas fumes weren't goin' anywhere. And unless you're in the habit of carrying this sort of thing in the bilge, this is the little baby that did the job." Sid holds out a brown callused hand, a Stanley razor resting on the palm.

Frank confiscates the knife and bags it. "Don't touch anything else, and don't let anyone on board till I get a CSI team out here. They'll take your prints—for comparison." On the way back to Centreville he says, "So that rules out the possibility of an accident. But beyond that, the field is wide open. Can you think of anybody who might want to hurt you or your boat?"

Nora hesitates. There are a couple of seniors who didn't graduate because they blew off her class. But she can't believe either of them would do this. The only person she's had a run-in with recently is Simon. *But he isn't a sailor. Besides, we agreed to let it go.* She shakes her head. "Not a soul. I'm glad to know I didn't cause the accident. But deliberate sabotage? Why me? And why now?"

"I suppose it could be a random act of vandalism—*Duet* just a target of opportunity. And the hell of that is, the more random the target, the more difficult it is to pin it on someone." Frank turns toward Nora. "How about Rebecca? Could she have been the target?"

"Oh, my God." Nora tries to get her mind around that possibility. And the implications. Richard Emery. Pete Fitzroy. And now Rebecca—or her. Is someone targeting West College people? That idea is just too far-fetched.

*   *   *

Nora wants nothing so much as sleep. Bill brought bread and soup, tossed a salad together, and served coffee ice cream for dessert.

He helped her eat, and afterwards he held her good hand and sat quietly at her side while they listened to the Pastoral Symphony and watched the night sky from the patio, listening to the the gurgle of the Corsica below. Bill said, "I could stay the night—help get you to bed—be here if you need anything. I would like to." Nora declined. He would get no rest, and she would feel like a burden. So he helped her out of her clothes and into a nightgown, put fresh ointment on her burns, changed her bandages, and said, "Call if you need anything. *Anything.* I'll bring something by for breakfast." His goodnight kiss felt almost fatherly. After he left, weariness settled in her bones, so heavy she could hardly move.

She skips her usual nightcap and turns in. She tunes in WBJC, classical music to sleep by, and flicks off the bedside light. She turns the good side of her face into the pillow and tries not to feel her body. Pain accompanies the beginnings of an itch, and small pin pricks circle the area where the IV's were inserted. But her thoughts cycle from body senses to threat. She drifts to sleep plagued by thoughts that someone tried to kill her or at least, didn't care if she died. Who?

Chapter Twenty-One

Nora reaches for the phone, stops. She hasn't really talked with Van since he brought lunch one day early in her recovery. The neglect hurts. *But, then, he might feel neglected, too.* She's been so involved with Bill, she didn't invite Van to sail all summer. She snatches up the phone and dials. The ringing seems interminable. Finally she hears a click and "Hendrick van Pelt."

Nora sucks in her breath. "Hi, it's Nora."

"Nora! This is a pleasant surprise. How are you?"

"Much better. A few weeks works wonders." She clears her throat. "Long time, no see. I thought maybe we could have a cup of coffee or something. Catch up."

"That is an excellent idea. Would you like to come here?" He pauses. "Or we could meet at Chums."

Nora had intended to invite him to her house. "Your place is fine. When?"

"Come now, if you wish. Or as soon as is convenient."

"I'll be there in about forty-five minutes."

Nora replaces the phone and exhales slowly. Those few stilted words in Van's rich baritone made her heart stutter. She sits there, letting that realization—and the implications—sink in. She spends half an hour making herself look as good as she can without looking as though she's made an effort. Her burns are much less livid, virtually gone. She applies a green tint to take the red out. The resulting brown spots stand out on her alabaster skin like gargantuan freckles. She washes off the tint and chooses a sage green silk shirt that covers most of the burn residue. She plaits her hair into the thick French braid she always wears sailing.

*　　　*　　　*

Van hangs up the phone. He's pleased at the prospect of seeing Nora and catching up on each other's news. But he had such an adrenaline rush that his hand trembled on the receiver. He goes to the kitchen to make coffee. His glance falls on Lissa's picture on the refrigerator door.

During his most recent trip to New York, cabbing into the city from Kennedy, the skyscrapers blocking the sun, people walking double-time, he felt glad he didn't live there. Lissa met him in the lobby of her apartment building, suitcase in hand. "Hi, sweetie! Guess what. The management finally got around to painting my apartment. But not to worry. I made reservations at the Warwick. My treat, of course."

"Of course *not*," he said. No gentleman would allow a woman to pay for the room. Still, the unexpected expense of a hotel was like sand in his boat shoes, a background irritation that grew as the evening progressed.

At Lissa's suggestion, they went to the Algonquin for drinks and dinner and afterwards another drink. The crowded little bar off the entrance was not to Van's taste. He cast a disappointed eye around the smoky room. "So, this is where the famous writers used to hang out."

"Absolutely." Melissa seemed invigorated. "Well, sort of. They gathered around an oak table in a little room on the other side of the lobby and played word games. Dorothy Parker was one of the regulars." Mention of an oak table made Van think about Nora sitting at her oak table, coffee mug in hand, a gentle breeze from the Corsica River whispering across the patio and lifting a wispy curl.

Lissa talked on, her hand on Van's forearm. Her eyes sparkled. He glanced surreptitiously at his watch, tired of the noise, the smoke. But Lissa's enthusiasm was catching. It lifted his spirits.

Leaving the bar, Van suggested they walk to the Warwick. "It is only ten blocks." As they walked toward 54th Street, conversation dwindled. In the silence, Van thought about Lissa. A career woman. A city girl. Could he live up to her expectations? Suddenly he felt embarrassed that he hadn't suggested taking a cab. It wasn't that he couldn't afford a cab. But the expense of their room, their dinner, their eight-dollar drinks—of anything and everything in the city—grated on him. He'd always been frugal—had had to be in the early years, struggling to support his growing family while paying for his own education, then college bills for four children. Being careful with money was something he *did*, not something he thought about. When he did take stock of his finances—especially at tax time—his usual thoughts were along the lines of how much better off he was as his salary went up and each child became self-supporting. Still, somehow, this trip made him feel poor. He hoped Lissa didn't know.

Van took Lissa's arm as the traffic light turned. Halfway down the mostly deserted block, Lissa slid her hand into his as a car pulled up along the curb. A passenger in the back seat rolled down the window and said something indistinguishable. Van started toward the car, Lissa's hand tugging him back. The rear door flew open and a big man jumped out—a man in a black shirt and a black leather vest, pointing a handgun at Van's gut. "Wallet," he snarled.

Van's heart raced. He kept his eyes on the man in front of him but searched his peripheral vision for Lissa. She stood like a statue in the middle of the sidewalk, gripping her shoulder bag. The man looked steadily at Van, holding the gun with easy familiarity. "Hurry it up! Let's have it. Now!"

Van pulled his wallet from his hip pocket and started to take money out, but the thief snatched the wallet and grabbed for Lissa's shoulder bag. Van lunged at him. The gun crashed down on Van's right arm and a backhanded swipe with the pistol barrel whipped his head sideways. Pain shot upward to his elbow, and his face hit the concrete sidewalk. The grit on the sidewalk sanded his cheek as the car sped away. As black edged in, Lissa bent over him. Her shoulder bag clunked his arm, the pain searing him almost back to consciousness.

Afterward, she told him that the whole episode, beginning to end, was over in half a minute. She had called 911. When the ambulance arrived at Bellevue B, Van was conscious, vaguely aware of a goose egg on his forehead, blood dried on the side of his face, and a pounding headache. Lissa gripped his hand painfully. A nurse pried her away and directed her toward the emergency waiting room.

Van's injuries—a broken arm and a slight concussion—were too minor to command a place at the head of the line. He waited for hours—the ER personnel fitting in a few minutes here, a few minutes there—between the young blonde who'd slit her wrists, the two teenagers who'd shot each other, the drunken couple who'd run a red light and been hit by a bus. Van had never seen so many bloody bodies. Pungent antiseptics and a meat-locker smell of ruptured guts mixed with booze and vomit. Van nearly threw up. The heart attacks and drug overdoses seemed almost peaceful by comparison. Behind his privacy curtain, Van heard distant sirens closing in on the hospital, screaming children, weeping relatives, shouting in English and broken English and languages he didn't understand or even recognize, a man moaning—just moaning, for thirty minutes—behind the next curtain. He had nothing to do but listen and remember the big hand pointing a pistol at his gut, swinging it at his head. Van was thankful to be alive. As hours wore on, he tried to put himself in another place, focusing on sailing and the peace of a quiet night at anchor. He thought of sitting topside with Nora—watching the stars, listening to the wind in *Duet's* rigging—and achieved a calm of sorts.

Back at the Warwick just before dawn, Lissa put him to bed with pillows padding his right arm. He'd declined more pain medication at the hospital but took it now. Fatigue had drained away any resistance he might otherwise have made to her fussing. She drew him close, his head on her shoulder. In spite of all the adrenaline that had pumped through his system, Lissa's warmth and comfort, combined with the drugs, seduced him to sleep. In his half consciousness, he murmured, "Thank you. For everything. I could stay here, just like this, forever."

Lissa stiffened, seemed to stop breathing, bringing Van back to the here and now. After a few seconds she laughed, an odd sound that seemed to catch in her throat. "You better watch yourself, fella. Saying things like that, a girl might get ideas—might think you'd just proposed and say yes before you could change your mind." She paused. "Van? Was that a proposal?"

Her words cleared the last haze from Van's brain. *Lissa— here and now—soft and comforting.* He said, "When I propose marriage, there will be no doubt about it in anyone's mind." He draws her closer. "So, you are still planning to meet my children at Thanksgiving?"

Lissa sighs softly. "Of course."

*   *   *

Van's thoughts turn to the phone calls he had with his four children to tell them about the mugging and invite them to meet the important woman in his life. Pieter, the oldest, offered a subdued "Thanksgiving. Cool. I'll be there." The remainder of the conversation was devoted to boats and Van's recovery. Van hung up unclear whether Pieter was pleased to be meeting Lissa or not.

Geertruyt focused almost exclusively on the facts, asking many questions about the mugging and Van's future with Lissa. Van had only partial answers for the latter. She ended the conversation with, "I hope she treats you well, Dad. You deserve some love."

Johannes' ebullient response was typical. "Way to go, Pop! I'll bet Lissa is some looker. I've always been kind of partial to Nora, myself, but hey, you gotta go with what feels good. If you need someone to prop you up over the Thanksgiving bird, I'm your man!"

Van couldn't immediately get in touch with Kirsten. An apprentice guide on float-and-paddle white water rafting trips on the Colorado River, she has access to a phone only when she gets to Phantom Ranch, halfway through the 226-mile, two-week trips. When she called and Van told her about Lissa, Kirsten started with "Oh, Daddy, I'm so happy for you," and moved quickly to questions about their plans. The fact that there wasn't much to be planned at this point didn't dampen her enthusiasm one whit. But she caught Van off guard when she asked, "So what does Nora think about this development?"

Van had paused, finally saying, "I haven't seen Nora since before I went to New York."

"This time last year, between sailing and the Slater murder, you two were practically joined at the hip. We all—Pieter, Trudy, and I—even Johannes—we all thought you and Nora were a hot item. We had a running bet on when we'd find ourselves with a redheaded stepmother." Van flinched. "So what happened with you guys anyway?"

"Nothing happened. She started dating Bill Baxter after the charter a year ago and I—we just sort of drifted in different directions."

"Daddy, get real. You are the least drifting person I know. Did you wimp out in the competition or did Melissa set up a cross-current?"

Van flushed and gnawed his lip. "I may have been—a convenient stopgap for Nora until someone more desirable came along."

"Humph. It didn't look that way to me. I thought you two were really good together. But if Lissa is what you want, go for it. I'll try to help matters along at Thanksgiving. Listen, I gotta go. Six people are waiting for this phone. Love you, Daddy."

*   *   *

Nora rings Van's doorbell. The seconds on the porch feel like forever. Eventually, she hears a fumble and a rattle and the inner door swings wide. Van pauses in the doorway, smiling. He opens the storm door awkwardly with his left hand.

Nora stares at the sling supporting Van's right arm, encased in a cast, and gasps, "Van! What happened?"

His smile turns rueful. "I went to the Big Apple and got mugged. It is painful but not serious. Come in. The coffee is ready."

Nora sits on the beige and blue striped futon sofa in the living room. *The Big Apple. Lissa.* Van comes in with two mugs of black coffee, the rich aroma surrounding her like a cloud. "So, tell me about it," she says, waggling her fingers toward his cast.

Van looks at Nora, then quickly away. "Lissa and I were walking uptown on 6th Avenue. I was being a tourist—thinking about the theaters and restaurants nearby, about noise and the smell of pizza. A car stopped. A guy seemed to be asking for directions. I was suckered. I went over to the car and got pistol-whipped and robbed. Pretty stupid, actually."

At the mention of the pistol-whipping, Nora feels weak. "My God! You could have been killed!"

Van shrugs. "But I was not. Just a broken arm and a few stitches in my scalp that would not even show except that they shaved that part of my head. But enough about that. Tell me how you have been. You look well."

Nora smiles. "Well enough. It seems I heal quickly. When I went back the week after I got out of the hospital, the doctor said I was already much better than he'd expected. Rebecca's out and about, with no apparent long term effects except a distinct aversion to sailboats. *Duet* is the only casualty still on the critical list."

"You told me Sid found a knife, that somebody cut the hose on your bilge blower. Any ideas who?"

Nora shakes her head. "Frank's been pressing me on that. I've wracked my brain to no avail. The CSI guys found gas in the bottom of the bilge and fibers presumed to be from the perpetrator's shirt. But no motive and no suspects. It's a little scary."

Concern is written across Van's face. He says, "It is more than a little scary."

"This may sound crazy, but I think everything that's happened around the College is related somehow—Emory's drowning, Fitzroy's death, my boat."

Van looks quizzical. "But nothing is related to anything else. What can it be but a combination of bad luck and coincidence?"

"Probably so." But she isn't convinced.

"So how are the repairs coming?"

"They're progressing. But slowly. The hull's mended but the engine's still in pieces. Has to be completely rebuilt. But she'll be worthy again before the season's over." She shoots a look at Van. "When she's ready, maybe we could take her out to celebrate. Maybe a little weekend run up to Still Pond."

Van's smile fades and he draws in a bushel of air. Expelling it slowly, he says, "Yeah, sure. By the way, Lissa is coming for Thanksgiving. To meet my children." The silence is short but thick.

"Well. That *is* news. I hope the holiday is all that you want it to be." Her smile feels stiff. She flicks a look in his direction, not quite meeting his gaze. "I'm amazed that you stayed unattached this long!" She sets her mug carefully on the coffee table. "Look, I just remembered that I have to—make a couple of phone calls." She stands. "We'll be in touch about the sail."

She walks quickly to the door, Van scrambling to accompany her. "Nora, I—"

She turns on the doorstep. "I'm glad things are going well for you and Melissa. I'm very happy for you." She smiles widely, clears her throat, and blinks. "Take care, Van." She puts her hand on his shoulder, brushes her lips across his cheek, and steps back. "Try not to get pistol-whipped every time you go to the big city." She whirls away, gone before Van can say more.

*   *   *

Van turns back into the house, his heart leaden, his breathing jagged. He hadn't meant to tell her that way. Hadn't meant to tell her at all, really, unless he actually proposed to Lissa. His thoughts roil. *Why should I get all torn up just because Nora invited me to sail?* He paces to the window and back. He slumps into his chair and curses the pain that shoots through his arm. He thinks back over everything Nora said, recalling her words and the tones in which she uttered them. She clearly grasps the implications of the Thanksgiving visit.

The ringing phone cuts into his thoughts. He jumps, jolting his broken arm again. "Hendrick van Pelt."

"Hi, sweetie. Guess what I've been doing." Lissa's voice is effervescent. "No, don't bother. You'll never guess. I just spent eight solid hours at Bridal Warehouse—less lunch time, of course—with my friend Marie. That's the most amazing place. They get all sorts of wonderful dresses—designer models and dresses from weddings that are canceled at the last minute—and twice a year they have these fabulous sales—dresses at five or ten percent of their original cost. Women wait in line all night to get in first but Marie knows one of the partners." Van wonders where this conversation is heading. "She bought a fabulous dress—cream satin with tiny cultured pearls embroidered on the bodice." She chatters on, heaping details of cut and fit and lace one on top of another.

She pauses and Van says, "It sounds like—a very special gown."

"Your enthusiasm is underwhelming."

Van smiles at her teasing. "It is just—I have no personal interest. I have not yet met Marie."

Lissa laughs. "We'll fix that the next time you're in town. And not being the groom, you can see the dress." She laughs. "You can imagine how I would look in a dress like that." She prattles on a few more minutes about work and why she can't get to Centreville for the weekend.

Van has little to say. When he hangs up, he rests his head on the back of the chair and closes his eyes. Two things press into his awareness: the pain throbbing in the side of his head and relief that Lissa won't be in Centreville for the weekend.

Chapter Twenty-Two

JIM PACES HIS OFFICE, WAITING for Frank to arrive at Old Main. He casts a worried glance at his vice president for finance. "Frank said burglary isn't really his bailiwick—but I persuaded him. God, Stan, why would anyone want to break into your office?"

Stan shrugs. "How would I know?" The faint whine in his voice irritates Jim. Frank's arrival, a detective in tow, stifles an angry retort.

Frank says, "Morning, Jim, Stan." He nods to both. "This is Sy Brown. He's in our criminal investigation division."

Jim extends a hand to Sy but lets it drop when Brown stands stiff as a fence post and doesn't make eye contact. He glances at Stan and Frank. Frank looks irritated with his subordinate, but a smirk flashes on Stan's face before a blank mask drops into place. When Jim speaks, his voice is cold and formal. "Thank you for coming, Frank. I appreciate it. As a trustee and all—I just felt a little more comfortable turning to you on a college matter. Stan's office is the only one that seems to have been broken into."

Jim leads the others across the suite. From the doorway to

Stan's office, he silently surveys the mess: desk and file drawers open, papers strewn about. The intruder even dumped the waste baskets.

Frank says, "Let's stay in the hall and give Sy a chance to do his job." He glances at Jim. "So what do you know about this?"

"Not much. When Stan opened his door this morning, he found this." Jim waves his hand in the direction of Stan's office. "He came to me immediately and I called you."

Frank turns to Stan. "Can you tell me anything more than that?"

Stan, wringing his hands and fidgeting, shakes his head. "I unlocked my door and there it was."

"Is your door usually locked?" Stan nods. "Besides the paper mess, is anything out of place?"

Stan pokes his head in the open doorway and peers around. "At night the file and desk drawers are closed and locked." He points to his right. "And that sliding panel has been moved. Usually it covers the wall safe."

"And you haven't touched anything?"

Stan flushes. "N-No, not really. I mean—well, maybe I scuffled some papers around on the floor when I checked the safe." He glances nervously from Frank to Jim. "I mean, of course I had to check the safe." Jim stifles an urge to roll his eyes. *Who doesn't know no one is supposed to touch anything?*

Frank stares at the wall safe. "That's a double-action safe. The dials have to be opened in sequence, right?" All three men look at the black door with *Morrell Safe Company, Baltimore, Maryland* in Gothic gold letters and two dials, with a heavy steel bar between them. "If we could limit our investigation to those who have the combinations to the safe ..." He shrugs.

Stan sputters, "Why, why, that's absurd. Nobody has the

combination except Jim and me and my assistant, and *he's* been here twelve years."

Frank says, "Length of service isn't really relevant."

Jim looks at his nervous vice president. *Stan may not be the brightest bulb in the pack, but surely he's honest.*

Stan continues, "Besides, if nothing's missing from the safe, it probably wasn't opened."

Frank's face is blank. "It's entirely possible that someone wanted *information*—not the documents themselves. What about keys?"

Jim explains that everyone who works in Old Main has keys to the front door: all the senior administrators, their assistants and secretaries—plus security and some physical plant personnel.

"And this office?"

Stan remains silent, staring out the window toward an old sycamore. Jim wonders fleetingly whether Stan is withdrawing from the entire proceeding. Or maybe he's embarrassed. Or worried that he'll be blamed. In any case, he doesn't answer.

Jim says, "Stan and his assistant have keys to this office. So does the janitor assigned to the building. A few people have campus-wide passkeys, including security personnel. And we have a cabinet of keys in the physical plant office so that workers can gain access as necessary." Saying this aloud, he realizes that security at the College is more an illusion than a reality.

Sy steps out of Stan's office. "I've dusted for prints, Frank—and there are plenty." He glances at Stan and Jim. "We'll need comparison prints from everybody who's been here recently." Remembering the litany of people with access, Jim groans inwardly. *This could disrupt the whole damn campus.* Sy continues. "The file cabinets and desk drawers weren't forced—but keys like that are a dime a dozen. Nothing on the window. There're scratch marks on the safe, maybe from picking the locks—or trying to. The tech guys can tell. As for the office itself, it was either a key or a pro opened that door. You can look around now."

Frank turns to Stan. "Okay, Stan, we need to know what's missing."

"How am I supposed to know that?" he whines.

"Look, Stan," Jim says through clenched teeth. "Go in and look."

Stan takes a step back, hands raised as if to fend off a blow. "Okay. Okay. Just give me a minute to go to the men's room." Jim sees Sy roll his eyes at Frank and shares Sy's exasperation.

*   *   *

Stan picks through the litter of papers, seeming reluctant to touch anything. After fifteen minutes, he says: "As far as I can tell, we're missing the budget, estimated revenues, the monthly financial statements for August." He pauses, looking defeated. "All my work in progress for the Finance Committee—down the drain. Glancing nervously at Jim, he adds, "And, uh, that draft we were working on yesterday … I left it on my desk last night and—it seems to be missing."

Jim blanches. *If that memo on faculty and administrative salaries gets out, there'll be hell to pay. Not that it would be justified. We pay faculty and administrators what is necessary to get the quality we need. Still, faculty always think what they do is more important than what any vice president does.*

Frank says, "Are any of these missing papers likely to cause problems?"

Stan shrugs.

Jim sighs and says, "All of them have the potential. The monthly financial statements include line items that are always controversial—the development travel budget, athletics. And then there's my discretionary fund. Some faculty actually think there shouldn't be one."

Stan stands near his office door, wringing his hands again. "That report for Brady. And the work for the Finance Committee. How am I supposed to reconstruct those with the meeting less than a month away? Nate Roth and Buck Brady—if one of them doesn't dump on me, the other one will."

Jim takes a deep breath, pushes his glasses up the bridge of his nose, and runs his fingers across his forehead. "Why the hell would anybody do this?"

Frank rocks back on his heels. "I'd expect someone who wanted financial info would just hack the computer system. So either the perp isn't computer savvy, or the important stuff is on paper. What do you have on paper that's so important someone would break in to get it?"

Jim doesn't hesitates. "Maybe it was just a student prank. Or some kind of random vandalism."

Frank eyes the president. "I suppose that's a possibility. But if it isn't?"

"I—the most sensitive item—among the ones we know about so far—is probably my draft recommendations on faculty and administrative salaries."

* * *

Jim mixes himself a rum and tonic and rests his head on the back of his recliner, eyes closed. *I came in here thinking I would be good for West College—that I could shape the institution—the curriculum, the building plan. And goddamn it, I will. But every Board meeting brings another disaster. Nate and Buck are going to blow their tops if they don't get those reports. And, Jesus, if that faculty and administrative salary memo is floating around . . .* He considers telling Bill about the draft salary recommendations, but all his instincts recoil. *The fewer people who know, the better.* For a few minutes he broods over the problems and accidents plaguing his presidency. He sighs and gets up to refresh his drink. *My recommendations to drop COLA and base salaries only on merit ... If that memo gets out prematurely, the Board might love it—but the faculty would have my head. Goddamn it—not even in a locked drawer.*

* * *

Rebecca drops her coat on a chair, her briefcase on the floor beside it. "Lord, what a week. One corporate meeting after another." She looks toward the drink at Jim's elbow. "Looks like you've started happy hour without me."

Jim closes his eyes and speaks quietly. "Stan's office was vandalized last night. A lot of confidential papers were taken." Jim tells her about the missing financial documents, the problems created for the upcoming Board meeting, the potential upheavals if the budget and the president's discretionary fund become public. He talks about the disruption the upcoming fingerprinting will cause.

Rebecca sits across the room, apparently absorbed by the patterns of light the setting sun makes through her glass of red wine. "Tell Stan to suck it up and reproduce the documents. As for the rest of it: anyone who gets upset over that sort of thing is just being juvenile. Don't let it get to you."

"Rebecca. You don't understand. All the years we've been married—haven't you learned anything about academe?" Jim shakes his head. "Anyway, the financials may be the least of my worries. Yesterday I gave Stan a list of proposed faculty and administrative salaries. That's missing, too. If it gets out, the controversy could split our nice college family wide open. And the Board will blame me for the turmoil. Jesus. It could bring college business to a standstill."

Rebecca scowls. "For God's sake, Jim. Don't be melodramatic." She pours another glass of merlot. "You're making a mountain out of a mole hill. Trustees are mostly business men and women. They don't like automatic salary increases, cost-of-living raises, any of that. They don't want to reward the dead wood. Shake things up. The Board will love you for it."

Jim looks at her. "I could lose a lot of faculty."

"Not the good ones."

Jim looks at his wife. "Haven't you listened to anything I've said?"

"Of course I listened. Someone took some financial documents. Big deal. You might be embarrassed about one thing or another. Students and faculty probably will raise a stink." Rebecca laughs. "But no one ever died of embarrassment. And as for the missing salary recommendations—it couldn't be that devastating. You dramatize everything." She turns toward the door, wineglass in hand. "I'm going to bed."

* * *

Jim sits alone, his thoughts floating. *Rebecca's been more bitchy than ever since the boat explosion. Will she get over it?* Jim shifts in his recliner, folds his hands across the beginnings of a paunch, and takes a deep breath. He imagines himself twice-divorced. He mixes another rum and tonic. *Maybe Stan doesn't have the mental horsepower for this job. But would it be fair to fire him so soon? Buck probably will blow a gasket if we don't have his reports. That's the way he is. But Nate will stand by me.* It's the only morsel of comfort Jim can find in his thoughts. *I need the comfort of Rebecca's body.* He goes up to bed and finds Rebecca fast asleep. Or pretending to be.

Chapter Twenty-Three

Frank stalks into Jim Sloan's outer office. When Jim's secretary smiles and shrugs and says, "I'm sorry, Captain, but without an appointment..." Frank says, "I'll wait." He doesn't smile before he sits down, rigidly upright, and stares stonily at the secretary. No one will want a uniformed officer hanging around the president's office any longer than necessary. She pinches her mouth into a tiny bow and frowns, but she taps on Jim's door and disappears within. She shows Frank into the president's office in less than ten minutes.

Jim stands when Frank comes in. "Hello, Frank. This is a pleasant surprise." His unsmiling face and wary gaze belie the words. "Sit down, sit down. So, what can I do for you?"

Frank sits, ramrod straight, feet on the floor. "You can stop yanking my chain and tell me everything you know about this burglary!"

Jim jerks back as if struck. "What do you mean?"

"Cut the bull! I know for a fact that your computer systems

have been hacked. Why the hell didn't you say anything about that?" Frank doesn't even try to hide his disgust.

Jim takes a slow, deep breath, adjusts his glasses, and says, "Where do you get your information anyway?"

His tone irritates Frank. "My sources aren't the point." He has no intention of getting the head of computer services in trouble for telling Nora about the problem. "Your chief financial officer's office is burglarized and his computer systems are simultaneously corrupted and you don't tell me?"

Jim slumps back in his chair. "When Stan realized that his files were corrupted, he called in Lew Denning to do the recovery. They were not successful. I didn't know about it till yesterday afternoon. Then I met with Denning myself." He sighs. "Lew assures me that we have a well-managed, sophisticated firewall with one of the most secure operating systems. But there's something called root kit tools out there—some of them available on the internet for free. I gather that it takes a good bit of knowledge to understand them, but they allow a hacker to get into the system and hide all traces." Jim rubs his forehead and sighs again. "The hell of it is, this wasn't necessarily an inside job—maybe not even a pro. Lots of people—including motivated students—do this sort of thing as a hobby." He looks like a man whose world is about to collapse around him. "I don't know what I'm going to say to the Board."

Frank sits back in his chair and crosses his legs, staring stonily until Jim fidgets. Then he says, "Thanks for leveling with me—finally. I don't think I need to take up any more of your time this morning." He stands.

Jim stands, too. "Uh, by the way, Frank. Jake Bentley called my office this morning. He wanted to know the dates of the trustee meetings for the next twelve months."

Frank says, "Really?" and thinks *This can't be good.*

*   *   *

Frank slams the car door and heads for his office, his stride long and hard. He passes the janitor's station without acknowledging George's welcoming smile and wave. He sweeps into his office like a cold wind and flops into the chair behind his desk, painfully aware of his rapid heartbeat. He takes deep, slow breaths, trying to control his body's signs of anxiety as he peers out the window at Jake's car parked in the space reserved for the sheriff.

He tries to ignore the knot in his stomach. So Jake is asking about trustee business. Frank shrugs and pulls a yellow pad from his desk drawer. "Dear Mama" is as far as he gets before the tightness in his chest steals his resolve to write to his mother about how the kids are getting along with Natasha Brown. *Shit. My self-discipline is shot to hell. I can't concentrate worth a damn.* Anger and helplessness consume most of his energy. Bill assured him that time would help. It hasn't. Not for Claire and not for the boys. Jessica is too young to be aware, but the twins have changed—more demanding, somber, not much fun to be around. Yesterday Mrs. Brown said, "The twins will be fine." Her words were soft and kind and they eased his spirits, at least for a while. But she also said, "Show more affection toward the boys. Play and laugh with them a little." Frank shakes his head and mutters, "Lord knows I'll try. But who's going to make me laugh?" He pushes his musings aside along with the writing pad. His throat feels tight. After a moment, he walks to Jake's office.

*   *   *

Jake looks up from his paperwork when Frank comes in, noticing that his captain's hair could stand to be trimmed, that his shoes are a little scuffed, and that the crease in his trousers isn't as sharp as it used to be. *Frank hasn't been himself for months. Is he going to pull out of this tailspin?* "Afternoon, Frank. How are you doing?"

"Okay, all things considered." Frank takes the chair opposite Jake. "So, you want to know about this burglary at the college?"

"Right." Jake drops some papers into a file drawer. "Shoot."

"For starters, I don't think fingerprints are going to get us anywhere. There are dozens, all over the office, and those we've identified belong to people who had reasons to be there, handling whatever they handled. The one set we haven't identified probably belongs to a former secretary who left Stan's office a few months ago. She still works for the college but is on maternity leave right now. Sy is confirming her prints." Frank shifts in his chair. "No sign of forced entry. A key to the office is missing from the Physical Plant key rack. We think probably it was used to gain entry. But no one in Physical Plant can remember exactly when it walked."

"Do you think it was an inside job? Did the perp wear gloves? What?"

Frank shrugs. "These days, everybody and his brother knows about fingerprints. But something doesn't feel right here. One thing I'm pretty sure of: it wasn't a student prank."

Jake lights a cigar and takes a couple of puffs. "Bad habit. I never should have started again." He grinds the stub in the ashtray and swivels in his chair. "So why not? You know how college kids are these days. You know what Saturday nights are like in Centreville. Christ, if I had my druthers, I'd move the whole damn college to Prince George's County and be glad of it."

"Lots of luck with that." Frank looks at Jake and runs a finger across his pencil-thin moustache. "For one thing, a prank would be all over campus by now—the what if not the who." He glances away. "It seems to me the real issue is the computer hacking." He tells Jake about his meeting with Sloan.

Jake whistles. "And they still haven't straightened it out?"

"Nowhere near. This could affect all of the business operations of the college—or it might screw things up even more broadly. And it did not have to be done on site. It's a two-part job. Maybe two people involved—or more."

Jake sighs. "It sounds complicated. And time consuming. Is computer hacking really our business?"

Frank says, "It has to be."

Jake drops his bulldog face into place. It is his preferred way of signaling those who know him that something unpleasant is coming. "Look, Frank, we've been friends a long time and I gotta tell you, I'm worried about you. I know fulfilling your responsibilities to West is important to you. But this damned burglary isn't the best use of your time." He holds up a hand to preclude an interruption. "The business about the computer hacking is suggestive, but it's not your beat and you've gotta get your priorities straight. You're paid by Queen Anne's County. You're the deputy sheriff, for God's sake! You said yourself that the computer hacking might not even be local. And it might not be related to the break-in at all. So drop it. And leave the petty vandalism to Joe and Sy. Just focus on the Fitzroy case." Jake pauses. Frank's jaw is clenched and he seems to be trying to harness his anger.

"Goddamn it, Jake, be fair! You've never had a more faithful or hard-working deputy. And you know it." He leans over Jake's desk and shouts, "The only damned thing you're interested in is getting re-elected!"

The uncharacteristic outburst stuns Jake. Frank stands stiffly before him. Jake breaks the heated silence. "How about we go for a mug of coffee and talk this out?"

"Not now." Frank stalks out of the office, slamming the door.

Jake leans back in his chair. *What's up? Of course, the kids are a* problem. And Claire. But he's got help at home. Being a trustee seems to be screwing with his head. If he doesn't get his act together soon, he's gonna be out on his ear. I can't carry him forever.

Within an hour Frank telephones his apology.

*   *   *

Frank leaves his office early. *What the hell happened to my judgment?* He walks along the river, thinking about his anger and the reasons for it. Everything started with Jessica's birth. He wonders whether his life will ever feel sane again. He feels guilty about spending so much time with Nora but he can't help himself. She seems to think all the things going wrong at West are related, but Frank just doesn't see it. Somehow, he has to get his focus back. Jake is right: burglary and vandalism take second place to murder.

Chapter Twenty-Four

October snow comes early to New Hampshire—wet and heavy—and continues all day. The house is cozy and warm, but the afternoon feels long. Allie's depression has grown steadily deeper in the months since Richard's death, her emotions spiraling down like the swirling flakes outside. She can't muster much energy for making supper. *Soup will do.* Even though Buck and her friends worry about her weight loss, she can't make herself care. She ladles hot soup into a bowl. With each spoonful, she wonders whether Richard would still be alive if she had allowed him to hope. *He must have committed suicide. Must have.* She cries, tears soaking into her napkin. *Come on, get your mind on something positive.* Buck called from Chicago, on his way back from Seattle. He knew about the storm pounding the North East. He said, "Don't worry. I'll make it home tonight." Now she stirs the bowl's residue, her spoon making miniature eddies. *Buck is my rock. That's what really matters.*

The roar of snow sliding off the eaves of the back room rips the evening silence. Allie parts the curtains and looks out on the white-bound world. The pines sag under the weight of snow and freezing rain. Power lines swing in the twilight wind like the slack strings of a huge musical instrument, making sounds both throaty and eerie. At 7:00, she turns on the TV to get an update on the weather in Boston and travel advisories at Logan Airport. She only half-listens. Thoughts of Richard keep intruding—how passionately they had loved, and his passion surviving all those years of silence. *I did love him once. But—Does moving on mean I'm shallow?* She stares at the weather map, unseeing. Images of trustees and spouses after Richard's inquest flash through her mind—some smiling knowingly, some averting their eyes. Their voices are loud in her ear, telling each other that they'd always known there was something wrong with the Brady marriage, that Buck was a fool for standing by her after all he learned about the affair. The thought drags her spirits lower. *I don't think the new antidepressant is working.* She glances toward the mantel clock—7:30. *Buck must be on the ground by now, if the fog has lifted at Logan. Two and a half hours home in good weather. How long will it take him tonight?* Her shoulders droop as she realizes that she is longing for the comfort of his presence. *Buck's as strong and reliable as anyone could hope for. And tonight I need him.*

A few minutes before 9:00, she sets out an empty glass, a bucket of ice, and a bottle of single malt scotch. She leaves a note on the kitchen table.

Buck,

Glad you're home. I'm tucked in upstairs reading. Come on up, and bring your drink.

Allie.

*   *   *

The phone wakes her. Startled, she rolls over and pulls the chain on the lamp beside the bed. Nothing happens. She pulls it a half dozen times, then gropes for the phone on the night stand. "Hello? Buck! Has something happened? Where are you?"

"Everything's fine. I'm a few miles away. I just wanted to hear your sweet voice—make sure you're all right."

Allie laughs. "I'm fine." She sits up, cold wafting across her shoulders, and pulls her nightshirt across her chest. She remembers that she fell asleep with the light on. "I was asleep when you called. I think we've lost power. I can't get the light on the nightstand to work. And the house seems awfully cold."

"Well, check some other lights and the thermostat. If the power is off, you can throw the switch on the backup generator."

"Yeah, I know. See you soon." She hangs up and slides back under the down comforter, pulling the flannel sheet up over her cold nose. *It's too cold to get out of bed. Buck can deal with the generator.* Allie snuggles deeper into the covers, listening to the wind and the night noises of the house. She hears a car and thinks for a moment that it might be Buck, then realizes that the sound is fading, that the car is driving away. Another wedge of snow roars off the eaves. *What if Buck slides off the road? I better tend to the generator myself. Damn.* She grabs the flashlight from the nightstand drawer, fumbles into her fleece slippers and robe. A faint smell, like cold fireplace ashes, tinges the air.

Allie opens the bedroom door to a light gray cloud. The suddenly strong smell triggers panic. She runs down the darkened stairwell, heart pounding, nostrils burning. She covers her mouth with the sleeve of her robe. Her lungs labor. *Why didn't the smoke detectors go off?* Moving toward the kitchen, she feels heat. She stops in the powder room, wets a towel and drapes it over her head and mouth. She hears a series of minor explosions. Turning, she runs toward the study off the front hall, gasping for air, feeling dizzy.

The telephone sits in the center of the flashlight's beam. Her hands shake as she tries to dial 911. The line is dead.

The front door swings open. "Christ, Allie, your house is on fire!" Payson Lamont, her next door neighbor, is shouting. "I've called 911. Let's get the hell out of here. Now." He grabs her arm.

Allie hears her dog bark, her mother scream. She pulls away, coughing and weeping. "Mom! Daddy!" She runs up the stairs as the fire roars from the kitchen toward the front of the house.

Payson starts after her. "Allie! They're not here! Get out now!" He takes only a few steps before staggering back toward the door.

* * *

Buck pulls to the shoulder of the road, stopping to clear the windshield of freezing slush before continuing north on Route 16. Eighteen miles to go. "Shit," he mutters. *The gasoline generator isn't going to work without power.* He hasn't yet hooked up the starter battery. Maybe he should call Allie again. He cracks the driver's window and wipes the inside of the windshield with his glove. As he turns off Route 16, an SUV skids around the corner, throwing slush and forcing him onto the shoulder. He stops long enough to clear the windshield again.

As he turns onto Daniel Webster Road, he hears a siren and, a few blocks away, sees the swiveling white and red light of an approaching emergency vehicle. In an instant his heart is pounding like a jackhammer. The tanker truck from West Ossipee slithers behind him, like an animal stalking prey. Buck sees the flames from half a block away. He skids to a stop, jumps from the Lincoln and races up the driveway, leaving headlights on, motor running. "My wife," he yells to Payson. "Where's Allie?"

Payson points toward the burning house. "Inside. She wouldn't come out, for Christ sake."

Buck races into the house, Payson and a jumble of other voices yelling after him.

"Allie! Allie!" He coughs out his first breath of smoke, taking the steps two at a time. Through the crackle of the flame he hears Allie's cries of "Mom, Daddy." He follows the sound of her voice, turns toward the rear hall window, and grabs her just as the ceiling falls. She tries to pull away. *My God, she doesn't know me.* His heart feels about to explode. Allie goes limp. *No, no,* his mind screams. The hall window shatters. Cold air rushes past. The bulb in the hall fixture explodes. Blood runs down his cheek. He gropes his way down the stairs and stumbles out the door, Allie unconscious in his arms.

An EMT from Center Harbor takes Allie from Buck. Three men from the Rescue Squad strap her to a stretcher, cover her with blankets. She doesn't respond to questions. The medic hooks her up to a ventilator, shoots IV fluids into her bleeding arm, and puts her in the waiting ambulance.

Buck strains against the man holding him back. "Is she OK?" he shouts as the ambulance door slams shut. He begins to shiver. Two more fire engines from the West Ossipee station nearly drown out his words.

The EMT says, "She has some second degree burns. She's semi-conscious. We've got to get her to the clinic in Center Harbor."

Buck holds back an impulse to grab him by the collar. "But is she going to be all right?"

"I can't say. Sorry. Right now, we've got to tend to you."

Buck yanks his arm away. "There's damn well nothing wrong with me!"

"Just take some oxygen and let me see to that cut on your face and the nasty bump on your head." The mask slipping into place muffles Buck's protest.

He looks around, taking in the commotion in front of his house. The fire chief steps out of the truck, a yellow slicker shielding him from the weather. Neighbors gather across the street where Payson Lamont holds forth. Buck catches the words, "Christ, the guys on that squad were quick. I couldn't get her to leave the house." Mostly the small crowd watches in silence, some looking regretful, others looking relieved.

The EMT makes quick work of swabbing the cut and examining Buck's skull. "To be on the safe side, we'll take you to a doctor."

"I'm not gonna see any damned doctor! Just take care of my wife!" Buck runs a hand through his hair, winces when he hits the lump. "I'll sign a release. Give me the damned form." Buck scrawls his name on the form and thrusts it at the scowling EMT.

"Okay, you're free to go." The EMT sounds sour.

Payson steps off the curb and over a couple of hoses hooked up to the tanker. "Jesus, Buck, I'm sorry."

"PL, what the hell happened?"

Payson stands shivering, wet and hatless. "I don't know. Rita and I were watching TV in the back room, sort of waiting for the storm to take out the TV cable, when our power went out. We talked a little, but when it didn't come back on, I went to the window to see whether anybody else had power. I thought I saw smoke coming out of the roof at the back of your house. I went outside and smelled it—nasty—chemical smoke. I tried to call Allie but her line was dead. I called 911 and then ran over. She was in the hall. I tried to get her to leave, but she pulled away from me, all wild-eyed, calling for her parents. She seemed disoriented, panicked. She ran back upstairs."

Buck rubs his forehead. "Her parents were killed in a house fire when she was little."

Payson shakes his head. "Geeze, Buck. She must have been… I'm so sorry. If you hadn't come when you did…"

"You did everything you could." Buck turns toward the fire chief. "Any chance of saving the house?"

"Maybe. Some of it, anyway. The wind's dropped and the storm is mostly rain now. Both should help." The chief looks at Buck. "If I were you, Mr. Brady, I'd get to the hospital. This smoke is toxic as hell."

*   *   *

By the time Buck arrives at the Center Harbor Clinic, Allie is already in the ER. He paces the waiting area. The ER doctor says her burns are mostly second degree, accompanied by fluid-filled blisters. "She'll recover. Skin grafts probably won't be necessary."

After another hour's wait, a technician ushers Buck to Allie's bedside. Bandages cover her right arm and hand and half of her face. Buck takes her left hand in his and kisses it. Allie's lips twitch. "I'm glad you're here. Will I be all right?"

Buck tries hard to look reassuring. He kisses her hand again and whispers, "Damn right!" It is all he can manage before his voice cracks.

He still holds Allie's hand when an attendant pushes her gurney toward the emergency room doorway, and the ambulance waiting to take her to the Hitchcock Burn Unit in Hanover. With the click of the door latch, she disappears from view. *I wish the damned thing looked less like a hearse.* He wipes his coat sleeve across his face, drives toward Hanover.

*   *   *

Buck sits through the night holding her hand, sometimes dozing but mostly thinking. "God, Allie," he whispers, "I should have been there. None of this would have happened if I'd been there, taking care of you." He listens to voices from the nurses' station, to all the sounds of the hospital. He hadn't realized it would be so noisy at night. He tries to take comfort from so many doctors and nurses within call. "You've got to get well, Allie. You've got to. You are my center." Allie stirs and he realizes that he spoke aloud. He clamps his mouth shut. Over and again he reviews their chain of recent disasters. *Why are we suddenly the most unlucky people in the world? How can I keep you safe, Allie?* Pain in his head derails his thoughts, steals his focus.

*   *   *

In the morning, knowing that Allie will recover, Buck tolerates a lecture by her attending physician on the physiology of the skin and how they calculate the amount of intravenous fluids a burn patient needs. When the doctor leaves, Buck asks her what she remembers about the fire, whether she wants him to bring anything—a real nightgown, perhaps, or a book. Allie turns her face to the wall and closes her eyes. He doesn't know what to do—or what else to say—or what her silence means. He stops talking. Before he leaves the hospital, he writes a list of things that need to be done: call their children, call his office, find out how much damage had been done to the house, see their insurance agent. Find temporary quarters—perhaps in Meredith, on Lake Winnipesaukee? Whether to attend the upcoming West College Board meeting is an afterthought.

He walks across the icy parking lot, his pace slow, his legs heavy, his back painful. He rests his forehead against the steering wheel. When he straightens up, he feels as if he's tapped a hidden reservoir of energy. "Fuck 'em." He turns the ignition key. "Nobody and nothing's going to get Buck Brady *or* his wife! Fuck 'em all." He swings out of the hospital parking lot and crumples his written list into a tight ball. He picks up his cell phone to call their children.

*   *   *

The fire marshal, a captain from the State Police barrack near Plymouth, and Sheriff Knute Coutermarsh are talking quietly when Buck climbs out of his car. Buck and a detective reach the cluster of men at the same time, as the marshal says that the fire was set. "We found all the usual signs of arson: several points of origin, residue of flammable liquids, and one hell of a hot fire.

"What you got there?" the sheriff asks, looking at the detective.

"Two wooden matches from near the garbage bin and blood from the telephone terminal box here below the kitchen window. Guess he caught a finger on the jagged edge by the seal. No prints though. Looks like the perp used latex gloves 'cause there's talc residue on the bottom of the box right where the lines into the house were yanked from the terminals."

"Anything else?"

"Yeah. I found a cigarette butt over there." He points to a spot a few feet away.

Buck says, "Can you get DNA?"

The sheriff looks at Buck as if noticing him for the first time. "Good mornin', Buck. Sorry about your house. Between the cigarette butt and the blood, we've got a mighty fine chance at DNA."

Buck stares at his house. "God, it stinks around here," he says, reaching for his handkerchief.

The sheriff turns back to his detectives. "Take these evidence bags to the van and then comb the yard. See if you can find anything else—anything at all. Maybe there's a footprint out in the yard that hasn't been trampled."

"Right."

The sheriff turns to Buck. "We're almost finished with the

preliminary investigation. Your insurance guy is free to visit the house any time after noon today." He pulls the zipper of his jacket a few inches down from his chin as he continues. "There's no doubt it was arson. And the telephone line into the house was torn from the outside terminal box."

"Christ Almighty. What about the goddamned smoke alarms?"

"The main control panel for the smoke detectors in the front hall looks as if it was tampered with, but the detectives need a technician from the firm that installed the system to determine exactly how it was done. Definitely a sophisticated job."

Buck massages his forehead. His gut churns. He tries to imagine people who would want to destroy him. *Who are they? And why me and Allie? If I ever find out who nearly killed my wife, I'll get the fucking bastard.*

Chapter Twenty-Five

"Rebecca." Jim tightens his grip on the kitchen phone but his voice remains mild. "You can't just 'pop in for dessert' when we've invited trustees to the house for dinner."

"*You* invited them, not I. *I* have work to finish." Her voice takes on the cold, legalistic tone Jim imagines she uses in the courtroom. "When we talked about my obligations as the president's wife, I agreed to be around for all the Board meetings. Even the *committee* meetings. This is just a dinner."

"This isn't a contract negotiation! You could have said no when I suggested it." Jim hears the pitch of his voice spiral upwards. "They'll be here in less than two hours! I expect you to be here, too." He hangs up the phone and wipes perspiration from his upper lip. *What are the chances?* He gazes through the window, across the back yard toward the river. The air seems as hazy as his focus.

The dinner party had seemed like a good idea: invite the Roths, the Bradys, Bill Baxter, and Adrian Livingston for a quiet dinner and try to smooth over some of the hostilities getting in the way of the Finance Committee. When Bill mentioned bringing Nora, Jim invited Frank to make an even number.

And now the whole damn thing is falling apart before it even gets started. Not that it's Buck's fault his house burned. And I'm damned sorry about Allie. But their absence knocks one hell of a hole in the primary purpose. And finding out about it just a couple of hours before... Just having a dinner will be all right—no one but Bill and Rebecca the wiser. Jim takes off his glasses and massages the bridge of his nose. *Could you have chosen a worse time to be a bitch, Becca?* Jim looks at his watch again. *How the hell will it look if you don't show up?*

Fifteen minutes before the guests are expected, Rebecca arrives. She sweeps past the door to the sitting room without speaking and goes upstairs. Jim draws a deep breath and exhales slowly. But his stomach stays clenched. He wills himself to relax. *She's a professional. No matter how pissed off she is at me, she won't let it show. She'll be a cordial hostess.*

She comes down just as the doorbell rings for the first arrival. She's changed into a silky beige tunic and pants, and wears a chunky necklace of carved wooden beads with long earrings to match. Her brown hair is pulled back and fastened into a fancy ponytail that hangs to her shoulders. If he didn't know otherwise, Jim would have thought she'd been preparing for the party all afternoon.

Jim and Rebecca stand side by side, smiling, as Jim opens the door to Bill and Nora. Behind his greeting and coat taking, the bell rings again. Nate and Priscilla arrive, closely followed by Frank and Adrian.

*   *   *

Gathered in the sitting room for drinks, everyone seems to keep a polite distance. Rebecca chats with Frank and the Roths. Jim engages Adrian, Bill and Nora in small talk, but keeps an uneasy eye on Rebecca's group. Priscilla's eyes look slightly unfocused and she seems to be enunciating with great care.

Jim says, "Too bad Buck and Allie aren't here. I'm not surprised, of course, given what happened. Right up till the last minute, Buck thought it might work out, but … You've heard that his house burned down two weeks ago? Allie's been in the hospital." Nora gasps. A few feet away, Frank snaps to attention. All eyes turn to Jim. "She inhaled lots of smoke, has some second degree burns." Jim looks down, swirls ice in the bottom of his glass. "He said he didn't want to talk about it till he has more to report, but she seems to be reliving the fire that killed her parents when she was a child. She's in a private facility now."

"Oh, God. That's awful!" There's no mistaking the genuine sympathy in Nora's voice. "How did it happen?" Everyone is listening.

"Buck was called out to Seattle on the spur of the moment and almost got weathered-in in Chicago on the way back. When I think what would have happened if he hadn't come home when he did …" Jim pulls his hand down his face and shudders. He repeats what Buck said happened and what the investigators found. "The smoke detectors, the phone lines, the accelerants. Whoever did it, they didn't care whether someone got killed. Maybe even wanted it."

Adrian Livingston says, "Surely not." He sounds shocked. But it's so contrary to his assume-the-worst nature that Jim wonders.

Priscilla turns to Frank. "When someone is killed, don't you look to spouses and family first? Isn't that a rule of thumb?"

Nate says. "Pris!"

Pris smiles loosely. "Just an observation."

Frank looks uncomfortable. "In cases of arson—in all crimes—there can be all sorts of motives. I've heard nothing to suggest that Allie was the target. Perhaps Buck was the intended victim."

"Who would be out to get Buck?" asks Nora.

Rebecca shrugs. "He does seem to rub people the wrong way." Jim glares at her.

Nora snorts. "But who would burn his house—endanger lives—because he's irritating?"

Pris says, "But Buck *is* the husband whose wife deceived him, whose marriage is hitting the rocks. Who else *would* want to hurt Allie?"

Bill breaks the stunned silence that follows. "Really, Pris. That was uncalled for."

Pris's jaw takes on a stubborn jut. "Who else had a reason to push Richard Emory overboard? Who else had a fight with Pete Fitzroy and then put him in a car with faulty brakes? People around Buck Brady end up dead!"

Nate, poised ominously on the balls of his feet, his expression fierce, moves toward Pris. Jim moans inwardly. Nate says, "For God's sake, Pris!"

She has a wine glass in one hand and a couple of drops splash to the floor. as she raises her hands in surrender. "Okay, okay. Maybe that was out of line. My apologies to all—especially to the Sloans."

Jim inhales deeply, realizes he'd been holding his breath. *Already she's had too much to drink. A piss poor apology, but if it defuses the situation, that's all that matters.*

"Really, Priscilla, there's no call to make a scene." Adrian Livingston sounds both disapproving and disdainful.

Frank's tone is cool and calm when he says, "Those incidents were widely separated in time, place, and method. Even if they're related, Buck seems devoted to Allie—in spite of everything."

Nora furrows her brow. "But there's been an incredible spate of incidents, hasn't there? Richard Emory drowned, Pete Fitzroy's brakes tampered with, my boat blown up, and now Buck's house …"

Jim thinks about the break-in at Stan's office but says nothing.

Frank speaks quietly. "Someone vandalized Stan's office."

Jim holds his breath, silently willing Frank to stop there, when Nora adds, "And Van was mugged. Good Lord, you'd think someone has it in for West College!" Her comment seems especially loud in the ensuing silence.

"That's preposterous," Jim says.

Everyone is talking at once—some suggesting reasons why the long string of incidents are unrelated and others proffering arguments for a master plot behind them all—when Rebecca announces dinner, and declares murder and mayhem off limits for further discussion.

Jim and Rebecca sit at the ends of the table. Bill, Nora, and Nate sit on one side, Pris, Adrian, and Frank on the other. The conversation meanders from one safe topic to another—the Superbowl prospects for the Baltimore Ravens, the league prospects for the various West College teams, the weather, the anticipated size of the freshman class, the Faberge exhibit in Philadelphia, the Baltimore symphony season.

Jim looks from one guest to another. Tension crackles beneath the polite conversations. Rebecca seems bent on not glancing his way. Pris eats mostly in silence, calling often for more wine, glaring at Nora every time Nate says anything to her. The only exchanges between Nate and Nora that Jim actually catches through the conversational crossfire are completely innocuous. But Pris barely takes her eyes off them.

When they return to the sitting room for brandy, the tension remains thick as fog. Pris is unsteady on her feet and everyone else is politely not noticing her inebriation. Nate finishes his brandy quickly and says, "Okay, Pris. Time to go."

"What if I'm not ready yet?"

Nate smiles and sets her brandy glass on the table. "Come on, old girl. You're about to turn into a pumpkin."

When he takes her arm, Pris pulls back as if to resist. Finally, she stands and says, "Well, just make sure you drive carefully. Everyone *else* on the Finance Committee seems accident prone."

When the Roths move toward the hall, the others rise and take their leave as well. Bill says to Jim, "You handled the evening as well as anyone could have. We'll talk things over sometime tomorrow, whenever we can get a few private minutes." Jim nods, dreading the prospect.

* * *

Jim tells the catering crew to finish the clean-up in the morning and joins Rebecca upstairs. She has already changed and is propped up in bed, a folder of contracts on her lap, a red pen in her hand. He had a half-formed intention of making love—or at least of having a little contact comfort. "Are you going to be reading long?"

"I told you when you called that I have work to do. I need to finish these mark-ups and messenger them to my office in the morning." She scowls. "What a waste that was! I put everything aside to be the happy hostess and the whole damn dinner was a disaster!" She seems about to say more but Jim leaves—goes back downstairs, pours a tall whiskey, and takes it to the porch.

Moonlight ripples on the Corsica. The peaceful flow of the river draws him closer. He walks to the water's edge and thinks about Richard Emory, about how it would feel to drown. *My presidency is falling apart around me. My marriage is falling apart. It isn't the Board that's jinxed. It's me.* He steps toward the river. Another step. Ripplets break gently on the shore. Another step. The cool, black water flows around his ankles and into his shoes. He smells the mud that sucks at his shoes and steals them from his feet as he takes another step. The river mud oozes through his socks, soft and inviting. Pain shoots through his foot when he steps on a sharp rock—a real, here and now pain. *Jesus Christ! Man up.* He backs out of the river, leaving his shoes in their watery grave.

Trooping back to the house, his step is lighter. Not that he wishes anyone ill, but without Buck, the biggest threat to a smooth Board meeting is lifted. He and Stan have a reprieve.

Chapter Twenty-Six

When Pris leaves the lecture hall at West College, night has fallen. Satan, Santa Claus, and a black cat careen past. Some things haven't changed since her own undergraduate days. She smiles wistfully and sighs. *It feels like two lifetimes since Nate and I traveled from door to door with the twins in tow and stood guard so bigger kids couldn't steal their candy.* As she drops the evening's program for "The Historical Roots of Halloween" onto the passenger seat, her irritation that Nate wouldn't join her for the lecture resurfaces. The press of Foundation business has never kept him from doing anything he really wanted to do. As she jams the key into the ignition, two acquaintances who attended the lecture hail her. One leans down to speak through the open window. "How about a night cap? We could stop at Doc's Riverside Grille."

The cocktails before dinner and the Chardonnay with the meal have long since worn off. "Sounds great. I'll follow you." Turning the key, she notices the slow, rhythmic shake of her hand. Nate always cautions her about drinking and driving. She pushes the thought aside and turns into the parking lot by the pub.

Doc's is noisy, the crowd decked out in Halloween costumes both traditional and bizarre. Pris finishes her first Old Fashioned as the waiter delivers a second round. Her thoughts wander to her favorite bridge partner—a lively competitor who, toward the end of every bridge evening, says, "Pris, sometimes too much is still not enough"—and then the two of them laugh and raise their glasses again. Pris smiles and sips her second drink. The three acquaintances reminisce about their college days and dissect the lecture they just heard on the "true" meaning of Halloween. Pris feels particularly witty and entertaining. It is 10:35 and several drinks later when she says her goodbyes and leaves for home. She hums, and unlocks the car on the second try.

Eventually she gets the seat belt fastened. She pulls out of the parking lot, heading for Route 301, feeling relaxed and in control of the world. "Bastard," she mutters as oncoming headlights blind her. She swings quickly back across the white lines, wondering which of the two is real. She squints ahead, sits more upright, but the white line continues to blur and go double. She opens the window, takes a deep breath of chilly air, and closes one eye so there is only one line. "You're tipsy. Pay attention." She makes a concerted effort to keep the car's path midway between the shoulder and the center line. "See, you *can* do it," she chortles, just before the car again veers left of center.

Another mile down the road, she brakes at the last minute and turns left. The tires of the car behind her send out a high pitched squeal as the driver swerves and leans on the horn. *Drive your hand right through the steering wheel, why don'cha?* She glances in the rearview mirror. "Fuck off. Just go fuck yourself." She half smiles. "It's more fun than blowing a horn." She giggles. "Or maybe that depends on whose *horn* you're blowing." She laughs again, and the two right wheels drop off the pavement. She corrects sharply.

When she realizes how close she came to crashing into the bridge abutment where Pete Fitzroy crashed, her heart thuds painfully. The driver of a car speeding toward her flicks on his high beams just before a curve in the road. *Christ, he's coming right at me!* Blinded, she swerves right.

A minute later a car comes up on her rear bumper, flashing high beams, tapping the horn. She slows down, but the car doesn't pass. She accelerates. It follows. As the road straightens, the car pulls out as if to pass, but lingers alongside while the driver makes obscene gestures through the open passenger window. Her glance is brief, just long enough to see that the driver wears white clothes and has a clown face, his huge red smile fixed and distorted. Wind from the open window whips off his red and white hat. She jerks her attention back to the road. But all she can see is a blurred pattern of light and dark. She swallows hard and glances left. *Why doesn't he pass? What the hell's he doing?* The clown's car is drifting toward her. She grips the steering wheel with sweaty palms and watches the pavement slide off to her left, the unpaved shoulder squeeze in from the right. When she finally sees his taillights, they are big as pumpkins. Fence posts fly by, suddenly turning into dried cornstalks. *Am I driving through a field of pumpkins?* She hears pumpkins exploding, feels the engine's heat through the floorboards.

The rest seems to happen in slow motion—cornstalks snapping, metal crunching. A yellow caution sign dances along the rear quarter panel and the car floats onto its left wheels. The dream explodes as the front end of the car buries itself in the trunk of a large oak.

* * *

Pris doesn't remember throwing up, but the smell of vomit almost makes her throw up again. She is slumped forward. The glare of headlights past the deflated airbag stabs her left eye. She hears a car stop, a door slam, footsteps. *What happened? How long have I been here?* Somebody raps on the driver's window. She pushes the button. Nothing happens. "It won't go down," she mumbles.

"What?" asks the silhouette at her window. He pulls on the door to no effect. "Are you hurt?"

"That clown ran me off the road," Pris mumbles. The man is holding a cell phone. She knows he's agitated, but she can't grasp the words that wash over her. "Yeah, she's on the Route 301, near the turn off to Queenstown... No, just one car... She's conscious—but bleeding around the face. Maybe other places, too... I don't know. I can't get the door open... She's incoherent... Yeah, I'll wait... No, no, I won't touch her."

The police arrive, lights flashing. An officer sets flares along the road. Pris hears an ambulance wail, sees more flashing lights. Someone pries open the door. *All these people. So much going on.*

"I'm aw right." Pris struggles to get the words out. Something warm and wet oozes from her forehead, drips from her nose and lower lip.

"I don't think so, ma'am." A flashlight beam flicks over her body. "Where does it hurt?"

"I dunnow."

"Can you move your head from side to side?" She responds by turning her head away from the flashlight beam. She tastes blood and feels throbbing deep in her head and chest. Fingers poke her neck and feel along the top of her spine. Hands pull at her. A soothing baritone says, "Easy does it. Easy. Go easy." The words are reassuring. And then she feels nothing. When Pris opens her eyes, she is out of the car and strapped to a stretcher, a brace fastened around her neck. She tries to say something but can't remember what she wanted to say. She keeps seeing the clown giving her the finger, seeing his face, his red and white hat. She whimpers. *If Nate had come with me, this wouldn't have happened. He wouldn't have let me drink so much.* She moans, pain the focus of her world.

* * *

"Mrs. Roth?" Pris feels like she's swimming to the surface from some great depth. She opens her eyes in spite of the pain in her head. She lies on her back in a hospital bed, hands clasped across her stomach. "Someone will look in on you later." Pris just stares at the ceiling.

Two police officers come in. The short, blond woman leans against the wall by the door. Frank stops by her bed. "Hello, Pris." He looks from the IV in her left arm to the monitor behind her head before saying, "Officer Barker and I need to ask you some questions. Can you talk? Can you tell us what happened?"

"I was just driving home when this clown ran me off the road."

"Did you get a look at the other driver?"

"I just told you. It was a *clown*—with red and white make-up! Or maybe it was a mask. Anyway, he gave me the finger as he passed—out the passenger side window—pumping his arm up and down. He wore white gloves. His hat blew off."

"Was he black? Caucasian? Asian?"

"Caucasian. Well, I mean, that was my impression. But I don't really know."

"But you're sure it was a man."

Pris scowls, then winces as pain shoots across her face. "It was a *clown*. That's all I know for sure."

"Was the driver alone in the car?"

"Of course he was alone! How else could I have seen him, giving me the finger out the passenger side window?"

"So there was nobody in the back seat?"

Pris plucks at the white sheet covering her lower body. "How the hell am I supposed to have seen into the backseat? Anyway, what difference does it make? That clown tried to kill me!"

"Calm down, Pris. I know you're in pain. But you must answer my questions. Can you tell us anything else about the driver? Anything at all. Or the car?"

Pris shakes her head and moans as pain throbs through her head and face. "Nothing. Except I think his hair was brown. Dark, anyway."

As they leave, Barker says to Frank, "It sounds to me like some partygoer having a little fun—maybe drinking, too. But given her condition, I doubt we could make a case even if we could find the driver."

She speaks quietly but Pris hears every word. She shouts at their backs, "But he tried to kill me!"

The night nurse comes in, starch-stiff. "Settle down, now. There's no need to disrupt the whole floor."

*   *   *

Pris is half-propped up in bed, trying to eat a little oatmeal and toast, when Nate comes into her room. "Oh, Nate! Thank God you're here. I called the house three times already. Where have you *been*?"

Nate stops by her bed and brushes her forehead with a kiss. "The doctor said the best thing was for you to get a good night's sleep. But I'm here now."

Pris's eyes fill with tears. "Oh, Nate, I was so scared. And I have these awful cuts on my face. Do you think I'll have scars? No one has told me anything. The doctor hasn't even been in this morning."

"I'm sure you'll be just fine." He gives her hand a brief squeeze, then stares out the third floor window overlooking the hospital parking lot, fists jammed into his pants pockets. "When the police called, they said your blood alcohol level was almost .32—not that far from comatose!" He casts a glance in her direction, then returns to his scrutiny of the parking lot. "You could have killed yourself, Pris—or someone else. If you don't shape up, your drinking *will* kill you—one way or another. And then what will happen to the twins?"

Pris glances at her rumpled, disheveled, bandaged form, pats her frizzy hair, and dabs her eyes with the edge of the sheet. "Nate, it was awful. This car ran me off the road *on purpose!* I know he did."

"How can you know anything, the state you were in? You could have hallucinated the whole thing."

"I wasn't that high! I know what happened! It was a man wearing clown make-up and a red and white hat. He gave me the finger!"

Nate looks at her with narrowed eyes. "Do you know how unlikely that sounds?" He shakes his head. "Pris, I can't take your drinking anymore."

Tears spring to Pris's eyes. "Don't leave me, Nate. I'll do anything. What do you want me to do? Go into rehab?"

Nate sighs. "We've been around that block three times already. I don't know how much more I can take." He starts toward the door. "I've got to get to the office. The doctor said they will keep you for tests and observation—twenty-four hours at least, probably detox. Call. I'll pick you up. Or send a car." He walks out without touching her again, without looking back.

Pris drops her head back onto her pillow and squeezes her eyes shut. *What if this is the last straw? What if he leaves me? What will I do if he leaves me?* She notices that her hands are sweaty and trembling. She rubs them on the sheet and tries to stop shaking but can't. "God, I need a drink," she mutters. Hearing herself, she blinks back tears. She hasn't even finished breakfast. *Maybe if I stop drinking—if I show Nate how much I love him—things will come right between us again.* Tears seep from under her closed eyelids. *I'll go to Dr. Marsden's clinic. Get straight.* She draws a deep shuddering breath. *That's what I'll do. As soon as I'm out of here, I'll dry out. And I'll do it by Thanksgiving.*

Thinking about the clinic—about the embarrassment and the gossip—about getting sober, and never taking another drink of alcohol—makes her hands sweat and tremble even more. Her breath comes in painful gasps. When the orderly comes in for the breakfast tray, Pris is curled into a fetal position, shaking and sobbing. The orderly calls the doctor.

Pris says, "I want to go into rehab. Now. Today."

"Mrs. Roth, you need to detox before any rehab facility will take you." He gives her an injection.

As the drug starts to take effect, as her tight muscles begin to relax and her panic begins to recede, she thinks that maybe a drug overdose wouldn't be such a bad way to die.

Chapter Twenty-Seven

Van looks across the dining table at Lissa, at the silky wing of hair lying across her cheek like a slice of midnight. *My God, she's gorgeous.* His children's kitchen banter as they share the after-dinner clean-up floats into the dining room, sweet music to Van's ear. Lissa, smiling, pulls him to his feet. "It's about time we had a real greeting," she murmurs and kisses him soundly. "Mmmmm. I feel an early-to-bed night coming on."

Van's beginning tingle of arousal fades. He clears his throat. "I have been thinking—with all the children in the house—I have been thinking I should bunk down here on the futon tonight."

"You can't be serious!" Her eyes search his face. "You are. You *are* serious." Her laugh sounds like a mixture of amusement and irritation. "Van, your children aren't *children*. Do you think they think we don't *do* it?"

"Of course not. But—I would feel—very awkward."

Lissa steps closer. "Well, let's see what I can do to make you a little more comfortable." She licks his ear.

Van draws back, glances toward the kitchen, and speaks more

quietly. "Lissa, I mean it. Sex—with my children in the house—and us not married—it is not something I can do."

"Oh, for God's sake! You are such a prude sometimes!" Her nostrils flare.

"And sometimes you are very inconsiderate."

Lissa's head snaps up. "What do you mean by that?"

"I mean the way you criticized my children all through dinner." He does not acknowledge that her criticisms of his children felt like criticisms of him, too. But at a gut level, his children are extensions of himself.

"What are you talking about?" She takes a step back.

The door to the kitchen swings open and Johannes pokes his head in. "Hey, Pops. We're gonna take in a movie. You guys wanna come?"

Van glances at Lissa. "Uh, no. We are—talking. Have a good time."

Johannes waggles his eyebrows. "You, too." The back door bangs. Van turns back to Lissa's tense face, wishing he could take back his last comment.

"Exactly how was I inconsiderate to your children?"

Van takes a deep breath and strives for a neutral tone. "Sit down. Have another glass of wine." He leads her back to the table and they resume their seats, he at the head of the table, she to his right. He leans toward her across the corner. "It is just that there were several instances that I thought awkward. For example, when you told Pieter he should Americanize the spelling of his name and then stopped him from talking about his current project at work."

Lissa looks surprised. "That wasn't a criticism. It was an observation. If his name is going to be pronounced 'Peter,' why not spell it that way? It would be simpler. And I didn't stop him from talking about his work at the boat yard. I just said that I hoped he wasn't going to go into the technical details of keel design and float tanks and all that rubbish."

"It is not rubbish to anyone who knows these things."

"Exactly."

Van chooses not to respond to her triumphant tone. "You told Geertruyt she should go by her middle name, get contact lenses, and change her hair style and clothing."

Lissa looks pained. "I didn't say it like that! I was very diplomatic. It's just that Mary would be so much easier. And more appealing. Geertruyt is—formidable. And it must be awkward, having to spell it out all the time, telling people to pronounce it 'Gare-troot'—all of that." Van feels defensive. He chose the children's names, had argued Sheila into recognizing his Dutch heritage rather than her Italian roots. "She has lovely blue eyes and thick, luxurious hair. But those glasses—loosely knotted hair held in place by a pencil—those clothes straight out of L.L.Bean… Any woman who majored in computer science and works as a systems analyst has enough to overcome. She doesn't need to look like a geek, too."

Van remembers Geertruyt's face going slowly scarlet, and his heart seems to fester again on her behalf. But she held her own very well. "I simply wanted you to know that the whole exchange made Geertruyt uncomfortable. And telling Kirsten she has a good face for TV, that you could get her a job with CNN for more money than she can ever hope to make teaching music in elementary school, that was a clear rejection of her values. Money is not important to her. And she likes living in a small town."

"Well, she might feel differently about that if you moved to New York."

Van stops toying with his napkin ring, tries to stop his surprise from sliding into anger. "We have never discussed me moving to New York."

Lissa leans closer and puts her hands over Van's. She smiles, her tone coaxing when she says, "Look, I didn't mean to be critical. It's just that I think Geertruyt and Kirsten could benefit from a little feminine guidance. And as for living in New York—well, no, we haven't discussed it. But things are pretty serious between us, and I hoped … Just think of the advantages the city has to offer—theater, music, the most amazing cultural diversity—not to mention the connections I could make for you and your children." She sits back, tucking a strand of hair behind her small, shapely ear. "There's nothing for me in Centreville, but there are a ton of colleges and universities in New York."

When did she start thinking I might move to New York? Van keeps his tone polite, but it comes out icy. "One does not lightly walk away from a tenured faculty position at a good school. I know Ph.D.'s who have spent years looking for full-time, tenure track positions."

Lissa shrugs. "If we were married, you wouldn't have to find something quickly. You wouldn't have to work at all if you didn't want to."

"Of course I would want to! I have paid my own way since I was a teenager!" Van grips his napkin ring, outrage close to the surface. He unclenches his hand and struggles to maintain a quiet, even tone. "I provided a home for Sheila. If I marry again, I shall do the same for my second wife. And my home is here."

Lissa sucks in a bushel of air. "You are so retro!" She leans back in her chair. "And as long as we're on the topic of dinner conversation, what about me? The way you all cut me out, talking about your family traditions—going on and on about what you eat and what you do for every holiday from Fourth of July to St. Patrick's Day. I've never felt more out of the loop in my life."

"Perhaps that conversation made us sound more rigid than we truly are. It is just that since my divorce—since the children left home—holidays are the only times we all are together. And family is important to me."

Lissa takes a deep breath, and her smile seems relieved. "You would be a good father!"

Something in her tone makes Van wary. "I had the impression that you do not approve of the way I have reared my children."

Lissa laughs and covers his hand with hers. "I'm not talking about *those* children. I'm talking about *our* children."

Van feels sucker-punched. "You think we would have children?"

Lissa looks disconcerted. "Well, I mean, if we were to marry."

Van licks his lips and takes another sip of wine. Once he'd had the vasectomy, Sheila had been completely uninterested in sex. Perhaps that was what led to her affair with the bartender at the yacht club. Van stares at his wineglass, searching for the right words. If he asks Lissa to marry him, of course he must tell her. But ... "Lissa. My youngest child is twenty. I cannot imagine a circumstance in which I would want to father another child."

"I never thought ..." Van hears tears in her voice and looks up. Lissa is chewing her lower lip. "I thought you liked children."

"I do. But my age—your age—your career."

"I'm only thirty-five. And you aren't yet forty-five. Of course my career is important, but it isn't the whole of my life. I always thought that when I found the right man—someone smart and handsome and kind—when the time was right ... You're that man. The man I want to father my children. This is the right time for me. For us." Lissa covers his hand with hers. "Van, will you marry me?"

The question leaves Van speechless. Of course he's thought about marrying Lissa. For the last couple of months, he's thought of little else. But he never imagined that she would be the one to ask the question. Live in New York? He is trying to decide what to say when Lissa continues. "Children are why I assumed—why it's important that we live together."

"In New York." Van shifts in his chair, stands, looks at Lissa.

She shrugs, offers a placating smile. "I *hoped* that you would move to New York. But if not, I guess we could commute."

"That is not my idea of a marriage."

"Well, Centreville is not my idea of a life." Lissa crosses her arms. She sounds wounded.

Van draws another deep breath. "I suggest we sleep on this and talk tomorrow."

"Don't start playing the calm, stoic male! Sleeping on it won't change a damned thing. Not for me, anyway." She studies his face. "If you don't want to marry me, say so. Now."

"We will talk about it in the morning." Van steps toward her. "Do not act impulsively."

"Who's acting?" She leaps up and rushes from the room.

Van hears her footsteps on the stairs. He sighs and moves slowly toward the downstairs bathroom linen closet where he has stowed his ditty bag and a new pair of flannel pajamas. Preparing for bed, he reviews their turbulent affair: the passionate sex, the joy of feeling so wanted, the excitement of sampling the big city offset by her tendency to take over without consultation. And now this business of children. *Could I deny my wife a child?*

* * *

Van settles onto the living room futon and pulls the fleece throw over his legs, keenly aware of the unfamiliar bind of pajamas on his usually naked body. The pajamas are necessary for his sense of propriety. His children would understand.

The kitchen door opens and his children's voices come quietly but clearly to Van. He hears them making microwave popcorn and setting up to play cards. In his mind's eye, he sees the familiar picture of the four of them settled at the kitchen table to play euchre. He hears the ruffle of shuffled cards.

Johannes says, "Why do you suppose Pop is sacking out in the living room?"

Geertruyt, sounding every inch the big sister, says, "That's none of our business."

Johannes laughs. "What does that have to do with a man's need to know?"

Pieter says, "We might as well make spades trump. Pick it up." Cards whisper on the table top.

"They didn't sound too happy after we left the dining room." Kirsten sounds pensive. "One for us."

Pieter's tone is dry. "They didn't sound too happy *before* we left, either. Two for us."

"Trouble in paradise?" As always, Johannes' voice holds a hint of laughter.

Kirsten chuckles. "We can only hope! Can you imagine spending every holiday for the rest of our lives with *her*?"

"Shhhh. Not so loud. Besides, I thought you liked her. One for us." The sound of cards being tapped on the wooden table accompanies Geertruyt's comment.

Kirsten sighs. "If I thought it'd make Daddy happy, I'd like Godzilla."

Johannes laughs. "What an image."

Kirsten says, "Seriously, can you imagine Daddy being happy with Melissa? She thinks I should abandon teaching—she doesn't even respect the profession. What's she doing on a college board of trustees anyway?"

Pieter says, "Our win. Another?" Someone shuffles the cards.

Geertruyt says, "I, for one, suggest that we do not count our chickens just yet. Dad is probably in the living room because we're in the kitchen. You know how he is."

Kirsten sighs mightily. "Yeah. You're probably right."

"Don't lose all hope. We'll see what the morrow brings," Pieter intones. In his normal voice he says, "Look, if no one wants to play more cards, how about a walk down to the river?"

"Sure."

"Count me in."

"Me, too."

Chairs scrape. The back door opens and bangs shut.

Van punches the blue and tan striped pillow Nora gave him for the futon. *When would I ever have known how they felt? Would Lissa really drive a wedge into my family? Maybe if I talk to her—low key, no anger—explain that I will try to make it as easy as possible for her to fit in ...* Van rolls onto his side. *But she wants children.* He remembers his children as toddlers, learning to control their own bodies, picking things up and putting them back; as preschoolers, paging through picture books and making forts under the table; as teenagers, arrogant and uncommunicative. He smiles. *Maybe another baby wouldn't be so bad. Sometimes vasectomies can even be reversed.* He read about a medical technique in which a fertility specialist removed sperm directly from a husband's testicles and artificially inseminated the man's second wife. *And if not, well, I wonder what she thinks about artificial insemination. But if she is determined to live in New York ... Getting her to see things my way would take some doing. But if I agree to having a child…* Van sighs and flips the pillow in search of a cool spot. *Maybe everything will be different in the morning.* Van punches his pillow again and turns onto his other side. *A future without Lissa in it feels very empty. What if I just take her up on it?*

*   *   *

Van makes a big pot of coffee and sits down with the morning paper. Soon Geertruyt and Johannes wander in, still in their pajamas, nod to Van, and rummage in the refrigerator. Each takes a section of the paper and reads while eating. Pieter and Kirsten pause only long enough to gulp huge glasses of orange juice. Kirsten says, "We'll eat after our bike ride." Once they bang out the back door, the kitchen returns to its usual morning silence.

The quiet reminds Van of his loneliness—loneliness usually unrelieved by the joy of his children's presence. He feels a pang of longing for a companion, for love to fill the empty spaces, to make alone not lonely.

Lissa comes into the kitchen wearing fawn-colored pants, a silk blouse the color of eggshells, black patent leather flats, and gold earrings. Van's first thought is that she is over dressed. He says, "Good morning. Would you like eggs? Cereal?"

"Just coffee and toast, thank you. Maybe a banana." She smiles at Van—a bright, tight smile. "I would like to go to the airport as quickly as we reasonably can. I'll have a better chance of getting a flight that way."

Geertruyt and Johannes look up, then quickly back at their newspapers. Van says, "It is Thanksgiving morning."

"Well, yes, I'd planned to stay till Sunday. But now I think I need to get back. Will you drive me? Or…?"

"Of course I will drive."

Tiger Heart

*   *   *

In the car, Van says, "We need to talk."

Lissa says, "Oh, I think we've said all that needs to be said for now." She turns on the radio. They drive the rest of the way to the airport barely speaking.

Van sets Lissa's travel bag on the sidewalk and kisses her on the cheek. She says, "Call me when you've thought things over." She walks into the terminal without looking back.

Van feels the empty space where she had been as he drives home. Thanksgiving with Lissa and the children should have been great. Try as he might, Van cannot think of anything he should have done differently. *What if Lissa really is the one? We have been good together.*

The miles sweep past. After a bit, he realizes he is feeling lighter. He starts whistling "Squid Jiggin' Ground." Suddenly he notices the tune—one on Nora's CD of seafaring songs. They've played it often during happy hour aboard *Duet. Maybe Nora will want to share turkey. Maybe she will have some advice about Lissa.*

Chapter Twenty-Eight

JIM TRUDGES UP THE GRANITE steps of Old Main, still smarting from the lash of Rebecca's tongue when she said, "Surely you aren't wearing *that* necktie." Remembering their argument the night before, his fury rises all over again. *When did she start thinking about an apartment in Baltimore? Would she really be in Centreville every weekend? How long would that last?* He hardly slept last night and his limbs feel as heavy as the old oak door he heaves open, its brass handle cold through his glove. Rebecca gave him the thin Italian leather gloves for his birthday—elegant, but useless against real cold. The door creaks and closes slowly behind him, pushing December cold into Old Main. *Stan ought to tell Physical Plant to do something about this door. A power assist or something. And it needs refinishing, too.* He pauses in the foyer to stomp snow from his galoshes and notices the rhythmic banging of the radiator. *Shit. Nothing's been done about replacing the heating system. He said he told Physical Plant to get on it.* Jim shakes his head. *He's so far from being on top of this job, half the time I think it's on top of him!* He unlocks his office door. *Well, after today, maybe I won't have to worry about that. No Stan, no Stan worries.* His smile tastes bitter.

Jim came into the presidency determined to make a success of it. Which depends, in part, on making a good impression—organized and businesslike. No piles of papers or stacks of reports clutter his office. No books overflow the bookcase. The only personal items are a six-inch-square Rubic's cube resting on top of a filing cabinet and Rebecca's engagement picture on the corner of his desk. Some days, his greatest comfort comes from looking at the bare surfaces.

He surveys the meeting preparations. Food Services has left fresh coffee, fruit, and pastries on the credenza. His secretary has placed yellow pads and pencils in front of five chairs around the conference table. A pile of folders tells him that Stan has been in already.

Nate Roth and Simon Hummel arrive, chatting amicably. They nod to Jim and continue their conversation while helping themselves to coffee. Simon inclines his head toward Nate, as if trying to catch the punch line of a joke, his sleek brown hair catching the light. Jim thinks, *Simon looks like a goddamned shampoo ad.* He wears custom-made suits, a shirt with monogrammed cuffs, matching socks and tie. Jim is wearing a tweed jacket and wool Donegal plaid tie. What a contrast. Rebecca had suggested a gray suit, a silk tie in muted shades. Not his style. He wonders whether Simon might be gay, but quashes the politically incorrect thought.

Stan arrives, takes a step toward Simon and Nate, stops, and stands awkwardly by the door. When Bill Baxter arrives, Stan sits down and opens a folder. *Why can't he get the social niceties right?*

Jim smiles, nods to those assembled, and takes his seat at the head of the table. He clears his throat. "Gentlemen. Thanks for coming on such short notice, especially at such a busy time of year. Although this isn't an established committee, you are the major players where college finances are concerned. I need your help—unofficially—first to determine whether there is any basis for Buck's concerns, and then to decide how to deal with him. Maybe a little time now will save us a lot of aggravation at the January Board Meeting."

Nate says, "Meaning Buck Brady is being a pain in the ass. Again." He looks like he's sucking lemons.

Jim glances quickly around the table. Simon smiles. Bill looks disapproving. Stan is making dollar signs on his yellow pad. "I can see Buck's point, actually," Jim says. "He wanted the five-year income history for the October meeting. Here we are, nearing the end of December, and we still don't have the report. He says if we keep stonewalling, he'll bring it up at the general meeting of the Board. Of course we're not stonewalling, but that's what Buck thinks."

"So why don't we have the report?" Bill's tone is mild, a polite request for information.

Stan sits up a little straighter. The papers tremble in his hand. "As you know—at least, I hope you remember—I did have a draft of that report, back in September, ready to go out for comment. But it was stolen, along with all that other stuff, when my office was vandalized." Stan glances around the table. Jim tries to look sympathetic and silently wills Stan to calm down. *We're both on the line here.*

Bill says, "And you didn't just print it again because ... ?" His tone is less mild now. Stan shifts in his chair.

Jim massages his brow, his spirits sinking. *Stan was my first hire at West. I'm responsible for this mess.*

Stan clears his throat. "Well, the computer system crashed right after that break-in. When Lew Denning got the system up again, the damned report was gone, along with a lot of other stuff generated in my office that week."

Nate says, "The system isn't backed up every night? What sort of an operation doesn't back up the computer files?"

Stan shifts in his chair and Jim has to force himself not to fidget. "The report was on my secretary's pc, and we don't have the software to back-up pc's that aren't part of the shared system. Denning's been agitating about our vulnerability. But something like that is a huge investment—time *and* money." Stan sips his coffee, runs his tongue over his upper lip. "I think … Denning thinks—maybe somebody hacked in or something. A few blocks of files had been zeroed out."

Bill slaps his pencil onto the table, a sharp little snap. Jim jerks upright. "Three *months* and you haven't reconstructed the report?"

Stan says, "Uh … Well, we've been working on it all along. But every time we get anywhere near done, something screwy happens."

Nate cocks one eyebrow. "Screwy?"

Jim's heartbeat quickens, his face flushes.

Stan says, "Sometimes all the column headings are dropped out. Or the columns are transposed. Sometimes everything is just scrambled. We've tried all sorts of things. Denning is stumped. We're afraid to put the file on another computer for fear of spreading a virus." Stan keeps his eyes on his file folder and licks his lips again. "So then I did the whole thing by hand." He nods toward the stack of papers in front of him. "But now I'm afraid the raw data might be corrupted."

Jim leans forward. "I explained all of this to Buck—that we'll get the report out as soon as we can. He was skeptical. And he isn't going to cut us any slack. He said it's serious, he's talked to people on the Finance Committee, he's talked to members of the Executive Committee, and no one's doing a damned thing about it—not even digging into the numbers." He settles back in his chair. "He believes we have a serious problem. He may think we are trying to cover it up. He'll take it to the full Board if we don't satisfy him that his concerns have been addressed."

Simon leans forward. "Exactly what concerns Mr. Brady?" His light tenor hangs in the air for a minute.

Jim draws a breath. "He questions the high returns we've had on our fixed-income portfolio. That's why you're here today, Simon—because you manage those funds. In particular, he wants a full audit of the part of our portfolio invested in foreign companies."

Nate grins. "Who but Buck Brady would be upset because the income is too high?"

Simon shrugs. "Everyone has a right to ask questions." He looks from Jim to Bill and back. "Although I was only generally aware of Mr. Brady's concerns, after your phone call, Jim, I took the liberty of putting together some information." He hands folders to each of the others. "Our systems are set up to run ten-year profiles. But it's cumulative and presented in reverse order, so you can focus on the five-year row if that's what you want."

Jim yanks open the folder. *Stan said the numbers couldn't be had. Didn't he even ask?*

Stan's eyes dart back and forth between his hand-written pages and Simon's polished print-out. He heaves a sigh and clears his throat. "Umm." Four pairs of eyes turn in his direction. "This is preliminary, of course, but—uh—my figures and Simon's figures seem to match. Simon has more detail. But everything is completely consistent." He passes around copies of his hand-written analysis.

Simon says, "I'd be happy to polish this up and present it in whatever form you like. I could have that done by close of business tomorrow if that would be helpful."

"Perhaps it would be." Bill looks brighter. Stan glares at Simon. *Hummel's playing hero for all it's worth. Angling for more business?* "Let's see what you have."

Simon goes over the report line by line. Stan looks like he's chewing on a wasp. No one finds anything that seems questionable—no abrupt changes or troubling trends over the entire ten-year period. The charitable remainder trust portion has done better than the fixed income endowment in general. "Because the college won't get the principle until the donors die, I've hedged those investments a little—very carefully of course—to try to boost the income by investing in private foreign holdings. Of course, I have not exceeded the twenty percent limit specified in the West College by-laws." He looks at Jim. "I cleared all this with your predecessor. I apologize if you feel I should have brought it up sooner."

"No, no. It's fine. And I expect that Buck will be satisfied, too, when he sees this." He clears his throat. "Now all that's left is to get the audit."

The group spends a few minutes discussing the best format for the report, then talks about Buck—how pushy he is, how abrasive, and how best to cool him off. Stan says nothing. Jim looks at the snow-covered branches of the hemlock outside his window. It's time to wrap it up and give himself time alone to think. He rises from his chair. "I'll call Buck and give him the gist of this, then over-night the figures to him."

Nate pushes back from the table. "That won't be necessary—the over-night, I mean. I'm going up to New Hampshire on Foundation business the day after tomorrow and I can deliver it.

Having one of us to walk him through the report might help keep him on track."

Bill looks at Nate. "Given the way you two get along, that's probably not a good idea."

Nate shrugs. "I can't shirk my responsibilities as chair of the Finance Committee just because I don't much care for Buck Brady. Besides, if I need to mend some fences, the sooner, the better."

Jim says, "The report is being sent to everyone anyway. Just leave it at that."

Nate looks chagrined but says nothing.

As the meeting breaks up, Bill says, "Jim, I'll be back in a minute. I need an update on—things."

"Sure. I'll be right here."

Stan, standing near the table with Simon, says, "Can you wait a minute? I'd like a word." As Nate and Bill leave, Stan says, "You had the data all the time. Why the hell did you let this mess go on for so long?" He is shaking, and seems oblivious to Jim's presence.

Simon raises his eyebrows. "What do you mean, let it go on? I didn't know there *was* a problem till Jim called to set up this meeting. Even then, he didn't tell me what was up—just that Buck had concerns and we needed to talk strategy."

"Don't give me that 'I didn't know' crap. If you didn't know, why did you show up with glossy reports in three colors—making me look like an ass?"

"I happened to run into Nate at a bar last night. He filled me in. I was just trying to help. And this is the thanks I get for staying up most of the night—for trying to be a Good Samaritan!" Simon's voice is low, too, but has taken on an edge. "*You* never asked me for data, let alone for reports. If you look like an ass, it isn't my fault."

He finishes buttoning his overcoat and stalks out the door. Stan picks up his folders and stomps out just as Bill returns.

Jim exhales and glances at Bill. "Stan may be something of a loose cannon." He shakes his head. "He may have to go."

Bill says, "This isn't the best time for us to talk. You and Stan need to get straight on what we're sending out. Have your secretary set up a lunch—sometime next week."

Jim nods. "Sure thing."

*   *   *

Alone in his office, Jim reviews the meeting. *Hummel's right. This mess is Stan's fault. Why the hell didn't he ask for the data weeks ago? Knowing that sort of thing is Stan's job. At least Brady will get his damned report. My ass is out of the sling on that, anyway. I just wish I didn't owe it all to an outsider.*

Leaving Old Main, Jim comes up behind Nate and Simon chatting on the steps. Nate claps Simon on the shoulder. "Way to pull that one out of the fire, Simon. Bill and Jim were smiling like cats with cream. Nice work! Will I see you later?"

"Of course. I'll bring the revised report." The men turn toward the parking lot with barely a nod to Jim. Two handsome men in their prime. Two rich, powerful men wearing camel hair coats and walking in effortless unison. *Huh. I thought they were barely acquainted. Rebecca's right. I can't read people worth a damn.* He buttons his tweed wool coat and strides toward Chum's, eyes on the path, thinking about how he will confront Stan, and when.

Chapter Twenty-Nine

NORA HURRIES UP THE SPIRAL steps of the Rusty Scupper, out of breath and a little anxious. She pauses on the top step, looks past the bar, and scans the tables along the glass wall that frames a view of Baltimore's Inner Harbor. Nate called her a few days earlier, to remind her that the progress report on the first phase of her research project is due soon, and to suggest that they have lunch to discuss it. Issues not related to her grant from the Roth Foundation have been on her mind for more than a week, and she's come with her own agenda. *If I tell him that Stan's early draft report contradicts the new one, would he think I'm trying to stir up trouble? Criticizing him for not being on top of things? Would he think I'm questioning his leadership of the Finance Committee? Overstepping my role?* She takes a deep breath and follows the hostess toward Nate's table. With each step over the gray-carpeted floor, she tells herself, "You can handle this."

Nate rises to greet her. "Nora. I hope the New Year has started well for you." Nate takes her extended hand and brushes her cheek with a social kiss.

She smiles. "Hello, Nate. It's good to see you." Her tension seeps out in slightly exaggerated flourishes as she sets her briefcase along the wall and hangs her shoulder bag from the back of her chair. Her fingers glide absently over the green leather menu cover and back again. She notices Nate watching, stops immediately, and turns her gaze toward the window. "There aren't many tourists in the off season."

Nate chuckles. "A pleasant change. I look forward to it every year—though it doesn't really make up for the end of the sailing season." Nora relaxes. Nate fills her wine glass from the bottle he's already sampled. He smiles. "I discovered this wine on my last trip to Italy. The grapes are grown in a small village just north of Sienna, in Tuscany. It's estate bottled. I hope you like it as much as I do." He picks up his glass. "Here's to the successful completion of the first phase of your research. And to your long and fruitful relationship with the Roth Foundation."

Nate's tone harks back to past compliments. Nora smiles as they clink glasses. "Yes, to the successful completion of the project." She clears her throat and glances up. "You come here often. Do you have any recommendations?"

Nate grins. "Let's ask Sam."

The waiter recites the daily specials: filet mignon with red wine and portobello mushroom sauce, grilled tuna with red pepper coulis, crab cakes with tarragon mayonnaise on the side. Nora recognizes the quiet baritone of the handsome waiter who has served them on other occasions. Her eyes flit to his three-fingered hand. She looks away, hoping he hasn't noticed her noticing. After they order, Nora says, "Did you and your family do anything special for Thanksgiving?"

Nate inspects his manicured fingernails. "Just a quiet family dinner before the boys went to a party with friends. Pris fell off the wagon early in the evening. When she passed out, I put her to bed and read myself to sleep." He sounds tired. The personal revelation embarrasses Nora. She blinks, remembering the rumors that Pris was recently in rehab, and wonders what to say. Nate rubs his forehead. His seems weary. He says, "I'm sorry. That was an ungentlemanly thing to say." He lowers his hand and looks at Nora. "And I've made you uncomfortable. I apologize." He stares at the cold gray water. "It's just—well—. You're a psychologist. You know how it is when someone—can't control an addiction." He speaks quietly and seems to be struggling for control. "There was a time—ten or fifteen years ago—or even five—when I thought I could help Pris. Now … maybe it's time I face reality."

Nora clasps her hands on the edge of the table and leans forward. "Oh, Nate. I'm so sorry."

"Not your problem. But thank you." He smiles crookedly. "The boys are great, though. Both of them will make the dean's list for fall semester. They've pledged my old fraternity—and seem to be developing some real leadership skills." While he talks about his sons' activities, Nora remembers life with her alcoholic mother—decades of broken promises, deceit, public embarrassments, and futility. *It's easy to forget that someone rich and powerful and handsome can still be miserable.* Nate's tone turns matter-of-fact. "They've gone back to campus now—just in time to let the old man get a head start on business. Foundation work always seems to quadruple right after New Year's, when the panel begins its review of new proposals—and just when I'm preparing for the January Board meeting at West!"

"That's great about the boys." Nora picks at her salad, searching for a way to broach the topic on her mind. Finally she blurts, "About the Board meeting—um—I'm not sure who to talk to about this. But you're chair of the Finance Committee, so … This is confidential, okay? Off the record?"

Nate pauses, a forkful of salad halfway to his mouth. "Of course. What is it?"

Nora takes a deep breath. "I have some concerns about Stan. I don't want to say anything to Jim because, well, he's Stan's boss. If it isn't anything serious, I wouldn't want to get Stan in trouble."

Nate lowers his fork. "You can count on me, Nora. Always. What's the problem?"

Nora clears her throat. "Did you notice anything—amiss—about the finance report for the upcoming Board meeting? I mean the special report on the history of our fixed income portfolio."

Nate twirls his wine glass, his gaze focused on a boat gliding slowly past in the harbor. "Amiss? What do you mean?"

Nora pats her lips with her napkin. "I mean, compared to reports from years past, does this one seem consistent?"

Nate shrugs. "I haven't looked at my Board packet yet. But I can't imagine there's a problem."

His tone is dismissive and Nora considers letting the matter drop. But she feels compelled to continue. "I came onto the Finance Committee only a year and a half ago, not long before Stan was hired. I don't have Board reports farther back than that, and we haven't had any similar reports—on the history of our fixed income portfolio—during my time."

Nate's scowl surprises Nora. "You wouldn't have one now if anyone was willing to stand up to Buck Brady's agitating. Pulling together a report on the history of the fixed income portfolio certainly doesn't top anyone else's priorities!" His sudden intensity makes Nora's heart thud and she hopes he doesn't notice the pulsing under her silk shirt. She looks at him, but says nothing. "Sorry for the outburst." Nate shrugs. "This seems to be my day for apologies.

I shouldn't let Brady get under my skin. Besides, I think things are going to be better in the future."

Nora looks at her plate. "As I was about to say, when I got this report, I was really surprised. I didn't remember the numbers looking so good. I pulled out the draft that Stan prepared last fall, just for comparison, and sure enough, the figures are substantially different."

Nate raises one eyebrow, cocks his head a little. "Stan gave you a draft? I never saw a draft report last fall."

Nora studies Nate with a psychologist's fascination, trying to identify the emotions flitting across his face. "It was—let me see—just before the October Board meeting. I happened to be in Old Main and Stan's secretary gave it to me, said it was going to be on the Finance Committee agenda. But it wasn't."

"You must have a copy of what Stan was working on before the break-in. He said everything was stolen. I'm surprised any copies of that survived."

"All I know is that I got the draft and then it wasn't on the agenda. I didn't think any more about it till now. It's a little hard to tell for sure because the data in Stan's draft weren't well organized—and the interpretative comments weren't coherent. But this new, polished report shows a lot more income."

Nate sits back. "You're something else, Nora. How many people would have kept a draft report all these months? Let alone be able to find it."

Nora laughs. "Lots of compulsive academics would have done the same." She looks at the steel grey water of the harbor, empty now but for a few commercial boats. "There have been so many red flags about Stan. I've heard that since the break-in, he hasn't been able to get the computer system to do anything right. I know the department chairs are livid. Our monthly expense reports are a shambles." She shakes her head. "It's hard to imagine that the same man put together the draft back then and the sleek finished product now."

Nate chuckles and looks aside. "He didn't. Simon Hummel did the new report, from the investment firm's archives."

"I thought it must have been someone else's work!" Nora sips her wine. "But anyway, the thing is this. I was hoping you would have some other reports—from Stan's predecessor—for comparison."

"I doubt it. This report is at Buck Brady's request—not a standard breakdown the Committee is accustomed to." Nate puts his hand over hers. "But give me the draft and I'll see what I can come up with."

His hand lingers on hers. She slips her hand away. "I don't have it with me. I wasn't even sure I was going to mention it." Nate searches her face. Nora rushes on. "But I'll send you a copy tomorrow. And while I'm at it, I'll send it to everyone on the Finance Committee. We're so close to the Board meeting already, people will barely have time to study it."

Nate frowns. "That could be problematic. Think about it. You said yourself that you aren't sure what it all means. And it was a draft. Who knows what Stan's final report would have been? Maybe his numbers are off because he hadn't put everything in yet. No one wants to pillory a man based on an incomplete draft."

Nora runs a hand over her hair, jams a pin into the figure-eight twist at the nape of her neck. "No, of course not. But ... I'll send it only to the trustees on the Committee, marked 'confidential.' You can call a closed session to thrash it out among yourselves. If there's nothing to it, fine. A closed session *is* trustees only, right? No Chair of the Faculty, no administrators?" Nate nods. "So there you are." Nora smiles, pleased with her solution.

After a beat, Nate says, "That could work, I suppose." He draws a hand down his face. "This could be one hell of a Board meeting."

The weariness in his voice touches Nora's heart. "Look, maybe I can help. Bill and I are going skiing in New Hampshire this weekend. I can deliver a copy of the old draft report to Buck and talk him down a bit. You know, point out nobody's stone-walling, urge him not to go off half-cocked till the Committee has had a chance to work everything out." Nora examines Nate's face. "What's bothering you?"

Nate shakes his head. "I like Stan. There have been a couple of times when I felt a little—uneasy—but—I always thought, you know, he hasn't been at West long, or maybe he's a nervous type. But it's difficult to imagine that anyone who's come this far in his career could create a draft that's grossly different from the real figures by accident." Nate sighs and sits up straighter. "But we aren't here to settle the question of Stan's competence or his honesty or anything else. We need to focus on your project."

Nora says, "Yes, of course." *Is he seriously thinking that Stan might be doing something criminal?*

*   *   *

On the drive back to Centreville, Nora's thoughts spin like leaves in a whirlwind, flitting here and there, landing for a moment only to take flight again. *Is Nate going to try to protect Stan? And if so, why? Especially if he really thinks Stan might be handing out false reports on purpose. Is he just sticking up for Stan because he doesn't want to admit that Buck has a point?* Over dessert and coffee, Nate said all the right, complimentary things about her work on the foundation-funded project, but tension whispered under his polite words. *Or am I just projecting my own tension?*

Nora drives on auto-pilot, the familiar landmarks passing

unnoticed. *His heart seems to be in the right place when it comes to college spending priorities. But he and Buck seem to be oil and water. And his home life must be hell. When I send him a copy, I'll include a nice cover note.*

When she turns off Rt. 301 at Queenstown to take the back road home, her thoughts are no more settled than when she left Baltimore. *Does he really think Stan is doing something illegal? And if he is, what?* By the time she pulls into the garage, she's convinced that taking a copy of the draft report to Buck is the right thing to do. He's the only one who seems truly concerned. She'll call Buck and suggest that they talk—briefly—before she meets Bill at the ski lodge.

Chapter Thirty

Nora slams down the phone. "Asshole. *He's* the one who brought up the financial returns in the first place! Why do I even bother?" Anger reddens her cheeks as she paces. Buck sounded disinterested—distant. What's his problem? Nora smacks her forehead with the heel of her hand. It must be Allie. Maybe she's worse.

She picks up the old draft report and wonders what it has to do with the one Nate delivered—with such confidence—just days ago. She stares blankly at the cover of Hummel's version as her fingers punch in Bill's home number. She absentmindedly tucks a hairpin into the figure-eight twist at the nape of her neck while she waits for Bill to pick up.

"Hi, Nora. What's up?"

"I'm *ready* to ski. Just a slight change in timing."

"Oh?"

Nora thinks she hears a note of caution in his voice and feels a stab of guilt. "Look, I'm sorry, but I'm going to be a little late.

I've arranged to meet Buck at the inn in Moultonborough this afternoon—Finance Committee business."

"Is this about the report Hummel put together for us?"

"Yes. I hope you don't think I'm stepping out of line, but I thought I might be able to smooth the way a bit." She clears her throat. "You could join us if you wish—though having the Chairman of the Board present might give our conversation more weight than it ought to carry."

Nora mentally counts to five before Bill says, "You go alone. Keep it less official. At this point, I don't want to be seeming to side with anyone."

She suppresses a sigh of relief. "Great. I'll change into ski clothes before I leave and meet you at the lodge before dinner. We should be able to make at least one run before we eat."

"I'll leave here in a half hour or so, maybe make a few runs this afternoon. The snow conditions are close to perfect. Let's plan on going out again after dinner. We haven't done any night skiing all winter."

If Bill is disappointed he won't show it. His ability to move on, not harboring ill feelings, is one of the qualities she cherishes in Bill. Her tension gives way to anticipation of time on the mountain with her lover. She pumps enthusiasm into her tone. "Okay, we have a plan!"

* * *

Bill finishes his second run. It's almost four o'clock when he bellies up to the bar in the lodge and orders a hot toddy. The exhilaration of skiing begins to give way to fatigue as he sits with his wool-socked feet propped on the window sill, ski boots aligned on the wooden floor by his chair. Thoughts of Nora and their relationship drift through his mind. She has told him she wants things to stay just as they are, and he has to admit, that's pretty damn good.

He sips his toddy and watches young skiers snow plow to a stop in front of the lodge before poling their way to the chair lift for another run. Skiing usually helps him set his cares aside, and today it is working its magic. Even problems with the new beer recipe seem less important. He rests his head on the back of the chair and closes his eyes. *Is it the skiing, or anticipation of time with Nora? When I am with her, everything seems so right.* He opens his eyes. A young couple clump past the window, red-cheeked and laughing, each wearing a "Just Married" placard.

As the afternoon wanes, Nora's absence starts a niggling anxiety. What's keeping her? What could she and Buck be talking about all this time? He flexes his toes, warm inside his socks. He'll count a hundred slow flexes, and if Nora hasn't shown up by then, he'll call. When he gets to seventy-five, and still no Nora, he slows the pace. *She'll be here any minute.* At one hundred, he reaches for his phone.

He tries her cell. No answer. He calls her home, just in case. No answer. He leaves messages both places. He slips on his boots and heads for the men's room. "Damn it," he mutters. He has visions of Nora dead on the highway, the victim of some southern driver who can't handle New Hampshire snow. He calls the Moultonborough Inn. Kevin, the bartender, tells him Buck left at least an hour ago, mad as blue blazes because the woman he was supposed to meet never showed. Bill cuts off the call. "Damn it!" Two city skiers in slick, designer clothes give him a look. With stiff fingers, he calls the Brady residence.

"Brady here." Buck's rough bass rumbles across the line.

"Hello, Buck. This is Bill Baxter. I'm calling about Nora. She was supposed to join me skiing after your meeting."

"Yeah, well, I haven't seen her. I waited more than an hour—because of the storm coming in and all—but she never showed. I figure she bailed on account of the snow. And frankly, I'm pretty pissed that she didn't call."

"That isn't like her. And she hasn't called me, either. Something must have happened." Anxiety tightens Bill's voice.

Buck says, "I'm sure she's all right, probably in a ditch with no cell service. But if there's anything you want me to do, just name it."

Bill rings off just as another call comes in: "Mr. Baxter, this is Kevin at the Moultonborough Inn. When my shift ended at 5:00, I found a cell phone in the parking lot. Maybe it belongs to the woman you're looking for. Probably not. But since you called earlier, I thought I should let you know."

"Thanks, Kevin. I'm glad you did. By any chance, did you notice a car with Maryland plates?"

"No, sir. No car. But the phone is at the bar. I come on duty tomorrow at 11:30 if you want to talk to me again. Have a nice night. Bye."

Bill's chest aches. His thoughts race. This is so unlike Nora. He calls the Moultonborough Inn again, tells the evening bartender about the cell phone. When he dials Nora's number, the bartender says, "It's ringing, but I can't pick-up. It's password protected." But now he knows she was in the parking lot. But did not see Buck. Should he go home to Maryland or wait at the lodge? Should he drive along her probable route and look for her car? She gets really pissed when anyone tries to offer help she doesn't think she needs. Impatient with the unaccustomed indecision, his cell phone shakes in his hand as he dials 911 for the New Hampshire State Police Barracks in Plymouth.

"This is Officer Coutermarsh. What is your emergency?"

*   *   *

Nora struggles against a terrifying dream, Van calling for help, her own voice calling, "Wait for me. I'm coming." The sound rouses her. "Van? What's happened? Where are you?" She reaches out. Nothing. She opens her eyes, looking for something familiar. The faint glimmer of the moon on the bedroom wall? The glow of the nightlight in the hall? Nothing. The whole world is alien, cold and dim. When she tries to move, her legs feel like stone. Slowly she realizes she's outside, lying in snow.

Minutes pass. *What the hell happened?* Her tension mounts as she tries again to move her legs. Her right thigh quivers, a faint echo of willful movement. *Sweet Jesus, am I paralyzed?*

As she comes fully awake, pain consumes her, stabs her head and neck. She feels a lump on the back of her skull, buffered by a gloved hand and woolen ski cap. She pulls off the glove and her bare fingers come away with something flakey. She touches a finger to her tongue. Dried blood. *I must have taken one hell of a fall. Where's Bill?* Then she remembers: she never made it to the ski lodge. She feels for her cell phone. Gone. "Damn," she mutters through stiff lips. She raises her head and feels dizzy. She runs her tongue over velvet-covered teeth and swallows the stale taste in her mouth. *How long have I been here?* She struggles to her knees. A sharp pain shoots through her torso. *Why am I out in the snow?* She moves slowly, twisting, hoping to find relief. Even her bones feel cold.

The day's cloud cover leaves everything gray and masks any hint of the sun's location. She sees vast stretches of snow. And mountains. She is in a shallow valley surrounded by pine-covered, rocky prominences. Fresh snow covers any signs of how she ended up on this mountainside. She moves fingers and toes, looking for evidence of frostbite, and makes faces against a cold west wind. *My legs.* She makes an effort to stand. Her right leg gives way and she falls to her knees. When the pain eases, she's wracked by nausea and dry heaves. Afterward, she eats snow to clear her tongue and slake her need.

She collapses. Her thoughts turn to the last things she can remember: the drive north, the snow starting as she crossed the New Hampshire state line, arriving at the Moultonborough Inn to meet Buck, and getting out of her car. Then … Then … "Damn it. Nothing."

Shivering turns her thoughts to survival. *Shelter. That's the first thing.* She hears nothing but the wind in the pines. "And go slow. No sweat. If you get wet, you'll never get dry. You'll freeze." She struggles up the hill, trying to spare her right leg. Pain shoots up to her buttock. Walking gets easier the farther up she goes, for the night wind has blown the fresh snow toward the saddlebacked valley and exposed the underlying crust.

Stiff and exhausted, she rests often and eats snow, faintly flavored with sweat from her hand. *Sweet Jesus. If I die here, I'll never see Van again. Or Bill. Or my sisters. I should have been there for them more—especially when they were little.* As the oldest, she'd taken on the mothering role during their mother's illnesses—and drunken failures to do what needed to be done. *If I get out of this, I'll do better.*

On the high ground, she stops for long, deep, slow breaths, and searches the horizon, hoping for some recognizable contour. A moonless, star-studded sky peeks through trees. *How did so many hours slip by?* She examines the feathery tips of pines and hemlocks, knowing—from her summers as a camp counselor—that they usually bend east. She snaps off a dead branch and marks a north-south axis. She hacks through the crust with a fallen limb and, shoveling with her hands, slowly digs a trench in the softer snow below. She breaks off pine boughs for a roof. As full dark descends, she wriggles feet-first into the snowy shelter, no bigger than a coffin. "Where the hell am I?" She falls asleep wondering whether she will ever wake again.

After a fitful sleep that feels no longer than a nap, she pokes her head out. She uses her elbows to inch out of the trench. *Lord, I'm hungry. I'd give my eyeteeth for some beef stew with mashed potatoes.* She sits on a granite outcropping to loosen the laces of her ski boots, hoping to improve circulation in her feet. She lumbers to a tree-barren rise, dragging her lame leg, making faces to test for frozen skin, wiggling fingers and toes. From the rise she looks north and recognizes the profile of Mt Liberty, Mt Hancock to its east. *The Kancamagus Trail can't be more than a few miles to the south. Damn this leg. Damn it to hell.* Hungry and exhausted, she pulls her scarf over her head, tucks it down her raised collar, and retraces her steps to the snowy bed.

The morning sun is a welcome reprieve from the cold black night and nightmares. But her head and leg throb, her torso hurts when she moves. Her right foot feels numb. When she rubs her toes to improve circulation, she sees that two of them are turning purplish, edging toward black. She pulls out the wool sock she's warmed against her belly, holds it momentarily against her cheeks, then puts it back on her foot. She reties the lace of her ski boot in a loose granny knot, the best she can do with ice-stiff fingers. "I'll never make the trail." She feels more helpless now than at any other time in her life. She thinks about never sailing with Van, about never lying with Bill again. A ragged sob rips her throat. Her despair melds into anger. "If I get out of here, I'll get the bastard who did this. I'll damn well get the bastard!"

As she labors to gather pine boughs, she considers a disgruntled student as a potential killer. Or maybe this is just one more strike from whoever has it in for West College. Nora touches her injured thigh through her ski pants and thermal underwear. The hand pressure triggers pain from hip to knee. Her rib is tender, and her head is not yet clear. *Was I drugged? Was that lump on my head a concussion?* She ignores her body's cries for relief and gathers more pine boughs. She arranges them in an open space on a pine-free knoll, fervently hoping. The green boughs on the white snow spell SOS.

* * *

Sunlight through the east window wakes Bill from a fitful sleep, the end of a seemingly endless night of worry and tossing. He snatches up the phone on the first ring. "Hello?"

"Mr. Baxter?"

"Yes."

"This is officer Coutermarsh from the Plymouth barracks. We found your friend's car just south of Lincoln off I-93." Bill listens intently, willing the news to be good. "The car was unlocked, key in the ignition. We've impounded it. It's too early to say much, but it looks like there might have been a struggle. We found some blood on the front seat, and…"

"My God." He grips the phone.

"Mr. Baxter?"

Bill draws a deep breath. "I'm here."

"There's a chance your friend was assaulted, maybe drugged."

Perspiration glazes Bill's forehead. "Did you check her cell phone?"

"We did. But there was nothing in the call history since a call to you midday yesterday. We'll keep you informed."

"I expect to stay here at the lodge till she's found. My cell phone is the best number. Thanks, officer." He can't escape images of Nora seriously injured—or dead. He has to *do* something—anything. He calls President Sloan and Frank to tell them the situation.

***

The day passes with no word from Nora and nothing further from the police. Bill phones his office and gives his secretary instruction on handling his obligations for the day. He dresses to hit the slopes, hoping to wear out his worry. But his heart isn't in it. Approaching the lift, he swerves left and trudges uphill. The cell phone in his breast pocket remains silent.

Back at the lodge, he has a drink. And another. He tries to think about happy times with Nora, but those thoughts slip sideways into worry. He tries talking to others in the bar. When he realizes he isn't really listening to anything anyone says, he turns in and tries to sleep.

The next morning breaks clear and sunny. Bill again phones his office.

His secretary says, "There's nothing you can do there. Maybe you should come back. The police can contact you here just as well as there."

"No. I want to stay close."

He dithers away the morning, trying to relieve his anxiety. He skips lunch. As the afternoon wears on, he fields queries from people in Centreville and paces from room to room, feeling caged and helpless. A few minutes past 3:00, his phone rings. "Baxter here," he says, his voice tight.

"This is the State Police barrack at Plymouth. Please hold for Officer Coutermarsh." His heart pounds as he waits, making silent promises to the Almighty.

"Mr. Baxter, I have good news. We found your friend. We've taken her to the Mary Hitchcock Clinic in Hanover."

"Thank God." He can scarcely breathe. "What happened? How bad is it?"

"We don't know what happened, but she was conscious when found."

"Where? Who found her?"

Coutermarsh speaks slowly and deliberately, New Hampshire heavy in his accent. "A member of the Forest Fire Patrol found her in the valley near Loon Mountain, just north of the entrance to the Kancamagus Trail. He saw an SOS in the snow from the watch tower—just a fluke he was even out there this time of year. But he snowshoed out to take a look. The chain that blocks the trail to vehicular traffic in winter had been tampered with. When he located Ms. Perry, he sent us his position on the GPS. The Rescue Squad took her to the hospital by helicopter about an hour ago."

"But will she be all right?" Bill's voice sounds loud in his own ears.

"I can't say, sir. But I'm sure you'll hear from the clinic before too long. You should wait by the phone until you do."

No way will he wait by the phone with Nora lying injured nearby. He is zipping his parka when the phone rings again.

"Mr. Baxter? This is Dr. Wortendyke at the Mary Hitchcock Clinic. Nora Perry asked me to call. I'm happy to tell you that I think she will be good as new in a month or so." Bill feels suddenly lighter. The doctor describes Nora's condition in general terms: dehydration, a concussion, hypothermia, frost bite on two toes of the right foot, a torn lateral meniscus of the right knee, and a hematoma of the right thigh. "We'll do our best to save the toes. The prognosis for everything else is excellent."

Speeding toward the Hitchcock Clinic, thoughts of the hole in his life if Nora were no longer in it spin through his brain. "Damn it, Nora, when did I start caring so much?"

Chapter Thirty-One

THE ADVENT CALENDAR ON VAN'S kitchen wall reads December twenty-third. Scents of pine and fir and his children's laughter fill the house. By dinner time, they've asked whether Nora will be joining them for Christmas, what present he plans to give her, and when he plans to see her. When he says, "I have no such plans," they intermingle lavish praise for "Dad's professor" with direct advice that he should make things up with her. Van wonders whether they planned the attack.

By dessert, all four are in full concerted rant. Kirsten says, "Daddy! What's *wrong* with you? It's been a whole month since you and Lissa called it quits. Are you saying you still haven't even *talked* to Nora?"

Van flushes. "Of course I have talked with her, checking on her recovery, and so on."

"So? How is she?"

"As far as I know, she has recovered from the exposure. But the end of the semester is always a bear. No time for socializing. I was grading exams until this morning." He thinks but does not say that probably she has been spending all her free time with Bill. Van has seen him in Centreville every day or so since Nora got out of the hospital. He hasn't mentioned to anyone how hurt he felt that she didn't call from the hospital. By the time Frank called to let him know about Nora's ordeal, Bill was already bringing her home.

Geertruyt eyes him speculatively, tugging on her brown ponytail. "Well, you aren't grading now. Call her."

"Give Pop a break." Johannes claps Van on the shoulder. "At his age, a man's recovery time is longer." He waggles his eyebrows. "But even *I* didn't suspect that it was *this* long." His siblings moan.

Van chuckles but his flush deepens. "I believe you have ridden that horse as far as it will go. Surely you do not intend to harass me all evening. How about caroling?"

They leave the table in a flurry of chair-scraping and dish-carrying and grab coats against the cold. Johannes stands tall and proclaims, "As you no doubt recall, it's my turn to determine where we sing." He clears his throat. "We'll start at Nora Perry's house."

His siblings grin, Kirsten ruffles his hair, and Pieter punches his shoulder, saying, "Way to go, Hans!"

Van groans. "You do realize that Nora's house is about three miles from here?"

"Then I guess we'd better bundle up some more," Johannes chortles.

Van suggests that they drive, at least part way. They crowd into one car and head out the campus gate toward town. Johannes says, "As officer in charge of this expedition, I designate Kirsten as our choral director, she being the only sibling trained in music. Excepting Pop, the world's best baritone."

Pieter snorts. "Dad's not a sibling, bozo."

Johannes adopts a pained expression and intones, "Oh, brother of mine, spare me your scorn. Do not flay me with the sharp sword of your tongue. Do not make me the brunt of public ridicule."

Pieter says, "I'll make you the brunt of my private fist if you don't knock it off." Everyone laughs.

Johannes parks at the mouth of the cul-de-sac leading to Nora's house. Van realizes how passionately he hopes that Bill will not be with her. They approach singing "The First Noel." With each step, Van steels himself for the encounter. The porch light flicks on and Nora appears in the doorway—alone. When their eyes meet, she smiles, and Van's sings more gustily. Through his mind flash scenes of chorus rehearsals with Nora and quiet times afterward at the pub. The carolers launch into "Hark the Herald Angels Sing." Nora joins in, singing joyously. When they finish, she says, "Would you like to come in and warm up? I have cocoa and eggnog."

While the others look from one to the other, Kirsten says, "Oh, we couldn't! I mean, thanks anyway, but we just had a big dinner. You're our first stop." She cuts a sideways look at Van. "We were hoping that we could recruit another female voice for this venture. Are you game?" Van smiles, hoping she accepts. Nora looks at him, her scrutiny brief, before she says, "I'd love to! Let me get my coat."

They carol for more than an hour, first at the houses near Nora's, then back on campus along Faculty Row and, finally, at the president's house. They end up in Van's kitchen making hot mulled cider. Having Nora in his house again—her mere presence—makes the evening right. He watches her laugh with his children and feels the peace he never had with Lissa.

Everyone seems to feel it. Pieter excuses himself to review a new hull design, due right after Christmas, but pokes his head back through the door to say, "This has been great. How about a reprise? Would you like to come to dinner on Christmas?"

Nora looks at Van. He says, "That would be terrific—if it would fit your plans."

She laughs. "As of now, that *is* my plan!" Van offers to drive Nora home, and as they prepare to leave, she asks whether she may bring anything.

Geertruyt says, "That fantastic minced fruit pie you made a couple of years ago."

Nora laughs again. "You got it." She gives Van a long, warm look. Words from a book Nora once gave him echo in Van's head: "When you find your place, you know it. It's quiet inside."

On the drive to Nora's house, Van says, "So, are you fully recovered from your time in the mountains?"

"Pretty much. I was afraid I'd lose the toes, so that's a great relief. All the other body parts seem to have recovered. But I still can't remember anything between getting out of my car in the parking lot and waking up in the snow. The doctor says I probably won't."

"When Frank called to tell me you had been mugged and dumped in the mountains, I—felt helpless. And beside myself with worry. I called the hospital, but by then you were on your way home with Bill."

"Really? Bill said he'd notified people in Centreville. I thought you knew."

"Had I known, I would have come to the hospital." Van clears his throat. "I am glad you will join us for Christmas. I thought you might be spending the day with Bill."

Nora shrugs. "He invited me to join him and his children and grandchildren. It just felt like too much family for me."

Van mulls over that comment, remembering his four children. Is it grandchildren that make it feel like too much family?

*   *   *

Over a dinner of leftovers the day after Christmas, Van says, "I am pleased that you all like Nora."

Johannes throws up his hands, pretending to defend himself, and says, "Hey, we just considered the options, Pop. We could do a whole lot worse than the redheaded Butcher for a stepmother!"

Van shifts in his chair. "Do not shop for wedding presents just yet! Nora Perry is not the marrying sort."

Late that night, remembering the moment as he drifts toward sleep, he sighs. *Marriage or no, life with Nora in it is greatly preferable to the alternative.*

In the week after Christmas, Van and Nora spend a lot of time together. They fall back into their old camaraderie quickly and easily. Nora makes dinner for him twice and he stays late, talking companionably. But home alone, awake in the night, when he thinks about how often they're together—about how easily she's once again become the center of his life—when he admits to himself that there is no place in the world he'd rather be than in Nora's company—his vulnerability terrifies him. His heart thunders against his ribs, cold sweat soaks the sheets, and each panting breath leaves him gasping for air. She has made no overtures. And she is still seeing Bill. *Your best bet, van Pelt, is to keep your feet on the ground and your mouth shut.*

On the morning of December thirty-first, Van lingers over his morning coffee. In less than a week, his life has turned over. He calls Nora. "I suddenly realize that we have not made plans for this evening. What would be your pleasure?"

Nora hesitates, then, "I'm so sorry. I'm going to a house party in Virginia."

With Bill, no doubt. Van holds his tone level. "I see."

"I should have mentioned it. But I assumed you had other plans."

"That is fine. No doubt you need to get started. Drive safely." As the call ends he tries to untangle the strands of disappointment and anger. *What did I expect? To pick up where we left off as if Bill and Lissa and all the months since then never happened?*

Van spends the day pounding together bookcases for Kirsten and trying to talk himself out of his funk. In the evening, he listens to Beethoven's Seventh Symphony and sips wine. He goes early to bed, determined to see less of Nora, to give both of them some space, to be more self-protective.

Chapter Thirty-Two

Priscilla reaches toward the end table, toward her tumbler—half full of Knob Creek. She cuts a sideways look at Nate at the other end of the sofa. He seems absorbed in his book. She drops her hand back into her lap. *Slow down, Pris.* She looks out the window, watches the snowflakes swirling around the streetlight. She glances again at Nate, still engrossed in reading. She lifts the crystal tumbler toward the table lamp, studies the changing amber patterns as she tilts the tumbler first one way and then another. The one remaining ice cube clinks against the side of the glass. *That ice cube could be me: surrounded by luxury, swimming in bourbon, and melting away.* Her smile is bitter. She brings the tumbler to her nose and sniffs. *Quit playing games, for Chris' sake. Just drink it. It's too late to climb back on the wagon tonight.* She sips the bourbon, savoring the taste and aroma.

Sliding closer to Nate, she lays her hand on his sleeve. "Why don't we light the fire, put on some music and—have a quiet time together?" She smiles, looking at him through half-closed eyes.

Nate glances at her and draws his arm away. "Not tonight, Pris. You're drinking."

"I haven't had much. And I won't have any more. Please," she wheedles. "We never talk any more."

He sighs. "You're not coherent when you drink." He stands. "Besides, we have nothing left to talk *about*," he says, walking toward the hall.

"Where are you going?"

Nate pulls on his overcoat. "Out."

"Are you meeting that Perry woman again? On *business*!" Tears and anger clot her voice.

"Give it a rest Pris. How many times do I have to tell you there's no other woman? There never has been. There never will be." The front door clicks shut behind him.

The sound hangs in the silence of the room and in her emptiness, more final than a slam. *Oh, Nate, I still love you so much. I still need you so much. God help me, but I do.* She wipes tears away with her sleeve.

She pours more bourbon, adds two ice cubes. *It's got to be more than my drinking.* She sinks into her favorite chair, frizzled orange hair spreading across the wingback. Thoughts of how life used to be float through her mind but soon give way to more recent memories—Nate smiling as he hands a drink to Allie, Nate looking flushed and happy with his arm across Nora's shoulders. Tears seep from her closed eyes. *It isn't just me! There's something more going on. And I'm gonna find out what!* She springs to her feet, spilling part of her drink, and heads for the stairs.

*   *   *

Priscilla slides a credit card into the slit between the doorframe and the door. "Come to mama," she mutters, biting her lower lip while jiggling the card. The lock snicks back and she smiles, pushing open the door to Nate's bedroom. *Never been easier.* She steps across the threshold. *He thinks locking the fucking door guards his inner sanctum. Hah!*

She drops into the leather club chair by the window and sips her drink. The moon casts pearly light on the snow, almost bright enough to read by. She looks around the room—burgundy, teal, and beige, solids and stripes, muted in the moonlight. Everything in its place. Not even a hairbrush on the dresser. Except for the golf and sailing trophies, it could be a room in an upscale hotel. *Damn trophies. They're more important to him than I am!* Pris stumbles to the trophy shelf. Seizing the biggest silver cup, she hurls it across the room. It lands on the bed with a soft, frustrating thump. She snatches it up for another throw and notices a blue-covered booklet and an envelope on the bed. She picks them up and plops down on the bed. Shaking her head, trying to focus, she turns the booklet over. "His passport. In a sailing trophy?" She picks up the envelope and turns on the bedside lamp. It contains a receipt from World Wide Travel and a contract confirming a private charter from Baltimore to the Cayman Islands, open departure date. She reads the receipt twice. Emotions she doesn't name knot in her chest.

She crosses to Nate's desk and pages through his calendar. *Nothing for tonight.* Leafing backward week by week, she finds lots of appointments with Simon, a few other regulars. The only woman's name she finds more than once is Nora Perry. They're all lunches. She picks up her bourbon and tries to think. *That doesn't prove anything. He'd have to note lunches. They're in the middle of his work day.* She searches the desk. Riffling through the file drawer, she finds bank statements, insurance policies for the house and car, receipts for taxes, credit card receipts. She squints at the folder of credit card receipts. *They say that if someone's having an affair, it will show up on the credit cards.* The papers make little whispering sounds as she shuffles through them. She finds nothing. She crumples the receipt from World Wide Travel into a tight ball and slumps forward in the chair, keening and rocking. *He's going away with her. He's leaving me. Oh, God! He's leaving!*

Several minutes pass while her grief slides back into the anger that propelled her into the bedroom in the first place. *Goddamn him to hell!* She pulls the West College directory from the shelf, punches in Nora Perry's number with a shaking finger. When the answering machine picks up, she shouts, "If you think you can fly off to the Cayman Islands with my husband, you've got another think coming, bitch! Leave us alone!" She slams the phone onto the desk. She hears beep-beep-beep-beep-beep-beep-beeeeeep and realizes that the receiver isn't on the cradle. *The story of my life: missed connection.* She mutters, "Goddamn fucking technology," and rattles the receiver into place.

*   *   *

When Nate returns, Pris is in the den, a bourbon in one hand, his passport and the crumpled contract in the other. She lurches to her feet, shaking the passport in his face. "There's no way in hell you're leaving *me*, Nathaniel Roth. No way in hell! I'll see you dead first!"

Nate draws back, looking stunned. He peers from her face to her hand and back again. His words fall like ice chips: "What *are* you raving about?"

"Don't act so sanctimonious, you sonofabitch! I'm 'raving' about you running off to the Cayman Islands!"

"Priscilla, get control of yourself. I'm not running off anywhere. You're talking nonsense."

"Nonsense? Nonsense? You call hiding your passport in a sailing trophy nonsense?" Her voice is shrill but she cannot stop. A pained look flashes across Nate's face. *He's going to try to talk his way out of this. I know it. But not this time!* She's so angry she shakes. Pris sets her tumbler on the end table, trying to control her body. Her glass lands half off the coaster and a dollop of bourbon sloshes onto the table. She grips the back of a chair for balance. When he takes her arm, she shouts, "Don't touch me!" and steps back. "And don't try to talk your way out of this, you bastard." She turns away from him, chest heaving.

Nate steps close behind her and puts his hands on her elbows. "Pris—"

She jerks around, one arm swinging against his chest. "Leave me *alone*." Nate steps back, shaking his head. Pris turns away again, elated at having struck back, struggling to keep her balance.

"Look at me, Pris. And listen to me." Nate speaks quietly.

"Why should I?"

"Because this isn't what you think. You need to hear what I have to say."

"I doubt that," she snarls. But she turns to face him.

Nate hangs his suit jacket on the antique ladder back chair and loosens his tie. He looks wistful. She stares at him as he talks, his words soft, his tone affectionate. "I'm not leaving you, Pris."

"Don't lie to me!" She holds up the passport and receipt, still clenched in her left hand. "I can read! I can add one and one and get two!"

"I'm not lying. We both know things haven't been good between us—not for a long time—so I was planning to surprise you with a trip to the Caribbean for your birthday."

He looks steadily at Pris, his head tilted a little—the same look as when he proposed and waited for her answer. Something quivers in her abdomen. "Don't play games with me, Nate." Her voice trembles. Her thoughts race, looking for something—anything—that would make his words believable.

Nate sighs, rubs his forehead. "I *was* hoping to surprise you, but …" He crosses to Pris and takes her hand. "Come sit down. Just listen." He leads her to the sofa and sits half-facing her, holding her hand in both of his. He keeps his eyes on their clasped hands when he speaks, his tone is intimate, an echo from the earliest months of their marriage. "I thought that if we got away from here—if we left the Baltimore winter behind—did some sailing, maybe scuba diving, lots of relaxation—I thought maybe I could help you get your drinking under control. Maybe we could make a fresh start."

Priscilla searches Nate's face, her heart thumping, her lungs struggling to breathe. "You want a fresh start? Really?"

"Really."

"So why was your passport hidden in the sailing trophy?" She speaks quietly, silently begging him to make her believe.

Nate squeezes her hand and laughs. "Of course I hid it. You thought I didn't know that you come into my room?" He looks at her, one eyebrow cocked, cups her face in his hands and kisses her tenderly. "You needn't worry, Pris. There is no other woman. You'll always be my wife." He folds her into his arms and rests his chin on top of her head. "You know, the surprise might be kaput, but I think this deserves a celebration anyway. How about if you slip into something silky? Come to my room. Soon." He kisses the tip of her nose. She watches his straight back and graceful gait as he leaves.

Pris snatches a bottle of champagne from the wine closet and two flutes and makes her way carefully to her room. She hurries to undress, frustrated by her clumsiness. She slips a sea-foam-green negligee over her ample body, thinking the Grecian style makes her breasts look voluptuous and her stomach less noticeable. *Will he still find me attractive?* She tries to remember when Nate last invited her to his room—or accepted an invitation to hers. A vision of other women Nate might have had sex with tries to surface but Pris pushes it down again. *He wants me! Tonight he wants* me.

* * *

When Pris arrives, flourishing the champagne bottle, Nate frowns. She says, "It's a celebration!"

He hesitates, and Pris fears she's made an awful blunder until he says, "Sure. It's a celebration," and pops the cork.

They sit by the fire in his bedroom, sipping champagne. Firelight winks on the crystal flutes. Nate talks quietly about all the things they'll do in the islands, his voice soothing. She drifts in a haze of alcohol and happiness. After awhile, Nate chuckles. "You seem to be fading, kitten. Come."

Priscilla's last awareness is lying with her head on Nate's shoulder, tracing finger patterns on the muscles of his chest while he whispers words of love, words she hasn't heard since the their boys were born.

* * *

The bright morning sunlight streaming through the window confuses Pris. Her room doesn't have an east window. Then she realizes that she's in Nate's room—in Nate's bed—and rolls onto her back. She squints at the ceiling, slowly remembering bits and pieces of the night before. She hears Nate singing in the shower and smiles. *I guess I wasn't dreaming.*

Nate emerges from the bathroom wearing a white shirt unbuttoned at the collar and grey suit pants, no shoes. His brown hair is still damp from the shower. The handsomeness of the man she married strikes Pris anew. He crosses to the bed, smiling, inserting his cufflinks. "How's my princess this morning?"

At the warmth in his tone, all her tension drains away. She

makes a pouty face. "Things would be better if you got back into bed with me!" She takes his hand, tugging him toward her.

Nate chuckles. "No can do. I have to go to work. Besides, after last night, I'd be useless to you anyway. I'm not as young as I used to be!"

Pris smiles back. She blushes, hoping Nate doesn't know she was too drunk to remember. She pulls the covers around her. "So you'll be home for dinner?"

"Absolutely. I have a late meeting, but I'll be home after. And we'll make plans for the trip." Nate glances at the clock. "About the trip … It would be best if you don't mention it to anyone." He looks at Pris and grins sheepishly. "We're going to play hooky from the Board Meeting and I'd rather not get a lot of grief about that beforehand."

"Miss the board meeting?" Pris arranges the sheet to camouflage her belly. "I thought you had to settle some big brouhaha over some report or other."

Nate grimaces. "That's why I decided to skip out. Buck Brady is going to be a royal pain in the ass and I just don't want to deal with it. Too bad *he* didn't get dumped in the White Mountains—and stay there."

"Nate! That's an awful thing to say."

"Just kidding." He ties a silk necktie and crosses to the mirror to adjust it. "If I spend a whole day—let alone two—in the same room with that asshole, I'll do something I'd regret." He turns to Pris. "Besides, it's your birthday. Nothing's more important than that." He kisses her lightly on the cheek and leaves.

Pris attends to an urgent need to pee, drinks three glasses of water, and climbs back into bed, wallowing in the happy beginning to the day. *I think I'll call down for a breakfast tray. Let the household help know that I sometimes share my husband's bed.* She smiles and reaches for the intercom.

*   *   *

Pris pushes the breakfast dishes aside to make space for a notepad. Munching toast and sipping coffee, she starts planning her wardrobe for the trip. At one point, she gazes through the window at the snow-laden trees. *Nate seemed so happy this morning. I wish I could remember.* She sighs. *I've got to cut back on the alcohol. And I will.* She rolls over, stretches, and buries her face in Nate's pillow, breathing deeply. She sniffs again. *Nate's aftershave doesn't smell like that!* Pain grips her heart and her old insecurities flood back. *Maybe it's the scent of that woman.* Fury makes her heart pound. *You fool! You let him wrap you around his little finger again.* She flings aside her packing list and jumps out of bed. She rummages through his medicine cabinet, looking for more traces of his lover. Nothing. In his sock drawer she finds two bottles of aftershave—the one he's used for years and a new one, the bottle nearly full. She sniffs the new aftershave. It's the scent on his pillow. She closes the drawer, shaking with relief. She picks up her notepad and leaves the room, quietly humming "Everything's Coming Up Roses."

Chapter Thirty-Three

VAN'S PHONE RINGS. THE CALLER ID flashes "Perry." He has not seen Nora since New Year's, though she has phoned three times. He sidestepped previous invitations, always with plausible excuses relating to workload or prior commitments, but excuses are wearing thin. And not seeing Nora goes against his heart's inclination. He answers the call, hoping she will suggest getting together. She invites him to dinner.

Van whistles through his teeth and dons his coat. Driving to her house, eagerness to see her throbs in his veins. *Just watch your step, van Pelt, or you will fall right back into the quicksand you were in after Christmas. Do not give that kind of power to a woman who will not commit.* Ringing the bell, his breath comes quickly. The door opens, revealing Nora's silhouette. Her hair is loose and back-lit, the tangle of curls seeming to invite his fingers.

*　　*　　*

Nora catches his look and bites her lip. "What?" she asks.

Van glances away. "I am happy to see you. As always."

Nora's heart pounds. *Get a grip. If he meant more than a common pleasantry, his voice wouldn't have been so flat.* She says, "Come in," and turns back into the house. *We need to clear the air.*

*   *   *

They sit by the fire, each sipping before-dinner scotch. They've discussed their classes for spring semester, the departures of Van's children, the next choral program—a dozen topics unrelated to their relationship. Nora glances sideways at Van. *We're adults. I'll ask him outright where we stand.* But before she finds the right words, Van says, "How is your grant progressing?"

Nora shifts mental gears. "Very well—though I can't say I've done anything to speak of since my *adventure* in the White Mountains. I had lunch with Nate in early December. It feels like a lifetime ago. He was quite positive—even said something about a long and fruitful relationship with the Roth Foundation." She summarizes the early results of her work. "So everything is great with the grant." She pauses. Eventually she says, "But…I don't quite know what to make of Nate."

"What do you mean?"

Van looks intently at her and Nora pauses again, tasting each word before it leaves her mouth. "He seems … contradictory … sometimes. On the one hand, he's supportive of faculty and of academic priorities. And there's no denying that the Roth Foundation supports a lot of good work. And I know life with Pris must be hell—the alcohol and all. But he *is* a married man, and he flirts with every woman in sight."

Van looks at her steadily. "Only with the good looking ones, actually. And you did not seem to mind his attentions, the last time I noticed."

"Why should I mind common social pleasantries? But … But sometimes he seems to presume an intimacy that just isn't there—and shouldn't be."

"Such as?"

Nora clenches her teeth, wishing she'd not opened this can of worms, resenting the defensive note that has crept into her voice. "Such as talking to me about Pris. I mean, their issues aren't exactly secret, but …"

"I am not surprised. Everyone finds you easy to talk to."

"Anyway, over lunch, when I mentioned that I have an old draft of the report that's on the Board agenda this time—the one Buck wanted—he got all—I don't know—watchful." Nora shrugs, and decides not to mention Nate holding her hand. "Look, forget it. Let's talk about something else." A vision of the smooth-faced, shiny New York woman Van might marry flashes into her mind. "So, what's the scoop on Melissa?"

Van seems to stiffen. He says, "She was here for Thanksgiving—as you know. She decided to leave early. I did not try to change her mind. I believe that, without having actually discussed it, we have mutually agreed that out relationship has no future." His tone carries half-sharpened barbs of annoyance. "Where do things stand with you and Bill?"

Nora takes Van's hand but stares into the fire. "I love Bill dearly." Van's hand spasms. She squeezes it. "He's a wonderful person, and he was an absolute brick when I was in the hospital. I'd do anything for him. But he wants to get married, and—let's just say, he knows I will never marry him." They remain silent for a moment. She shifts. "Look, I don't want to get into a discussion of Bill or Melissa. But there are things we need to talk about. *I* need to talk about anyway." She takes a deep breath. "I was really angry—and hurt—when you stalked out after seeing Bill here." She glances away. "You didn't even return my calls for awhile." She tries to relax, struggles to maintain a quiet, even tone. "And I was hurt that you didn't visit me in the hospital this last time, that you showed no interest in—in me."

Van listens quietly, but his face looks like a storm brewing. Eventually he says, "I told you, I did not know until you were on the way home. I *wanted* to come then. But Bill seemed to be taking care of everything." His words push close upon each other. Nora's head snaps up. Van grimaces and draws a deep breath. "I need you in my life. I need you and I want you in my life." He looks pained, and sounds as though the words are being wrung from him.

Nora sgrips his hand. Tears flood her eyes. "Oh, Van. I need you, too."

"When Frank said you had been drugged and dumped during a blizzard, I had nightmares." Van shakes his head and massages his brow, as if trying to ease a headache. Eventually he grins crookedly. "Even though I know you are a survivor."

Nora laughs. "A long history of camping in all seasons helps!" She straightens. "We need another drink."

Van stands. "Let me get it." He squeezes her shoulder on his way to the kitchen. As he sets their glasses on the table, he kisses Nora's cheek and murmurs, "Thank God you are alive and well." He sits down. "Surely you have thought about it. Perhaps you talked about it with Bill. Or Frank. But with me you have been silent. We must consider why someone tried to kill you."

"Why would anyone do any of the things that have plagued people at the college? I've said for months that someone is targeting the Board."

"Why not kill outright? Why rely on explosions and fire and faulty brakes? Why leave you alive in the mountains?"

"My key was in the ignition, the gas tank empty. The police think it was supposed to look like I'd run out of gas and died going for help." Nora shudders and sips her scotch. "But of course I had no idea my car was close by."

Van frowns. "No sensible person would just walk out into a winter night. One would phone for help. Or bundle up as best one could in the car and wait for rescue." He takes her hand, rubbing his thumb across her knuckles.

"They found my cell phone in the parking lot at the Moultonborough Inn—as if I'd dropped it getting out of my car. But I never went into the Inn. Surely the police would have been suspicious."

"Thank God you were able to keep your wits about you. What bothers me the most is that the attacks on you—and on the Bradys—must be part of a bigger plan. So many incidents. So many people. What if whoever is doing this kills again?" Van reaches for Nora's hand. "What would I do if something more happens to you?"

Nora kisses the hand that covers hers. She keeps her tone intentionally light. "Fortunately, nothing is going to happen to either of us. Expecting disaster is just being paranoid." She wonders whether she believes her own words.

"Humpf. A little paranoia could be a very healthy thing."

Nora feels Van's gaze as she moves toward the kitchen. "I'm not up to doing the veal, but I can throw together a light supper."

"Anything is fine." Van pulls a hand down his face. "Think about the time line. In May, the brakes on Buck's rental car were tampered with and Pete Fitzroy hit that bridge abutment. In July, *Duet* was blown up. Then Stan's office was vandalized in early September. Then the Bradys' fire. At Halloween, Pris was run off the road. And then you again."

"And in August, you were mugged." Nora sets a tray of fruit, cheeses, paté, and crusty bread on the table. "But the very first thing was when Richard Emory drowned. If there's a common cause here, he's probably part of it."

"Maybe." Van opens a bottle of red wine and pours. "But I am not convinced that my mugging and Richard drowning are part of the pattern. Falling overboard in rough seas could be accidental. If that was accidental, the malice started in May."

Nora stares at Van. "That's my point: Richard Emory's death is not clear-cut. What if his drowning *was* murder? I was supposed to look like I froze to death by accident, but it must have been attempted murder. I *was* drugged. Everything is connected to West." Nora picks up the cheese knife.

Van takes a bunch of grapes. "We must think about this logically. If the incidents are related—far flung as they are in time and place—then finding a common thread between any two of them should help unravel the knot."

"Richard Emory was on a boat, my boat was blown-up. Someone who sails is doing this?"

Van scratches his chin. "Since his office was vandalized, Stan's computer system has been screwed up. A computer professional?"

Tackling the problem with Van, Nora feels hopeful. "How about someone with a lot of mechanical skills—cutting my bilge blower line, the brakes on Buck's rental car, picking the locks at Old Main—Stan's office—everything at the Bradys' house …" She pauses. " All we know is that somebody has a lot of skills and really gets around!"

Van straightens his back and turns to Nora. "Perhaps more than one person is involved." He grins. "If there is only one perp, he is one very talented dude."

From Van's lips, *dude* and *perp* sounded comical. Nora

appreciates his efforts to lighten her mood and returns his smile. The clock chimes and she says, "Good grief. Look at the time."

"Time flies whether you are having fun or not." He grins.

"How about a brandy? And maybe some nuts to finish off. It was a very light supper." Nora pours, and Van helps carry. They sit by the fire, sipping and nibbling in silence until Nora says, "Motive. That's always the key." Van nods. She continues. "Jealousy, hate, revenge? Self-defense, need, greed?"

They mull over each one, but Nora draws little comfort from the effort. None seems relevant to all the incidents.

While they talk, Nora's thoughts keep returning to Van's mugging. Ever since she first heard about it, she's shuddered to think that he might have been shot—even killed. "You know, your mugging is different from all the other attacks in one major way: you actually saw and heard and touched your attacker."

"Hmmm." Van rests his head on the chair back and closes his eyes. "Yes, it was the most intimate of the incidents. It was also the least complex—just brute force, snatch and run. It was a white man, approximately my age—or maybe younger. But not a kid. He was dressed in solid black. And he was in good shape—well-muscled. His voice was deep and resonant—but cold enough to freeze the Bay. He sounded like a man who could kill without hesitating." Van shakes his head. "I can see him still—the street light glinting on the gun, the way he gripped it, only a thumb and two fingers."

"Why would he hold a gun that way? It makes no sense."

Van opens his eyes. "He only *had* a thumb and two fingers on his left hand."

Nora stares at Van. "That sounds like Three-finger Sam. Why would an ex-con from Baltimore be mugging people in New York City?"

"Who the hell is Three-finger Sam?"

Nora's words tumble over one another. "He's a waiter at a restaurant on Baltimore harbor. He's well-built, good-looking, and has a wonderful voice. He's called Three-finger Sam because he lost two fingers in juvenile detention. Though, technically, what he has left is a thumb and two fingers, not three *fingers*."

"Nora, slow down and focus. What do you know about ex-convicts in Baltimore?"

"When you put it like that, not a thing! But I happen to know about this *one*. Nate introduced us. *He* knows Sam because Sam lives at a halfway house for ex-convicts and parolees that's funded by the Roth Foundation."

Van says, "Which fingers are missing? From which hand?" After Nora tells him, after they've compared their descriptions of the mugger and the waiter, on all the details they can remember, Van says, "So someone closely connected to West College has befriended the man who attacked me. I cannot accept that as coincidence."

"But *why*? Why would he be targeting Nate's friends and acquaintances?"

"Perhaps Nate put him up to it. After all, *he* is the one with ties to the College. Is he connected to each of the incidents? And if so, how?"

Nora retrieves a yellow pad and pencil. When she returns, she catches Van's smile. *He's probably thinking, Nora and her lists!* She smiles back, but continues making three columns headed Fellow Trustees, Finance Committee, and Other Relationships. Together they enter each victim's name according to his or her connection to Nate.

Jumbled memories flash through Nora's mind: Nate sitting across from her at the Fourth of July party, the look on his face when he asked whether she'd brought the draft report to the restaurant, the explosion on *Duet*. She shudders.

Van seems to read her mind, for he squeezes her hand. When he says, "The explosion might have killed you," his voice is husky. "And then the White Mountains. You could be in danger now."

Nora looks away. Her laugh is shaky. "Three-finger Sam isn't going to come here. He doesn't know I know anything. Assuming I *do* know anything."

"I'm going to stay here till this thing is settled. I want—I want to protect you."

She pats his forearm. "And I thank you for that. But even if Sam or Nate—or whoever—did come here, I can protect myself. I have a stun gun. Frank insisted—last summer, after *Duet*. He showed me how to use it. It stops an attacker in his tracks but isn't lethal." She struggles to sound matter-of-fact. "A woman living alone needs to be able to protect *herself*. Besides, what about your mugging? You're in as much danger as anyone." Nora shakes her head. "We can't really know unless we can figure out *why?*"

Looking at the lists, Van says, "The biggest cluster is around finances. Assume there is one big motive there—financial—plus a few attacks that are camouflage."

"Finances! I know what it is! Sort of." Nora clutches Van's arm. "It's that report—on the charitable remainder trust part of the fixed income portfolio. Buck has been asking about that for months." She leaps up and paces. "Right before Buck was supposed to have a report, Stan's office was vandalized. No report was forthcoming. And now we have what's supposed to be the finished product, but it's widely divergent from the draft I got last fall." She pauses and looks at Van. "When I told Nate that I had this draft and that there were big discrepancies, he wanted to handle it himself. When I said I would send it out directly, he … Well, nothing tangible, but he wasn't happy." Excitement bubbles up. *Just like old times, trying to solve a crime with Van.*

Van leans on his elbows. "If Nate is involved in some sort of financial crime, and Buck was stirring up trouble, that would be a reason to shut Buck up. Allie and Pete Fitzroy were just bystanders. And Richard Emory was an accountant. He and Nate were together quite a bit on *Endeavor*. Maybe Emory tumbled to it first, and Nate pushed him overboard in the storm, thinking that would be the end of it."

Nora says, "We've got to tell Frank. Now!"

She turns toward the phone but Van catches her hand. "Now? It is after 9:00."

Nora pulls away and heads toward the kitchen, throwing over her shoulder as she goes, "Last night, I got this message from Pris on my answering machine. She didn't leave her name, but I know it was Pris—and she was drunk. She said something like, 'You bitch! If you think you're going to fly off to the Cayman Islands with my husband, you've got another think coming.' I just shrugged it off. There's no reason for her to think such a thing, so I just chalked it up to alcohol and jealousy. But what if Nate *is* about to leave the country!" She punches in Frank's number.

Chapter Thirty-Four

Nora grips the phone, scowling. Frank says, "We'll make arrangements with law enforcement in Baltimore to pick up Three-finger Sam for questioning ASAP. But we'll have to proceed cautiously with Nate. After all, Nora, you have no proof. None. We can't move against a man with his money and connections without something a lot more concrete than your intuition."

"But he's about to leave the country!"

"So you think—based on an anonymous drunken message you believe his wife left." Nora snorts, but he talks on. "Now don't get your panties in a bunch. We'll keep an eye on the airport. If he shows up there, that will be reason enough to question him. In any event, I'll talk with him tomorrow. All I'm saying is that no one's going to go off half-cocked and arrest him tonight."

When Frank rings off, Nora slams down the phone, still smarting from his condescension. She turns to Van, still scowling. "He acts as if I'm over-reacting! Like I'm a half-witted child—or an hysterical woman!" She clenches her fists. "They might not arrest Nate at all."

Van puts his arm around her and says, "Dear heart, don't worry. I will stay. I will protect you."

She twists out of his embrace. "Don't you start, too! I've had enough male supremacy for one night." She faces him, arms akimbo. "I'm not *afraid*. I'm *angry*. And I can take care of myself!"

"That is not what I meant. *I* am worried. Any sensible person would be."

"So you agree with Frank. I'm not sensible!" They argue, one of those senseless arguments that doesn't address the real issues. Van's every offer of comfort or support infuriates her more. Finally she says, "This is my house! And I want to be alone in it!" She regrets the words as soon as they leave her lips, but it is too late to call them back.

Van's face turns stony. "Fine. Call me if and when you wish." He picks up his coat and leaves.

*   *   *

Alone, Nora's anger quickly gives way to self-recriminations. At heart she realizes that picking a fight with Van had sprung from two roots, deep in her own history. His tenderness, his words of love—much as she wanted them—made her hope that he cared as much as she. And that caring makes her vulnerable. Her family is littered with women who cared too much, who counted on a man's love and tenderness and ended up heart-broken and destitute. By age twelve, she had sworn she would never be one of those women. That, combined with her fierce need to be self-sufficient, made her drive Van away tonight. Will he come back?

Nora flings herself into her recliner and turns her thoughts to something less painful than a breach with Van. She reviews the incidents, the back-and-forth with Van. Someone is targeting people at the College. Someone blew up her boat. Someone drugged her and dumped her in a blizzard. Someone sees her as a threat.

For the first time, a creeping anxiety about future attacks takes hold. *Here I am, alone, getting jumpy as a cat on hot coals, with no one to blame but myself. Damn it, why did I have to dig in my heels tonight?* Nora turns on the patio light. Icy crystals coat the dried leaves of pin oaks and the needles of pines, glistening against the darkness that hangs over the river. The ice-covered leaves of a low-hanging branch tap the upper panes of the patio door. She's a lighted target in the winter night. She flicks off the outside light and draws the curtains. She brews a pot of tea and sits in semi-darkness, trying to face down her anxiety. "Get a grip," she mutters. "It's your own fault you're here alone."

The warmth of the teapot handle contrasts with the chill along her spine. Thoughts of quiet summer nights anchored in a calm cove fail to bring ease. In time she empties the dregs from the teapot and draws comfort from a line from Shakespeare—"Or, in the night, imagining some fear, How easy is a bush a bear."

The phone rings. She jumps, her pulse racing. Her "Hello?" is breathless.

"Hello, Noni." Frank's voice is such a relief that she feels weak in the knees. "I wanted to let you know that the wheels are in motion. The Baltimore police are on their way to pick up Three-finger Sam. They've got officers at the airport, too."

"That's great." *Maybe I was too hard on Frank.* "Thanks for letting me know."

"Ummm. About Nate—I *will* talk to him in the morning. But—in the meantime—perhaps I should stay with you. Just in case. Even if it isn't Nate or Sam, it's *someone*. I could leave the kids with Claire overnight."

Having someone there would be wonderful. But she's already sent Van away. "You're a good friend. I appreciate the offer. But it isn't necessary. Really. There's no reason to think I'm in any more danger tonight than I have been—or will be—any other night. And I have the stun gun handy." When she hangs up, the implications of Frank thinking she might need protection sink in.

Nora paces, scolding herself for letting her previous anger at Frank spill over to Van—too gentlemanly to strike back. *I wouldn't feel so guilty if he'd blown up, too. But no, he just withdrew.* She wonders what he must be thinking, wonders whether their on-off relationship is too fragile, too bumpy to bring either of them peace and contentment. She picks up the telephone to call him, stares at it, then puts it down.

She listens intently to the night sounds of the house, flinching every time the wind scratches twig fingers across the windows. She remembers the blast that sank *Duet*—the sheer power of it—the oily water on her body, in her mouth. There had been no warning. She thinks of the Bradys and imagines the crackle of a small fire being whipped into a bigger fire by the night wind. She stares out the kitchen window, struggling to breathe normally, straining to see whether all the moving shadows under her garage light are wind-tossed trees. The wind drives thick clouds off the moon, revealing a car parked near the entrance to her driveway. *Oh, my God.* She peers toward the car, sees a dim glow of dashboard lights and a black silhouette against the charcoal night.

She races to the bedroom, snatches up the stun gun, and reaches for the phone just as it rings. "Hello!"

"What's wrong? Noni, what is it?"

"Oh, Frank, thank God! There's a car parked by my driveway. It wasn't there a few minutes ago. Someone is—just sitting there." Saying this, Nora starts to feel foolish.

Frank's tone is soothing. "It's all right. He's one of my men."

"One of yours?"

"Hear me out now. I respect your decision not to have me stay over. But given everything that's happened—If you're right—Well, I couldn't live with myself if I let anything happen to you." He pauses. "My gut tells me things are coming to a head." When he speaks again, the words come in his captain's voice: "If my putting a man there makes you angry, get over it."

Nora's relief bubbles up on a laugh. "Of course I'm not angry. Frank, thank you. I'm more jittery than I care to admit. Your officer is a welcome comfort."

"Are all the doors and windows locked?"

"Yes, of course."

"And your stun gun? Where is that?"

"In my hand. It'll be within reach until the sun comes up tomorrow." Nora chuckles weakly.

"Try to get some sleep. I'll call in the morning."

Nora hangs up. She starts to return the stun gun to her bedside stand but carries it back to the sitting room. She holds the trigger in for a second—testing—and listens to the reassuring crackle of the current. *Is it Nate? Or Three-finger Sam?* Nora checks all the doors and window locks. *But why? What is it about that damn report? Nate knows boats. He could have cut the hose to the bilge blower.* She pours scotch with a shaky hand and peeks through the kitchen blind. The cop is still there. *Thank God. What if someone's on his way here now?* She closes the window blind, but leaves the outside light on. She makes another round of the doors and windows, re-checking locks, closing all the curtains and blinds, knowing the compulsion is irrational but feeling driven. She draws heavy drapes across the patio doors. She can't think of anything else to do to feel less exposed.

Turning on the TV, she sips scotch and chooses the all-night movie network. *Seven Brides for Seven Brothers* is just coming on— one of her favorites. After fifteen or twenty minutes, she feels less tense. She downs the residue in her glass and pours more whisky over fresh ice. Head back, eyes half closed, she listens, following the story line by the dialogue. Her right hand feels for the stun gun stuck between the cushion and the arm of her chair. For a moment, she regrets her lack of self-control in pouring another drink, but that washes away almost before it surfaces. She takes another sip, closes her eyes on the scene of the six brothers holding onto their kidnapped brides while Adam whips the horses toward the snowy mountain pass, the men of the town in hot pursuit. Half-conscious of the dialogue, Nora rides in the front of the sleigh, watching the snow-covered trail bend slowly into a dark mountain pass. When the sleigh stops, Richard Emory leads her into a darkened theater, down the aisle to a seat in the front row. On the screen, Van is struggling to save someone in a roiling avalanche, the snow melting into a raging sea. A man in the adjoining seat pulls a large fur coat across his lap, leans toward her, and says, "Nora, how nice of you to come." She turns, looks into Nate's distorted face—white skin, gouged cheeks, burning eyes. A pistol gripped by a thumb and two fingers appears over his shoulder.

Nora wakes to her own muffled scream. She shivers, chilled by a night sweat. She touches the stun gun, glances at the diluted scotch, reaches toward it but withdraws her hand. *Probably not good for keeping the night terrors at bay.*

In the bedroom, she drops her damp clothes in a heap and feels a cold draft across her breasts. *Where's that coming from?* She listens. The wind howls down the chimney. *I must have left the fireplace damper open.* She quickly pulls on green fleece pajamas.

She is about to climb into bed with her stun gun and a much-read copy of *Pride and Prejudice* when the telephone rings. "Hello. Hello?" She hears breathing. A muffled voice mumbles, "Sorry. Wrong number." A click, then silence. Her heart pounds, her chest feels tight. Her mind searches for reassurance that she hasn't overlooked any precaution. She slips her feet into fleece-lined moccasins and hurries down the hall to peek through the kitchen window. The police car is there, but something seems different. She stares, finally realizing that she can no longer see a person silhouetted inside. "Oh my God," she whispers.

Nora wipes her damp palm on her pajama leg and dials Van.

"Nora, are you all right?" He sounds wide awake.

"Yes, I'm fine. I mean—Frank stationed a patrol car near my driveway and ..."

"Is it gone?" The tension in his voice is nearly palpable.

"No, it's here. But ..." Tears tighten her throat. "Oh, Van, I just got this call—a wrong number, probably, but now I can't see the policeman in the car. I'm frightened."

"I am on my way." The line goes dead.

The panic in Van's voice is contagious. *Shit! I left the stun gun in the bedroom!* Nora is halfway to the bedroom when she feels a cold draft on the back of her neck. She half turns, glancing toward the kitchen. The door between the garage and the kitchen is open. She runs. An arm comes around her neck, nylon tightening against her throat. She gasps for air, struggles against the solid arm inside the padding of the jacket sleeve. Pain shoots down her back. She struggles to keep from falling as her attacker tightens his grip, pulling her head down to his waist in a chokehold. He shakes her, a mad dog shaking his prey. Her fingers scrabble at the sleeve, trying to get a grip.

"This is it, bitch. You're gonna be sorry you ever got in my way. You and all the other fucking bastards at West." The voice is familiar—but low and growling. Who? He grabs a handful of hair, jerking her head lower. *My God, I'm going to die.* She stomps the heel of her moccasin-covered foot on his instep. He loosens his hold. Nora twists free and drives her knee into his crotch.

Her attacker doubles over and falls to the floor, moaning. Nora spins toward the bedroom but he catches her left ankle. She struggles to twist away, arms flailing, loses her balance, and crashes down. She lands hard on her back, knocking the wind out of her still-laboring lungs, twisting her right leg under her body. She hears the pop even over their panting. Pain shoots through her knee and for an instant she thinks she's going to faint.

Simon Hummel scrambles forward and pins her, one knee on her chest. "You bitch." He slaps her hard, splitting her lip. She tastes blood, metallic and salty. "You fucking bitch! You couldn't leave the damned report alone!" He backhands her, whipping her head to the other side. She drives the heel of her hand against the point of his chin, knocking him off her chest. She struggles up and limps toward the bedroom, Simon cursing and panting behind her. He catches her, picks her up in a bear hug, and throws her onto the bed. "You castrating bitch! Thinking Nate wanted to fuck you." Slaps punctuate the insults. *Rape? He's going to rape me first?* He plants one knee on her chest. Cracking ribs send searing pain through her right lung. "The fun and games are over." She's barely conscious when he pulls a coil of nylon line from his jacket pocket and stretches it across her neck. Nora's vision shrinks to pinpoint focus. Simon's leering face seems to be floating farther away. Her scrabbling fingers finally find the stun gun. She holds in the trigger and presses the prongs into his side. He jerks, convulses, and falls sideways. Nora pushes his body off her and tries to clear her vision. He moans and shakes his head as if confused. The effects will wear off in a few minutes. *How long has it been?* She presses the stun gun to his thigh and holds it there for a slow count of three. She struggles upright but when she tries to limp to the dresser, her right leg gives way. She belly crawls to the dresser. Every move sends pain shooting through her lungs. She hauls herself up to her left knee, throws things every which way, grabs several stockings. The effort to tie his ankles together, roll him onto his stomach, and secure his wrists behind his back, leaves her lightheaded from the pain.

Someone pounds on the front door, calls, "Nora. Nora!" *Van. Thank God!* He pounds again. Crawling to the front door seems to take forever. She's trembling so badly she can hardly undo the deadbolt and flop aside. A gust of cold air kisses her damp forehead as everything goes black.

Chapter Thirty-Five

Nora looks from Van to Frank to Bill, all gathered around her hospital bed, and tries to smile brightly. "My, my. Three handsome men bearing flowers! But really, we've got to stop meeting like this." Her mouth feels like cotton and the words come out husky and hesitant.

Frank slides a vase of yellow roses onto the windowsill, brushes a kiss across her forehead, and moves to the foot of her bed. "How are you doing, Noni?"

"About as well as you see."

Van sets a dish garden on her bedside stand and gently squeezes her hand. "The doctors told us nothing except that we could visit this afternoon. All very proper, of course—but frustrating nonetheless." He looks hollow-eyed and solemn.

Bill adds his bouquet of mixed blooms to the windowsill, kisses her cheek, and pats her shoulder. "What did the doctors say, my dear?"

"Ummm. Four broken ribs. One punctured a lung and it collapsed, so they had to put a tube in there to get the air out of where it shouldn't be and back where it should. They fixed the tear." Focusing is difficult. *It must be the pain meds.* She tries to smile. "Fortunately, no holes in my heart or aorta or anything, so I guess I'll live. That's the good news." She squeezes Van's hand. "Would you give me a sip of water?" Van holds the cup of ice water so she can drink through the bent straw. But her dry mouth returns almost immediately. "The bad news is that they can't actually do anything for broken ribs, just wait for them to heal—and prescribe heavy-duty pain pills. And it will probably go on for a couple of months."

Bill taps her bandaged right knee. "What about this?"

"That's some sort of cuff to get the swelling down. I have an ACL tear—my anterior something ligament—and some small fractures and bone bruises and things. They'll fix it with arthroscopic surgery, maybe later today, maybe tomorrow." Nora stifles a yawn. "I won't be tripping the light fantastic any time soon. They say I'll be on crutches for about three weeks, walking in about a month."

Bill slaps a folded newspaper onto the bed. "And Hummel is claiming it was self-defense!"

Nora tries to focus on the newspaper: **SIMON HUMMEL, PROMINENT FINANCIAL MANAGER, ARRESTED ON ASSAULT CHARGES. Suspected Involvement in Numerous Other Crimes.**

> Simon Hummel, senior partner in Smith Hummel Clark Peterson Associates, a prominent leader in Baltimore social and business circles, was arrested early Tuesday morning at the Centreville home of West College professor Nora Perry. Hummel entered the Perry home after forcing a locked garage window and a fight ensued. Perry claims that Hummel beat and choked her and was trying

to kill her when she used a stun gun to subdue him. Hummel says he was angry with Perry for insulting him and rejecting his sexual advances, but meant only to scare her until she attacked him, at which point he had to defend himself. Both parties were taken to a nearby hospital.

An officer from the Queen Anne's County Sheriff's Office who was guarding the Perry home was knocked unconscious and suffered a mild concussion. He did not see his attacker. Hummel denied involvement. He is being held without bail on evidence that he is a flight risk. (See related story, **Night Flight,** Page 2.)

Nora has no energy to read further. "So what happened to Three-finger Sam?"

Frank chuckles. "I told you we were going to pick him up. He's a convicted felon named Samson Davis. We told him that DNA testing linked him to the Brady arson." Frank shrugs and grins. "We don't have the actual results yet. That takes time. But we faked him out—and gave him a plea bargain. Davis claims Hummel paid him a total of $50,000 for the various crimes against people associated with West College. He claims that when he tampered with the brakes on Brady's rental car, he didn't intend to kill anyone—and I quote, 'Maybe just bang Brady up a little. It was a mistake that Fitzroy was driving that car—that he died. But after that, I had no choice but to do whatever Mr. Hummel said. He paid me every time, but I never had a choice.'"

Bill snorts. "But you have the case tied up in a bow, right?"

"Sam, yes. It could be a little dicier with Hummel. His attorney claims none of those charges can be substantiated. His line is that there is no evidence against Hummel but the uncorroborated word of a convicted felon whose testimony has been bought by a plea bargain. He had no reason to perpetrate these monstrous crimes." Frank's lip curls contemptuously. "His attorney says—and I quote—'The incident at Professor Perry's house was purely personal and cannot be tied to any of those other unfortunate events.'"

Nora tries to stay focused but feels loopy. She may need to hear it all again. But now she says, "What about Nate?"

"Baltimore police staked out BWI Airport, on the lookout for Nate. No luck until Hummel was paged to meet his party at the bar in the international terminal. They knew Hummel had been arrested nearly two hours before. So they found Nate with a pile of luggage and a flight plan to the Cayman Islands. Part of the luggage was Hummel's."

Bill says, "So you have him."

"Maybe not. He told police that he and Hummel are good friends who'd planned a vacation together in the Caribbean. They held him for questioning—all they could do at that point. Roth refused to say anything and called his attorney, who says Nate has done nothing wrong and has no comment on Hummel's arrest or the alleged crimes."

"But he was in on all of this with Hummel!" In her outrage, Nora bolts upright, but falls back gasping at the pain.

Van squeezes her hand. "Getting upset will just make you feel worse."

Bill says, "He's right. You just need to take it easy right now."

"And we'll see what we can find to tie them together." Frank looks from one to the other. "Any ideas?"

Nora flaps the hand that isn't tethered to the IV drip. "There's all that to-do about the financial statements and reports. Nate *and*

Simon must have been trying to keep anyone from knowing. But what if Nate claims he doesn't know anything about any fraud?"

Van lets go of Nora's hand and paces the small space between the bed and the door. "Maybe the tie is Richard Emory." He faces Frank and Bill. "He was an accountant. Perhaps he said something to Nate during the sail on *Endeavor*. They talked a lot."

"Right!" Bill turns to Nora. "Remember when we were strolling the deck, looking at the moon decorating the water, and the two of them were in some sort of huddle by the stern rail? As I recall, Richard was saying something like, 'I'm a damned good accountant. I know my business.' That's when I said it was too good a night to be talking business, or something like that."

Van scratches his chin. "Are you suggesting that Nate had a reason to push Richard overboard?"

Bill shrugs. "If Nate and Simon were in some scheme together, maybe so."

Van stops pacing. "Buck has been all over the financial reports. That must be what set off the attacks on him."

Nora nods. "I think they were lovers."

All eyes swivel to her and the three men say, "Who?"

Their chorus makes her giggle. "Simon and Nate! The way Simon yelled at me during the attack. And Pris' jealousy. She had no reason to be jealous of me, but I'd bet dollars to donuts she had reason to be jealous of somebody. I bet they both are gay and in the closet." Nora scrubs a hand down her face. "It all makes so much sense. Hummel manages the whole portfolio and Nate chairs the Finance Committee."

Frank gets that gleam in his eye that says the end is in sight. "What better cover than a pitiful wife, two children, and flirting with every attractive woman in sight? I'll get a warrant for Emory's office. A big firm like that, they've probably kept all his files. Maybe he kept evidence."

Chapter Thirty-Six

Nora set's two mugs of coffee on her oak table and sinks into the chair across from Pris. A twinge of pain shoots between her not-quite-healed ribs and she winces. Two months and she's still not right. She gazes steadily at Pris and summons a neutral tone. "Your call surprised me."

Pris looks away, pink suffusing her face. "Yes, I suppose it did." She inhales deeply. "I needed to talk with you because—because I've been so unfair—so mean that night I was in drink-and-dial mode. You've never been anything but kind to me. But I—I suspected you. Anyway, I want—I *need*—to apologize."

She must mean her message on my answering machine. "I never expected an apology."

"No, I'm sure you didn't. But making amends is part of my Twelve-Step Program." Pris smiles wryly. "I pretty much bottomed out when Nate was arrested. But now I've finished rehab."

Pris' hair is shorter than Nora remembered, and has more brown highlights. The hunter green sweater suits her. Nora says, "You're looking good. How are you feeling?"

"Fine. I'm feeling fine. And I've lost fifteen pounds already."

"That's terrific!" Nora squeezes her forearm. *God, I love it when a beaten-down woman gets her act together!* "I'm really pleased for you. Pulling yourself together takes a lot of strength."

Pris shrugs. "Some things aren't so bad." She smiles again. "I'm talking with the Roth Foundation attorneys about whether I can take over there, if need be. The Foundation does so much good. The work is fascinating. I could provide continuity. Who knows? Maybe I'll take Nate's seat on the West College Board as well."

Nora sips her coffee, thoughts racing. *Completely out of touch! I suppose her personal fortune might carry some weight with the Foundation. But she's had no experience heading a big organization. And what makes her think West College would want a constant reminder of Nate and Simon and all that?* Finally she says, "Having goals to work toward is a good thing. Just be sure you have a Plan B in case something doesn't work out."

Pris swirls the coffee in her mug, her smile fading, and Nora thinks perhaps she spoke too bluntly. Before she can muster anything more positive to say, Pris resumes. "I saw Nate this morning. God, it's awful—seeing him in jail. He looks so gaunt, so broken. In some ways, waiting for the trial is the worst part." She glances out the patio window. "I don't know how we're going to get through this."

Nora tries to read Pris's expression, searches for something noncommittal to say. "Life is going to be painful for you and your sons for a long time. How are they holding up?"

Pris sighs. "They've left school. The spring semester had hardly begun, but the scandal … The boys are pretty bitter. They won't even visit Nate. Most of our friends aren't speaking to us anymore."

"That's terrible! You need support now more than ever."

Pris smiles weakly. "When people find out I'm not getting a divorce, they just—withdraw. Nobody seems to understand."

"You're staying married?" Nora tamps down her incredulity. "I can't say *I* understand that, either."

"No, I guess you wouldn't." Pris fidgets. "But I want you to. Nate really isn't a bad person."

Attacking a weak woman goes against Nora's heart. She tries to maintain a neutral tone when she says, "How can you believe that?" But hints of exasperation and disbelief leak through.

Pris wrings her hands. "You've been through so much and I know in some ways you blame Nate, but it really isn't his fault. He's—everything's been so awful for him."

"Pris, get real!" Nora's fury vies with fascination. "How can you say it's not his fault?"

"None of this would have happened if his parents had accepted him for who he is!" She glances at Nora. "It's always the parents, isn't it?" Her laugh sounds forced. "Nate says they didn't understand about homosexuality. I try to tell him that was a different era. But he can't forgive them. When he turned thirty, with no marriage in sight, they started talking about his 'choices' threatening his inheritance. He never admitted to them that he was gay, but they seemed to know. It got so bad—well, he gave in—and married me."

Nora stares at Pris. Being gay and in the closet is no excuse for the things Nate did. "Pris, his entire life was a lie!"

"Exactly! Think how awful that must have been for him. And I was so naïve. I never, not even once, so much as wondered." Pris's tears spill over. "All those years, I thought it was me—that I was the problem in our marriage. But Nate ... He's grateful that I gave him two wonderful sons. And he does love me. It's just—he could never love any woman—that way. But even if I'd known, I think

I would have married him anyway. It wasn't always bad—not in the early years." Pris blots her tears with a crumpled tissue. "He tried so hard. But our marriage—the boys—none of that was enough for his parents. In the end, they tied up all their money in the Roth Foundation and trusts for the twins. Nate never got over that." Nora tries to stifle an incredulous snort. Pris looks pleadingly at her. "I don't mean just the *money*. It was the rejection. My inheritance must have made it worse—a constant reminder." Pris looks at her hands, clenched on the table, and drops them into her lap. "I think, in a way, that's what must have driven him to steal from the college—not having money of his own outright—money he was entitled to. It really wasn't his fault."

Nora bangs the tabletop so hard that it jars her aching ribcage. "Pris, wake up! People died because of his greed! His lover nearly killed *me* right in this house!"

"But Nate didn't know—Circumstances just all came together. All he wanted was a second chance at life. Simon talked him into the money scheme. Nate never knew he would do all those awful things!" Nora stands abruptly, knocking over her chair. Pris looks at her with frightened eyes. "Please, just try to understand. Inside, he's really a good man. Think of all the good he's done in Baltimore."

Nora stares at her. "You think good works balance out murder? He pushed Richard Emory overboard. He must have. Because of him, Pete Fitzroy is *dead*, and Allie and Buck and Rebecca could have been. *And* me."

Pris juts out her chin and presses her lips into a thin line. Finally she says, "*But he took care of me*—all those years—when I was drinking. He's my strength to stay sober now. I'm doing everything I can to help him. There's no evidence Richard Emory was pushed overboard. And everything else was Simon, using Sam.

Nate didn't know! Our lawyers say there's a good chance Nate can go free."

"How can you believe such a thing? Between Simon's and Sam Davis's testimony, there's no way in hell he'll get off."

Pris looks startled. "You haven't heard?"

Nora feels suddenly wary. "Heard what?"

"Simon won't testify against Nate. Sam is the only one who's cut a deal. Plus, the search of Richard Emory's files turned up nothing." Pris shrugs and looks embarrassed. "Our lawyers say that without something linking Nate to Richard's drowning—or at least knowledge of the fraud—the case against him is practically nonexistent. Simon is the one who actually fiddled the books and transferred money—and paid Sam. And as for Sam, even if he *could* implicate Nate, who would take the word of a convicted felon who's getting a plea bargain over that of a well-regarded man like Nate?"

"He won't get off if I have anything to say about it!"

Pris gnaws her lip. "The lawyers say there's reasonable doubt. Nate didn't even know Simon was coming here to scare you."

"I can't believe you're going along with this." Nora paces, shaking her head. "How can you possibly stand by him?"

Pris shrugs one shoulder. Nora thinks she looks defeated. Or maybe just tired. "I can't do anything else."

Waves of irritation and anger wash over Nora. She stops in front of Pris, feet planted, arms akimbo. "Leave my house. Now."

Pris's face crumples and tears flow freely. "I'm sorry. I'm just so sorry."

Nora can't help relenting a little. "I wish you no harm, Pris. But I can't listen to any more of this."

She closes the door behind Pris and sinks into her recliner, thought and feeling clamoring for attention. Glancing at the clock, she mutters, "Damn. I'm going to be late."

Dressing for dinner, she tries to focus on the evening ahead. Van's formal speech, his precision, his logic—everything about him is comforting. Just what she needs. He's taking her to the Imperial Hotel in Chestertown for dinner. Not their typical evening together.

* * *

Van smiles thinking of the evening ahead. He's going to take the plunge, tell Nora how he feels, perhaps actually propose. Thoughts of money float to the surface. He carries enormous debt. Although all of his children had tuition exchange and scholarships, college for four kids on a faculty salary took all his resources and then some. He'd just paid off his own educational loans when Pieter matriculated at Middlebury. He's never owned a home of his own, or a new car. He still barely manages to fund his 403-b retirement account.

Nora would never think him interested in her money. But other people might. He's embarrassed by the thought. Mentally, he shakes himself. *The issue here is not money. The issue is, would she marry me?* He dons his tweed jacket, knots his tie, and examines his reflection, approving what he sees. *If she refuses, I shall have to make-do. The most important thing is whether she loves me.* Van checks his watch, and whistles as he heads for Nora's.

* * *

On the drive to Chestertown, Nora describes her visit from Pris. She turns in her seat to face Van. "So Nate has a good chance of staying out of jail. Can you believe that?" Nora's laugh sounds bitter. "He admits telling Simon about my suspicions, but claims he had no idea that Simon would attack me—had no knowledge of any of the crimes Simon and Sam Davis committed."

Van grips the steering wheel. "That is too farfetched! Surely the jury will see it."

"His lawyers claim Nate was just a poor deluded guy in love with a no-gooder. It might not even get to a jury." Nora brushes back a tendril of loose hair. "Pris standing by him makes it that much harder to paint him as a villain—the supportive, loving wife, claiming it wasn't really his fault versus the known felon and confessed thief. Plus all the good work he's done through the Foundation." Nora shakes her head. "Van, she's pathetic. And infuriating. She can't seem to recognize—to acknowledge—that he stayed with her for his own benefit, not for hers."

Van glances at Nora's scowl. "She sees nothing wrong in all that he has done?"

"In her heart, I think she knows. But she *excuses* him." Outrage laces her words. "I've just had a close encounter with a wife, and I definitely don't want to be one." Van's spirits plummet. "I don't want to be dependent. I don't want to be vulnerable. I don't want to give up control of my space, my money, my time—my life!"

Van nods. "Yes. I see that." He stifles a sigh. "We shall not settle Nate's future tonight. But if there is anything linking Nate and Richard, we will find it."

Nora's face brightens. "Never say die!"

Chapter Thirty-Seven

Frank slumps in one of the armed chairs at Nora's oak table, legs sprawled, coffee mug balanced on his midriff, brows pulled into a scowl. Van's feet are tucked under his chair, ankles crossed. He leans on his elbows and stares solemnly into the brown depths of his mug. Nora eases her still-battered body into a chair between the two of them. A lopsided grin quirks her lips. "We could be the personification of Frustration, Hopelessness, and Dejection!"

"What's to be happy about? A year and a half after Emory drowned and we have nothing—nada, zip, zero, bupkis. We searched his office, his home office, both computers, and his other electronic devices. Nothing suspicious to, from, or about Roth or Hummel or anything hinky."

Van glances up. "Friends? Confidantes?"

"Apparently he wasn't a confiding kind of guy."

Nora scowls. "But there must be *something*. Richard was obsessive compulsive. It was obvious in everything from his neckties to his tiny, precise printing. Everything comes back to finances, and Richard was in the middle of West College finances. And all the rough stuff started after—probably with—his death. I'm telling you, he must have left something behind."

"Noni, I absolutely trust your professional instincts. But we need more than instinct." Frank pulls a hand down his face. "I have the feeling Carol knows something she isn't telling." His gaze rests absently on Nora, slowly turns speculative. "Maybe what we need is the woman's touch."

"You think we can bond just because we're both women?" Nora feels her hackles rising.

Van says, "Hold off on the high dudgeon. Consider how Pris opened up to you. And you were there when Carol needed support, back on *Endeavor*. You should consider stepping in."

"C'mon, Noni. Just give it a shot. Bring some of that psychology to bear."

"I'm not a clinician!"

"But you know people," Frank says, as Van chimes in with, "People talk to you."

Nora looks from one to the other. "What the hell? Let's brainstorm an approach."

* * *

Maneuvering onto I-97, heading for Rt. 50 and the Bay Bridge, Nora calls Frank. "Pay dirt! It seems Richard kept journals! I have the ones for the two-and-a-half years just before he drowned. Want to come to my place for a good read?"

* * *

Nora serves coffee to Van and Frank, and offers cookies, then picks up Richard's last journal. She rifles the pages of the half-written journal. In small printed script, so neat it could almost be typewriting, are the last words Richard Emory wrote. Nora reads aloud: *I can't share Carol's bed again. Maybe a room in the basement.*

White walls. Carol moving in the room above. Every night the same. Should have left when I had the chance. "No wonder Carol found this too painful to give to anyone."

"Is there any mention of Nate?" Van asks.

Nora finds the entry for Saturday, Aug. 4. "Here's the first day on *Endeavor*. I'll start there." She skims the pages. "Lots of stuff about seeing Allie, guilt about Carol, etc., etc., etc. But listen to this. He told Nate that Simon Hummel was cooking the books."

Let N have it with both barrels. H has 10% of charitable remainder trust in foreign holdings, not audited since purchase. reported earnings too high. I know my business. Income reports faked. H has skimmed a couple of mil at least.

Nora says, "There's more. It seems Nate was skeptical, taking a wait-and-see line."

Frank whistles. "A couple of million *at least*."

Van fist-pumps the air. "We have him!"

Nora's smile feels like it will split her face.

Frank says, "Not so fast. We need more."

"There *is* more, on August fifth. Listen to this." Nora speed-reads a couple of pages, then says, "He starts with a bunch of stuff about talking with Allie, but listen to this."

Dragging ass back to Endeavor I saw NR and SH coming out of bar. H manages portfolio. R chairs Finance Committee. Makes total bloody sense. Now they know I know, better tell pres. Or police. And watch my back.

Nora snaps the journal closed.

Frank says, "It's promising. Let's take a look at the other journals. He must have had suspicions long before the sail."

*   *   *

The three of them work through Richard's journals, deciphering the abbreviations and numbers, tracing the accumulating connections. When they finish, Van taps the yellow legal pad. "Here we have, by date, the journal entries that reveal Richard's growing suspicions and conclusions over the last thirty months."

Nora says "All but tied up in a bow! You've got him, Frank."

Frank shakes his head. "Afraid not. For one thing, I don't have jurisdiction in water deaths. Emory's death is the bailiwick of Natural Resources Police, remember? But jurisdiction is moot. But this isn't nearly enough."

"Why ever not?" Nora jumps up and paces by the table.

"The bottom line is that there isn't a shred of evidence that Richard Emory was murdered."

Nora massages her temples with the heels of her hands. Her voice trembles when she says, "So all this is for nothing."

"Don't take it so hard. Look at what we do have. This seals the case on Simon's theft. And we can blow a hole the size of the moon in Nate's assertion that he had no suspicion of Simon's shenanigans. At the very least, we should be able to put Nate away on conspiracy, financial fraud. Add in their personal relationship and we may be able to get him on accessory to the other crimes." Nora and Van exchange disappointed looks. "He'll get jail time. But how much? Where?" Frank shrugs. "Who knows?"

The words taste bitter when Nora says, "Hope for a hanging, get a slap on the wrist. I guess we should feel lucky that he'll get prison time."

Frank smiles. "I know it doesn't satisfy your moral outrage, Noni. But sometimes you settle for whatever bit of justice you can salvage." He stands. "Besides, as best we can tell, Hummel was the worse perp. And we've got him six ways to Sunday."

Frustration roughens Nora's voice. "What's the point? Damned if I ever help solve another murder!" She bangs their mugs into the sink, feeling as riled as a summer storm on the Chesapeake.

Van cocks one eyebrow and grins. "Until next time."

The End